Rufus Anderson

History of the Missions of the American Board of Commissioners for Foreign Missions to the Oriental Churches

Vol. 2

Anatiposi

Rufus Anderson

History of the Missions of the American Board of Commissioners for Foreign Missions to the Oriental Churches

Vol. 2

Reprint of the original, first published in 1872.

1st Edition 2023 | ISBN: 978-3-38212-835-7

Anatiposi Verlag is an imprint of Outlook Verlagsgesellschaft mbH.

Verlag (Publisher): Outlook Verlag GmbH, Zeilweg 44, 60439 Frankfurt, Deutschland
Vertretungsberechtigt (Authorized to represent): E. Roepke, Zeilweg 44, 60439 Frankfurt, Deutschland
Druck (Print): Books on Demand GmbH, In de Tarpen 42, 22848 Norderstedt, Deutschland

Republication of the Gospel in Bible Lands.

HISTORY

OF

THE MISSIONS

OF THE

AMERICAN BOARD OF COMMISSIONERS FOR FOREIGN MISSIONS

TO THE

ORIENTAL CHURCHES.

BY

RUFUS ANDERSON, D. D., LL. D.,

LATE FOREIGN SECRETARY OF THE BOARD.

IN TWO VOLUMES.

VOL. II.

BOSTON:
CONGREGATIONAL PUBLISHING SOCIETY.
1872.

RIVERSIDE, CAMBRIDGE:
STEREOTYPED AND PRINTED BY
H. O. HOUGHTON AND COMPANY.

CONTENTS.

CHAPTER XXXII.

THE BULGARIANS OF EUROPEAN TURKEY. — 1862-1871.

CHAPTER XXXIII.

THE ARMENIANS. — 1861-1863.

CHAPTER XLIII.

The Armenians. — 1869–1872.

CHAPTER XLIV.

The Armenians. — Education. — 1872.

MISSIONS

TO THE

ORIENTAL CHURCHES.

CHAPTER XXIV.

THE ARMENIANS.

1846–1855.

SEVERAL European governments, and especially England, performed an important part in securing civil and religious freedom to the Protestant Armenians.[1]

In March, 1846, Sir Stratford Canning, English Ambassador at Constantinople, reported to his government thirty-six evangelical Armenians as persecuted by the Patriarch. To this he added personal efforts to meliorate their condition, which resulted in promises from Turkish officials and the Patriarch of better treatment, promises that were by no means fulfilled.

Agency of Sir Stratford Canning.

Upon learning that the Armenian Protestants had been organized into a church, he transmitted to

[1] This is impressively set forth in the *Correspondence respecting the Condition of Protestants in Turkey,* published by order of Parliament in 1851, pp. 154 folio.

Lord Palmerston, the Foreign Secretary, their declaration of reasons for so doing, and their confession of faith.

Agency of Lord Cowley.

The Hon. H. R. Wellesley, better known as Lord Cowley, on taking the place of Sir Stratford during his visit to England, cordially took up the unfinished work of his predecessor, and urged upon Lord Palmerston the importance of procuring from the Porte a recognition of the Protestant Armenians as an independent community. He showed that, in spite of the liberal assurances extorted from the Patriarch, they were exposed to daily injury and insult, and would continue to be so until recognized by the Porte as a distinct community among its Christian subjects. At the same time, he forwarded a copy of an able declaration by the American missionaries of their objects in coming to Turkey, which they had made to the Porte through Mr. Carr, the American Minister. Lord Cowley was instructed by Lord Palmerston, "to bring the situation of these people earnestly under the consideration of the Porte, and urgently to press the Turkish government to acknowledge them as a separate religious sect." In December the Porte freed the Protestant Armenians from the rule of the Armenian Patriarch, so far as regarded their commercial and temporal affairs, and allowed them to appoint an agent, who should manage their affairs with the gov-

Instructions from Lord Palmerston.

Action of the Porte.

ernment; and also to keep separate registers of marriages, births, and deaths. The Chevalier Bunsen, the well known Prussian Ambassador in Paris, now entered into the work, and recommended, that their recognition be as durable and complete as that of the other Christian nationalities. To this proposal Lord Palmerston cordially assented; but the Turkish officials were, as usual, disinclined to go forward.

The Chevalier Bunsen.

On the 19th of November, 1847, Lord Cowley had the satisfaction of announcing, that the Grand Vizier, wishing, as he said, to do something that he knew would be agreeable to his lordship, before he should leave the country, had obtained the Sultan's permission to issue a vizierial letter in his Majesty's name, which would establish their independence at once.[1]

Lord Cowley's success.

At the suggestion of Lord Cowley, the Porte promised to send letters to five different pashalics where there were Protestants, requiring them to act in accordance with the letter; in which was granted the privilege of toleration to all Protestant subjects alike, whether from the Armenian, Greek, Syrian, or Roman Catholic Churches, or from the Jews.

This letter was of great importance under the existing circumstances; but the privileges it conferred might all be taken away on a change of ministry. Accordingly Sir Stratford Canning, on his return to

[1] This letter may be found in *Missionary Herald* for 1848, p. 98.

Further protection obtained by Sir Stratford.

Constantinople in 1850, lost no time in commencing negotiations for a more stable basis of protection, and succeeded in obtaining an Imperial Firman with the autograph of the Sultan, in behalf of his Protestant subjects; giving to their civil organization all the stability and permanency that the older Christian communities enjoyed in Turkey. It was issued in November, 1850; and translated into English, reads as follows: —

The Firman.

"To my Vizier, Mohammed Pasha, Prefect of the Police in Constantinople, the honorable Minister and glorious Councillor, the model of the world, and regulator of the affairs of the community; who, directing the public interests with sublime prudence, consolidating the structure of the empire with wisdom, and strengthening the columns of its prosperity and glory, is the recipient of every grace from the Most High. May God prolong his glory!

"When this sublime and august mandate reaches you, let it be known, that hitherto those of my Christian subjects who have embraced the Protestant faith, in consequence of their not being under any specially appointed superintendence, and in consequence of the patriarchs and primates of their former sects, which they have renounced, naturally not being able to attend to their affairs, have suffered much inconvenience and distress. But in necessary accordance with my imperial compassion, which is the support of all, and which is manifested to all classes of my subjects, it is contrary to my imperial pleasure that any one class of them should be exposed to suffering.

"As, therefore, by reason of their faith, the above mentioned are already a separate community, it is my royal compassionate will, that, for the facilitating the conducting of their affairs, and that they may obtain ease and quiet and safety, a faithful and trustworthy person from among themselves, and by their own selection, should be appointed, with the title of 'Agent of the Protestants,' and that he should be in relations with the Prefecture of the Police.

"It shall be the duty of the Agent to have in charge the register of the male members of the community, which shall be kept at the police; and the Agent shall cause to be registered therein all births and deaths in the community. And all applications for passports and marriage licenses, and all petitions on affairs concerning the community that are to be presented to the Sublime Porte, or to any other department, must be given in under the official seal of the Agent.

"For the execution of my will, this my imperial sublime mandate and august command has been especially issued and given from my sublime chancery.

"Hence thou, who art the minister above named, according as it has been explained above, wilt execute to the letter the preceding ordinance; only, as the collection of the capitation tax and the delivery of passports are subject to particular regulations, you will not do anything contrary to those regulations. You will not permit anything to be required of them, in the name of fee, or on other pretences, for marriage licenses, or registration. You will see to it that, like the other communities of the empire, in all their affairs, such as procuring cemeteries and places of worship, they should have every facility and every needed assistance. You will not permit that any of the other communities shall in any way interfere with their edifices, or with their worldly matters or concerns, or, in short, with any of their affairs, either secular or religious, that thus they may be free to exercise the usages of their faith.

"And it is enjoined upon you not to allow them to be molested an iota in these particulars, or in any others; and that all attention and perseverance be put in requisition to maintain them in quiet and security. And, in case of necessity, they shall be free to make representations regarding their affairs through their Agent to the Sublime Porte.

"When this my imperial will shall be brought to your knowledge and appreciation, you will have this august decree registered in the necessary departments, and then give it over to remain in the hands of these my subjects. And see you to it, that its requirements be always in future performed in their full import.

"Thus know thou, and respect my sacred signet! Written in the holy month of Moharrem, 1267 (November, 1850).

"Given in the well guarded city Constantiniyeh."

At the request of Sir Stratford Canning, thirteen of the leading Protestants called upon him, on the occasion of his procuring this charter of rights; and for nearly an hour he addressed them on their duties and responsibilities, in their present position in the empire. He told them that they ought to thank God that they were the first to be relieved from the shackles of superstition, and made acquainted with the pure Gospel of Christ. He told them that many eyes were upon them, and that they ought to excel all others in the land in faithful obedience to the government, in a brotherly deportment to those of other religious opinions, and an example of uprightness in every relation. Again and again did he exhort them to act, in all things, according to the principles and doctrines of the Gospel.

Good counsel to the Protestants.

Three years after this, on the 6th of December, 1853, on his return to Constantinople as Lord Stratford de Redcliffe, the same noble friend of religious freedom, wrote to the Earl of Clarendon, that he had endeavored in vain

Dilatoriness of the Turkish government.

to obtain the official transmission of the firman to the Pashas throughout the empire. This was strikingly characteristic of Turkish procrastination. But he was then able to state, that the Porte, "out of consideration for his repeated representations," had officially transmitted the firman to all Pashas where a Protestant society was known to exist.

Another concession by the Sultan.

In 1854, his lordship obtained the concession from the Turkish government, that Christian evidence, in matters of criminal jurisdiction, should stand on the same footing everywhere in Turkey as the testimony of Mohammedans; thus removing a great wrong, under which the rayahs of the empire had labored for centuries.

Agency of the American Minister.

While gratefully acknowledging our obligations to the representatives of other nations, I should also record, that our brethren, both in the Armenian and Syria missions, were under continued obligation to Mr. Carr, our Minister at the Porte, for personal protection as American citizens. He acted with decision whenever their rights were invaded. In the repeated efforts made to remove them from the country, his reply to the formal demands of the Porte was, that he had power to protect the missionaries as American citizens, but not to remove them; and furthermore, that while papal missionaries from France and Italy were permitted to reside in Turkey, Protestant missionaries from America must also have the same privilege.

Here we may properly pause, and consider what God had wrought, not alone through the agency of the churches, but with the coöperation of the great powers of the earth. Twenty years before, Messrs. Smith and Dwight did not find a single clear case of conversion in their extended travels through the Turkish empire. How many and great the subsequent changes! First came the national charter of rights, given by the Sultan in 1840; which, among its other results, destroyed the persecuting power of the Armenian aristocracy. Next came the abolition of the death penalty, in 1843, and the Sultan's pledge, that men should no more be persecuted for their religious opinions. Then, after three years, came the unthought of application of this pledge to the Armenian Protestants, when persecuted by their own hierarchy. In the next year followed the recognition of the Protestants as an independent community. Finally, in 1850, came the charter, signed by the Grand Sultan himself, placing the Protestants on the same national basis with the other Christian communities of the empire.

Greatness of the changes.

How wonderful this progression of events! So far as the central government was concerned, missionaries might print, gather schools, form churches, ordain pastors, and send forth other laborers, wherever they pleased. Attention had been awakened, and there was a disposition to inquire, renounce errors, and embrace gospel truths. There was a progressive change in fundamental ideas; a gradual reconstruction of the social system; a spiritual reformation. At least fifty places were known, scattered over Asiatic Turkey, in all of which souls had been converted through the truth, and where churches might be gathered. Ten churches had been formed already, and in part supplied with pastors. Aintab, scarcely known by name five years before, numbered more Protestants than even the metropolis, and was becoming one of the most interesting missionary stations in the world.

Divine agency recognized.

In this remarkable series of results we recognize the hand of God, who makes all earthly agencies subservient to the great work of redemption; so that secular agencies come as legitimately into the history of the republication of the Gospel in Bible lands, as do the labors of the missionaries. They were among the ordained means; and the leading agents cannot fail to command our grateful admiration.

The danger.

The danger at this time was, that the reformation so auspiciously begun, would pass its grand crisis before the central lights had grown bright enough, and a knowledge of the Gospel been sufficiently diffused in the empire. There was everywhere a curiosity to know what Protestantism was, and to hear what the missionaries had to say; but this curiosity, regarded as a national feeling, was in danger of dying out. In the year 1851, the President of the National Council of the Armenians said to Mr. Dwight: "Now is the time for you to work for the Armenian people. Such an opportunity as you now enjoy may soon pass away, and never more return. You should greatly enlarge your operations. Where you have one missionary, you should have ten; and where you have one book, you should put ten in circulation." Constantinople, Smyrna, Broosa, Trebizond, Erzroom, and Aintab, were already occupied as stations. It was proposed at once to occupy Sivas, Arabkir, Diarbekir, and Aleppo. Mr. Adger, after a laborious and most useful service in the literary department of the mission, was constrained, by his health, in 1847, to retire from the field.

The statement of Lord Stratford, that three years were allowed to pass before the Sultan's firman was transmitted to the provinces, will account in part for the fact that persecution did not cease. In general, whenever evangelical views entered for the first time into a place, a battle was to be fought, and the first recipients of these views were sure to suffer more or less from the hands of their former co-religionists. But relief was almost sure to come on an appeal to the capital; and thus there was a gradual progress towards the full protection of the Protestants as a distinct community.

Why persecution continued.

The accession of missionaries during the time

now under review, was as follows: Joel S. Everett, in 1845; Isaac G. Bliss, in 1847; Oliver Crane, in 1849; Joseph W. Sutphen, in 1852—who died before the close of the year; Wilson A. Farnsworth, William Clark, Andrew T. Pratt, M. D.; George B. Nutting, Fayette Jewett, M. D., and Jasper N. Ball, in 1853; Albert G. Beebe, George A. Perkins, Sanford Richardson, Edwin Goodell, and Benjamin Parsons, in 1854; and Alexander R. Plumer, and Ira T. Pettibone, in 1855. All these were married men, except Mr. Pettibone. Mary and Isabella, daughters of Dr. Goodell, returned to the mission within the last two years.

New missionaries.

In June, 1848, Pera was again ravaged by fire, and Messrs. Dwight, Homes, and Schauffler lost their houses, and most of their effects.

Pera again ravaged by fire.

In October of the same year, seven persons were added to the church at Aintab, five of whom were women. In this month, Dr. Azariah Smith returned to that station with his wife, and made it his permanent abode.

The Aintab station.

The church at Aintab had a commendable zeal for the spread of the Gospel in the surrounding villages; but their colporters were never suffered to remain long in a place, the Armenian magnates persuading the Turkish authorities to send them away as vagabonds. They now resorted to an ingenious expedient for protecting

Native zeal for the spread of the Gospel.

themselves with the authority of law. Five men, who had trades, went forth to different towns, with their tools in one hand and the Bible in the other. Wherever they went they worked at their trades, and at the same time preached Christ to the people. The experiment succeeded wonderfully. They could no longer be treated as vagabonds, and the spirit of religious inquiry spread in all directions. The congregation in Aintab became so large that two houses were opened for worship at the same time, and urgent appeals came from Killis, Marash, Oorfa, Diarbekir, Malatia, Harpoot, Arabkir, and other places near and remote.

Activity of the mission.

Mr. Crane succeeded Mr. Schneider at Broosa. Mr. Benjamin made a missionary tour from Smyrna to the interior of Asia Minor; Mr. Schneider made one to Aintab, on a temporary mission; Messrs. Goodell and Everett to Nicomedia and Adabazar; Mr. Peabody into the province of Geghi; Mr. Homes to Nicomedia; and Mr. Johnston to Tocat. The building occupied by the Seminary at Bebek became now the property of the Board. The printing at Smyrna, in Armenian, Armeno-Turkish, Hebrew-Spanish, and Modern Greek, amounted to twenty-one thousand copies, and five million five hundred and eighty-two thousand pages. There was printing done at Constantinople, but the amount was not reported. Among the works in process of publication was D'Aubigne's "History of the Reformation."

The persecuting Matteos had now finished his career as Patriarch. Before the close of 1848, he was convicted of frauds upon the public treasury, and of forgery, and was degraded, and passed into retirement on the shores of the Bosphorus.[1]

Matteos deposed from office.

Three additional pastors were ordained during the year which closed with May, 1849; Baron Mugurdich, at Trebizond, Baron Hohannes Sahakian, at Adabazar, and Baron Avedis, as co-pastor at Constantinople. The reader is aware that Hohannes received the greater part of his education in the United States. He possessed a delightful spirit, and developed far more talent than he was commonly credited with in America, where he could communicate his thoughts only through the medium of a strange language.

Native pastors.

The mission suffered a painful bereavement on the 14th of November, 1850, in the death of Mrs. Hamlin, at Rhodes, whither she had gone with her husband in the hope of relief.[2]

Death of Mrs. Hamlin.

Another bereavement occurred at Aintab in the death on the 3d of June, 1851, of the Rev. Azariah Smith, M. D. Such was his peculiar adaptation to different fields, that he had labored

Death and character of Dr. Azariah Smith.

[1] *Missionary Herald*, 1849, p. 42; *Report*, 1849, p. 115.

[2] See an account of her last sickness in *Missionary Herald* for 1851, p. 82; also in her Memoir, *Light in the Dark River*, by Mrs. Lawrence.

in many places, but had a special attachment for Aintab. The uncommonly rapid development of the active Christian graces at that station was largely owing, under God, to his skillful efforts, and he wished there to spend the remainder of his days. In this he was gratified. He returned from laboring at Diarbekir greatly in need of quiet. But finding so much to be done in the absence of Mr. Schneider at the annual meeting in Constantinople, he allowed himself no relaxation. His labors for the last six weeks of his life were incessant. A violent fever did its work in a fortnight. At the outset he gave specific directions as to the treatment of his case, feeling that soon he would be unable to prescribe for himself; and expressed a wish that no native physician should be employed, as there was no competent one to be had at Aintab. While in full possession of reason, he spoke of his departure with the composure of one on a short journey, and soon to return. As the native brethren came in one by one and in companies, he reminded them how often he had preached to them salvation through Christ alone. "In his lucid intervals," says his missionary brother, "and even in his delirium, his soul seemed intent on measures for the good of this people. At last he appeared to be at the gate of heaven. When no longer able to articulate words, he would utter faint syllables expressive of his growing rapture. Then he would move his lips as if in prayer; and, again, for minutes together, he would attempt to sing. It was a blessed privilege to be by his side." Mr. Dunmore was present at the funeral, and says: "The chapel was crowded, and the roofs of the surrounding buildings were covered. There was abundant proof of the presence of grief-stricken hearts in gushing tears, and sobs were heard throughout the assembly. There were six or seven hundred present, and nearly as many accompanied us to the grave. I scarcely ever saw in America a more quiet and solemn procession. In the Protestant burying ground, by the side of his only child, lie the remains of our dear departed brother."

Miscellaneous matters.

The Rev. George W. Dunmore and wife had joined the mission early in 1851, and proceeded to Diarbekir by way of Aintab. Broosa was now left for a time, as Nicomedia and Adabazar had been, to the care of a native pastor, under the superintendence of the Constantinople station; and useful evangelical tours were performed by different brethren.[1]

The law forbidding the residence of foreigners in Constantinople proper having become a dead letter, two of the brethren took up their abode near the "Seven Towers," amid an Armenian population, and a third evangelical church was formed in February, 1852, in the suburb of Has-Keuy.

[1] See *Missionary Herald* for 1851, pp. 24–32, 78–81, 160–162, 232–236

Among the miscellaneous labors of the brethren at the capitol, was the distribution of letters received at the mission post-office from the European mails. Not less than fifteen hundred letters were thus disposed of in the year 1851, as the Turks had no arrangements for distributing letters that came by steamers. There was also much other secular labor for the brethren at this central station.

Difficulties in the church at Trebizond occasioned the calling of an ecclesiastical council, — the first one convened in the Turkish empire. Pastor Simon was present from the first church in Constantinople, pastor Hohannes from Adabazar, and Mr. Dwight from the mission. Pastor Hohannes was chosen moderator, and pastor Simon scribe; and Mr Dwight describes them as managing the case with admirable tact and prudence. The results were satisfactory.

First ecclesiastical council.

Marsovan began now to claim special attention. It stands in one corner of a lovely plain hemmed in by mountains, and then contained eight hundred Armenian houses, with twice that number of Turkish families. The story of the entrance of the Gospel into this place is so interesting that it deserves to be recorded. Pastor Simon visited it in September, 1851, on his return from the council at Trebizond, and learned that, eighteen years before, a respectable inhabitant made a pilgrimage to Jerusalem, and bought in Beirût a few

The Gospel introduced at Marsovan.

Armeno-Turkish tracts, not knowing what they were, only that they were written in his own native tongue. He read them carefully on his way home, and liked them so well that he retained them; but not until Protestants and Protestant books were anathematized in the churches did he learn their origin. They had been printed in Malta under the supervision of Mr. Goodell. Soon after this, Der Vartanes, on a missionary tour through Armenia, spent a night at the convent in Marsovan. This man was present in the evening, and recognized the similarity between the teachings of the stranger and his favorite tracts, but did not dare to speak out before the Vartabed. He managed, however, to see the good priest alone, and with great difficulty they contrived to unite in prayer under a tree in the garden. This was the only evangelical prayer he ever heard till Mr. Powers visited the place in March, 1851. We need not say how cordially he was received by the owner of the tracts; nor by him alone, for the missionary could scarcely get a moment to himself day or night. No wonder Mr. Powers felt that God had good things in store for this people. When he returned in July, he was disappointed in not being met by his friend, till he learned that six weeks before he had been dragged from his bed at midnight, and sent a prisoner with four others to Amasia, a town twenty-four miles distant. There for two weeks they were shut up with the vilest criminals, and one day they were chained together, two and two. The charge brought against them by the governor and council of Marsovan was, that they had made a violent assault upon the court. Nor would the Pasha of Amasia, who, according to Turkish custom, had "eaten" a large bribe, listen to any denial of the preposterous accusation.

The outrages which they suffered at length produced such an excitement at Marsovan, that the primates hastened to give an order for their release. The spirit of religious inquiry now greatly increased, and a large number signed a petition to be set off from the Armenian Church as Protestants.

Mr. E. E. Bliss visited Marsovan in October, and was there three months. His presence was greatly needed. There had been a decline of piety, and only a small number of the Protestants retained their interest in spiritual things. Conversation turned not so much on the truths of the Gospel as on the errors of the Armenian Church; nor so much on these as on the corruption of their priesthood and the exactions of the government. All were convinced of the truth of Protestantism, but its particular charm was in its promise of good for the life that now is. There was an obvious need of more persecution.

Is visited by Mr. Bliss.

During the first month, Mr. Bliss preached every evening in the week, and twice on the Sabbath. The audiences ranged from fifty to

A needed persecution

two hundred and fifty, and there were increasing evidences of interest in the preaching. Then came tribulation because of the word. The power of wealth and political influence was enlisted against the truth. The taxes of those who had joined the Protestant community were more than doubled, and those who could not or would not pay them, were thrown into prison. Indeed, former scenes in Constantinople were now repeated in Marsovan. No mercy was shown, except on the one condition of leaving the Protestant meetings. When day after day passed and brought no relief, the feeble began to yield. One by one they made their submission to the Vartabed, and received his blessing. Only four stood firm.

Unexpected relief.

But now the Lord sent a partial deliverance, in an unexpected way. An authoritative copy of the Sultan's firman was sent from Constantinople, by a brother who was ignorant of the circumstances. No such copy had before reached that part of the interior, so that any official who pleased could ignore its existence. The news of its arrival brought out the affrighted Protestants from their hiding-places. Many whose sympathies were with them, were as joyful as themselves. Before night five or six, who had submitted to the Vartabed, bore to him a written recantation of what they had done; and he, having heard of the firman, received the recantation and was silent. After that there was comparative peace, and the number attending on the preaching of the missionary increased.

I have dwelt on these developments at Marsovan, as an illustration of what, in various degrees, was experienced in other places at this stage in the reformation; as in Marash, Kessab, Demirdesh, and Adana. Wherefore this statement.

Mr. Wood, of this mission, being detained in the United States by the failure of his wife's health, was elected, in 1852, a Corresponding Secretary of the Board, to reside in the city of New York. The widow of Dr. Azariah Smith had remained in active labors at Aintab, but disease now obliged her to retire from the field. Miss Maria A. West took charge, with Mrs. Everett, of the girls' boarding-school at Constantinople; and Miss Melvina Haynes, a sister of Mrs. Everett, gave herself to a species of labor among Armenian females, which has since risen to importance in the missionary field. Mrs. George B. Nutting died at Aintab, July 9, 1854. Various notices.

In the Reports of the Prudential Committee to the Board for 1852 and 1853, a hundred important towns and villages are named, into which the reformation had gained entrance.

Pastor Simon, of the first church in Constantinople, spent a summer at Aintab; but his absence was the occasion of serious injury to his own charge; and so it was at Adabazar. Missions by native pastors.

Pastor Hohannes of that church, with teacher Simon, of Nicomedia, devoted eight months to a missionary tour through Asia Minor. Their course was by way of Smyrna and Beirût, to Kessab, Aleppo, Killis, Aintab, Marash, Oorfa, Albestan, Cesarea, Marsovan, and Samsûn; thence by steamer to Trebizond; thence to Erzroom, Khanoos, Moosh, Van, Bitlis, and back again through Diarbekir, Harpoot, Arabkir, Egin, Divrik, Sivas, Tokat, Amasia, Marsovan, and Samsûn. An inspection of the map will show that these brethren traversed Asia Minor by three lines, visiting all its most important places. They spent a considerable time in many of them, and everywhere found ready listeners to their message. In numerous places there were inquirers, who needed only leaders to withstand the fire of persecution.

Death of Mrs. Everett.

The mission suffered a sore bereavement in the death of Mrs. Everett at Constantinople, in December, 1854. She possessed a transparent and beautiful character, with eminent capacity for usefulness.[1]

Death of Mr. Benjamin.

Mr. Benjamin also died at Constantinople, the next year, at the age of forty-four. He was nine years in the mission to Greece. His labors in the Armenian Mission,—first at Smyrna, and then at Constantinople,—were mainly through the press, in which he was eminently

[1] See *The Missionary Sisters*,—Mrs. Everett and Mrs. Hamlin,—written by Mrs. Benjamin.

useful. He had a clear conviction, in devoting his life to giving the Armenians an evangelical literature, that he was doing the work to which his Master called him. Nor did he overrate the importance of this branch of the work. His missionary experience in another field was of much value in guarding him against mistakes. At Pera, in addition to his literary labors, he preached statedly in modern Greek to a small congregation.[1]

[1] See an obituary notice of Mr. Benjamin in the *Missionary Herald* for 1855, pp. 142–147.

CHAPTER XXV.

THE ARMENIANS.

1855–1860.

The Crimean war subservient to the Gospel.

THERE are times when the movements of armies are evidently made subservient, in divine Providence, to the progress of the Gospel; and the history of missions to the Oriental Churches would be imperfect without some notice of the Crimean war of 1854 and 1855. The historian of that war has shown, that it originated in the desire of Nicholas, Czar of Russia, to secure certain rights in the "holy places" at Jerusalem (in which he was opposed by the Roman Catholic government of France), and to obtain a formal recognition of himself as protector of the millions in Turkey professing the Greek religion.[1] But for the seasonable return to Constantinople of Lord Stratford de Redcliffe in 1853, there is reason to fear, that the extraordinary persistence of the Czar might have been successful,

Origin of the war.

Providential interposition.

[1] See volume first of Kinglake's *Invasion of the Crimea.* He describes very minutely how the English nation was drawn into the war; but it is not necessary to go into that subject here. The nation was doubtless much influenced by its desire to uphold the Turkish government in order to keep open its communication with India.

and that the protectorate would have been used to destroy the evangelical missions.[1]

The author was in the interior of Asia Minor a short time while the Crimean war was in progress, and heard of reports among the people, — circulated, as was believed, by Russian agents, — that if Nicholas were victorious, he would secure the withdrawal from Turkey of Protestant missionaries. Exasperation caused by the failure of his negotiations with the Sultan, brought on the war; and the fall of Sebastopol was a more direct benefit to the missions, than it was to the nations that fought against it. But for the result then obtained, at vast ex-

Probable consequence of Russia's success.

Effect of the fall of Sebastopol.

[1] Some idea of the spirit in which such a protectorate might have been exercised, may be obtained from two out of a number of kindred articles of the Russian Penal Law:

"Article 206. Whoever is found guilty of having induced others to secede from the Greek Orthodox Confession, and to join another Christian Church, will be condemned to the loss of the rights of his social position, to transportation to Tobolsk or Tomsk (Siberia), or to the punishment of the lash, and one or two years of imprisonment in the house of correction.

"Article 207. Whoever endeavors, by preaching or writing, to seduce members of the Orthodox Church to join any other Christian community, will be punished the first time, with the loss of some of his special rights, and imprisonment for one or two years in a house of correction; the second time, with imprisonment in a fortress from four to six years; the third time, with the loss of all his personal and social civil rights and status, and transportation for life to Tobolsk or Tomsk (Siberia), with imprisonment of one or two years."—*New York Observer* for August, 1871.

pense of treasure and life, very different might have been the prospect of a successful republication of the Gospel in Bible lands.

The mission in 1855.

The number of missionaries in the Armenian Mission in 1855, was twenty-six. One of these was an ordained physician, and there was a physician unordained. There were twenty-eight female assistant missionaries, three of whom were unmarried. Of the Armenian helpers, thirteen were pastors and preachers, and sixty-four were lay-helpers. The stations, — called such because missionaries resided at them, — were fourteen. Twelve of these were north of the Taurus, and two were south of that range.

Schools.

Constantinople, Tocat, and Aintab had each a training-school for native preachers and helpers, and there was also a girls' boarding-school at Constantinople; and thirty-eight free schools were scattered over the field. Nine years after the organization of the first evangelical church, the number of churches was twenty-three. The church at Aintab was the largest, containing one hundred and forty-one members. Kessab, a long day's journey south of Antioch, where no missionary had ever resided, had a church of forty-one members. The first edifice for Christian worship in the Ottoman Empire, erected on a new site, was the stone

Church organization.

Church building.

church at Aintab. Prior to this, Christians had only been allowed to repair their old churches, and to rebuild on the old sites. The obtaining of this new indulgence was probably owing, in a measure, to the influence of the Crimean war. The dedication service, early in 1855, was attended by more than twelve hundred persons, and more than eleven hundred were present on the following Sabbath.

The printing. The printing reported for this year amounted to thirty-five thousand volumes, and nearly five millions of pages, in the Armenian, Armeno-Turkish, Greek, Greco-Turkish, and Hebrew-Spanish, but chiefly in Armenian. A religious periodical was issued every two months called the "Avedaper," or "Messenger." Dr. Dwight was editor of this, but the general supervision of the press, after the decease of Mr. Benjamin, devolved on Dr. Riggs.

Editions of the Scriptures. Octavo and duodecimo editions of the Armenian Bible were going through the press, as was also an octavo Bible in Greco-Turkish. The New Testament had been issued in the ancient Armenian, in the Ararat dialect or Eastern Armenian, in the Ararat and Ancient Armenian in parallel columns, in the Greco-Turkish, and in the Armeno-Turkish. The Gospel of Matthew was issued in the Koordish language, and the Psalms in the Bulgarian. A demand for the Bible in the Turkish language came from almost every part of the empire.

The book depository was removed from Pera across the Golden Horn into the old city of Constantinople, and the Moslems made no objection. More than twenty boxes of books were sent to a single place in the interior within the space of a year and a half. At one time two boxes were ready for Diarbekir, one for Cesarea, one for Aintab, and another for Jerusalem.

The book depository.

In this work the misssion was liberally aided by the American, and the British and Foreign Bible Societies, by the London Religious Tract Society, the American Tract Society, and more recently by the Turkish Missions Aid Society. Mr. Barker, agent of the British and Foreign Bible Society, and the Rev. C. N. Righter, of the American Bible Society (who died not long after at Diarbekir), did much to promote the work of Bible distribution in the countries around the Mediterranean and Black Seas; and the Constantinople Bible Society employed a French and English colporter among the soldiers of the allied powers. More Bibles and religious books went into the hands of Mohammedans from the depository of the mission during the years 1854 and 1855, than in all the previous years of its existence. Twenty thousand copies of the Bible were scattered through Turkey in that space of time.

Aid from abroad.

The transfer of Dr. Riggs to the department of the Press made it necessary to suspend the Greek department in the Seminary at Be-

Greek students in theology.

bek, and four of the six Greek pupils were sent to Dr. King at Athens.[1] Another became a teacher in Demirdesh, and another went to the United States to complete his professional studies.

Five Armenian students had been licensed to preach, and sent to Adrianople, Cesarea, Sivas, Diarbekir, and Kessab. Another, having the ministry in prospect, was a teacher in the new training-school at Tocat, under Mr. Van Lennep. A similar school existed at Aintab.

Licentiates.

The accession of missionaries from 1855 to 1860 was as follows: In 1855, Orson P. Allen; in 1856, George A. Pollard, Tillman C. Trowbridge, and Misses Mary E. Tenney and Sarah E. West; in 1857, Crosby H. Wheeler, Charles F. Morse, Oliver W. Winchester, Jackson G. Coffing, George H. White, and Julius Y. Leonard; in 1858, Theodore Byington, George Washburn, and William Hutchinson; and Herman N. Barnum, who, being at Constantinople as a traveller, made an offer of his services, which was accepted in this year; in 1859, William W. Meriam, Joseph K. Greene, James F. Clarke, George F. Herrick, and Henry S. West, M. D., and Miss Myra A. Proctor; in 1860, Alvan B. Goodale, M. D., William F. Arms, Zenas Goss, William W. Livingston, and Lysander T. Burbank.

Accession of missionaries.

[1] The author regrets being obliged to say, that these all disappointed the expectations of their benefactors.

Messrs. Washburn, Trowbridge, Pettibone, Barnum, Herrick, and Goss came to the mission unmarried; Mr. Washburn afterwards married a daughter of Dr. Hamlin, Mr. Barnum a daughter of Dr. Goodell, and Mr. Trowbridge a daughter of Dr. Riggs.

Mr. Everett, a devoted servant of Christ, was called to his rest on the 5th of March, 1856, after a sickness of a few days. His orphan children returned to the United States in charge of Miss Haynes, the sister of their mother. Messrs. Isaac G. Bliss and Edwin Goodell, in consequence of the failure of health, were released from their connection with the Board. The former afterwards recovered his health, and returned to Turkey as agent of the American Bible Society, in which capacity he has rendered very valuable service. Antioch and Aleppo were transferred from the Syrian to the Armenian Mission. At Erzroom the war drove away, not only the church-members, but most of those who were interested in the truth. Mr. Richardson removed to Arabkir to supply the place of Mr. Clark, who had been called to the seminary at Bebek; left without a teacher by the death of Mr. Everett and the temporary absence of Dr. Hamlin. At Marash, in consequence of the war and the proximity of the rough mountaineers of Zeitoon, the missionaries were at one time in no small danger.

Death of Mr. Everett.

Miscellaneous notices.

The beheading of a young Armenian, who had

rashly declared himself a Mohammedan, and then repented of his rashness, and the consequent successful efforts of Sir Stratford Canning, in procuring a pledge from the Sultan that no person should be persecuted in Turkey for his religious opinions, were described in the first volume.[1] This was in 1843 and 1844. Ten or eleven years later, there was another beheading at Adrianople for a like cause, and another at Aleppo; and the same high-minded statesman was again aroused to effort, not only for a more effectual abrogation of the death penalty itself, but to obtain for the Protestant Christians freedom from persecution, and for the Christians generally the privileges that were enjoyed by their fellow-subjects of the Moslem religion. The eighty folio pages of documents on the subject, which were presented to both Houses of Parliament in 1856, form an important and interesting chapter in the history of those times. The principal writers, in addition to Lord Stratford de Redcliffe and the Earl of Clarendon, were the Earl of Shaftesbury, Lord Cowley, Sir Culling Eardley Eardley, President of the Turkish Missions Aid Society, the Rev. Cuthbert G. Young, its Secretary, and Mehemet Fuad.

Renewed agitation about the death penalty.

As the result of all, a Hatti Humaïoun, or Imperial Firman, was issued by the Sultan in February, 1856. When read in public, the

The Hatti Humaïoun.

[1] Vol. i. p. 135.

Sheik el Islam, the highest Moslem ecclesiastic, invoked the divine blessing on the Imperial Edict; but probably without an apprehension, either by himself or by his government, of the full significance of the instrument. By many of the Mohammedans it was regarded as opening the door for them to become Christians. Not a few of the Armenians and Greeks were displeased with it as favoring Protestantism; and this fact did not escape the sagacity of Mohammedans.

The Imperial Rescript, as translated from the French, is as follows: —

"Let it be done as herein set forth.

"To you, my Grand Vizier, Mehemed Emin Aali Pasha, decorated with my Imperial Order of the Medjidiyé of the first class, and with the Order of Personal Merit; may God grant to you greatness, and increase your power!

"It has always been my most earnest desire to insure the happiness of all classes of the subjects whom divine Providence has placed under my imperial sceptre; and since my accession to the throne I have not ceased to direct all my efforts to the attainment of that end.

"Thanks to the Almighty, these unceasing efforts have already been productive of numerous useful results. From day to day the happiness of the nation and the wealth of my dominions go on augmenting.

"It being now my desire to renew and enlarge still more the new institutions, ordained with the view of establishing a state of things conformable with the dignity of my empire and the position which it occupies among civilized nations; and the rights of my empire having, by the fidelity and praiseworthy efforts of all my subjects, and by the kind and friendly assistance of the great powers, my noble Allies, received from abroad a confirmation which will be the commencement of a new era, it is my desire to augment its well-being and prosperity, to effect the happiness of all my subjects, who in my sight are all equal and equally dear to me, and who are united to each other by the cordial ties of patriotism, and to insure the means of daily increasing the prosperity of my empire. I have, therefore, resolved upon, and I order the execution of, the following measures.

"The guaranties promised on our part by the Hatti-Humaïoun of Gul-Hané, and in conformity with the Tanzimat, to all the subjects of my empire, without distinction of classes or of religion, for the security of their persons and property and the preservation of their honor, are to-day confirmed and consolidated; and efficacious measures shall be taken in order that they may have their full and entire effect.

"All the privileges and spiritual immunities granted by my ancestors *ab antiquo*, and at subsequent dates, to all Christian communities or other non-Mussulman persuasions established in my empire under my protection, shall be confirmed and maintained.

"Every Christian or other non-Mussulman community shall be bound, within a fixed period, and with the concurrence of a commission composed *ad hoc* of members of its own body, to proceed, with my high approbation and under the inspection of my Sublime Porte, to examine into its actual immunities and privileges, and to discuss and submit to my Sublime Porte the reforms required by the progress of civilization and of the age. The powers conceded to the Christian Patriarchs and Bishops by the Sultan Mahomet II. and his successors, shall be made to harmonize with the new position which my generous and beneficent intentions insure to these communities.

"The principle of nominating the Patriarchs for life, after the revision of the rules of election now in force, shall be exactly carried out, conformably to the tenor of their firmans of investiture.

"The Patriarchs, Metropolitans, Archbishops, Bishops and Rabbins shall take an oath on their entrance into office, according to a form agreed upon in common by my Sublime Porte and the spiritual heads of the different religious communities. The ecclesiastical dues, of whatever sort or nature they be, shall be abolished, and replaced by fixed revenues for the Patriarchs and heads of communities, and by the allocation of allowances and salaries equitably proportioned to the importance of the rank, and the dignity of the different members of the clergy.

"The property, real or personal, of the different Christian ecclesiastics shall remain intact; the temporal administration of the Christian or other non-Mussulman communities shall, however, be placed under the safeguard of an assembly to be chosen from among the members, both ecclesiastics and laymen, of the said communities.

"In the towns, small boroughs, and villages, where the whole population is of the same religion, no obstacle shall be offered to the repair, according to their original plan, of buildings set apart for religious worship, for schools, for hospitals and for cemeteries.

"The plans of these different buildings, in case of their new erection, must, after having been approved by the Patriarchs or heads of communities, be submitted to my Sublime Porte, which will approve of them by my imperial order, or make known its observation upon them within a certain time.

"Each sect, in localities where there are no other religious denominations, shall be free from every species of restraint as regards the public exercise of its religion.

"In the towns, small boroughs, and villages,

where different sects are mingled together, each community inhabiting a distinct quarter shall, by conforming to the above-mentioned ordinances, have equal power to repair and improve its churches, its hospitals, its schools, and its cemeteries. When there is question of the erection of new buildings, the necessary authority must be asked for, through the medium of the Patriarchs and heads of communities, from my Sublime Porte, which will pronounce a sovereign decision according to that authority, except in the case of administrative obstacles. The intervention of the administrative authority in all measures of this nature will be entirely gratuitous. My Sublime Porte will take energetic measures to insure to each sect, whatever be the number of its adherents, entire freedom in the exercise of its religion.

"Every distinction or designation tending to make any class whatever of the subjects of my empire inferior to another class, on account of their religion, language, or race, shall be forever effaced from the administrative protocol. The laws shall be put in force against the use of any injurious or offensive term, either among private individuals or on the part of the authorities.

"As all forms of religion are and shall be freely professed in my dominions, no subject of my empire shall be hindered in the exercise of the religion that he professes, nor shall be in any way annoyed on this account. No one shall be compelled to change their religion.

"The nomination and choice of all functionaries and other employés of my empire being wholly dependent upon my sovereign will, all the subjects of my empire, without distinction of nationality, shall be admissible to public employments, and qualified to fill them according to their capacity and merit, and conformably with rules to be generally applied.

"All the subjects of my empire, without distinction, shall be received into the civil and military schools of the government, if they otherwise satisfy the conditions as to age and examination which are specified in the organic regulations of the said schools. Moreover, every community is authorized to establish public schools of science, art, and industry. Only the method of instruction and the choice of professors in schools of this class shall be under the control of a mixed council of public instruction, the members of which shall be named by my sovereign command.

"All commercial, correctional, and criminal suits between Mussulmans and Christian or other non-Mussulman subjects, or between Christians or other non-Mussulmans of different sects, shall be referred to mixed tribunals.

"The proceedings of these tribunals shall be public; the parties shall be confronted, and shall produce their witnesses, whose testimony shall be received, without distinction, upon an oath taken according to the religious law of each sect.

"Suits relating to civil affairs shall continue to be publicly tried, according to the laws and regulations before the mixed provincial councils, in the presence of the governor and judge of the place. Special civil proceedings, such as those relating to successions or others of that kind, between subjects of the same Christian or other non-Mussulman faith, may, at the request of the parties, be sent before the councils of the Patriarchs or of the communities.

"Penal, correctional, and commercial laws, and rules of procedure for the mixed tribunals, shall be drawn up as soon as possible, and formed into a code. Translations of them shall be published in all the languages current in the empire.

"Proceedings shall be taken with as little delay as possible, for the reform of the penitentiary system as applied to houses of detention, punishment, or correction, and other establishments of like nature, so as to reconcile the rights of hnmanity with those of justice. Corporal punishment shall not be administered, even in the prisons, except in conformity with the disciplinary regulations established by my Sublime Porte; and everything that resembles torture shall be entirely abolished.

"Infractions of the law in this particular shall be severely repressed, and shall besides entail, as of right, the punishment, in conformity with the civil code, of the authorities who may order, and of the agents who may commit them.

"The organization of the police in the capital, in the provincial towns, and in the rural districts, shall be revised in such a manner as to give to all the peaceable subjects of my empire the strongest guaranties for the safety both of their persons and property.

"The equality of taxes entailing equality of burdens, as equality of duties entails that of rights, Christian subjects, and those of other non-Mussulman sects, as it has been already decided, shall, as well as Mussulmans, be subject to the obligations of the Law of Recruitment. The principle of obtaining substitutes, or of purchasing exemption, shall be admitted. A complete law shall be published, with as little delay as possible, respecting the admission into and service in the army of Christian and other non-Mussulman subjects.

"Proceedings shall be taken for a reform in the constitution of the provincial and communal councils, in order to insure fairness in the choice of the deputies of the Mussulman, Christian, and other communities, and freedom of voting in the councils. My Sublime Porte will take into consideration the adoption of the most effectual means for ascertaining exactly and for controlling the result of the deliberations of the decisions arrived at.

"As the laws regulating the purchase, sale, and

disposal of real property are common to all the subjects of my empire, it shall be lawful for foreigners to possess landed property in my dominions, conforming themselves to the laws and police regulations, and bearing the same charges as the native inhabitants, and after arrangements have been come to with foreign powers.

"The taxes are to be levied under the same denomination from all the subjects of my empire, without distinction of class or of religion. The most prompt and energetic means for remedying the abuses in collecting the taxes, and especially the tithes, shall be considered. The system of direct collection shall gradually, and as soon as possible, be substituted for the plan of farming, in all the branches of the revenues of the State. As long as the present system remains in force, all agents of the government and all members of the medjlis shall be forbidden, under the severest penalties, to become lessees of any farming contracts which are announced for public competition, or to have any beneficial interest in carrying them out. The local taxes shall, as far as possible, be so imposed as not to affect the sources of production, or to hinder the progress of internal commerce.

"Works of public utility shall receive a suitable endowment, part of which shall be raised from private and special taxes, levied in the provinces which shall have the benefit of the advantages arising from the establishment of ways of communication by land and sea.

"A special law having been already passed, which declares that the budget of the revenue and expenditure of the state shall be drawn up and made known every year, the said law shall be most scrupulously observed. Proceedings shall be taken for revising the emoluments attached to each office.

"The heads of each community and a delegate, designated by my Sublime Porte, shall be summoned to take part in the deliberations of the Supreme Council of Justice on all occasions which might interest the generality of the subjects of my empire. They shall be summoned specially for this purpose by my Grand Vizier. The delegates shall hold office for one year; they shall be sworn on entering upon their duties. All the members of the council, at the ordinary and extraordinary meetings, shall freely give their opinions and their votes, and no one shall ever annoy them on this account.

"The laws against corruption, extortion, or malversation, shall apply, according to the legal forms, to all the subjects of my empire, whatever may be their class and the nature of their duties.

"Steps shall be taken for the formation of banks and other similar institutions, so as to effect a reform in the monetary and financial system, as well as to create funds to be employed in augmenting the sources of the material wealth of my empire.

"Steps shall also be taken for the formation of roads and canals to increase the facilities of communication and increase the sources of the wealth of the country. Everything that can impede commerce or agriculture shall be abolished. To accomplish these objects, means shall be sought to profit by the science, the art, and the funds of Europe, and thus gradually to execute them.

"Such being my wishes and my commands, you, who are my Grand Vizier, will, according to custom, cause this Imperial Firman to be published in my capital, and in all parts of my empire; and you will watch attentively and take all the necessary measures that all the orders which it contains be henceforth carried out with the most rigorous punctuality."

How regarded by Lord Stratford.

Lord Stratford, in replying to a congratulatory address from the missionaries, declared his agreement with them in the opinion, that something great had been gained; though he believed the principles involved would require persevering efforts to carry them into practice. He said that he was himself but an humble instrument in the hands of divine Providence, and that he had never felt the hand of God so sensibly in any other measure he had carried through, as in this, which, after he had given it up for lost, had succeeded all at once, in a way that filled him with astonishment.[1]

[1] That the Hatti Humaïoun was really intended to include the death

The plenipotentiaries of Great Britain, Austria, France, Russia, Sardinia, and Turkey, assembled in February, 1856, at the close of the Crimean war, to negotiate what is known as the Treaty of Paris. It is evident from the Protocols of their Conference, that, having the Earl of Clarendon and Lord Cowley among them, they were intent on giving weight and perpetuity to this firman of the

Recognized in the treaty of Paris.

penalty, is made exceedingly probable by the official correspondence which preceded it, and which was in fact its procuring cause. Only a few brief extracts can be given in this note.

Includes the death penalty.

Referring to the punishment of death as applied to apostates from Islamism, the Earl of Clarendon, English Minister of Foreign Affairs, writes thus to Lord Stratford de Redcliffe: "As the Turkish empire is, by treaty stipulations, to be declared part and parcel of the European system, it is quite impossible for the powers of Europe to acquiesce in the continuance in Turkey of a law, and a practice, which is a standing insult to every other nation in Europe."

Again, on the 17th of September, 1853, the Earl of Clarendon writes thus to Lord Stratford: "Her Majesty's Government distinctly demands that no punishment whatever shall attach to the Mohammedan who becomes a Christian, whether originally a Mohammedan, or originally a Christian, any more than any punishment attaches to a Christian who embraces Mohammedanism. In all such cases the movements of human conscience must be left free, and the temporal arm must not interfere to coerce the spiritual decision."

Referring to the Imperial Rescript, February 12, 1856, Lord Stratford says, writing to the Earl: —

"If no one is to be molested on account of the religion he professes, and no one to be punished as a renegade, whatever form of faith he denies, I do not see what room there can possibly be for any practical persecutions in future within the limits of the Sultan's empire." See *Correspondence respecting Christian Privileges in Turkey*, in *Parliamentary Papers for* 1856, pp. 15, 24, 25, 33, 55, 60, 66, 67, 77–80.

Sultan, by a formal recognition of it in the treaty. This was done in article ninth, after much deliberation, and with the full concurrence of all the plenipotentiaries, including the representative of the Sultan.[1]

How estimated by the missionaries.

The Hatti Humaïoun of 1855 was much more than a confirmation of the Imperial Firman of 1850, nor was it a dead letter. A year afterwards Dr. Jewett, while admitting that it was inefficient in certain respects, declared it to have been in an important sense, a quickening spirit. "Never," he says, "within the same space of time, has there been as much religious discussion with the Mussulmans as since the issue of the late firman, and never before, I think, has there been such a spirit of religious inquiry among Mohammedans, and readiness to discuss the merits of the Christian

[1] "NINTH ARTICLE. His Imperial Majesty the Sultan, having, in his constant solicitude for the welfare of his subjects, issued a firman, which, while ameliorating their condition without distinction of religion or race, records his generous intentions towards the Christian population of his empire, and wishing to give a further proof of his sentiments in that respect, has resolved to communicate to the Contracting Parties the said firman, emanating spontaneously from his sovereign will.

"The Contracting Powers recognize the high value of this communication. It is clearly understood, that it cannot, in any case, give to said Powers the right to interfere, either collectively or separately, in the relations of his Majesty, the Sultan, with his subjects, nor in the internal administration of his Empire." See *Treaty of Paris*, March 30, 1856, in *Parliamentary State Papers*, vol. lxi. p. 20. Also, appended, *Protocols of Conferences*, pp. 8, 13, 51, 57, 58.

religion, as has been evident during the past year. It has awakened hope of a good day even for the Moslems." A few years later, Dr. Goodell, speaking of it says: "To the Protestant communities here, and to all who live godly in Christ Jesus, this Hatti Humaïoun is a boon of priceless value. Heretofore its principal use was to secure us from the molestation of these corrupt churches, but we have now begun to test its importance with reference to the Mohammedans themselves. Only a few years since, the headless bodies of apostates from the Mohammedan faith might be seen lying in the streets of the great city. But now such apostates may be seen at all hours of the day walking these same streets without any apparent danger, urging the claims of Christianity even in the very courts of the royal mosques, and teaching and preaching in the chapel, in the private circle, and sometimes even in the palaces of the great, that Jesus Christ is Lord, to the glory of God the Father. And all this wonderful security is, under God, owing entirely to the Hatti Humaïoun." He adds, "It is said that the Turkish government is sometimes guilty of violating some of the great principles of that document. And who that knows anything of human nature, or of the history of our race, ever supposed they would not be guilty of it? To suppose the contrary would be to suppose the Turk advanced very much farther towards perfection than any other nation on the face of the earth."

A correspondence arose, about this time, in the old Armenian Church, between those who inclined towards the Papal Church and those who were opposed, and it was gratifying to see that the principal Armenian newspaper, published under the sanction of the Patriarch, drew its arguments almost wholly from the Scriptures, scarcely anything being said of the Councils, or of the Fathers.

Indications of progress.

The out-stations of Nicomedia, Adabazar, Rodosto, Baghchejuk, and Broosa were prosperous. A Protestant Greek community at Demirdesh stood firm under persecution, though without a spiritual guide. The Pasha did little for their protection, but divine Providence had other instruments for their deliverance. The French Vice Consul, having to feed immense herds of cattle for the French army, selected the principal Greek Protestant of the place as the most competent overseer, and empowered him to employ the needful agents. This brought to his feet some who had beaten him and even threatened him with death. He freely employed them and paid them honestly, thus returning good for evil.

The training-school at Tocat was composed of pious young men who made considerable progress in their studies. A footing was gained at Tarsus and Bitias, south of the Taurus range, and a native pastor was ordained at Kessab. Here was a Protestant community of more than four hundred.

At Aintab and in its neighboring villages, after

only nine years of labor, there were twelve stated religious services, nearly half of them conducted by native preachers, two thousand Protestants, old and young, two hundred and sixty-eight church-members, a large congregation on the Sabbath, three promising young men in the pastoral office, and two more prepared for that office. The year 1856 was one of unbroken prosperity in all temporal concerns at Aintab. The influence of this prosperity, however, had its usual effect in developing a love of the world, and a feeling of self-consequence, resulting in some perplexities within the church. Such results are known in much older communities, and ought to be expected in the early religious life of such a people. Between the pastor Kara Krikor and his people there was all that could be expected of mutual confidence and harmony, and his monthly salary was paid with a promptness unusual in such cases.

Progress at Aintab.

The death of Mrs. Schneider on the 29th of September was a great loss to the mission. This excellent woman had an earnest desire for the salvation of every one she met, and old and young listened with pleasure to her instructions. It became known, soon after her decease, that three or four small companies of native sisters had begun of their own accord to hold meetings in various quarters. The progress among the women of Aintab had been great. When the first missionary arrived,

Death of Mrs. Schneider.

only one woman was known who was able to read. It was now ascertained that nearly three hundred could read the New Testament.

The boarding-school pupils at Constantinople received a pupil this year from each of the following places — Trebizond, Diarbekir, Rodosto, Haskeuy, Scutari, and Baghchejuk. The chief difficulty in teaching was the want of suitable text-books in the modern language. In addition to the usual studies, the pupils were allowed an opportunity to acquaint themselves with domestic duties, and they did it in most cases with hearty good-will. Dr. Goodell exercised a fatherly care over the institution.

Girls' school at Constantinople.

During most of the year Mr. Clark had charge of the Seminary at Bebek. The prescribed course of study embraced four years in the scholastic department and three in the theological, and was designed to secure to the pupils a systematic training. The qualifications required for entering, raised the character of the common schools connected with the mission. During vacations the students were required to support themselves. The average number was forty-five, and it was necessary to reject no less than sixty applicants, mainly from inability to support them. Among them were Bulgarians, Albanians, Wallachians, and Servians. Seven students were in the theological department, and three others went through a part

Seminary at Bebek.

of the course, one of whom was a Turk, and another a Greek. Dr. Hamlin gave instruction in this department after his return, assisted by Dr. Schauffler in Turkish. Nine of the students in the seminary were church-members, and others gave evidence of piety.

The growth of the Armenian Mission, along with its great extent of territory, required a division for the more convenient administration of its affairs. Hence a Southern Armenian Mission was organized in November, 1856, having the Taurus for its boundary on the north, and embracing the stations of Aintab, Marash, Antioch, Aleppo, and Oorfa. Its printing was to be done at Constantinople. The members of this mission were Messrs. Schneider, Pratt, Beebee, Perkins, Morgan, Nutting, Cotting, and White. The field of the Northern Mission extended from the Balkans in European Turkey to the eastern waters of the Euphrates.

Division of the mission.

The "Turkish Missions Aid Society" was formed in England in 1854; "not to originate a new mission, but to aid the existing evangelical missions in the Turkish empire, especially American." The funds contributed to the American missions were given expressly for a Native Agency; and important aid has thus been rendered down to the present time. The funds of the Society having suffered diminution in 1857, Dr. Dwight was invited to visit England. He arrived

Turkish Missions Aid Society.

Dr. Dwight visits England.

in March of the following year, and visited the principal cities, in company with the Secretary. "I was everywhere received," says Dr. Dwight, "with the most overflowing kindness, and my simple story was listened to with the most intense interest. Clergymen and laymen of all evangelical denominations were usually present at the meetings, which were held on week days, and I saw nowhere anything like a sectarian spirit, but uniformly the very reverse. Ministers of the Church of England, as well as others, publicly advocated the plan of aiding the American Mission in Turkey, rather than sending forth a mission of their own." Valuable as the coöperation of this Society has been in the bestowment of funds, its moral influence in Turkey, as a visible illustration of fraternal feeling among Protestant Christians of various names and countries has been of far greater value.[1]

A remarkable man.

An account was given, in a former chapter, of the conversion, in 1842, of a "Papal Armenian.[2] His name was Bedros Kamaghielyan, and his death occurred in 1857, fifteen years afterward. His conversion was remarkable, and so was his subsequent life. He was for some years an efficient helper at Salonica among the Jews, and

[1] The aid afforded by the Turkish Missions Aid Society to the missions of the Board in Western Asia, has averaged about ten thousand dollars a year.

[2] Chapter ix. p. 130. See, also, *Missionary Herald*, 1857, pp. 387–390.

ever after that, he was a successful assistant of Dr. Dwight in Constantinople. Eminently wise to win souls to Christ, it is believed that many, among the different races in Turkey, will rise up and call him blessed. The first Turkish convert who became a preacher, received his first impressions from Bedros at Salonica. Years later, the missionaries learned that the origin of an interesting work of grace among the Greeks of Cassandra, in that region, was traceable to him. Though suffering from bodily infirmity in the later years of his life, his labors were unceasing for the salvation of souls, and for the edification of the church. He was noted for his humility and self-denial, and his piety was a steady glow of light. His views of the gospel method of salvation were clear, and his manner of presenting it exceedingly happy. He was eminently a peacemaker in the church, and his good sense was in constant demand in the settlement of difficulties. As a deacon in the Yeni Kapoo church he was constantly looking after the sick and infirm, visiting families in the Protestant community, and instructing their women in the doctrines and duties of Christianity. When attacked by his last sickness, Bedros very soon received the impression that it would be fatal. Once, in great bodily suffering, he exclaimed, "O, what a Saviour is my Saviour! He scatters all my darkness, and gives me peace." At another time, he wished the missionaries might all be called to his bedside, that he might declare to them his great joy, and what things the Lord was doing for his soul. A Mohammedan of some distinction, who had often had religious conversations with Bedros, called upon him without knowing of his sickness. The sick man, though in extreme bodily weakness, spoke very faithfully to his visitor, and told him of his joy in view of death, and his hope of going to be forever with the Lord Jesus Christ, and added: "This is the only way of peace and salvation, and Christ is the only Saviour of sinners for you, and for me, and for all the world." The eyes of the Turk filled with tears. He had never seen a Christian die before; and to hear a man talk with so much gladness of his departure from the world overcame him, and he hurried from the room. An aged Moslem called, who had known Bedros, and gave some evidence of being a Christian. Going to his bedside, his eyes streaming with tears, he embraced and kissed him in the most affectionate manner. Dr. Dwight closes his statement with the following testimony: "Thus has passed away one of the choicest spirits this world ever saw. I feel that I have many lessons to learn from his quiet, humble, and most useful life; and I trust that his death may be greatly blessed to all the missionaries, and to all the people."

The second Mrs. Hamlin died suddenly, on the 6th of November, 1857. Though not permitted to give her dying testimony, the

Death of Mrs. Hamlin.

record of her life was that of a meek, lowly, and quiet spirit; diligent, faithful, and affectionate in every duty.[1]

Station at Arabkir.

The region, of which Arabkir is the centre, was now rising in importance. The territory dependent on this station for instruction extended from northeast and southwest, along the western bank of the Euphrates, one hundred and seventy-five miles, with a population of one hundred thousand; about equally divided between Armenians and Mussulmans, with few Greeks, no Roman Catholics, and no Jews. A large number of the Mussulmans were known as Kuzzelbashes. The field was first occupied in 1853, and churches had been organized in three cities and two villages, all of which enjoyed the stated preaching of the Word.

Sivas and Tocat.

Sivas, west of Arabkir, and Tocat on the northwest, were missionary centres of populous fields, extensively accessible; the former containing a population of more than a hundred thousand, and the latter of nearly half a million, — Armenians, Turks, Kuzzelbashes, Koords, and Greeks.

Harpoot.

Harpoot lies east of Arabkir, on the other side of the Euphrates. Mr. Dunmore commenced this station in 1855, and was alone in this city of twenty-five thousand inhabitants; the failure of his wife's health having obliged her to return to

[1] See Memoir, *The Missionary Sisters*, written by Mrs. Benjamin.

the United States. He had been usefully employed here nearly three years, — the last with Messrs. Wheeler and Allen, — when, having a taste for exploration and pioneer labors, he was transferred, in 1858, to Erzroom, with special reference to the region south of that city; and Messrs. Wheeler and Allen were joined at Harpoot, in 1859, by Mr. H. N. Barnum. The city is the centre of a population of about one hundred thousand, and stands on a lofty hill, looking to the distant range of the Taurus on the south, and scores of villages on the intervening plain. Northward, across the eastern branch of the Euphrates, is the still loftier range of the Anti-Taurus; while the distant horizon to the east and west is shut in by mountains. Arabkir was occupied for several years by Messrs. Clark, Pollard, and Richardson, but in 1865 was included in the Harpoot field.[1]

Geghi.

Geghi is about ninety miles from Harpoot, in the direction of Erzroom. It was visited by Mr. Peabody and Mr. Bliss in 1848 and 1851. Mr. Peabody found the Vartabed of the place and ten of the people deeply interested in reading the Scriptures. Mr. Wheeler visited Geghi in the summer of 1858 and found the truth much opposed, but taking a firm hold among the sixteen hundred Armenians of the place. He was touched by their earnest entreaties to remain with them a few months;

[1] Mr. Wheeler's *Ten Years on the Euphrates.*

or if that might not be, that he would leave his native helper till some one else could come among them. As with the Apostle Paul at Troas, the eagerness of the people to hear led him to protract his labors on one occasion, till an hour and a half past midnight, and on another till the breaking day.

The year 1859 was signalized by a revival in the Bebek Seminary. At its commencement, nearly half the students were regarded as hopefully pious, and these all seemed at once to have new views of spiritual things. The Holy Spirit not only revived the graces of such, but put forth a converting power. Within a few weeks nearly all the students gave credible evidence of piety. There were several cases, also, of hopeful conversion in the girls' boarding school; and similar awakenings were reported at Marsovan, Yozgat, Baghchejuk, Broosa, and Marash. At the last place thirty-seven were added to the church at one time, making eighty-six by profession since the beginning of 1858.

Revival of religion.

Mr. Parsons had received frequent complaints from the brethren of Nicomedia, that their girls had not been properly cared for by the teacher, and from the teacher that the brethren were intermeddling. He answered by withdrawing all aid until they could agree among themselves. The effect was immediate. They began to pay a tuition fee, and made special efforts to render the school attractive. The number of pupils was in-

Girls' school at Nicomedia.

creased to seventy-eight, and the school ceased any longer to need aid.

Destructive fire at Tocat.

A fire destroyed the mission premises at Tocat in 1859. The flames were so rapid as not only to consume the buildings, but the clothing and bedding of the pupils, the books and apparatus of the school, a portion of the furniture of Messrs. Pettibone and Winchester, who had been recently placed at the head of the school, and all the effects of Mr. Van Lennep, including a large and valuable library, and a manuscript Armenian translation of a commentary on the Bible, made, and to have been printed, at the expense of the Prince of Schönberg. In view of this calamity, it was deemed expedient to close the training-school. A similar one was opened in the fall of the same year, at Harpoot. Mr. Clark returning to the United States, Dr. Hamlin renewed his connection with the Bebek Seminary.

Mr. Dunmore's explorations.

Mr. Dunmore, after describing a tour he had made of twelve hundred miles from Erzroom to Oroomiah in Persia, and from thence, on his return, through Russian Armenia, gives the following summary of his missionary travels: "I have travelled on horseback over six thousand miles in Turkey, and one thousand in Persia and Russia, between two and three hundred on goat skins upon the Tigris, and over fifteen hundred by steamer, without sickness by the way, without accident, or the loss of an article of value. And I have never taken a guard when travelling alone, for protection from robbers. Surely we may safely trust Him who says: 'Believe in God, believe also in me.'"[1]

The missionaries at Cesarea were much encouraged by the progress of the work there. Mr. Leonard thus writes: "The church, though constantly dismissing members to other churches, still maintains its numbers by fresh accessions from without, and is at the same time evidently advancing in consistent, intelligent Christian character. Here are some noble exemplars of faith and piety, who search the Scriptures daily, and adorn their doctrines by a godly life. I have often wished I might introduce some of our American friends into our teachers' meetings on a Sabbath afternoon, or to the Sabbath-school at the intermission of public worship, where nearly the whole congregation remains, exhibiting a zeal and aptness in the discussion of religious truths scarcely surpassed in the most favored churches in New England. The weekly woman's prayer-meeting is sometimes left entirely in the hands of the native sisters, and any one of half a dozen is always ready without embarrassment to take the lead, discoursing very appropriately from her Turkish Testament. This, I am told, is a rare thing in Turkey, where woman has been so long held in ignorance and degradation."

Church at Cesarea.

The reader will remember the Patriarch Matteos,

[1] *Missionary Herald* for 1859, pp. 306–313.

and his degradation in 1849. After ten years passed in retirement, he was elected Catholikos of all the Armenians, and removed to Echmiadzin. His election to such a post at this time was significant, but the probability of his being able then to hinder the reformation did not create serious apprehension.

Matteos the persecutor.

Mrs. Beebee died peacefully at Marash, on the 28th of October, 1858, after protracted sufferings, and her husband returned some months after to the United States with broken health, and was released from his connection with the Board.

Death of Mrs. Beebee.

CHAPTER XXVI.

THE ARMENIANS.

1860–1861.

THE fleets and armies of Europe had retired, and the Turk felt in a measure freed from a troublesome guardianship; which had, however, greatly promoted both religion and reform in Turkey. The fact that the war had materially weakened Russian influence at the Porte, may have been among the reasons that induced England now to relax its hold on the government of the Sultan. As a consequence, French diplomacy was decidedly in the ascendant, and lent its influence to promote Papal schemes. "The Armenians," writes a well informed missionary, "accept a declaration of the Bible as ultimate, and as the Protestant missionaries made the Bible the basis of all their work, and accustomed the people to refer to it for authority in all spiritual matters, the Papists have been shut up to the use of political measures to gain adherents. This they have done by espousing the cause of any party in litigation on condition that he should register himself a Roman Catholic. This influence was very powerful throughout the country, as it

One result of the Crimean war.

was supported by the intervention of the French embassy, and led to violence and persecution in various parts of the empire, especially at Mardin, where the papal power was comparatively strong."

Anticipating the history, it may be said, that the Franco-German war changed all this. The Turkish government then no longer feared the French, and hence no longer lent itself to Papal intrigues. The dogma of the Papal Infallibility has been also a severe blow to the Oriental Papacy.

No one was more competent than Dr. Dwight to testify concerning the state of religious opinions among the Armenians of the metropolis. Writing in February, 1860, he said it would be hard to find an intelligent Armenian in Constantinople, unless among the ecclesiastics, who did not acknowledge that there were many errors in the Armenian Church, and that the evangelical system was the best.

Religious opinion in Constantinople.

About the same time, he found a great change for the better at Rodosto, on the northern shore of the Sea of Marmora. The evangelical brethren had suffered many indignities from the Armenians, but now even the magnates were disposed to cultivate friendly relations with them. This he attributed, in great measure, to the wise and yet firm demeanor of Apraham, the native preacher, who afterwards became pastor of the Rodosto church. He was a native of the place, and

Change for the better at Rodosto.

was once a deacon in the old Armenian Church, and a candidate for the offices of vartabed and bishop. His first knowledge of the truth was gained while in the Armenian monastery at Jerusalem. From thence he came to Bebek, where he studied theology. He was an exception to the rule, that a prophet has no honor in his own country, for without compromising the truth, he had gained the respect of all. He showed his missionary friend a list of eighty families, upon which he called in regular order. Though most of them belonged to the old Armenian Church, they received him kindly. The missionary called with him upon two of these families prominent in the Armenian community, in one of which they spent an entire evening. A copy of the Bible, in the modern language, was in the house, and was brought forward, read, and commented upon, just as if this had been a Protestant family.

Dr. Dwight attended the examination of the Protestant school at Rodosto. More than half of the pupils were from non-Protestant families; and an audience of two hundred and fifty expressed very general satisfaction with the attainments of the pupils. On the Sabbath he administered the Lord's Supper. A large number not connected with the church, were present, and gave close attention to the preaching. Many must have come from mere curiosity, but the missionary never preached with greater certainty that he had the sympathies of his audience.

In the following July, events showed that the new influences had in some way reached all classes of Armenians in the metropolis. An aged Protestant died and his body was borne by his friends to an Armenian cemetery, which hitherto had been open to all bearing the Christian name. Now, however, a mob, composed of the very lowest class of Armenians, seized the coffin, and forcibly carried it out of the burying-ground, where it remained four days. The mob increased to thousands, and kept possession of the ground day and night. The American and English Ambassadors were at length roused, and remonstrated with the Porte and the Patriarch. The burial was assented to, and the Seraskier, or Minister of War, came with several hundred troops. A place was selected for the grave within the cemetery, but the mob, at the first blow of the pickaxe, rushed forward with a savage yell. The troops were ordered to resist, but not to fire. After twenty or thirty had been wounded, the mob fell back. The Patriarch and other dignitaries of the Armenian Church now came upon the ground, and gave their sanction to the spot selected for the burial, and the grave was dug. Just then the Seraskier, for some unexplained reason, ordered the grave to be filled, and another to be dug outside of the cemetery, in the middle of the public highway.

Outbreak at the metropolis.

The Protestants declined taking part in the burial in such a spot, though entreated to do so by the Seraskier, but remained and looked on in silence, while Mussulmans dug the grave, put the coffin into it, and filled it up. As soon as this was done, the mob rushed forward and trampled spitefully upon it, in the presence of the Pasha and Patriarch. The representatives of the Protestant powers now united in a strong remonstrance to the government; and Stepan Effendi, the civil head of the Protestants, was speedily notified, that ground would be given them for cemeteries wherever Protestants were found.

A remarkable native helper.

A native assistant died at Baghchejuk, near Nicomedia, early in the year, who had from the beginning been intimately connected with the work in that place, and was called the "prince of colporters," on account of his success in distributing the Scriptures. Being by nature an earnest man, when converted he became zealous in disseminating the truth. As he was respected through all the region, there was great anxiety among the Armenians to regain him, and an ex-Patriarch visited Baghchejuk, in the hope of bringing him back. Promises and threats were equally vain, and the storm of persecution finally burst upon him. His vineyards and mulberry orchards were cut down, and much of his property was wrested from him. He was beaten and stoned, and his name cast out as vile. When they were building the church he brought a basket full of stones and brick-bats, which had been thrown through his windows, to be incorporated in the foundation wall. He described the effect of persecution in his own case, thus: "The truth in my heart was like a stake slightly driven into soft ground, easily swayed, and in danger of falling before the wind; but by the sledge-hammer of persecution God drove it in till it became immovable." "His working power," says Mr. Parsons, the resident missionary, "like everything else in his possession, was consecrated to Christ. With great self-denial on his part, two hundred piasters a month (about eight dollars) enabled him to give all his time to street preaching, and the sale of the Scriptures. As a bookseller he was eminently faithful and successful. Not contented with sitting in the book-stall waiting for purchasers, he used to shoulder a basket of books, and go through the streets and lanes of town and city, offering for sale the 'Holy Book;' the 'Book that would not lie;' the 'Infallible Guide;' and proclaiming, in a loud voice, its divine origin, man's need of it, and its light-and-life-giving power. This he did as time and strength permitted, from Broosa to Angora, and from Bilijik to the Black Sea. He everywhere either carried with him, or had near at hand, a supply of Bibles in the Turkish, Armenian, Greek, and Jewish languages. Probably not less than one hundred thousand persons have heard from him the proffer of the word of life."

"The word of God," continues Mr. Parsons, "was his constant companion. He was so familiar with it, that he could turn with facility to any passage desired. He walked with God. He was a man of prayer. His happiest moments were seasons of devotion — private, social, and public. I should say, rather, that next to the work of bringing others to Christ, his delight was in prayer and praise. He has rested from his labors, but his works do follow him. Before he died, he could rejoice in a rich harvest from his own sowing, but a greater harvest is yet to be reaped from the seed so widely scattered by his hand. He has gone, a sheaf of the first-fruits of the work in Baghchejuk. He 'came to his grave as a shock of corn cometh in in his season.'"

Mr. E. E. Bliss passed through Marsovan on his way to Harpoot, and found that the rampant hostility of eight years before had died out.[1] Instead of the hootings and stonings, which then greeted his arrival, he was met, a long way out, by a goodly company to escort him to his lodgings. On the Sabbath, in place of the little company assembled in a lower room of his own house, he now preached to a good audience, in a large and commodious chapel.

Great change in Marsovan.

"I spent," he says, "a few days at Sivas, where I was eight years ago, and found the small room,

[1] See chapter xxiv.

where ten or fifteen then met for God's worship, exchanged for a large upper room, filled with an audience of more than a hundred. And as we went onward to places we had never before visited, it was a continual feast to see the extent to which the work of God had spread in the whole country. In almost every place where we stopped for the night, however obscure the village, some would gather around us as brethren in the Lord. They were often coarsely dressed and rude of speech, undistinguishable in appearance from the mass around them; but a few words of conversation would show that their souls had been illuminated by the truth."

Changes elsewhere.

The annual meeting of the Northern Armenian Mission for 1860, was held at Harpoot, east of the Euphrates, seven hundred and fifty miles from Constantinople. And it was a significant fact, that the delegates from the metropolis were able to communicate with their families over the telegraph wires, destined to connect London with Calcutta.

Telegraphic communications.

The distance from the capital, and of the stations from each other was so great, as to render it difficult to assemble in the annual meetings, that were indispensable for an effective administration. At this meeting, what had been known as the Northern Mission, was divided into Western and Eastern, and Erzroom, Harpoot, and

The mission further divided.

Arabkir composed the Eastern Mission. The Southern Mission then took the name of the Central; and the stations of the Assyria Mission were united to the Eastern. It will be convenient to use the names Western, Central, and Eastern in designating territory, but we shall, as far as possible, treat the three divisions as constituting one great mission.

The church at Harpoot received its first native pastor at this annual meeting. He was one of several young men, who left Diarbekir for Constantinople, eight years before, for the purpose of obtaining a Protestant education at Bebek. They were subjected to many revilings on their way, and few showed them any kindness. Some who were in sympathy with them deprecated their removal from Diarbekir, as the withdrawal from that place of the little light which had begun to shine. Now, having completed the course of study at the Seminary, Tomas, one of that company, was preaching the Gospel every Sabbath in Diarbekir, and was to become pastor there; and Marderos, another, combining great excellence of character, was made pastor of the flourishing church at Harpoot.

First native pastor at Harpoot.

Mr. Dunmore, when he commenced the Harpoot station, five years before, found not a single Protestant in that city. It was now only three years since the arrival of Messrs. Wheeler, Allen, and Barnum, and there were thirty-

Rise of the Harpoot station.

nine church-members, and Harpoot was fast becoming an important centre of influence. There were schools in ten of the thirteen out-stations, eleven of which were supplied with preaching on the Sabbath by the missionaries and students of the Seminary, and in all the surrounding regions there was an increase of attendance on preaching. Women learned to read, and groups were found studying the Bible. In the numerous villages of the Harpoot plain and outlying districts were many faithful disciples of the Lord Jesus. The spirit of freedom had gone forth, as was seen in the growing activity of laymen, and the consequent decline of superstition and ecclesiastical despotism. Instruction was communicated to large numbers of both men and women, and it was beginning to be regarded as disgraceful for adults of either sex not to be able to read.

Theological school.

The theological school contained twenty-four pupils, of whom eleven were from the vicinity and ten were married men. The students devoted their winter vacation of four months to preaching and teaching, and in term time they preached at out-stations.

Dr. Dwight's second tour in the East.

Mrs. Dwight, after twenty-one years of eminently useful service, died at Constantinople in November, 1860. Dr. Dwight's family being thus broken up, he commenced, with the approval of his brethren, a tour through Syria and Asiatic Turkey, intending to go over much of the ground he had traversed with Dr. Eli Smith in their explorations thirty years before.

How great the changes in the intervening period! Then, for fourteen and a half months, he was unable to receive tidings from his wife, whom he had left in Malta. Now, from beyond the Euphrates, he could have communicated daily with Constantinople by telegraph. Then, no fellow-laborers were to be found between Smyrna and the little bands of German and Scotch brethren soon after to be driven away from Russian Armenia and Georgia, and nowhere did they meet among the people any religious sympathies in unison with their own. Now, the survivor found missionaries scattered over the land, and he scarcely entered a place where some one, at least, did not greet him with a joyful welcome. Then, the object was to explore an unbroken scene of spiritual death. Now, it was to confirm living churches, and help forward a growing spiritual work.

Changes between the first and second tours.

The tour was extended as far as the Nestorian mission, and occupied about eight months. Reviewing this journey of almost unprecedented interest, Dr. Dwight could not refrain from using the language of Christian triumph: "I have visited," he says, "every station of the Board in Turkey and Persia excepting those among the Bulgarians. It has been my privilege to see all the missionaries and their families, — a rare body of men and women, of whom our churches and our country may well be proud, — and also to become personally acquainted with hundreds and thousands of the dear Protestant brethren and sisters of this land — God's lights in the midst of surrounding darkness; God's witnesses even where Satan dwelleth."

Dr. Dwight was at Marash in April, and this is his own vivid description of what he saw there: "This place is indeed a missionary wonder! Twelve years ago there was not a Protestant here, and the people were proverbially ignorant, barbarous, and fanatical. Six years ago the evangelical Armenian church was organized with sixteen members, the congregation at that time consisting of one hundred and twenty. On the last Sabbath I preached in the morning to a congregation of over a thousand, and in the afternoon addressed nearly or quite fifteen hundred people, when forty were received into the church, making the whole number two hundred and twenty-seven. Nearly one hundred of these have been added since Mr. White came here, two years ago. One old woman of seventy-five years was admitted who was converted only four months ago. She was previously a bigoted opposer, but now she seems full of the love of Christ. Her emotions almost overpowered her on approaching the table of the Lord.

Triumph of the Gospel at Marash.

"The church-members here impressed me from the first as men who thought more of the spiritual than the temporal. The Holy Spirit has been evidently at work here during the whole of the year, and especially through the past winter, and conversions are constantly taking place. The burden of conversation among the brethren is in regard to praying and laboring for the salvation of souls.

"On the Sabbath the half of the body of the church was filled with women packed closely together on the floor. The other half, and the broad galleries around three sides of the house, were completely crowded with men. A new church is needed immediately in the other end of the town. I bless God that He brought me here, and I feel almost like saying, 'Now lettest thou thy servant depart in peace.'"

It should be said that this visit to Marash was in the midst of a revival. The resident missionary, Mr. White, describes the work as being chiefly among the Armenians and Roman Catholics. "Every night they met in the houses of the Protestants and spent hours, sometimes even till near morning, examining the Scriptures and comparing them with the corrupt teachings of their own churches. Our young men were very active, laboring both day and night, so much so, that the Catholic bishop said he could not understand it; that if the young men were paid for thus laboring, the missionaries had not money enough; and if they were not paid, they had a love which he could not understand. Many of his people, however, seemed to comprehend it better than he did, and are now regular attendants at our church."

Tribute to the wives of missionaries.

The veteran missionary pays a noble tribute to the wives of the missionaries at the several stations of the central mission: "I felt myself rebuked when I saw the earnest, self-devoted spirit of my missionary sisters, who are laboring in Aintab, in Marash, in Antioch, in Aleppo, and in Oorfa, for the salvation of their degraded sex; thinking little of the sacrifices they have made in leaving America, to live in such a country as Turkey. It would be difficult to find in Christendom a more happy class than these, our helpers in Christ Jesus. The holy object which fills their hearts lifts them above the distracting and embittering influences of external circumstances."

Change at Diarbekir.

The change at Diarbekir, during the score of years since Dr. Grant and Mr. Homes barely escaped with their lives, had been truly wonderful. Drs. Dwight and Schneider and Mr. Nutting, on their approach from Oorfa, were met, eighteen miles out, by a deputation of Protestant brethren on horseback; and, a few miles further on, by another detachment, headed by Mr. Walker and the native pastor; and when near the city, by a third on foot, thus giving them a sort of triumphal entry. Nor, during their whole stay, was there anything to awaken a feeling of insecurity, but convincing evidence, that Protestantism had a strong hold on many minds.

Dr. Dwight noticed a decline of the Turkish population in the region of the Euphrates. Several entire quarters in Diarbekir, formerly Turkish, had passed into Christian hands, and the process was going on. Armenians, Jacobites, and Protestants were buying Turkish houses, but seldom did a Turk buy one of theirs; and around the outskirts of the city there were extensive Turkish quarters all in ruins.

Decline in the Turkish population.

Mrs. Dunmore had come to the United States in 1856, in consequence of the failure of her health, and was never able to return. Her husband continued his self-denying labors four years longer, until, seeing no prospect of her recovery, he believed his duty required him to follow her. It was then a time of civil war in his native land, and his public spirit led him to accept an invitation from a regiment of cavalry to be their chaplain. A detachment, with which he was connected, was surprised early in the morning of August 3, 1861, and he fell, shot in the head before he was fairly out of his tent.[1]

Death and character of Mr. Dunmore.

In courage, enterprise, tact, and efficacy, Mr. Dunmore stood in the front rank of missionaries. "He did not write much of what he did," says Mr. Walker, his successor at Diarbekir. "He cared not

[1] See *Missionary Herald*, 1862, p. 321.

to be known. But he cared for the souls of this poor people, and for Christ's kingdom. I think that few missionaries are so well fitted for the work, and very few labor with the same zeal and self-denial. To few is it given to accomplish so much. There is comparatively little accomplished in Diarbekir, Arabkir, Harpoot, and Moosh, which is not, under God, due to this brother. His influence will long be felt in these parts. Paul was his model, and there are few who come so near to that exemplar. He had wonderful power in attaching the natives to him. He could sympathize deeply with them, and aid them as few can. His heart was in the work here, and it was a very great trial for him to return to America. His fearless journeys among the Koords in this land, led us often to feel apprehensive for his life. The Lord forgive the Texan, whose bullet cut short a life so valuable."

The missionary force.

In the years 1860 and 1861, the ill health of either husband or wife deprived the mission of the labors of Messrs. Clark, Hutchison, Parsons, and Plumer, and their families. Mr. and Mrs. Peabody returned to their native land, after a faithful service of nineteen years. Dr. Schauffler also terminated his official connection of twenty-nine years with his missionary associates, and entered the service of the American, and the British and Foreign Bible Societies in the work of Bible translation for the Turkish Mohammedans. Miss Tenney was married to Dr. Hamlin, who had been released from his connection with the Board to take charge of a Protestant college in Constantinople, though without any change in the great object of his labors.

Mr. Williams reoccupied Mardin in the year 1861. This was then, as now, the capital of the Syrian Church, and the natural centre of operations among the Arabic-speaking people in Eastern Turkey. It embraced Mosul, and multitudes of towns and villages scattered over a wide region, and required more than one missionary; though that one was a man of first-rate abilities and eminent devotion to his work. It was put in connection with the Armenian Mission, partly because its missionary policy was the same, and partly because it seemed necessary to work that whole field from one central station, and by a small number of missionaries, and because it would require the moral support of the larger mission in its neighborhood.

Mardin connected with the eastern mission.

A training-school was commenced at Mardin in the following year, on the plan of the one at Harpoot, with a class of eight hopefully pious young men. The congregation had doubled since Mr. Williams' return and Protestantism had a more favorable position; but as yet the intellect accepted the truth more readily than did the heart.

Training-school at Mardin.

Trebizond had only a native pastor, and the day-school was reported as one of the best in Turkey. Khanoos, southeast of Erzroom,

Other portions of the field.

had been faithfully cultivated for some time by the native pastor, Simon, who was now removed to Moosh, where he would have a better field. Erzroom was again without a missionary in consequence of the necessary removal of Mr. Trowbridge to the capital.

Scripture translations.

In addition to notices of versions of the Scriptures in the preceding chapter, it should now be stated, that Dr. Goodell had completed the great work of his life, — the translation of the Bible into the Turkish language, as written in the Armenian character and spoken by the Armenians. The version was from the Hebrew and Greek; the New Testament had received three distinct revisions, and the Old Testament one. His principal helper, for thirty years, was Panayotes Constantinides, who died March 11, 1861. "He had greatly desired," writes Dr. Goodell, "to live to see the end of the revision, and we pressed on together, returning thanks at the end of every chapter, that we had got so far on our journey. But his strength failed him on the way, and when there was but little further to go, he laid himself down, and the angels carried him to his home in heaven." Dr. Schauffler had nearly completed a translation of the New Testament in Turkish, with the Arabic or sacred character, and after much difficulty had obtained the consent of the government to its publication. Dr. Riggs had reached the books of Kings, in addition to the Psalms, in his version of the Scriptures in Bulgarian, and had also given time to preparing and editing Bulgarian tracts.

The amount of publication in the year 1860, in the Armenian, Armeno-Turkish, Bulgarian, and Modern Greek, was 164,500 copies, and 13,296,000 pages. The total expenditure was $15,789, from the following sources: — Publications.

American Bible Society	$3,473
British and Foreign Bible Society	1,243
American Tract Society, New York	2,646
American Tract Society, Boston	674
London Tract Society	1,175
American Board of Commissioners for Foreign Missions	5,462
Other sources	1,116
	$15,789

Among the books published were a Reply to Archbishop Matteos in Armenian, a Commentary on Matthew, Hymn-Book, Theological Class-Book, and Geography, — the last at the expense of Haritûn Minasiyan, an Armenian printer. The Word of God was more in demand than any other book. The Armenian Bible, with marginal references, electrotyped and printed in New York by the American Bible Society, was highly prized. The American Tract Society had also electrotyped and printed several works for the mission, which were admired for their beauty, and were furnished more cheaply than they could have been prepared in Constantinople.

CHAPTER XXVII.

THE ASSYRIA MISSION.

1849–1860.

Origin of the mission.

MOSUL is related to the Syria Mission in language, the written Arabic being essentially the same in both fields; but there is considerable difference in the language of preaching and social intercourse. "Near Mosul, and especially on the east of the Tigris," writes Dr. Leonard Bacon, after his visit to Mosul, "the language is Syriac, or as they there call it, *Fellahi*, the peasant language. In other districts, Turkish and Koordish are spoken by many nominal Christians. The people in Mesopotamia are very different from those in Syria. They are of other sects. Instead of the Greek Church, the Greek Catholic, and the Maronite, we find, as we travel east of the Euphrates, and especially as we approach the Tigris, the Jacobite, the Syrian Catholic or Romanized Jacobite, the Nestorian (almost exterminated), and the Chaldean or Romanized Nestorian. And the condition of these sects, as it respects the feeling of strength and pride, is very unlike that of the sects in Syria.

The Maronite Church, and the Greek Catholic, are strong and proud in their relation to Rome, and in the feeling that they are protected by the great papal powers in Europe. The Greek Church may be likened to a Russian colony in the Turkish empire. But the more eastern sects, remnants of what were once the great Oriental Church, are in far different relations, ecclesiastical and political. The Jacobites, like the Nestorians, feel themselves weakened and depressed. The Syrian Catholic and the Chaldean are not very firmly united to Rome, and are little affected by European influences. Nor is this all. The nominal Christians of Mesopotamia are of a very different race and blood from those of Syria. The Greek element, which characterizes the Arabic-speaking Christians west of the Euphrates, — an element of subtlety of disputation, and of intellectual pride, — is not so prominent in these more Oriental communities. For these and other reasons, I cannot but think that this field should be occupied by the brethren of the Mosul station, and be regarded as entirely distinct from that of the Syria Mission. Mosul, as a centre of missionary labor, is much more nearly related to Oroomiah, than to Beirût, or Aleppo."[1]

The visit of Messrs. Perkins and Stocking to Mosul, in May, 1849, has been already mentioned.[2] That visit did much to prepare the way for Mr.

[1] *Report of the Board for* 1851, p. 82. [2] Chapter xx.

Ford, of the Aleppo station, who went there at the close of 1849. He was kindly received by Mr. Rassam, the English Consul, and had a joyful greeting from the little band of "gospel men," who welcomed the return of their long lost privileges of Christian instruction. Of the fifty who soon called upon him, about twenty appeared to be decidedly evangelical, and ready to stand by the Gospel at all hazards, though few of them gave evidence of a work of grace in their hearts. Twenty more were enlightened and favorably disposed; and the remaining ten might be regarded as indifferent or hostile. This little band was the remainder of those who had been brought under the influence of the Gospel, when our brethren of the Mountain Nestorian Mission were detained in the mysterious providence of God, to labor and suffer there. Yet the Lord had not forsaken them, for Meekha, the ingenious mechanic, who had learned the truth from Mr. Laurie, had given them the benefit of his steadfast piety and diligent instruction.

Mosul re-occupied.

The reader knows, already, what led to the temporary occupation of Mosul by the Board, in 1841. Its relinquishment in 1844, was chiefly in view of the fact, that the Episcopal Church of the United States had a mission then in Turkey, with the avowed object of laboring among the Jacobites of Mesopotamia.[1] That mis-

Why it had been relinquished.

American Episcopal Mission.

[1] This was first known through Dr. Grant, who forwarded a copy

sion having been withdrawn from the Turkish empire, the operations of the Board were naturally extended again to Mosul, to look after the fruits of former labors, as well as to meet the exigencies of the mission in western Koordistan.

The Rev. Dwight W. Marsh arrived at Mosul on the 20th of March, 1850, going by way of Beirût, Aleppo, Aintab, Oorfa, and Diarbekir; from this last place he floated down the Tigris on a raft supported by inflated goat-skins, in less than four days to his new home. He describes the river as breaking through between bold precipices, and scenery delightfully and unexpectedly romantic. Mr. Schneider was his travelling companion from Aintab to Diarbekir, and Mr. Ford was at Mosul to greet him on his arrival. The Rev. William Frederic Williams removed from the Syria Mission to Mosul in the spring of 1851, going in company with Dr. Bacon and his son Mr. Leonard W. Bacon, then travelling in the East. Salome Carabet, the eldest of the girls in Mr. Whiting's family at Abeih, went

The mission of the Board reinforced.

of a letter from seven of the American Episcopal Bishops to the Syrian Patriarch at Mardin, as evidence of the fact. After stating the object in sending the Rev. Horatio Southgate to reside for a time at Mardin, with the hope of associating two others with him, to which no exception could be taken, the Patriarch was informed by the letter, that Mr. Southgate "will make it clearly understood, that the American Church has no ecclesiastical connection with the followers of Luther and Calvin, and takes no part in their plans or operations to diffuse the principles of these sects."

with Mr. Williams, to take charge of a school of thirty girls.

Experience of Dr. Bacon in the Koordish mountains.

Dr. Bacon's visit to Mosul was in compliance with a request of the Prudential Committee, that he would make his tour of relaxation and improvement the occasion of visiting the several stations of the Board in Western Asia. The attempt to proceed from Mosul to Oroomiah through the mountains by the most direct route, was unsuccessful. The two travellers, in company with Mr. Marsh, soon after crossing the Zab, were set upon by Koordish robbers, who had been requested by an Agha, near Akra, to kill them. So imminent was the peril, that they united together in prayer to God, led by Dr. Bacon. Some Moolahs seeing this, interceded for their lives, and though they could not hinder their being plundered, they succeeded in sending them safely to another Moolah, three hours distant, who was revered for his sanctity; and it was through his resolute protection, under God, that they effected a safe return to Mosul. Mr. Rassam gave information of the outrage to the English Ambassador, and the Pasha, in the following year, having received orders from Constantinople, sent three hundred men, with three cannon, against the robber, who was compelled to pay the full value of the losses, and much more besides to the government.[1]

Punishment of the robbers.

[1] *Missionary Herald*, for 1851, p. 295, and 1852, p. 388.

The Assyria Mission was so named for geographical reasons. Its most northern station at this time, was Diarbekir. Dr. Grant passed through this city with Mr. Homes, in 1839, Messrs. Hinsdale and Mitchell passed through it in 1841, and Mr. Laurie in 1842. The city was visited by Mr. Peabody in 1849, when he found several persons awakened by reading the Scriptures and other books, brought there by colporters. It was visited again by Mr. Schneider in the following year, who reported that nearly fifty Armenians were accustomed to meet on the Sabbath for reading the Scriptures. These were then subjected to a severe persecution, and they sent to Constantinople for a vizierial letter, which was granted, but brought little relief. Dr. Azariah Smith organized a small church at Diarbekir in the spring of 1851. It included both Armenians and Jacobites; but only those were to be received who gave satisfactory evidence of piety. As soon as this restriction was announced, the most influential Syrians in the congregation resolutely set themselves to secure admission to the church for all Protestants of good moral character. For a time their efforts to unite the congregation in opposition prevented attention to their ordinary business; and but for the conservative spirit of the Armenian portion, perhaps the audience, as a whole, would have gone back to their churches. In the end all were persuaded to listen to a discourse on the

How the Gospel came to Diarbekir.

Church organized.

subject, by Dr. Smith, and the character of the young ruler, in Luke xviii. 18–30, was unfolded in connection with Acts ii. 43–47. The exhibition of a church, as an association of men devoted, body and soul, time and wealth, to the extension of Christ's kingdom, was new to them. That repentance involved the ceasing to live for selfish and worldly ends, and that faith in Christ included the consecration of our energies to his service, was no part of their old creed. And though these truths had been previously preached by the missionaries, the practical connection in which they now came up made them more impressive.

Arrival of Mr. Dunmore.

Mr. and Mrs. Dunmore, after spending some months at Aintab, arrived at Diarbekir in November, 1851. They were accompanied by Stepan, a graduate of the seminary at Bebek. This man, not long after his arrival, was rudely arrested by a Turkish officer as a Protestant, and cast into a prison, where he spent the night with vagabonds and thieves. The Pasha refused Mr. Dunmore a hearing, but at once ordered Stepan's release.

Mr. Dunmore had not yet a free use of the Turkish, which was the language spoken by the Armenians; but an average of more than seventy persons came on the Sabbath to hear Stepan, and new faces were seen at every meeting.

Soon after the arrival of Mr. Dunmore, a young

man of talents, named Tomas, who had long been vacillating, boldly declared himself a Protestant, and though his bishop offered him the monthly reward of two hundred piastres for two years, paid in advance, if he would leave the Protestants, his reply was: "Go tell the bishop that I did not become a Protestant for money, and that I will not leave them for money, even should he give me my house full of gold." Tomas was then nineteen years of age, and had an orphan brother and two sisters dependent on him. He had been a prosperous silk manufacturer, but after he became a Protestant, both nominal Christians and Moslems refused to trade with him, and he was impoverished. It was decided to send him to the Bebek Seminary, with his younger brother; and to send his older sister to the Female Seminary at the same place; while Mr. and Mrs. Dunmore took the youngest, a bright little girl of six years. In this young man we have the future native pastor of the church in that city.

The future native pastor.

The persecutions inflicted on the Protestants at Diarbekir were similar to those described elsewhere. But not only were the native converts, in this remote city, oppressed in every possible way, but the missionary reports himself as being grossly insulted, and even stoned in the streets whenever he went abroad.

Persecutions.

About this time Mr. Marsh performed a missionary tour to Mardin, through Jebel Tour, a branch of the great Kûrdish range of mountains which crosses the Tigris above Jezirah, and goes westward toward the Euphrates. These rugged, though not lofty mountains, cover fourteen hundred square miles, and form the stronghold of the Jacobites. Their ecclesiastical capital is Mardin. "High up the mountain's side," writes Mr. Marsh, "with a steep descent of six or seven hundred feet to the plains, the city wall mounts up still higher, three hundred feet or more; and a large castle on the mountain top crowns the view." Here he found several persons favorably inclined, and recommended the place for a missionary station.

Mr. Marsh's visit to Mardin.

The Rev. Henry Lobdell, M. D., and wife, reached Mosul in May 1852. They came through Aintab, Oorfa, and Diarbekir. Such was the desire of the people of Aintab for a missionary physician to take the place of Dr. Smith, that four hundred and twenty of them signed a petition in a single evening, requesting him to remain; but he felt constrained to give them a negative. He speaks with pleasure of his brief sojourn at Oorfa, which he describes as beautifully situated on the west side of a fertile plain, and retaining many marks of its ancient greatness.

Dr. Lobdell's experience at Aintab and Oorfa.

In the ten days which Dr. Lobdell spent with Mr. Dunmore at Diarbekir, he was impressed by the hold the reformation was taking in that place. At the same time, he and his missionary brother had a startling illustration of its hostility to the Gospel. They were looking at the great mosque of the city, formerly a Christian church, and in the words of Mr. Dunmore, "As we were standing in front of it, in the public highway, examining its architecture, several lads came up and began to insult us and to order us away. We did not notice them, but went further from the mosque, and stopped to examine some old marble pillars. Soon, however, we found a rabble about us, who began to jerk our garments. I then turned and spoke to them, and they instantly rushed upon us like tigers. They seized Dr. Lobdell's hat, threw it into the air, and began to beat him. One ruffian seized me by the throat. By main strength I loosed his grasp, and was moving off, when two men tried to wrest my cane from me, but did not succeed. We retreated as fast as possible, but when we got out of the reach of their hands, they resorted to throwing stones, some of them weighing two or three pounds. One hit Dr. Lobdell in the side, and we saw no alternative but to run for our lives. We went immediately to the Pasha, taking one of the largest stones with us, and made a statement of the facts in the presence of the council. He refused to do anything more than to send a man to inquire who was in fault, the ruffians, or we! He said he knew nothing about us."

Outrage at Diarbekir.

In a tent supported by a raft of one hundred and

twenty inflated goat-skins, Dr. and Mrs. Lobdell floated down the Tigris to Mosul. "The Arabs, who swam out upon their goat-skins, and the Kûrds armed to the teeth upon the shore, were alike unable to touch us, as the river was unusually high and swift. I do not remember having enjoyed four successive days so much. The scenery is grand, equaling that of the far-famed Hudson. It might not wear as well, but it is unique and wonderful." Mr. and Mrs. Williams were there to welcome them.

Descent of the Tigris.

Mr. Marsh was absent on a visit to his native land, from whence he returned with his wife in May, 1853. He was accompanied as far as Aintab by Rev. Augustus Walker and wife, and from thence to Diarbekir, by Messrs. Schneider and Walker. Mr. Dunmore's congregation had then risen to nearly two hundred hearers.

Diarbekir a year later.

Mr. Marsh was especially struck, on returning to Mosul, with the greatly improved singing of the congregation, which he thought was now better there than at Diarbekir, Aintab, Constantinople, or Beirût. This was due to the unwearied pains taken by Mr. Williams, though the people seemed to have a better ear for music than elsewhere in Western Asia.

Congregational singing at Mosul.

Dr. Lobdell found his medical profession a great assistance to him as a preacher of the Gospel. Jacobites, Papists, and Moslems came

Dr. Lobdell as a medical missionary.

in considerable numbers, and he preached the Gospel alike to all. He was overworked, and it was perhaps a favor to him that the judge was stirred up by Popish priests, as the Moslems affirmed, to forbid the Mohammedans coming to his preaching. The judge was willing that they should call upon him for medical aid, if he would not preach the Gospel to them; but the doctor declined administering to the body, unless he could, at the same time, explain to them "the words of Jesus" (which all Moslems professed to receive) for the benefit of their souls.

Salome Carabet returned to Syria, very much in the manner of Rebecca of old, to become the wife of the young pastor at Hasbeiya; and the female school was thus deprived of its teacher.

A visit by Dr. Lobdell to the Yezidees in October, 1852, developed interesting and valuable information. Their doctrines he regarded as a strange fusion of Mohammedanism and Christianity with the philosophy of the older Persians.[1] The Yezidees.

In June, 1853, Dr. Lobdell travelled through Koordistan to Oroomiah. One of his objects was the improvement of his health; but he greatly desired, also, to confer with the brethren of the Nestorian Mission, and to preach the Gospel in the regions between. He took with Dr. Lobdell's visit to Oroomiah.

[1] See *Memoir of Dr. Lobdell*, pp. 213–227; also *Missionary Herald*, for 1853, pp. 109–111.

him a native, who not only spoke the Syriac and Arabic, but the Turkish and Koordish.[1] "He came to us," wrote Dr. Perkins, "for the benefit of his impaired health. Yet was he buoyant as a lark, being overjoyed to find himself in our happy circle, after his perilous journey across the mountains." Two days after his arrival he was seized with a fever which proved severe and obstinate. But he recovered, and was able to give much thought to the somewhat peculiar method of proceeding in that mission; in which no separate Protestant community had been formed, and no church organized; though the missionaries had the communion by themselves, to which they invited only those whom they believed to be truly regenerated. His preconceived opinions had been somewhat adverse to the plan, and he and his brethren at Mosul had adopted other methods. But he wrote to the Secretaries of the Board his approval of the main policy of his brethren in Persia, as justified by their peculiar circumstances, and ratified by the blessing of Heaven. He specified some things in which he thought more decided measures might be taken; but advised that the mission be left to follow the leadings of Providence, until a crisis should come in the Nestorian Church, and then to act as they should deem wise at the time.

His view as to the ecclesiastical policy of that mission.

Before returning, Dr. Lobdell made an excursion

[1] *Missionary Herald*, 1854, pp. 18–22.

of three weeks in the province of Azerbijan, going as far as Tabriz. It was while he was at Gawar, on his way home, that Deacon Tamo was liberated from his long imprisonment. Messrs. Rhea and Coan accompanied him to Mosul. Dr. Lobdell represents the two highest peaks of the Jelu Mountains as distinctly visible from Mosul. Every step through Koordistan reminded him of the devotion, courage, and energy of Dr. Grant.

His return to Mosul.

Some difficulties existed in the Protestant community at Diarbekir, growing out of the old leaven of baptismal regeneration, from which the church itself had not been thoroughly purged. The church then contained eleven members, — eight men and three women. Six of the men were Syrian Jacobites, and four of these were formerly deacons in their church. The difficulties encountered by Dr. Smith in 1851, when he declared his intention of admitting to the church none but such as were truly pious, and baptizing only them and their children, were now revived.

Difficulties in the church at Diarbekir.

In view of these things, a meeting of the Assyria Mission was held at Mosul for ten days, in March, 1854. It was then decided that Messrs. Marsh and Lobdell should return with Messrs. Dunmore and Walker, and assist in reorganizing the church at Diarbekir. Out of twenty candidates whom they examined, eleven were accepted; and, in the presence of three hundred persons, were

The church reorganized.

organized into a new church, with a creed and covenant.[1] Dr. Lobdell had a hundred Christian patients daily while there; but the Pasha still continued to refuse protection, and the missionaries were still hooted and stoned in the streets. They believed, however, that the Gospel had taken such hold in the city as to insure its ultimate triumph.

Singular conflict of interests.

The church was subjected to a severe trial, immediately after its reorganization. The Mosul brethren had to return to their own work; it was necessary for Mr. Dunmore to join his sick wife at Arabkir; and as it was unsafe for Mr. and Mrs. Walker to be left alone at Diarbekir, they went to Aintab for the summer. The Koords robbed them on their way, but they returned in the autumn, accompanied by David H. Nutting, M. D., and wife. Mr. Dunmore remained at Arabkir till the spring of 1855, when he commenced the important station of Harpoot. The missionaries at Diarbekir now enjoyed the very welcome protection of W. R. Holmes, Esq., the newly appointed English Consul. Dr. Nutting's professional services to the Pasha, in a dangerous illness, soon after his arrival, gave him an introduction to almost all the officers of the government and influential Moslems in the city, and ob-

Strength out of weakness.

[1] I find, in the archives of the Board, an extended analysis of the baptismal question by these brethren, in its bearing on the Oriental Churches.

tained for him a public expression of the Pasha's gratitude. Instead of stonings in the streets, without redress, as under the preceding Pasha, the missionaries received respectful treatment, and had free access to all classes. Mr. Walker found the state of things better than he anticipated. Certain disaffected members of the Protestant community had repented of their errors. Persecution had not shaken the faith of any in the church. During the winter the congregation increased to two hundred. In April, 1855, six were admitted to the church, and not less than four hundred and fifty persons were present. The accessions were not only from the Armenian and Jacobite Churches, but also from the Catholic Church, though fierce persecution and imprisonment were the consequence. A large portion of the Jacobite Church were convinced of the truth, and of the emptiness of their own rites and ceremonies. Some openly avowed that they retained their connection with their old church merely to fight against it, hoping to turn the whole community to Protestantism. The people demanded that the Bible should be read in the church in Turkish or Arabic, instead of the ancient Armenian and Syriac, which were, to most of them, dead languages; and the Jacobite bishop was forced to yield. Finding, at length, that this must rapidly undermine the priestly influence, he secretly removed the Scriptures from the church. But the word of the Lord was not bound, for the deacons or readers carried their own Bibles.

At the out-station of Hainè, Stepan, the native preacher who had come to Diarbekir with Mr. Walker, was enabled by divine grace to maintain his position. The Pasha at one time ordered him to leave, but he thought it right to disobey. At a subsequent period, being stoned and beaten in the streets, he was obliged to flee, and the Protestants suffered much oppression. Through the energetic efforts of the Consul at Diarbekir, the persecuting governor was deposed, and another appointed.

Native preacher at Haine.

Across the river from Diarbekir is Cutterbul, a large Christian village, where were twenty Protestants, with several church-members; and the missionary, in his occasional visits, gathered almost as large a congregation as the one at Mosul. The preaching would have been acceptable in Turkish, or Koordish, though the people preferred the Arabic. Cutterbul was but a sample of what the villages on all sides of Diarbekir might have been, were the station fully manned.

The Gospel at Cutterbul.

The Protestants at Mosul obtained no relief from their oppressive taxes until January, 1854; when, through the efforts of Lord Stratford de Redcliffe, a firman was addressed to the Pasha for their protection. The Pasha then ordered an equitable rate to be made for them, which

Relief at Mosul.

encouraged the Protestants, and disheartened their enemies. The year was one of progress. Five were added to the Protestants, and two to the church, while there was a decided improvement in the attention given to preaching. The boys' school prospered, with forty pupils. Women were to some extent instructed in reading the Bible by the scholars, who went from house to house for the purpose. Thirty adults were taught at their houses, and thirty others attended the male school regularly. The church-members gained a reputation for strict honesty, temperance, and general excellence. The mere existence of a church upon an apostolical basis, worshipping God in simplicity, told with force against the corrupt hierarchies.

Special dangers growing out of the war.

The excitements at Mosul during the Crimean war, were often intense. At one period there was great danger of an outburst of Mohammedan fanaticism, so that the Christians were in terror for their lives. Stringent orders from Constantinople aroused the local authorities to do their duty, and the insolence of those ready for deeds of blood was checked. Early in May, 1854, a volunteer reinforcement of two thousand Koords for the Turkish army, was quartered in the city, and certain outrages indicated an approaching massacre of Christians and Jews. The evil was averted by the bold decision of the English Consul, who went to the Pasha, and demanded that the Koords be sent at once out of the city. They were soon on their way to the seat of war.

Mosul was regarded as free from miasma; but the heat of the summer days was exhausting to the foreigner, and the natives also suffered. For a hundred days in 1853, the mercury stood, at two o'clock in the afternoon, as high as 98°; and for eighty days it ranged from 100° to 114°. The highest point in the shade was 117°. It was much the same in the following year.

Excessive heat.

As the summer advanced, the health of Mrs. Williams declined, and it became obvious that she could no longer endure the excessive heat. She was desirous of removing to a cooler climate, and Dr. Lobdell went with her and her family to the mountains. When they were near the Zab river, they met Dr. Wright from Persia, who had come with the hope of conducting them to Oroomiah. The rest is told in the words of Dr. Lobdell. "We could go no farther, and on the 29th of June, at sunset, were on our way towards Mosul; our sick friend being anxious to go there to die, but most of the time unconscious of the incidents and fatigues. On the last day of June we reached Akra; a litter was made, twelve Christians bore it, and the next morning at six o'clock, while moving on the road, that litter became a bier! An hour farther, and a rough box was made ready for her we had loved. The children knew not what had

Death of Mrs. Williams.

happened. At evening, the box was bound upon a mule, and we rode silently for fourteen hours, and crossed to the ruins of Nineveh shortly after sunrise. The flag of the English Consul was thrown over the body as we crossed the Tigris. A narrow house had already been prepared for it outside the walls (not even the dead body of a Moslem could have been carried within the gates); Mr. Marsh had a short service; and there we laid the wife, the mother, down to her last sleep." [1]

The Crimean war inflamed Mohammedan fanaticism all over Western Asia. Such was its influence in Persia, that the missionaries requested Dr. Lobdell, in view of his recent visit, to go to Bagdad, and represent their critical situation with reference to the Persian government to Mr. Murray, English Ambassador to Persia; who was to be there in January, 1855, on his way to his post. He accordingly commenced his voyage down the river on the 10th of January, upon the customary raft of skins, and on the fourth day reached Bagdad. The ambassador arriving on the 8th of the following month, Dr. Lobdell had a satisfactory interview with him, which probably led to the subsequent visit of Mr. Murray to Oroomiah. His return was by post-horses in fifty-eight hours. The road made a long curve to the east to avoid the

Dr. Lobdell visits Bagdad.

[1] Memoir of Dr. Lobdell, p. 330.

Arabs of the desert. The nearest route would have been on the west side of the Tigris.

Ten days after this, Mr. Marsh and Mr. Williams went to Diarbekir to attend the second annual meeting of the mission. The next day Dr. Lobdell prepared a sermon, talked with a crowd of papists, preached to eighty-five patients, delivered his sermon to the church in the evening, and went to bed with a chill and fever. On the day following, he wrote his last letter, and made his last entry in his journal. He gradually grew worse, and was at times delirious. A message was sent for the absent brethren, but, owing to the disturbed state of the country, it was the twentieth day of his sickness, and only five days before his death, when Mr. Marsh reached Mosul. As he entered the room, the Doctor threw his arms about his neck and wept. The church-members prayed earnestly for his recovery, and were eager to serve as watchers. He passed easily away, as the Sabbath was closing, on the 25th of March, 1855, to his eternal rest. His age was twenty-eight.

Sickness and death of Dr. Lobdell.

Dr. Lobdell's life was short to fill four hundred pages in Professor Tyler's excellent Memoir, but the volume is none too large. His life, measured by activities and results, was long. His character was many sided, and every side glowed with consecrated ardor. He made the most of himself as a man, a scholar, a Christian,

His character.

and a Christian missionary. Like the Apostle Paul, "forgetting those things which are behind, and reaching forth unto those things which are before," he pressed "toward the mark for the prize of the high calling of God in Christ Jesus."

He had a strong desire to go as a missionary to China, but the author, in his official correspondence, though seldom venturing to oppose such predilections, was so impressed with the difficulties to be overcome at Mosul, and with Dr. Lobdell's adaptation to that field, that he called his attention to it, and soon received the reply that he would go, as soon as he could get ready; and from that time the new field grew in his affections. That he could or would have done more for the kingdom of Christ, in any other sphere of labor, no one who attentively considers his remarkable life will venture to affirm.

Dr. Henri B. Haskell succeeded Dr. Lobdell at Mosul, and reached Diarbekir, with the Rev. George C. Knapp and wife, appointed to that station, in April, 1856. The Christian worship at Diarbekir had now assumed a regular form. There were four services on the Sabbath. At the first, an hour after sunrise, fifty persons assembled for prayer and praise, and the meeting was conducted by two native teachers; one reading his own translation of Doddridge's "Rise and Progress" in Turkish; the other, after having read through Dr.

Religious services at Diarbekir.

Goodell's "Notes on Matthew," and a volume of his sermons in Turkish, had commenced reading discourses of his own. The second was at the time of "noon cry" from the minarets, when Mr. Walker or Baron Tomas, now returned for a time from Bebek, preached to about two hundred persons, who listened more attentively than most American congregations. At the ninth hour (three o'clock in the afternoon) Baron Tomas met a Bible-class of sixty or eighty of the more intelligent Protestants. The last preaching service, at the tenth hour, was usually attended by a hundred or a hundred and fifty persons. From forty to seventy persons were present at the Friday evening meeting. The monthly concert was well attended, and with increasing contributions. Mrs. Walker had a Wednesday afternoon meeting for the women, at which from twenty to forty were present.

The Gospels in Koordish.

The Gospels had been translated into Koordish by the native helper at Hainè, and copies of Matthew had been received from the press in Stamboul. As soon as the good deacon Shemmas could get the box containing them from the custom-house, he retired to his room and poured out his soul in thanksgiving to God for his great mercy, and prayed that He would now greatly bless his Word in this new tongue.

The church at Diarbekir was doubled in 1856, and all belonging to the mission, both male and female, found full employment in imparting instruction. Baron Tomas returned to Bebek, to spend two years in the study of theology.

Excepting the death of the second Mrs. Williams, on the 25th of December, there was nothing in 1857, specially demanding attention.

Mr. Williams spent the summer of 1858 in Mardin, intending to occupy it as a new station, and returned in November to make it his permanent residence. He found the people, as he expected, exceedingly bigoted, yet hardy and intelligent. There was an important advantage in the pure mountain air of the place. The language was Arabic, as at Mosul. More than half of the twenty thousand inhabitants were nominal Christians; there were three Arabic-speaking villages within six miles, and the whole of Jebel Tour was accessible. He found the Romish Church stronger than he had expected, having a Papal-Syrian patriarchate just established within the city. He was received by the ecclesiastics with bitter denunciations. For a time, no one dared to acknowledge himself a Protestant, though many Mohammedans called upon him, and seemed to appreciate his very intelligent and gentlemanly conversation and manners.

New station at Mardin.

Subsequently a papal priest, to whom, in former years, he had given a Bible, joined himself to the missionary, and patiently endured severe persecution. But the most encouraging

Remarkable case of conversion.

case was that of an influential merchant named Meekha. He was originally an Armenian, and, thirty years before had become a Papist, and carried over one hundred houses with him. He was the champion of the papal party. His conversion was on this wise. The priest just mentioned had sown much Gospel truth among his disciples, and among them was a son-in-law of Meekha. At length the old man, provoked by an instance of dishonesty and falsehood in his bishop, and unable to read himself, sent for his son-in-law to read to him the Gospel. The young man was kept reading for three days, until the Gospels and Epistles were all finished. Amazed to find his religion opposed by the whole spirit and teachings of the divine oracles, Meekha sent for the priests and they came. "Prove me your doctrines from the Bible," said he. Convinced, from their manner of reply, that they had nothing to say, he ceased from the worship of the Virgin, and declared himself a Protestant; and his wife was as sincere and earnest as he. Though father, mother, and three unmarried daughters were excommunicated, and subjected to continued insults, their souls were overflowing with joy and thankfulness that the Gospel had come to them.

Speaking of this family, Mr. Williams says: "I have never witnessed such amazed eagerness as that with which, for the first time, they comprehended that salvation is without money and without price —

absolutely free and gratuitous. It was to them *news* — good news; and when I call to mind Meekha's impetuous temperament, and see him listen with such docility to Christ's teaching, I cannot but hope that, though imperfectly sanctified, the 'good work' is begun in him, which God's grace will complete. He accepts no new truth without a challenge, and nothing short of a 'Thus saith the Lord,' will give it currency with him. At one of my evening lectures I alluded to Isaiah's statement, 'All our righteousnesses are as filthy rags,' when two or three spoke up: 'What 's that?' On repeating it they were incredulous, and demanded chapter and verse. I gave it to them next day, and it has taken hold of them like iron. I have seen Meekha since throw that verse into a crowd of opposers with such force as to start them from their seats with an emphatic 'God forbid,' and the most positive denial that such a verse could be in the Bible. When I turned to the passage, and put the book into their hands that they might read it for themselves, they could not believe their own eyes, but continued poring over it, reading carefully from the head of the chapter; and this very day some of them came in to ask what it meant, and so changed in their manner I could hardly believe my eyes. Before, obstinate, dogged, unreasonable; now, meek, docile, and asking what the will of the Lord is. One said, 'That went like a dagger to my heart, and I slept none all that night.' And when to-day, I turned to Rom. iii. 26, Eph. ii. 8–9, and Rom. iv. 1–4, they listened as children. Truly the word of the Lord *is* a sharp sword, piercing to the heart."

Mr. Knapp's health forbidding a longer residence at Diarbekir, he commenced, in May, 1858, a new

New station at Bitlis.

station at Bitlis, a healthy place several thousand feet above the level of the sea. Dr. and Mrs. Haskell were with them during the latter half of the summer, and spent the summer of 1859 at Mardin; but Mr. and Mrs. Marsh and Mrs. Lobdell decided to remain at Mosul. In May, Mr. and Mrs. Marsh were called to part with their second and only surviving child. A fortnight later, Mrs. Marsh herself had a severe attack of

Death of Mrs. Marsh.

fever, but soon recovered. The fatal attack was three months later, and her death occurred unexpectedly. The thermometer in the early part of the night before, stood at 113°. During the day it was 120°; and on the night of her death it was 100° on the roof, where they slept. She had had a slight illness for a few days, and it now became a burning fever, with delirium, and all remedies proved vain. She died on the 12th of August, at the age of thirty-two, after a residence of six years at Mosul, as an earnest and faithful laborer. Her mother and her only sister had died before reaching the age of thirty, and it is possible Mrs. Marsh might not have lived as long in her native land, as she did at Mosul. "Yet it is probable," as her husband wrote at the time, "that the heat, so unusually extreme, cutting the leaves from the tree in our court by thousands, and causing many natives of the country to fall dead by the roadside, was the immediate occasion of her death."

Mrs. Lobdell found reason, in the necessities of her children, for returning to America, and in April, 1860, she bade adieu to the little band of women, who, for eight years, had sat at her feet to learn of Jesus. She reached her native land in August, in company with Mr. Marsh.

Return of Mrs. Lobdell with Mr. Marsh.

Mosul remained unoccupied during the summer, the heat at that season being found too great for endurance; though the climate is agreeable for nearly three fourths of the year. The summer retreat prepared by Dr. Lobdell at Deira, near Amadiah, was distant seventy miles, or four days' travel, and it required at least nine days to reach Mardin.

Difficulties in the way of occupying Mosul.

There were but two or three places in Turkey where missionaries, up to this time, had had such marked success as in Diarbekir. The church, at the close of 1859, numbered sixty-one, and after the April communion, seventy-three. Rarely did a communion pass without some additions. Protestants were a recognized power among the people, and their influence was extending. Books were eagerly sought after and paid for. Illegal taxes

Great prosperity at Diarbekir.

had nearly ceased in the city itself. After a weary struggle of nine years, the assessment of the tax-roll for the Protestants was made upon a satisfactory plan, which bid fair to be permanent. The commercial standing of the Protestants was above that of any other sect, though there were no wealthy men among them. But the increase of the congregation had been retarded by the want of sufficient accommodations for public worship. The lamented removal of Mr. Holmes, the English Consul, to a more desirable consulate in European Turkey, while it was a great loss to the mission, threw his house upon the market, and it was purchased for a place of worship at less than half its cost. It required only slight alterations, and could be indefinitely enlarged. The members of the church subscribed a thousand dollars towards its purchase, and a certain amount was granted by the Board. The school for boys, and the one for girls, were both eminently a success. At Cutterbul, half the village was Protestant and the rest more than half so, and the place of prayer would not hold the congregation.

Close of the Assyria Mission.

In 1860, the stations of the Assyria Mission were brought within the field of the Eastern Turkey Mission, and the Assyria Mission ceased to have a separate existence.

CHAPTER XXVIII.

THE NESTORIANS.

1851–1857.

THE return of Mr. Stoddard, accompanied by his wife and Mr. and Mrs. Rhea, was mentioned in the first volume. He thus describes the manner of his reception: "While crossing the plain of Oroomiah, we arrived at a village twelve miles from the city, where a company of our brethren and sisters, with their little ones and many of the Nestorians, greeted us with tender emotions. A tent had been pitched, and a breakfast prepared; and we all sat down on the grass, under the grateful shade, to partake of the repast. Our hearts were full. During the three hours which we spent at this village, Nestorians of all classes, many of them our brethren in Christ, were continually arriving; and when, soon after noon, we set out for the city, our progress resembled more a triumphal procession than a caravan of weary travellers. Every mile increased our numbers. Our way was often almost blocked up by the people who came to meet us, some on horseback, some on foot; bishops, priests, deacons, village teachers, members of the seminary, with whom I had many times wept and prayed, all pressing forward in eager haste to grasp our hands, and swell the notes of welcome. Three years ago, they followed us out of the city, holding our horses by the bridle, and begging us not to leave them, while their mournful looks bespoke the sorrow of their hearts. Now I was returning to them with restored health, to identify my interests with theirs. I brought with me the salutations of many thousand Christians in our native land, and was accompanied into the harvest-field by new reapers. As I turned from thoughts of the past, and looked on the animating scene around us, the contrast almost overcome me."

Death of Judith Perkins.

This was in 1851. In October of the following year, Dr. and Mrs. Perkins, going to meet Mr. and Mrs. Crane, and Sarah Stoddard, on their way from Trebizond, experienced a severe affliction in the death of their only surviving daughter, a very interesting girl. The journey was expected to be of advantage to the health of Mrs. Perkins and to their two children, Judith and Henry; and it was due to the new-comers that some one, acquainted with the language and country, should aid them through the long and tedious route from Erzroom. After a ride of thirty miles, they were unexpectedly exposed to a pestilential atmosphere at Khoy, where they spent the night. All went well with them until they had crossed the plain of Khoy, and the mountain beyond, and passed their last resting-place, when the beloved daughter showed signs of cholera. They could not rest there under the burning sun, and there was no water near; so they were obliged to proceed three or four miles further, to the Moslem village of Zorava. The nature of the disease was now painfully certain. The Mohammedan villagers were terrified and inhospitable. They would not even allow a morsel of bread to be sold to the faithful Nestorians who accompanied the family, nor even barley for their tired, hungry horses. And when the limbs of the child were cold and stiffening under the power of the deadly disease, they would not sell one stick of wood to warm water for her; but again and again ordered the heart-stricken travellers to leave the village with their dying child. As a further aggravation, after the father had twice administered laudanum, the vial containing the medicine disappeared from their tent, and could no more be found. There were all the usual accompaniments of the cholera, and in that high region the night air was cold. Collecting dry weeds, they managed to kindle a fire, and heated a stone which they placed at her feet.

The spirit of the child was quiet, and beautifully resigned to the will of God. There had been no doubt as to her piety before her sickness, and the whole scene was all that could have been expected of an older person. At length the end came. "Breathing shorter and shorter for fifteen or twenty minutes," writes her father, "she gently slept, as we believe, in Jesus, at three o'clock on the morning of September 4, 1852, aged twelve years and twenty-six days."

The bereaved and afflicted family was now a hundred and forty miles from home; but home was the place for her burial. The mother washed the corpse with her own hands, and dressed it for the grave. As no coffin could be obtained, the loved one was sewed in a strong oriental felt of the size and form of a bed-quilt, and placed upon a bed, and two willow sticks, cut from the margin of the brook, were sewed upon the sides of the bed, and it was then bound to the back of a faithful horse; the panic-stricken villagers calling upon them all the while, "Depart, depart." With what different feelings were they received on their return, by their large circle of weeping friends! One of the Nestorians, who had accompanied the family, standing by the grave, artlessly described to the Nestorians the affecting scenes he had witnessed, and all were bathed in tears. "In all the families of the village," wrote Miss Fidelia Fiske, "Judith had taken a deep interest, and several of the middle-aged women had been taught by her in the Sabbath-school. Indeed, she had greatly endeared herself to all the scores and hundreds of Nestorians who knew her, and was a universal favorite among the people. A Nestorian of a distant village said, on hearing of her death,

"There was none like her, — so beautiful, so wise, so pious. She would pray like an angel."[1]

The Gospel made its way among the Nestorians amid many discouragements. Yet there was progress. Even in the mountains of Koordistan, where the brethren could do little more than watch the leadings of Providence, there was much that was hopeful. It was an indication of promise, that the people of Memikan, the mountain station, notwithstanding their sufferings for the sake of the Gospel, did not falter in their adherence to it. Strangers, after listening to the reading and reciting of the school children, sometimes went away exclaiming, "Glory to God! There is nothing bad in all this." Religious worship was well attended. Even in the busy season, when the laborers were in their fields before dawn, and worked till late, a goodly number attended the daily evening service. Nor was it here, only, that a listening ear was found. In a tour among some of the largest neighboring villages, the missionaries were kindly received. Some sat from morning till the setting of the sun, giving earnest heed to the preaching. Could the people have been assured that they had nothing to fear from the civil power, they would have braved their ecclesiastics. Even as it was, the missionary pursued his work without molestation, and was treated with uniform respect by the authorities.

Progress in the mountains.

[1] See *The Persian Flower; A Memoir of Judith Grant Perkins of Oroomiah, Persia.*

Progress on the plain.

On the plain of Oroomiah, there was more preaching than ever before, and the line of demarkation between an evangelical church and a dead Christianity, was becoming more and more distinct. Mar Yohannan boldly discarded many customs of his Church, and then seemed disposed to go as fast in the work of reformation as his people could be induced to follow; and there was the same spirit among the helpers of the mission.

The seminaries.

The two seminaries were coming under a stricter discipline, and aimed at a higher standard of scholarship. About half of the forty students under Mr. Stoddard were hopefully pious, and some of them gave high promise of usefulness. One was appointed to succeed the bishop of the largest diocese in the province. Several were from different mountain districts, and one was from the valley of the Tigris.

The number in the female seminary had increased from forty to fifty, and it was delightful to witness the intelligent zeal of some teachers in the Sabbath-schools. The ten who graduated in March were all hopefully pious, well educated, and quite refined, and most of them were expected to become teachers in their own villages.

A suggestive case of piety.

The description given by Mr. Stocking of a very aged priest, whom he saw among the hills north of Gawar, encourages the belief that the Holy Spirit sometimes makes the faintest rays of Gospel light effectual to salvation. The man was nearly deaf, and bending under the weight of a century or more, according to the statement of the people, but was able to converse intelligently about events which happened two or three generations before. "We were much surprised," writes Mr. Stocking, "at the correctness of his views in regard to some of the cardinal doctrines of the Scriptures, and particularly as to the necessity of an evangelical faith, in distinction from one that was dead, and of the work of the Holy Spirit in renewing and sanctifying believers. Though not remarkable for his learning, he appears to have been taught by the great Teacher himself; for he had never before seen a missionary. As I left him, to see him no more, he affectionately took my hand, and said he had one request to make, which was that we would remember him in our prayers at the mercy-seat. He also requested a New Testament in the ancient and modern Syriac, for his village, which we sent to him."

Scenes on an extensive tour.

In August, 1851, Mr. Coan, accompanied by Priest Dunka and Deacons John and Khamis, visited the districts of Jeloo, Bass, Tekhoma, Tiary, and Diss, and discoursed to more than four thousand persons. A part of this ground had never been trod before by a missionary. The ecclesiastics were, as usual, the greatest opposers, but there were two pleasing exceptions. In Alsan, a village of five hundred souls, there was one priest who, at first, seemed reserved, but as his prejudices were removed, he became, with his people, an attentive listener. The missionaries tarried four or five hours, preaching the Word to the hungry multitude. The people, in little companies, conversed about what they had heard, and publicly upbraided their priest for letting them remain in such ignorance. He made humble confession, and expressed a desire to send his little boy, a bright looking lad, to Oroomiah for instruction. At another village, they found a decidedly evangelical priest. That his influence over his large village was good was apparent in the quiet and orderly behavior of the people, and their attention to the Gospel. Indeed, they were accustomed to the word of exhortation daily at their evening prayers. This priest had a small school every winter, to which several lads resorted from neighboring districts.

A very different scene was witnessed in the village of Mar Ziah, which was thronged with ecclesiastics who obtained their livelihood by begging. "They were dressed," Mr. Coan writes concerning them, "in scarlet and silk, and were exceedingly haughty in their bearing. We met the people in the churchyard, but, after a few words, there arose such a tumult as I hope never to see again. For an hour or more, the place was like a pandemonium. Some wished to hear what we had to say; but others, with savage fierceness, flew at them, yelling at the top of their voices, and looking as if ready to drink their blood. In the course of an hour or two their rage had spent itself, and after a few words of solemn admonition, we left them." At another village, scarcely three miles distant, where was no priest, a few persons assembled in a room where the missionaries stopped, and their solemn and tearful attention was very unlike the noisy scene they had just left. One young man begged, with tears, to receive a copy of the Gospel.

Nazee was one of three Tiary girls who came to Oroomiah after the massacre of the mountain Nestorians, and in the seminary became hopefully pious. She was now living at Chumba, and having heard of the coming of her missionary friends, was standing on the bank of the impetuous Zab, awaiting their arrival. There was no fording the torrent, but the travellers ventured across on two single string pieces, bending under them at every step. She greeted them joyfully, and hastened to prepare a place for their lodging. While she was gone, the Malek came and took them to his house. Nazee was disappointed, but followed, eager to hear every word. During the address to the villagers assembled on the roof, it was affecting to see the eagerness with which she listened. Though others left she could not leave, and not till near midnight did she bethink herself, and apologize for keeping Mr. Coan up so late after

Nazee, a Christian girl at her mountain home.

a fatiguing day's journey. She was a light in her village, by which the deeds of the wicked had been reproved, and she had consequently suffered much persecution. Some friends in America, interested in the account which had been given of her while in the seminary, had sent her articles of dress; but her neighbors assembled and maliciously tore them into fragments before her eyes. She bore it meekly, and only prayed for them. She expected fresh insults because of the kindness shown her in the present visit. Long before light, on the day they were to leave, she was with the visitors, anxious to improve the few moments left for Christian conversation; and she followed them, lonely and sad, to the river's side. There they kneeled by the roaring stream, and commended her to the Great and Good Shepherd.

Altitudes of different objects and places.

Mr. Stoddard mentions the visit of Mr. Khanikoff, a Russian scientific gentleman, in the summer of 1852, to obtain information concerning the elevations and climates of these districts. Lake Oroomiah was ascertained to be about four thousand one hundred feet above the ocean, and the city four thousand five hundred feet, the plain sloping down gently towards the lake. Mount Seir rises two thousand eight hundred and thirty feet above the city, and seven thousand three hundred and thirty feet above the ocean; differing not greatly, in real height, from the White Mountains in New Hampshire. The mission residence, on the mountain side, is a thousand feet above the city. The mountains of Koordistan, some of which are capped with snow through all the year, often rise to the height of twelve thousand feet, and one peak is supposed to be fourteen thousand feet above the sea. Mr. Khanikoff afterwards became Russian Consul General at Tabriz, and proved himself a sincere and valuable friend to the mission.

A Russian friend.

Failure of health constrained Mr. Stocking to return, with his family, to the United States, and he was never able to resume his missionary labors. Since his lamented decease, a son has taken his place among the Nestorians.

Mr. Stocking's return home.

It should be gratefully acknowledged, that violence towards missionaries has almost everywhere been the exception, and not the rule. It has been so even in Koordistan. But Mr. Cochran, while travelling with several Nestorians through Nochea, was assailed by five robbers in the employ of a Koordish chief, named Seyed Khan Bey. As Moslems the assailants were of course reckless of the life of Christians; and, for a time, the party were apprehensive of being murdered. But at last, while the freebooters were intent on their prey, the company fled up the steep mountain side, leaving their effects. Their horses were afterwards recovered.

Case of robbery.

The year 1854 opened with a revival in both the

Another revival.

seminaries. At the commencement of it, scarcely half the students in either of the institutions gave evidence of piety, which was an unusually small proportion. The thought of this, and especially that several of the senior class were about going forth into the world without Christ, led to earnest prayer, and to efforts which were followed by an immediate blessing. The special religious interest continued several weeks, and extended to the large village of Geog Tapa, but the results appear not to have been distinctly reported.

The eighteen young men who graduated in 1854,

Seminary graduates.

were of higher promise than any previous class. Several of the performances at their graduation were very gratifying, particularly the valedictory addresses, pronounced by a young man of eighteen, which would not suffer in matter or manner, Dr. Perkins thought, by the side of similar addresses at any American college. Nearly all were hopefully pious, and were returning to homes widely distant from each other.

In some parts of the field there was much enthu-

Extraordinary enthusiasm.

siasm. In Geog Tapa, for example, about seventy adults had commenced learning to read. The mode pursued there and elsewhere, was to induce teachers, scholars in the village schools, and other readers to teach adults, by the promise of a Bible, Testament, or other book, if they were successful. At an examination, the forenoon was devoted to the girls' school, taught by two graduates of the female seminary, and the afternoon to the Sabbath-school. Such a crowd of Nestorians was present, that it was necessary in the afternoon, to meet in a grove. The first class examined in the Sabbath-school consisted of men from twenty to seventy years of age, headed by the chief man of the village. Then followed a class of women, fifty or sixty in number, from forty to fifty years of age. These classes, not being able to read, had been taught orally. Next came a class of men, about twenty in number, and a class of twenty-three women, who had recently learned to read. These had been taught individually by boys connected with the village schools, each of whom received a copy of the Old Testament as a reward. On the plain of Oroomiah seventy-three free schools were reported, with more than a thousand boys, and one hundred and fifty girls and women as pupils.

In Gawar, two schools embraced fourteen boarding and thirty-two day scholars. Fourteen of these were from Jeloo, Bass, and Tekhoma districts. Among them were four deacons, four from the family of the bishop of Jeloo, and nearly all were from prominent families. They were wild mountaineers, and in some things difficult to manage, but they acquired knowledge rapidly and with delight; and the constant study of the Bible wrought a perceptible change in them. In the Bootan districts, hitherto inaccessible to missionary influence, there was now a strong desire for schools, and for the labors of evangelical teachers.

Books.

The New Testament in the modern language was beginning to be circulated among the people; a much enlarged edition of the hymn book had been issued, and a volume, entitled "Scripture Facts," had a wide circulation. Mr. Perkins had completed a translation of Doddridge's "Rise and Progress," and was engaged in translating Barth's "Church History."

Death of Mr. Crane.

Mr. Crane died at Gawar on the 27th of August, 1854, at the commencement of a career of bright promise. So ardently was he beloved by the people there, that at the funeral service the whole assembly repeatedly broke forth into weeping. The afflicted widow was called, within a week of her husband's death, to mourn also the loss of a beloved son, and removed to Mount Seir, where she was a valued helper in the mission. She returned home in 1857. Mr. Rhea and Miss Harris were united in marriage in October, and spent the winter at Gawar.

Audacity of papal missionaries.

The audacity of the papal missionaries, backed by the French embassy, was marvelous. The American mission having been importuned to open a school in the large village of Khosrova, in Salmas, where popery predominated, two young men, graduates of the seminary, were successively sent thither. The first was several times driven away, through the instigation of the Lazarists, and those who were friendly to the mission also became objects of persecution. The second was assailed by the mob, headed by the French chief of the Lazarists, and by a bishop. These two men, with their own hands, threw him into a canal, and called on the people to drown or kill him. He was mercifully delivered, but narrowly escaped with his life. The matter being reported to Mr. Abbott, the English Consul at Tabriz, the chief of the Lazarists, with some fifteen of his satellites, went thither, and apprehending a cool reception from the Consul, whose protection the Lazarists enjoyed in common with the American missionaries, he applied for assistance to the Russian Consul, proposing to transfer his passports to his hands. Mr. Khanikoff refused, and severely rebuked them for their conduct. Mr. Abbott obtained an order from the Governor of Azerbijan to lay heavy fines on the Mussulman deputies of Khosrova for withholding protection, and on the principal papists for their acts of violence, with the requirement of bonds for future good behavior.

English and Russian protection.

Messrs. Abbott and Stevens, English consuls at Tabriz and Teheran, kindly exerted their protecting influence, and Mr. Cochran subsequently spent a week at Khosrova, and had his house thronged every evening with from fifty to a hundred and fifty people, eager to listen to the preaching of the Word. The ecclesiastics raged, and stirred up the agent of the master of the village (who lives in Tabriz) to endeavor to drive our brother away; but the attempt failed. Sixty houses gave their names and seals, wishing to become Protestants. They were exceedingly desirous of having a missionary, and even threatened, good-naturedly, to take one by force to live among them.

Mr. Cochran at Khosrova.

The reader may remember what Dr. Lobdell said of the course of this mission in respect to the forming of distinct churches.[1] Dr. Perkins, writing in May, 1855, gives the following account of the progress of the reformation towards that result: "Our communion occurred about two weeks ago, and nearly one hundred communicants sat down to the table of the Lord, including our mission. It was a solemn and delightful season. Among the native brethren present were Mar Yohannan and Mar Elias; and most of the others, of both sexes, were educated and quite intelligent; but, what is of far greater importance, they were, as we trust, true Christians. It would be easy at once to triple the number from those who, in the judgment of charity, are the children of God; but we think it better to introduce them somewhat gradually and

Matter of church organization.

[1] Chapter xxvii.

cautiously to the ordinance; while, at the same time, we would not too long allow any of the sheep and lambs of Christ's flock to suffer for want of this important means of grace. It is exerting a powerful influence on those who participate in it, and on many others; and it cannot fail ultimately to produce the effect either of redeeming the ordinance from abuses, as administered in Nestorian churches, or drawing off the pious part of the people to a separate observance of it. We are quite willing that the scriptural administration of the ordinance to the pious Nestorians should work out either of these results, in the legitimate time and way, or both of them, as the Lord shall direct."

Some months later, notice was given that, in the future, instead of personal invitations, the door would be thrown open for all who should consider themselves worthy candidates. Uniting with the missionaries would thus seem more like a voluntary and public profession of religion. None were to be received, however, to the communion without a private examination. On one sacramental occasion about one hundred united with the missionaries, and more than thirty of them for the first time. A large number were also present as spectators, many of them deeply interested.

Deacon Guwergis of Tergawer, the well known "Mountain Evangelist," died on the 12th of March, called suddenly from earnest and most useful labors to his reward. Death of Deacon Guwergis.

Hostility of the Persian government.

The course of the Persian government towards the mission and its friends, at this time, was very unsatisfactory. Asker Khan, a general in the Persian army, was appointed to investigate the truth of certain charges brought by the papists against the American missionaries, and early evinced a most unfriendly feeling towards them, and a partiality for their accusers. Indeed, he took no pains to conceal his hostility, and did all he could to stop the schools and other evangelizing agencies. But

Powerful protection.

the missionaries had the aid, as far as aid could be rendered, of the Hon. C. A. Murray, the English Ambassador, and of Mr. Abbott at Tabriz, and Mr. Stevens at Teheran, and also of Mr. Khanikoff, the Russian Consul General at Tabriz. The disturbed state of political relations, and especially the want of harmony between the English and Persian governments, made it impossible for these friends to accomplish what they desired to do in their behalf. After withdrawing from Teheran, Mr. Murray visited Oroomiah, and the correspondence which then passed between him and the missionaries, showed his desire to aid both the suffering Nestorians and the missionary work. In his absence, the Russian Consul General became their protector,— "at first," as he said, "unofficially, but with very good heart; and officially, whenever he should have the right so to do." It is remarkable, and reveals a protecting Providence, that no department of labor, with the exception of village schools, very materially suffered at this time.

In February, 1856, there began to be indications of the special influences of the Holy Spirit in some of the villages occupied by native helpers; and very soon there were marked indications of another work of grace in the two seminaries. The feeling in both the schools became very general. The voice of prayer was heard on every side; and a large proportion of those who were not pious, appeared to be seeking in earnest the way of life. On the 30th of March, Mr. Cochran reported that, with the exception of those most recently admitted, nearly all were hoping that they had passed from death unto life. In the villages, also, there were cases of peculiar interest.

A new revival.

Mr. and Mrs. Rhea were alone in Gawar. In the autumn it was deemed advisable, in view of the insurrectionary state of Koordistan, that they should withdraw for a time. They at first felt it their duty to remain; but the progress of events soon made it plain that Gawar was an unsuitable place for a lone lady, especially when winter should render it impossible for her to remove. Mr. Rhea, while at Oroomiah, continued, as far as possible, to superintend the labors of the native helpers in Memikan, and he returned the next summer, with Mrs. Rhea, to their mountain home. The Koordish chieftains, who had proudly

Gawar vacated for a time.

Discomfiture of the enemy.

boasted, that they would put their heels upon the necks of the poor Christians, were soon fleeing in dismay before the advancing Ottomans.

Mr. Stoddard wrote, in September, 1856, that for six months, in consequence of the withdrawal from Persia of the English Ambassador, the missionaries had been without any political protection, and at the mercy of a hostile government, yet there was perhaps never a time when their work presented a more cheering aspect on the whole. The seminaries, being on the mission premises, suffered less annoyance than did the village schools, which were scattered widely over the plain. The teachers in these schools had many of them been educated in the seminaries, and were altogether superior as a class to what they were a few years before; and thus the standard of instruction was raised, and more religious influence was exerted over the pupils. Nor was there ever a time when more people were brought within the sound of the gospel, or when there were more stated attendants on preaching. And much use was made of the Monthly Concert on the first Monday of the month. The whole day was devoted to the natives. "Early Monday morning," writes Mr. Stoddard, "some of our friends arrive from the nearer villages, and others are continually dropping in during the forenoon. At about the dinner hour, nearly all are assembled. We occupy considerable time with them in private, or in

The Lord their protector.

little companies, each one attending to the helpers under his care, in hearing the monthly reports of their labors and trials, their hopes and fears, and intermingling the reports with religious conversation and prayer. At three in the afternoon we assemble, and spend an hour or two in public religious exercises. In the evening a similar meeting is held, when the natives not only speak freely, but often occupy nearly the whole time, leaving the brother who has charge of the meeting little to do. It very often happens, also, that after the meeting has been together two hours, there are several who feel that they want to be heard, if but for a few moments." These monthly occasions Mr. Stoddard enjoyed exceedingly, and came to look upon the "First Monday" as the great day of the month.

The monthly concert.

In October, Messrs. Stoddard and Cochran and Miss Fiske made a tour of three weeks in the mountains of Koordistan. At Gawar they were joined by Mr. and Mrs. Rhea, and visited the districts of Ishtazin and Bass. From that point Messrs. Cochran and Rhea extended their journey to Amadiah, and returned to their party at Tekhoma, a week later. Thence they passed through the districts of Tâl, and up the Zab to Gawar. The fact that American ladies traversed in safety the gorges and precipices of central Koordistan, was an encouragement to native helpers and their families to reside in those difficult regions; but such tours were too fatiguing, probably, to be often repeated.

Mountain tours.

The object of the visit to Amadiah was to make further explorations with reference to the formation of a station on the western side of the mountains. The mass of the people were on that side, and could not be advantageously reached from Oroomiah. The eastern district was fast becoming supplied with pious helpers, and it seemed very desirable for that section of the country to share in this initiatory work, before anything occurred to hinder it. The convictions of the brethren as to the desirableness of commencing a station there were much strengthened, and Mr. Cochran offered his own services for that purpose.

Search for a western station.

November was ushered in by an event deeply interesting to the mission families; a public profession of religion by the three eldest children of the mission; and hope was entertained as to the piety of some of the younger.

An interesting event.

Asker Khan, agent of the Persian government at Oroomiah, now became more troublesome than ever, resorting to every form of annoyance in his power. At the instance of Mr. Khanikoff, Dr. Wright and Mr. Stoddard visited him at Tabriz, to see what could be done to induce the government to check the doings of its agent. But in this they failed, though the Consul did all he could to assist them. Even the Turkish Consul volunteered his aid, but almost in vain. Through Mr. Khanikoff, they learned that the orders from Tehe-

Violence of government agents.

ran to the Kaim Makam required him to forbid the labors of the missionaries in the province of Salmas; to see that no school was established save in the two places where missionaries resided; and that the number of the schools should not exceed thirty, nor the number of pupils one hundred and fifty. He was to require that no girl receive instruction, at all events, in the same school with boys. The missionaries were not to induce any person to change his religion, and were to enter into a written engagement not to send forth preachers. Books conflicting with existing religions in Persia were not to be printed, and native teachers and preachers were to be approved by Mar Yoosuf and Mar Gabriel, two unprincipled and bitter opposers of evangelical religion. Such were the orders issued, it is believed at the instigation of the French, by the Prime Minister of Persia, and Messrs. Stoddard and Wright, unable to secure even delay in carrying them out, returned to Oroomiah. The mission now, at the suggestion of the Consul, made a formal application for protection to the Russian Ambassador at Teheran.

How these agents were removed.

Asker Khan was assassinated six days after the return of the brethren from Tabriz, by a Koordish chief at Mergawer. But his coadjutor, Asker Aly Khan, governor of the Nestorians, pursued the same persecuting course, urged on by the Kaim Makam at Tabriz. The career of the

Kaim Makam, however, was now short, for in January, 1857, the populace of that city, exasperated by his oppression, rose in a body, broke into his palace, plundered it, and compelled him to flee for his life. He was subsequently summoned to Teheran, and on his approach to that city, was stripped of his honors, mounted on a pack saddle, and thus led to prison, while a fine was imposed on him of a hundred thousand tomans.

CHAPTER XXIX.

THE NESTORIANS.

1857–1863.

THE sojourn of three weeks at Tabriz had been a source of constant anxiety to Messrs. Stoddard and Wright, and the former had premonitory symptoms of fever on his way home. But he was not apprehensive on that account, and finding Mr. Cochran and two of the native teachers disabled by sickness, he devoted much time and labor to the Seminary, and to the correspondence which had accumulated in his absence. Yet fever was threatening, and on the 22d of December, ten days after his return, he became decidedly ill. On the 25th he was confined to his bed, where he lay for two and thirty days, while the fever ran its fatal course. He died in great peace January 26, 1857, in the thirty-ninth year of his age. The public funeral services were in Syriac, and his remains were borne to their last resting-place by graduates of the seminary, whose conversion dated back to the first revival.

Death of Mr. Stoddard.

The mind of Mr. Stoddard was cast in a fine mould. The older members of the Board remember him at the Annual Meeting in Pittsfield in 1849. My own thought at the time was, that were an angel present in human form, his appearance and deportment would be much like those of Mr. Stoddard. A calm, seraphic joy shone in his face, and all that he said and did was just what all delighted to hear and see. His presence did much to give a character to that meeting. Mr. Stoddard had a frail body, and an almost feminine grace of person, like the popular impression of that disciple who leaned on the bosom of his Lord; but, like that disciple, he had strength of principle and inflexibility of purpose. His consecration to the missionary work was no sudden impulse. It was the result of repeated, and sometimes unexpected, meetings and conferences with Dr. Perkins, whose sagacious eye had marked him for a missionary. But the question once settled, it was settled for life. He went whole-souled into the work, and never doubted that his call to it was of God. His talents, which were of a high order, and his learning, which excited the admiration of Persian nobles and princes, were unreservedly consecrated. "He goes among the churches," said the lamented Professor B. B. Edwards, of the Andover Seminary, "burning like a seraph. So heavenly a spirit has hardly ever been seen in this country."

His character.

Mr. Stoddard's daughter Harriet followed him to the grave within two months, at the age of thirteen, a victim to the same disease. She

Death of his daughter.

was sustained by the same calm trust in Christ, which lighted up the last hours of her excellent father.

Dr. Perkins wrote in 1857, that when the mission was commenced, twenty-four years before, hardly a score of Nestorian men were able to read intelligently, and but a single woman, the sister of the Patriarch. The people had no printed books, and but few copies even of portions of the Bible in manuscript, and these were all in the ancient Syriac, and almost unintelligible. Their spoken language, the modern Syriac, had not been reduced to writing. Their moral degradation was extreme. Still there was a remarkable simplicity in their conception of religious doctrines, and a remarkable absence of bigotry in their feelings, as compared with other oriental sects, and they were very accessible to the missionaries. The change had been great. Of the fifty-six in the male seminary when he wrote, thirty were hopefully pious; and so were ninety-one of the one hundred and fifty who had been connected with it. These were the fruits of seven revivals. Of the one hundred and three who had been connected with the female seminary, sixty, or more than one-half, gave good evidence of conversion; and the same might be said of three fourths who were then in the school. A large portion of the young men who had left the seminary, were either preachers of the gospel, or very competent teachers in the village

Retrospective view.

school; and the greater part of the religious graduates of the other seminary were married to those missionary helpers. This seminary had been blessed with eight revivals. The instruction in both institutions had been almost wholly in the native tongue.

The entire Bible had been translated into the spoken language, which the mission had reduced to a written form; and two thousand intelligent readers, the result of the schools, had been supplied with the sacred volume. Indeed, the Scriptures had been printed and given to the people in the ancient Peschito version, as well as in the spoken tongue. To these were added valuable works on experimental and practical religion, for the use of the schools, and to meet the wants of a community in the early stages of a Christian civilization.

Though separate churches had not been organized, none but pious Nestorians, for the last two or three years, had been admitted to communion with the mission church. The number who had thus communed was about two hundred, and it was thought that from one hundred and fifty to two hundred more were worthy of a place at the Lord's table.

The French Jesuits and their emissaries had been a sore trial, but their success had not been great; and they had probably been useful, by stimulating the mission and the pious Nestorians in their Master's service.

Mrs. Rhea had been two years a member of the

mission as Miss Harris, and three as Mrs. Rhea. Her active and useful life closed on the 7th of December, 1857, at the age of twenty-nine years and five months. "Her sick room," says Dr. Wright, "was a hallowed place, where the Sun of Righteousness shone with wonderful brightness."

Death of Mrs. Rhea.

Another revival of religion occurred in both the seminaries, at the opening of the year 1858, which was extended to Geog Tapa and other villages. Miss Fiske, in charge of the female seminary, relates a fact of much significance. She writes: "Some of the girls' pious friends came to pray with them yesterday, and I was led to inquire how many of them have a pious father or mother (or both), or older brother or sister; and I was surprised to find, as I think you will be to know, that about two thirds of them have such praying friends. I contrast this with the facts respecting their friends in 1846, and feel that we ought to be thankful and humble before our God, for what he has done for them."

Decisive indication of progress.

Mr. Rhea spent the winter of 1857 and 1858 on the western side of the Koordish mountains, and everywhere found an open door for preaching to the rude dwellers among the rocks. In Shermin, Usgan, and Argin, Nestorian villages southwest of Amadiah, he was cordially welcomed to their houses and churches, and had large congregations that gave earnest attention to his preaching. Snow fell eleven out of fifteen days, and when ready

A winter in western Koordistan.

to return to Amadiah, he found the way entirely blocked up. Mr. Marsh having joined him from Mosul, they spent a number of days among large papal villages in that region, where they found ample opportunity for preaching the Gospel; and several individuals seemed earnest inquirers after the way of salvation from the power of sin. With reference to

Mosul and vicinity.

Mosul and vicinity, Mr. Rhea writes: "I am deeply impressed with the evidence, that the labors of the mission here have not been in vain, and that their results are not to be measured by the number of names on the church roll. The Jacobite Church here is now shaken to its foundations; and it cannot be doubted, that whatever of feeling after something better exists among many of its members is owing to the steady light of the Protestant church streaming in upon its darkness." He was absent six months, and for one third of this time was in Mosul.

The mountain field.

He regarded the proper field of the mountain branch of the Nestorian Mission as extending from Amadiah on the north to Mosul on the south, and from Akra on the east to Bootan on the west; including the mountain districts between Gawar and Amadiah. The Christian population was one in respect to nationality and language, and was a remnant of the once great Syrian Church. The language was the same substantially as that spoken in the eastern districts.

As the result of these explorations, Mr. Rhea

made an eloquent appeal for more effective labor in Western Koordistan, which was published in the "Missionary Herald," but cannot be sufficiently condensed for these pages.[1] His health had suffered in his mountain tours, which resembled those performed by his eminent predecessor, Dr. Grant. This rendered it necessary for him to spend a year for recovery in his native land, where his missionary addresses were well received. Two other members of the mission, second to none in the field, — the venerable Dr. Perkins, and Miss Fidelia Fiske, — were obliged to visit the United States in 1858; the former to care for the health of Mrs. Perkins, who, after burying six of her children, had accompanied Mrs. Crane to America, taking her only surviving child; and the latter, in consequence of a disease, which proved fatal after a few years. Dr. Perkins was also accompanied by Mrs. Stoddard, and three children of the mission.

An appeal.

Mr. Rhea's appeal had not been without effect. The Rev. Thomas L. Ambrose joined the mission near the close of 1858, the Rev. John H. Shedd and wife in 1859, and the Rev. Henry N. Cobb and wife in 1860, with direct reference to the mountain field; and the Rev. Amherst L. Thompson and Rev. Benjamin Labaree, with their wives, and Frank N. H. Young, M. D., in 1860, to strengthen the force on the plains, to-

New missionaries.

[1] See *Missionary Herald*, 1858, pp. 317, 318.

gether with Misses Aura Jeannette Beach and Harriet N. Crawford. Mr. Thompson had given much promise of usefulness, but died at Seir, August 25, 1860, only fifty-four days after his arrival. Miss Beach was to be associated with Miss Rice, who had rendered efficient service in the girls' Seminary as the associate of Miss Fiske, but was then alone and overburdened.

Death of Mr. Thompson.

The unexpected but providential withdrawal of so many older laborers, at this juncture, was not favorable to a more enlarged occupation of the field; and the plan of forming a station on the western side of the mountains, was not carried out. The height of Amadiah above the plain of Mesopotamia, and its salubrity in summer were found to have been overestimated; and further researches made it evident, that the demands of so trying a mountain field were more than the average health of missionaries would be able to endure at any season of the year. Indeed, impaired health obliged Mr. and Mrs. Cobb, who had been specially designated to the mountain district, to return home within two years; and, to their own great regret and that of their associates, they have never been able to rejoin the mission.

Failure of the plan of a western station.

Failure of Mr. Cobb's health.

The Nestorian helpers, as a class, were pronounced able and faithful men, remarkably so for Orientals. But they could not fully take

Nestorian helpers.

the place of missionaries. "They do nobly," wrote Mr. Coan, "if properly directed and watched over, better perhaps, in some circumstances, than we can; but it is not the work of a day, nor a year, thoroughly to eradicate the habits of life of those who are brought up in gross superstition."

Tenth revival in the seminary.

Early in the year 1859, the seminary for young men was blessed with its tenth revival, in which a third of its pupils were hopefully converted. There had then been eleven such spiritual refreshings in the seminary for girls. In most of these outpourings of the Spirit, as now, the villages were more or less favored. The effects of these revivals were by no means limited to the souls converted. An enlightening, softening, elevating influence affected the masses. The young men from the seminary were generally of good abilities, having been selected from a large number of candidates, and many of them were distinguished for piety; and quite as much might be said of the other seminary.

Literary treasure of the Nestorians.

More than fourteen millions of printed pages had been distributed among the Nestorians. The Old Testament with references formed a part of this literary treasure; and the New Testament was about being issued in that form.

Marriage of Mar Yohanan.

Among the novelties to be recorded was the marriage of Mar Yohanan, in violation of the canons of the Nestorian Church. The bishop had been connected with the labors of the mission from the beginning. He pleaded the example of Luther and the Apostles. The step was one of his own choosing, and taken in the face of many threats, as well as the imputation of unworthy motives; but the "evangelicals" almost universally approved his course. The excitement was much less than had been apprehended; and another of the bishops, after some time, followed his example.

Advance towards church organization.

In 1860 the observance of the Lord's Supper, instead of being confined to the missionary stations; was held, once in four months, in the various villages where the converts resided, and about a score of virtually reformed churches were thus planted and watered in as many different places. The native pastor was held responsible for the persons whose names were presented to the missionary, as suitable to be admitted to the Lord's table. Mr. Coan speaks of those little churches, as being such in fact, "scattered in the different villages, as so many moral light-houses in the surrounding darkness."

Death of the patriarch.

Mar Shimon, the Nestorian Patriarch, died near the close of 1860, at the age of fifty-nine, and after having been thirty-five years in office. His successor was a nephew, eighteen years old, and a youth of amiable disposition. The patriarch had stood variously affected towards the mission, but was, for the most part, unfriendly. The effect of the Gospel in diminishing the superstitious reverence of the people for him, was one of the causes of his hostility.

About this time, a spirit of unlooked-for liberality was manifested among the Nestorians. It should be borne in mind that the people are poor, that the man worth five hundred dollars is counted rich, and that probably no Nestorian is worth two thousand dollars. The indications in our own country were at that time very unpromising; and when the prospective embarrassments of the Board were stated at the monthly concert in Geog Tapa, John, the pastor, urged the people to support their own missionary in the mountains, and one of the audience rose and pledged nearly a month's support. Others contributed unwonted amounts, and soon the whole congregation was in a blaze of enthusiasm. Those who could command money gave money, others contributed wheat, or other produce, and even women took off their ornaments and gave them. At the monthly concert the next day in the city, the people were more aglow than at Geog Tapa, and gave on a larger scale, though frequently reminded that they were poor, and urged not to give more than their cooler judgments would approve. The amount contributed was five hundred dollars. They seized upon the figure of "a bride" — more forcible in Persia than in America, — which Mr. Coan had used in his address; and

Extraordinary outburst of liberality.

one and another contributed for her "shoes," "dress," and other things, until the "church," the "Lamb's wife," had a very comfortable outfit.

This outburst of benevolent effort was too sudden and excessive to last in the same measure. The advantage gained by the elevation thus reached, was the practicability of keeping the converts up to giving according to their ability, which is the Gospel standard. Dr. Perkins, writing two years later, thought there was a real gain by this effort, though it had reacted somewhat. Most of the pledges were redeemed after the next harvest and vintage.

Dr. Dwight was eighteen days at Oroomiah during his Eastern tour in 1860 and 1861. Mr. Wheeler had accompanied him from Harpoot. Some important changes in the practical working of the mission, made at the Annual Meeting, threw a greater responsibility on the native pastors. They were to have the responsibility, not only of administering baptism, but of the Lord's Supper; and the children of none except communicants were to be baptized. The relation of pastor and people was thus made more prominent and distinct. Dr. Dwight declares himself satisfied by what he saw at Oroomiah, that nothing more than this was needed to complete the organization of the reformed church. He had had the impression, for years, that sooner or later the converts among the Nestorians, like the same class

Dr. Dwight's visit to Oroomiah.

His opinion of the church policy of the mission.

of persons among the Armenians, would be organized into separate churches, wholly distinct from the Nestorian Church. The excommunications and persecutions that had led to that result among the Armenians, he seemed to think would not occur among the Nestorians; and it was evident to him that the old ceremonies of the Church were silently vanishing away, and that reformed services were taking their place, as the result of a fundamental change in the minds of the people. A distinct theological class was to be formed in the seminary of promising young converts, and no more men were to be educated in that school than could afterwards be profitably employed. The conclusion was also reached, in view of past experience, that the mountain regions should not be occupied by American families; reserving them as the peculiar field of the reformed church of the plain; as a training-school for their missionary spirit, and a necessary outlet for their pious zeal.

Improvements.

The native preachers and helpers held a two days' meeting at Oroomiah while Dr. Dwight was there, in which several important subjects were discussed. He liked their appearance, admired the spirit of many of them, and was greatly moved by the extraordinary fire of their eloquence, though he understood them only through an interpreter. He was specially impressed by the childlike piety of the venerable Mar Elias.

Appearance of the native preachers.

Mr. Breath, the ingenious and efficient missionary printer, died of cholera on the 10th of November, 1861. He had so far succeeded in training native printers and book-binders, that there was no further call for such workmen from the United States. Mrs. Breath returned home, with her three children, in the following year.

Death of Mr. Breath.

Some uneasiness was created about this time by rumors, that priests of the Russian Church were coming to Oroomiah to proselyte Nestorians. They did not come; but emissaries were sent by them secretly, who made large promises, that deceived many; yet the evangelical party, with two or three exceptions, kept aloof from the affair. The proposal was that the Nestorians should renounce their religion, and receive the seven sacraments of the Greek Church; the inducements held out being such as the payment of their taxes for some years, and salaries to all ecclesiastics and head men of the villages. The Persian government at length became somewhat alarmed by these proceedings, and the English Consul, Mr. Abbott, having demanded the official interference of the authorities at Tabriz, measures were adopted promising some degree of relief to the oppressed and therefore discontented Nestorians.

Apprehended aggressions from Russian priests.

I have passed in silence, for the most part, the long series of efforts by the Persian government to embarrass the mission, since they appear to have been generally prompted by bribes from emissaries of the Papal Church, and proved strangely inoperative.

Another interesting revival of religion occurred in the two seminaries in February, 1862. It seems to have been marked rather by an increase of grace in the church-members, than by the number of converts. The first months of 1863 and 1864 were also distinguished by special religious interest, extending to many of the villages on the plain.

More revivals.

On Sabbath-morning, December 6, 1863, the good old Mar Elias died, more than four score years of age. Until within a week of his death, he was accustomed to walk to town to attend the monthly concert, a distance of five miles, and for many years he had visited the villages of his diocese on foot. He was sick only three days, and his mind was clear. When asked by the young men about him for his dying charge, it was, "See that ye hold fast to God's Word." An immense concourse gathered from the surrounding country to do honor to his memory; and Dr. Perkins preached from the text: "My father, my father! The chariot of Israel and the horsemen thereof."

Death of Mar Elias.

As a most cheering illustration of what Nestorians may yet become, through the grace of God in the Gospel, I quote largely from an account of the venerable man, by Mr. Rhea.[1]

His character.

[1] See *Missionary Herald*, 1864, pp. 146, 147.

"While our good old bishop was not an educated man, — his knowledge in books extending little beyond the Word of God, — and had but ordinary intellectual ability, he was still one of the most interesting characters among the Nestorians. There is no name among them that will be more fragrant; none that deserves a more honored place in the annals of his Church. The singularity of his position here, thirty years ago, — devout, spiritual, God-fearing, and active, when a deep night hung over his whole people, — like a mountain beacon, whose summit had caught the first beams of the sun, which was soon to flood all below with its glory; his prophetic anticipation of the coming of missionaries; his joy in welcoming them; his peculiar attachment to them and their families; his true-hearted devotion to them as God's ministers, and to their work, through all kinds of vicissitudes; the charming guilelessness of his character, ingenuous as a child; his wonderful love for the Word of God, making it his meditation by day and by night, — not able to pass two or three hours consecutively, without drinking from this well-spring of life; the child-like gentleness of his character, — though, when stirred in God's behalf, he showed a lion-hearted courage, tearing down the pictures and images which Papal hands had stealthily hung on the walls of his church, and pitching them indignantly from the door; his love of sound doctrine, holding forth the word of life in his humble way, always and everywhere, his face never so full of spiritual light as when rehearsing a conversation he had just had with some Mussulman friend, to whom he had opened the Scriptures, and talked of the kingdom yet to fill the whole earth, — the brotherhood of all races, — the one flock and the one shepherd; his silent patience, in a land of cruel wrong, under heavy burdens, borne uncomplainingly for many years; his wonderful spirituality, all things earthly being but the types of the heavenly, — the one, by resemblance or contrast, constantly suggesting the other, so that he could not be reminded that he was late to tea without the quick reply, 'May I not be late at the marriage supper of the Lamb,' or 'Jesus will gather us all in, in season;' all these traits of Christ-like beauty combined to make a character which, in this weary land, was a constant rest to the toil-worn missionary, — an influence for good, continually streaming forth into the darkness of spiritual death around him. God, who accurately weighs all men, only knows how much his kingdom in Persia has been advanced by Mar Elias, than whom the Nestorian Church never had a more spiritual and evangelical bishop."

Armenians on the plain of Oroomiah.

Almost five thousand Armenians inhabit the plain of Oroomiah, and the attention of the mission was gradually turned towards their spiritual enlightenment, with a prospect of ultimate success.

At a general meeting of native helpers, in March, 1863, a Church Manual, or Directory was adopted; "in the observance of which," Mr. Cochran writes, "we have all that is essential to a reformed church, with reformed pastors; and in the possession of the substance, we can afford to dispense with the shadow of new organizations. . . . . The prospect, we believe, was never brighter than at present for the ultimate evangelization of the old Church."

Manual for the reformed church.

During the thirty years from the arrival of Dr. Perkins, five of the twenty men and seven of the twenty-four women, who had joined the mission, had died; and five men and nine women had for various causes been obliged to retire from the field, leaving in the mission seven male and nine female laborers. In this time, the vast unknown of men and things where dwelt the primeval race, had become well known. A great work of exploration had been performed. So far as knowledge of the field was concerned, many a valley had been exalted, many a hill brought low. This was indeed preliminary work, but it was indispensable, and was no small share of what is involved in the conquest of the country for Christ. The seven missionaries then in the field had more than fifty Nestorian fellow-laborers in the gospel ministry, graduates of their seminary, and the nine female missionaries rejoiced in scores of pious young women from their

Retrospect of the mission.

seminary, abroad as wives, mothers, and teachers, doing a work perhaps not second in importance to that of the pious graduates of the other school. Nor should we overlook the reduction of the spoken language to writing, the translation of the Holy Scriptures into it, and the multiplication of books to the extent of seventy-nine thousand three hundred volumes, and more than sixteen millions of pages. Of the half a score and more of revivals in the seminaries, Dr. Perkins affirms that they would compare with the purest revivals he had ever witnessed in America.

Miss Rice in sole charge of female seminary.

The return of Miss Beach to the United States threw the whole care of the female seminary on Miss Rice. She was afterwards materially aided by Mrs. Rhea, and from time to time by other members of the mission.

Care of the English government for the Nestorians.

The interest taken by the English government in the oppressed Nestorians, should be gratefully acknowledged. Mr. Taylor, English Consul at Diarbekir, was sent early in 1864 through the Nestorian districts of Koordistan, to ascertain their grievances, and report to the Ambassador at Constantinople; and Mr. Glen, a pious attaché to the British Embassy in Persia, spent several months on the plain of Oroomiah for a similar purpose.

CHAPTER XXX.

THIRTY YEARS AMONG THE JEWS.

1826–1856.

The first missionary sent by the Board to the Jews in the Levant, was the Rev. Josiah Brewer, who, while connected with the Board, was supported by the "Female Society of Boston and Vicinity for promoting Christianity among the Jews." Sailing from Boston, September 16, 1826, he proceeded to Constantinople by way of Malta and Smyrna, expecting there to find every facility for learning the Hebrew-Spanish language, spoken by the Spanish Jews. But disturbances, growing partly out of the Greek revolution, so hindered his gaining access to the Jews, that he deemed it his duty to turn to some more open field of missionary labor.

The first missionary.

After the retirement of Mr. Brewer, the ladies assumed the support of the Rev. William G. Schauffler, who became his successor. He was a native of Stuttgart in Germany, but early removed, with his parents, to a German colony near Odessa. He came to this country through the

The second missionary.

agency of the Rev. Jonas King, and spent several years at the Theological Seminary in Andover, to prepare himself for a mission to the East. He was ordained at Boston in November, 1831, and embarked soon after, going by way of Paris, where he attended the lectures on the oriental languages and literature, for which that city was then distinguished. He had been familiar with the French language from his youth, and, having an aptitude for such studies, applied himself successfully to the Arabic and Turkish. His health beginning to fail after some months, and the cholera making ravages in the city, he resumed his journey through Germany to Odessa, and thence by water to Constantinople, where he arrived on the last day of July, 1832.[1]

Arrival of Mr. Schauffler at Constantinople.

The greater part of the Jews in Constantinople are descendants of the eight hundred thousand who were expelled from Spain in 1492, and their language is the Hebrew-Spanish; or the Spanish with a mixture of Hebrew words, all written in the Spanish Rabbinical alphabet. As soon as Mr. Schauffler had acquired this language, he began the careful revision of a Hebrew-Spanish translation of the Old Testament, already in print, but not intelligible to the common people. He found the Jewish mind in an unquiet state. Eight years before, as

The Constantinople Jews.

[1] For Mr. Schauffler's account of his residence at Paris and this journey, see *Missionary Herald* for 1833 and 1834.

many as a hundred and fifty had renounced Judaism at one time, but nearly all were soon driven back by persecution. Several of these now requested baptism, and were ready to suffer for the sake of becoming Christians; but they seemed incapable of understanding that anything more could be required of them than an exchange of external relations, and gave little evidence of piety.

Baptism of a German Jew.

Near the close of 1834, Mr. Schauffler baptized a German Jew, whom he named Herman Marcussohn, having formed his acquaintance in South Russia, sixteen years before. As he could not there profess Christianity except by joining the Greek Church, he had come to Constantinople, bringing letters to Mr. Schauffler, and was engaged by him as a literary assistant.

Religious excitements.

Religious excitements were not wanting. Three young Jews became anxious for Christian baptism, and both the Greek and Armenian Patriarchs refusing it, they fell into the cold embrace of the Papal Church. Three others expressed the same desire; and ten young men took advantage of the death of the civil head of their community to flee, as was supposed, for the sake of greater freedom in religion. Mr. Schauffler's varying and perplexing experience constrained him to believe, that private charity, and sacrifices for individual Jews, should be employed very sparingly.

The year 1835 was chiefly employed in revising

the Hebrew-Spanish version of the Old Testament, and in preparing a Lexicon in the two languages. He also commenced a series of tracts in Hebrew-German. To some extent there was among the Jews a hearing ear, and to a greater extent the absence of an understanding heart. The German and Polish Jews were less bigoted and more intelligent than the Spanish Jews, but were more greedy of gain, and more indifferent to religion. On the great day of atonement they allowed Marcussohn to address them in their synagogue on the Christian religion; the rulers of the synagogue having first given him a seat on the platform among themselves, where they read their Scriptures and prayers, and where sermons were delivered.

A visit of some months made by Mr. Schauffler among his friends at Odessa, in 1836, resulted, through divine grace, in a revival, as has been already stated, among the German population, and was not without good effects upon the demoralized Jews of that city. During his absence, his revision of the Psalms in Hebrew and Hebrew-Spanish was printed at Constantinople, under the superintendence of Mr. Farman, a missionary of the London Jews Society. A relative of the chief rabbi called on Mr. Schauffler after his return, and took a hundred copies for distribution, and he thought his chief might be induced to give his *imprimatur* to the contemplated edition of the

Visit to Odessa.

Psalms in Hebrew-Spanish.

Old Testament; but from some unknown cause, the chief rabbi became a fierce opposer of the Psalms, and prohibited the use of the edition.

Goes to Vienna to print the Old Testament.

In May, 1839, Mr. Schauffler left for Vienna, to superintend the printing of the Old Testament for the Spanish Jews. As he was leaving, the caique, in which himself and family, including an infant child, were going off to the steamer, upset, and the whole party narrowly escaped drowning. His visits to Odessa, in going and coming, were the occasion, as before, of spiritual blessings to the people. His family expenses were paid by the Board, but the printing was at the charge of the American Bible Society. He was absent nearly three years, returning in August, 1842; and in that time carried through the press three thousand copies of the Old Testament in Hebrew-Spanish, in two volumes quarto, containing fifteen hundred pages. The Hebrew occupied every alternate page. He also printed five hundred copies of the Hebrew-Spanish Pentateuch, in two volumes, 16mo., with the Hebrew on the opposite page. The Sefardim, or Spanish Jews, having the New Testament previously, were now favored with the whole inspired volume in their vernacular tongue.

The Hebrew-Spanish Bible.

Unsuccessful opposition.

Notwithstanding the anathemas of Jewish rulers, the three thousand copies of the Psalms, printed in 1836, were nearly exhausted in

1844, and the book was in great esteem among the people. A vain effort was made by the rabbis to suppress the Vienna edition of the Old Testament. Only a few of the hundreds of copies in the hands of the people were delivered up, and it was believed that those confiscated by the rabbis found their way again into circulation.

About this time, the "Committee of the General Assembly of the Church of Scotland on the Scheme for the Conversion of the Jews," made a grant of £2,162 (about $10,000) to this mission for the circulation of the Hebrew Scriptures, the purchase of rabbinic type, and the publication of school-books and tracts for the Jews. This, while it generously enlarged the operations of the mission, afforded no relief to the treasury of the Board.

Generous aid from Scotland.

Such were the calls for the Hebrew-Spanish Old Testament, that more than twelve hundred copies went into the hands of the Jews previous to June, 1843. One rabbi requested twenty copies for poor Jews in Roumelia; another, and he the chief rabbi, asked for ninety copies for six destitute places; and another, the rabbi of Orta Keuy, made repeated solicitations for thirty copies for schools in that suburb, and for twenty additional copies to place in reading rooms, where Jews come together in a social manner, on their Sabbath, to read the Bible.

Demand for the Scriptures.

Calls for religious conversation were frequent, but

there was painful evidence, that in most cases the object was more selfish than spiritual. There appeared to be a general dissatisfaction with Judaism, but no proper knowledge of Christianity. Poverty and distress were the principal occasions of these calls. A few appeared to be interested in more fundamental truths; and they attentively read McCaul's "Old Paths," a controversial work that exposes the absurdity of rabbinism. The chief difficulty with all was in respect to the divine nature of the Messiah.

The grand difficulty.

The Spanish Jews, numbering seventy or eighty thousand souls in Constantinople, afforded a field for the faithful sower, rather than the cheerful reaper. The tyrannical rule of their rabbis rendered them less accessible, perhaps, than any other people in Turkey, the Moslems alone excepted; and intellectually they were among the most degraded races in the East. Yet they stood higher in their morals than did the Turks. They had but few books; and until the issue of the edition under Mr. Schauffler's superintendence, they had no copy of the Old Testament in their vernacular tongue, that was accessible to the people at large. Two editions of the Old Testament, in Hebrew-Spanish and Hebrew and Chaldee, with Rabbi Solomon Jarchi's commentary in opposition to Christian doctrines, had been published in 1816, at Vienna, in six quarto volumes. Now the Christian church, while

Present duty of Christian churches.

waiting for a wider entrance among the people, was called on to provide the books that would be indispensable when that entrance should be secured. Among those most needed now, were a Hebrew and Hebrew-Spanish vocabulary of the Old Testament (then in preparation); a Spelling Book for schools; a short Hebrew Grammar; a brief Arithmetic; a Geography of the Bible, and a Natural History of the same; various religious tracts and essays on prophecies, especially those concerning the Messiah; and a translation of McCaul's "Old Paths" into Hebrew-Spanish.

The Ashkenazim, or German Jews, were only about two thousand, and were chiefly young men driven from Moldavia by the Boyars, and from Russia by the law of conscription that threatened them with the hardships and perils of a soldier's life. This department was under the charge of Mr. Allan, a missionary of the Free Church of Scotland, in connection with Mr. Schwartz, a converted Jew.

The German Jews.

The Protestant Armenians showed a deep interest in efforts for the conversion of the Jews, and were forward to render their aid. Nor could Jews or Mohammedans be wholly uninfluenced by the change then going on in the Armenian churches of the metropolis in respect to the use of pictures; the greater part of which had been removed, and the patriarchal church, in place of them had set the example of having passages of Scripture painted in large letters on the walls.

Interest of Protestant Armenians.

Besides the Spanish and German Jews in Constantinople, there was a small body of Italian Jews who were generally destitute of all religion. Then as there were many Germans in the city, Mr. Schauffler held a stated service for them, in which his labors were blessed to the hopeful conversion of some. The attendance was often composed largely of Israelites. In the closing month of the year 1844, he baptized a Jewish physician.

The Italian Jews.

Service for the Germans.

The Jews are probably more strongly prejudiced against the Gospel, than any other people. Their whole literature is anti-Christian. So are their education and internal religious policy. The great effort of Jewish learning for fifty generations, has been to prevent the Old Testament from suggesting Christian ideas to the Jewish mind. Hence a Jewish mission requires an extraordinary amount of preparatory work, in the first instance; though its main objects and duties afterwards will differ little, if at all, from those of other missions.

Why so much preparatory work needed.

Mr. Schauffler was specially adapted to the preliminary work in Jewish missions, growing out of the peculiar state of the national mind. What this was, up to the year 1845, has been sufficiently indicated. In that year, a second edition of the Pentateuch, in Hebrew and Hebrew-Spanish, was printed at Vienna; and a new edition, of five

New editions of the Scriptures.

thousand copies of the Old Testament in the same languages, was commenced at Smyrna. The American Bible Society, which bore the expense of these editions, also authorized the printing of a Hebrew and Hebrew-German version of the Old Testament, for the German Jews.

The testimony of Mr. Schauffler is so explicit on a point of great importance in a mission of the Jews, as to justify the following quotation: — Important testimony.

"My own observation from the first, has established this fact, that whenever a Jew is truly converted, the hope of seeing all Israelites settled in Canaan sinks to the level of many other secondary ideas; and Christ and him crucified, — Christ risen, ascended, and reigning in glory, Christ and his kingdom, wherever its centre may be, — becomes the all-absorbing theme. In other words, such Jews I have always observed to be just what true converts among ourselves are; differing from us only in this, that they cherish that desire for the conversion of Israel, which we ought also to cherish, and of which Paul has left so splendid an example. Half-converted men, in whom the carnal pride of the old Pharisee has never been broken down by a divinely wrought sense of the guilt of unbelief in Christ, who, when they were baptized, thought they did Christ and his people an honor; these, of course, never fail to consider themselves as something special in the kingdom of Christ, and they expect to be treated by Him accordingly. These make an exception. There are, also, truly converted men among the proselytes, who cherish that notion. They are those who have been under the influence of missionaries, who make them a 'royal race,' amid the divinely designated 'royal priesthood' (than which nothing can be higher) of Christ's true people. We are all apt to believe what magnifies ourselves. But I have observed no inherent tendency that way among truly converted Jews, and never found it necessary to make efforts to eradicate such carnal hopes."

Change of relations to Constantinople Jews.

The particular relations of the Board to the Spanish Jews in Constantinople underwent an unexpected change in the year 1846. Owing to the protracted and unavoidable delay in providing associates for Mr. Schauffler, the brethren from the Free Church of Scotland had so far taken possession of the ground, as to render another mission in that city inexpedient. Whatever cause there may have been for regretting this after the Board had obtained the men, no blame was attached to our more zealous brethren of the Scotch Church. Mr. Schauffler would continue to reside in Constantinople, and would render valuable aid to all the missions to the Jews in those parts.

Attention was now directed to Salonica (the ancient Thessalonica), which had been visited by Messrs. Schauffler and Dwight some years before. The city was visited again by Mr. Schauffler in July, 1847, and he urgently recommended occupying it as a Jewish station. The number of rabbinical Jews residing there was estimated at thirty-five thousand, or about half of the whole population. The number of their synagogues was fifty-six. The Jews were diffused throughout the city, and not confined, as in Constantinople, to certain quarters. There was, therefore, a good degree of intermingling in civil life with other people. The natural consequence was, that a Salonica Jew did not evince the shyness so common elsewhere, in approaching Christians, or in entering their houses. They were thankful for the gift of the Old Testament in a language they could understand. Moreover, the centre of rabbinical learning was at Salonica, and not at Constantinople; which made the assent given by the Salonica rabbis to the correctness of the Hebrew-Spanish version, the more influential.

Attention turned to Salonica.

The Jewish population.

The Rev. Messrs. Eliphal Maynard and Edward M. Dodd, appointed to this mission, reached Salonica, with their wives, in April, 1849, going by way of Constantinople. Mr. Schauffler was to remain at the metropolis, but accompanied them to Salonica and was with them seven weeks, helping them much towards a successful entrance

Missionaries to Salonica.

on their work. Both of the brethren devoted themselves to the Hebrew-Spanish. Mr. Dodd gave, also, some attention to the Turkish, with a view to the Zoharites, or Moslem Jews, numbering about five thousand; all of whom seemed to rejoice that missionaries had come there to reside. He describes them as among the noblest of the inhabitants of the city, and as very ready to talk on religious subjects, with less self-conceit than the rabbinical Jews.

The Zoharites.

The Prudential Committee, on sending forth these brethren, stated the more important facts, principles, and usages, which should be kept constantly in mind in their mission to the Jews.[1] The relations of that people to Christ's kingdom were believed to be the same with those of all other people; and they were no more shut out from that kingdom by a "judicial blindness," or more really "cast away," than any other perverse and wicked nation. The obstacles to be overcome among them were substantially the same with those in the Oriental Churches. The relations sustained to the spiritual blessings of the Abrahamic covenant being no longer of blood, but of faith, these blessings must be common alike to believing Jews and Gentiles. Never again, in the spiritual kingdom of God, will there be circumcision or uncircumcision, Greek or Jew. Never again will there be a need of

Relations of Jews to Christ's kingdom.

[1] More fully stated in the *Missionary Herald* for 1849, p. 101.

bloody rites, a mediating priesthood, and a showy ritual. Never again will there be a theocracy with a sensuous external economy, limited to a single nation. Never again, in the kingdom of God, will he be accounted a Jew, in the evangelical sense, who is one outwardly, nor that be accounted circumcision which is outward in the flesh; but he will be a Jew, who is one inwardly, and is, of course, heir to all the spiritual promises made to the Jews in the Old Testament; and circumcision is of the heart, in the spirit, and not in the letter. On these broad, fundamental Scripture principles, rested the whole superstructure of our mission to the Jews.

The prevalent idea, that judicial blindness came upon Israel in consequence of their crucifixion of the Son of God, precluding their conversion as a people until the arrival of some great prophetic era, seems without any proper Scripture warrant. They were blinded only "in part;" only "some" of the branches were broken off; they are not "cast away" as a people; and when the rest of mankind shall embrace the Gospel, and come into the kingdom, the Jews will do the same.

The practical inference drawn from all this was, that the same general course should be pursued in Jewish missions, which is proper in missions to any other unevangelized people. They must be instructed as to the oneness of Christ's body, the church, and the equal membership of all

The practical inference.

true disciples. If a church be formed of Jewish converts alone, it should be in full communion with all other Christian churches.

Manual labor schools and hospitals for the Jews, employing converts merely for the sake of giving them employment; boarding-schools to serve as houses of refuge for the children of converts; expenses incurred for shielding converts from persecution or for teaching them trades; were not regarded as within the range of missionary work; but the converts were, in general, to be left, as the Apostles left them, to meet the consequences of their conversion upon their persons, their families, and their business, as God in his providence and by his grace should enable them.

Mr. Maynard was removed by death from his labors within five months after his arrival. In company with a New England clerical friend, he made a tour into the delightful region of Thessaly for relaxation and health. Unconsciously they exposed themselves to malaria, and both took the same fever; of which Mr. Maynard died at Salonica, and his friend at Athens. Mrs. Maynard soon afterwards returned home. The place thus early vacated was filled, in the following summer, by the Rev. Justin W. Parsons, who was accompanied by his wife.

Death of Mr. Maynard.

A new missionary.

The Salonica Jews had scarcely more than the shadow of education. A school taught in the principal synagogue contained about a

The people without education.

thousand pupils, but with the least possible intellectual value in the instruction. Half as many more were in private schools, where Hebrew and Hebrew-Spanish were taught, but nothing like Grammar, Geography, or History. In a small select school, supported by rich Jews, Italian (the commercial language) and French were taught. Familiarity with the Talmud was regarded as the perfection of knowledge, so that a man needed to know nothing else. "Oh," said a beardless youth to a missionary, "if you had only read our Talmud, you would throw all your books into the fire." Salonica was famous for its books, but they were servile imitations of the Talmud. The spoken language was essentially Spanish, but with a deficient vocabulary, and greatly corrupted with Turkish and Hebrew words, while subject to constant change. Consequently the many books and tracts in Hebrew-Spanish, which were published by the English missionaries in Smyrna, were comparatively useless at Salonica, because of the difficulty of understanding them. These Jews therefore needed missionary schools.

Their capacity for self-righteousness.

The excessive self-righteousness of this people, as described by Mr. Dodd, disclosed a serious obstacle to missionary success among them. "Two thousand years of punishment," he says, "have not destroyed the feeling, that they are the beloved of heaven. They pray, morning, noon, and night, and that too in the holy language. They always ask a blessing on their food. They neither eat nor touch any unclean thing. Except they wash their hands oft, they eat not. When they fast, it is by entire abstinence from food. They read the Word of God almost continually. In passing through the bazaars, you may see the shop-keepers taking up the Bible to read in their leisure hours; and if a visitor has to wait for you a few minutes, with a Bible within reach, you will certainly find him reading it, though it be in an unknown tongue; and once a year they sit up all night to read through the law. Their recognition of Providence is excessive. Every event is referred to God. He is thanked for every good; submission to his will is expressed in every trial. Every hope is uttered conditionally, in dependence on him; and his aid is invoked in trouble as frequently, and with as little meaning, as many Christians speak of fortune, or luck. As to the outward semblance of piety and devotion, I do not think another such people can be found. Like their fathers, they seek God daily, and delight to know his ways. As a nation, they take delight in approaching God. 'Is not the Lord among us?' 'No evil shall come upon us.' Talk to them of God's glory, and they will answer by quoting some beautiful Psalm of David. Talk of man's sinfulness, and they will repeat Psalm 51st, with seeming penitential devotion. Speak of God's wrath against sin; they will assent readily, but add, that he is pitiful, remembering that we are dust. Thus the missionary is baffled. Let him search the Word of God to find expressions that shall penetrate to their consciences; the Jew is familiar with them all, and repeats them every day in his prayers. They either mean nothing, or through a talmudic gloss, aided by self-righteous blindness, they foster his confidence in the mercy of the God who is his peculiar friend, and loves him more than he loves the Gentile world, or even his own justice and truth."

Mr. Parsons also says, after a visit to Seres, a city fifteen miles northwest of Salonica: "The Jews of Seres have the same blind submission to the rabbis, the same prejudices, the same evasions of the truth. Gold is their God, and traffic is their religion,— one would say, who should meet them only in their fair. But in their prayers, and their Sabbath observance, the deceiver makes them appear to themselves the holy favorites of heaven, separate from the nations."

Literary labors of Mr. Schauffler.

Mr. Schauffler had now printed his Hebrew grammar, and commenced the printing of his Hebrew lexicon. The edition of the Pentateuch was nearly exhausted.

A new missionary.

The Rev. Homer B. Morgan and wife reached Salonica in February, 1852. The brethren were of the opinion, that while for two thirds of the year the climate of that city was tolerably healthy, the low portions, where the Jews and Greeks chiefly resided, were subject to malaria. The missionaries, therefore, would have resided in the more elevated parts occupied by the Turks, but could neither hire nor purchase houses in that quarter. The best they could do was to live in the upper stories of their houses. Mr. Dodd suffered from a bronchial affection, and sought to recruit his health by an excursion into Thessaly, where he enjoyed some excellent opportunities for preaching the gospel, both to Jews and Gentiles.[1] Mr. Parsons visited the part of Macedonia, which lies northwest of Salonica, and then extended his journey to Sophia, the capital of Bulgaria.[2]

Insalubrity of the climate.

The health of Mr. Dodd did not improve, and he repaired first to Malta, and then, with the consent of the Committee, to the United States. In August, 1852, a month after his departure, Mr. and Mrs. Parsons, and Mr. and Mrs. Morgan were all prostrated by intermittent fever. Mrs. Morgan did not yield to the disease, till she had exhausted her strength in caring for the others; and then, after a short illness, during most of which she was unconscious, she was removed to her heavenly home. Mr. Parsons was at one time very low; and the three survivors were subjected to such frequent returns of fever during the winter, that they were advised by

Dangerous sickness.

Death of Mrs. Morgan.

[1] *Missionary Herald* for 1852, pp. 235–238.

[2] *Ibid.* pp. 78–83.

physicians to spend the spring and summer on the Bosphorus. They left the station in charge of native helpers, and removed to Constantinople. Until sickness came, their labors had been uninterrupted. Their circle of acquaintance was constantly increasing, and they were generally regarded by the Jews as their sincere friends. They were expected in their visits to declare and make personal applications of gospel truths. A little volume upon the inspiration of the Old and New Testaments, by Mr. Dodd, was favorably received by many of the Jews.

Removal to Constantinople.

It was not deemed expedient for the brethren to resume their residence in Salonica. Mr. Morgan and Mr. and Mrs. Parsons removed to Smyrna, where they shared with their English brethren in labors among the Jews. They hoped to continue to occupy Salonica through Armenian native helpers, and to visit it themselves in the healthy season. Mr. Morgan was married to Mrs. Sutphen, of the Armenian mission, at the close of 1853, and on the return of Mr. and Mrs. Dodd to Smyrna in the autumn of 1854, they went to Salonica, expecting to remain there during nine months, and then to retire before the miasma of summer. Mr. Morgan was welcomed by his Jewish acquaintance, and found that the spirit of inquiry had spread, and that there was greater boldness on the part of a few. But whatever their secret conviction of the truth, none

Salonica but partially reoccupied.

confessed the Saviour openly. The first fruits ripened elsewhere. A family of three fled to Malta, and were baptized there; another, a converted rabbi, came to Smyrna, and became a teacher. There had been a considerable advance in female education, since Mrs. Dodd had, with great difficulty, persuaded a Jewish girl to encounter the odium of learning to read. Some prominent rabbis were teaching their daughters, and the tide seemed evidently turning.

Labors among the Smyrna Jews.

The Jews of Smyrna were found to be more worldly, and less given to religious thought, than the Jews of Salonica. But an avowedly Christian school of near twenty pupils was sustained during the year 1854, and taught by the converted rabbi above mentioned. The teacher was known to be a proselyte. The New Testament was read daily, and biblical instruction occupied a large place. It was hopeful that Jews were found willing to place their children in such an atmosphere. A boarding-school was opened for a few of the more promising boys belonging to the day-school. The parents of five actually signed a contract binding them to the missionaries for three years. This they did after the most explicit declarations, that while the boys would be trained for the highest usefulness and happiness in this world, they would be carefully instructed in the way of salvation through Jesus of Nazareth. The experiment could not proceed without opposition. The chief rabbi interposed. The eldest boy in the school manifested an inclination to embrace the Christian religion, and was beaten, dragged to the synagogue, and compelled to go through the form of worship. He was then put in irons procured from the mad-house. He afterwards fled to Constantinople, where he was baptized by one of the Scotch missionaries. The teacher was also thrown into prison, on a false accusation. A young Jewish physician appeared fully to embrace the truth, and was not moved by the most cruel threats, or flattering promises. Mr. Parsons was greatly encouraged.

Labors of Mr. Schauffler.

The instruction of inquirers at Constantinople had passed mostly into the hands of English and Scotch missionaries to the Jews, while Mr. Schauffler's labors were chiefly literary. He was preparing a new translation of the Psalms into Hebrew-Spanish, in a more popular style; but could hardly expect entire success, owing to the peculiarities of the language as spoken by the common people in different places. His translation of the Old Testament into Hebrew-German, after revision by Mr. Koenig, of the Scotch Free Church Mission, was printed by the American Bible Society. He was able to preach in various languages, and did not neglect employing his talent in that direction. The printing of his Hebrew Lexicon was completed in 1854.

The reader will scarcely be prepared for the relinquishment of this mission, which took place early in 1856, though not in consequence of failing success. The Armenian and Jewish missions, at their united annual meeting in the spring of 1855, recommended that the Board relinquish to some other society the Jewish stations of Salonica and Smyrna. Constantinople, as such a station, had been practically relinquished some time before. At a conference of missionaries in Constantinople in November of that year, on occasion of a visit from the Foreign Secretary of the Board, the subject was carefully considered, and the question was decided according to the personal convictions of the brethren in the Jewish mission. The result was in favor of relinquishing the Jewish field to the English and Scotch Societies; and of the younger members of the mission devoting their strength to the Armenian field, the exclusive right to which had been conceded to American missionaries by the general consent, as it were, of Protestant Christendom. It had become certain that the Board could not command laborers enough to do anything like justice to both fields; while the English and Scotch churches manifested a special interest in laboring for the conversion of the ancient people of God; and there were both English and Scotch missionaries in Constantinople, and English missionaries in Smyrna; and others from the Established Church of Scotland were ready to occupy Salonica.

Why the mission was relinquished.

Mr. Schauffler subsequently devoted himself to labors for the Moslems, many of whom were becoming interested in the spiritual form of Christianity presented in the Protestant Armenian communities, that were springing up throughout the empire. Mr. Schauffler to labor for the Moslems.

CHAPTER XXXI.

THE BULGARIANS OF EUROPEAN TURKEY.

1857–1862.

The geographical
brings it directly in contact with European civilization. Its interior may easily be reached from the Bosphorus, the Sea of Marmora, the Dardanelles, the Grecian Archipelago, the Adriatic Sea, and from the Danube flowing down from the heart of Europe. The Mohammedan population is estimated at four millions, and three fourths of these are supposed to be of Christian origin, and less firmly wedded to the Moslem faith than the remaining million of Osmanly Turks. And even these, born and educated on the borders of Europe, in the midst of divers Christian races, must form a character different from that of the Asiatic Turks in other parts of the empire.

The geographical position.

Moslem population.

Of the various races in European Turkey, the Bulgarians, properly so called, who are estimated at four millions, speaking the Bulgarian language, claim our first attention. They inhabit not only Bulgaria proper, extending from

The Bulgarians.

the Danube to the Balkan Mountains, but also an extensive region south of these mountains, reaching to the Bosphorus, the Marmora, and Albania; and embracing a good part of ancient Thrace, Albania, and Macedonia.[1]

The Bulgarians are of Slavonic origin, and their race is among the oldest in Europe. In the latter part of the fifth century they crossed the Danube, and gave their name to the country between that river and the Balkan Mountains. In subsequent ages they extended their conquests into Thrace and Macedonia, and, encamping before the walls of Constantinople, sought to drive the Byzantine emperors into Asia Minor. In 712, the Bulgarian troops defeated the armies of the Eastern Roman Empire, and laid siege to Constantinople. Three years later their king concluded a commercial treaty with the Emperor Theodosius III. which is said to have remained in force for a long time. In the year 814 the Bulgarians again invaded the Roman Empire, captured Adrianople, and carried a bishop named Manuel, with others of the citizens, into captivity. This person formed the

Their origin and early history.

[1] On the map, this country is called *Bulgaria, Roumelia,* and *Macedonia. Roumelia,* formerly called Moldavia and Wallachia, north of the Danube, is peopled by a race supposed to be descended from the old Roman military colonies. The language has an affinity to the Latin. *Servia* is peopled by Slavs, who speak substantially the same language with the Bulgarians. The population of Roumania is estimated at 3,864,000, and that of Servia at 1,078,000.

companions of his captivity into a church, and they remained true to their faith, and labored earnestly for its spread. Having made proselytes among the Bulgarians, the bishop and many of the captives suffered martyrdom. Somewhat later, a captive monk, named Constantine Cypharas, endeavored to carry forward the work thus commenced; but the Greek empress, Theodora, for some special reasons, was led to redeem this monk, and procure his return to his native country. At this juncture, a sister of the Bulgarian king Bogoris was residing at Constantinople, whither she had been conveyed as a captive in early youth, and where she had been educated as a Christian, and the effort to secure the return of the monk resulted in her being sent back to her friends. She now labored to gain over the king, her brother, to the Christian faith. Circumstances at length favored her pious efforts, and she sent for Methodius of Thessalonica, a monk and a skilful painter. He was afterwards joined by his older brother Constantine, or Cyrill, surnamed the Philosopher, on account of his learning. Cyrill reduced the Slavonic language to writing, taught the barbarous nation the use of letters, and translated the Scriptures into that language. In the year 861 he baptized king Bogoris. The king undertook to force his people to change their religion and they revolted. He succeeded in suppressing the rebellion, and showed the superficial

Their conversion to Christianity.

nature of his Christianity by the cruel revenge he took on the leaders of the revolt. Then the nation followed the lead of their king, and has ever since been nominally Christian. Neander says, that Cyrill was distinguished from all other missionaries of that period, by not yielding to the prejudice which regarded the languages of the rude nations as too profane to be employed for sacred uses, and by not shrinking from any toil which was necessary to master the language of the people among whom he labored.

The Bulgarians wavered for a time, according to the sway of their political interests, between the Greek and Latin Churches, until finally they decided wholly in favor of the former, and a Greek archbishop and bishops were set over them.[1]

Their ecclesiastical relations.

In the year 924, Simeon, the Bulgarian monarch, compelled the Byzantine Emperor, Romanus I., to recognize the National Church of Bulgaria as wholly independent of the Greek Hierarchy. This independence, after about fifty years, was partially destroyed by a Greek Emperor; and in 1018, Basil II. restored the supremacy of the Patriarch of Constantinople. The kingdom was revived in the latter part of the twelfth century, but was again overthrown in 1393, by the Sultan Bajazet I. Mohammed II., when

[1] Neander's *Ecclesiastical History*, vol. iii. pp. 307–316, Torrey's Translation; and Dr. Murdock's Note to p. 51 of Mosheim's *Institute of Ecclesiastical History*, vol. ii.

he subverted the Eastern Empire in 1453, made the religious chiefs of the Christian sects responsible, not only for the spiritual administration of their respective flocks, but also for that of a large share of their temporal affairs, — such as public education, civil suits, contracts, wills, and the like. The Bulgarians appear for a time not to have been formally recognized by the Turks as belonging to the Greek Church, and of course were not subject to its Patriarch; but the Fanariote Greeks succeeded at last in making the Porte believe that, being of the same religion with the Greeks, they should be placed under the direct authority of the Patriarch of Constantinople; and this was effected in the year 1767. Thus the Bulgarians lost their religious independence.

Their aversion to the Greek hierarchy.

Since then, they have ever cherished an intense dislike of the Greek bishops, whose aim has always been to extinguish every remnant of national feeling, and obliterate all traces of their origin. They earnestly desired to have the Bible and the church-services in their own vernacular language, while the Greek Patriarch and his bishops insisted upon using only the ancient Greek. The people desired to have their children taught in the schools through the language of their own homes, while the bishops insisted that the instruction should be in the Greek language. They desired that their bishops and other ecclesiastics should be chosen from among themselves; but the Patriarch forced upon them Greek bishops, men of a foreign tongue, and foreign habits and sympathies, whose whole aim was to keep the people under the galling yoke of ecclesiastical tyranny.[1]

What the Bulgarian people specially desired was ecclesiastical independence; and, in order to be freed from their forced dependence on the Greek Patriarchate, their leading men sometimes inclined to go over to the Pope. This of course was favored by the intrigues of the Jesuits, and politically by all the power of France. This awakened state of mind led many to examine the teachings of Scripture, and compare them with those of the Greek and Papal Churches; and some made inquiries of the missionaries at the several stations, as to Protestantism; and the question naturally arose, whether it would not be as well to become Protestants, as Roman Catholics.

Their danger from the Papacy.

Intervention of Protestantism.

The Greek Patriarch was decided and bold. In 1861, he summoned the Bulgarian bishops to appear and answer for themselves before his great ecclesiastical Council at Constantinople; but they refused, declaring that they owed him no allegiance. The summons was thrice repeated, but in vain; whereupon the bishops were anathematized, and it was resolved to banish them to Mount Sinai. This was prevented by the interference of the Protestant Ambassadors, and the Bul-

Struggle with the Greek Patriarch.

[1] *Missionary Herald*, 1858, p. 322.

garians rallied to the defense of their bishops. Three thousand of them gathered at one time in one of their churches in the metropolis, and were prevented from proclaiming a Free Bulgarian Church only by the intervention of the Turkish government. Meanwhile the Bulgarian nation was agitated with the discussion of religious doctrines and ecclesiastical relations, and the Papists flooded the land with their publications. When the anathema against the bishops was sent to the Bulgarian towns, the people in some places would not allow it to be read, and publicly burnt it. They even caused a counter anathema to be read against the Greek Church. They doubtless regarded this matter as wholly a religious one; but, in an evangelical point of view, it was little more than a national movement for securing their rights. Sentiments were sometimes uttered, however, which strongly reminded one of the commencement of the Reformation in Germany. "The religion of the Greeks," says Mr. Crane, "has been denounced as contrary to the Bible, and the Scriptures eulogized and recommended to the people. In their printed speeches we have seen no instance, in which they have called upon Mary and the saints for protection, but many in which they have called upon God to vindicate their cause."

Roumelia was partially explored in 1857 by Dr. Hamlin, accompanied by the Rev. Henry Jones, Secretary of the Turkish Missions

First exploration of Roumelia.

Aid Society, then visiting our missions in Turkey. From Rodosto to Adrianople, a distance of seventy-two miles, they saw but few Bulgarian villages. Yet what came within their observation was of special interest. "Wherever we saw flocks, we saw Bulgarian shepherds; and wherever we saw cultivation, we saw Bulgarian laborers. They are indeed spread all over Roumelia, as laborers and shepherds, and the industry of the country is in their hands. The land is generally of excellent quality. It lies spread out in beautiful levels, and undulating, gently rising hills. In the neighborhood of villages it is covered with rich fields of grain, but elsewhere, for successive miles, it is roamed over by flocks of sheep, which, however, cannot crop a tithe of the grass. It is a beautiful region, waiting for the taste and intelligence of virtuous industry to make it a paradise."

Dr. Hamlin's report.

We have also a charming view given us of the hundred miles of country between Adrianople and Philippopolis, as it presented itself to the travellers in the opening of spring. "The Greek race disappears entirely from the soil, and the predominant race is the Bulgarian. So entirely unconscious are the people of the Balkan's being the boundary, that when I spoke of Bulgaria, I was repeatedly corrected by the remark, 'You are now in Bulgaria.' The soil along our route is of the finest quality, and large villages were occasionally seen on our right and left, with magnificent views of cultivated lands and vast pastures, the snowy Balkan summits bounding the north, and lower ranges of hills the south. The fields, clothed in the brightest verdure of spring, gave promise of unsurpassed abundance; and in view of the inspiring scenes before us, we could not forbear exclaiming, with the Psalmist: 'Thou crownest the year with thy goodness, and thy paths drop fatness. The pastures are clothed with flocks; the valleys also are covered over with corn; they shout for joy, they also sing.'"

Dr. Hamlin speaks thus of the people: "In the midst of this fertility, we had only to cast the eye upon one of the villages in order to feel that cruel oppression and spiritual darkness are upon the people. In some of the Bulgarian villages we saw no window, nor even a place for one, in a single house. The country being destitute of forest trees, there is no timber, except what is brought from a great distance, and so they construct their dwellings of the lightest material possible. They are generally of wicker work, plastered within with mud. A large mud chimney and a door are the only openings. And yet the Bulgarians, in these miserable cottages, are the cleanliest people in the world. Excepting the rice cultivators, who dress expressly for their muddy work, we saw not a ragged Bulgarian between Adrianople and Philippopolis. Their clothes are of home manufacture, coarse, strong, whole, and clean. The unembarrassed, kind, respectful bearing of the people, men, women, and children, must impress the most cursory observer. An impudent laugh, an over-curious gaze, or a rude remark, we did not meet with from old or young. We could hardly say this after going ten steps into a Greek or Turkish village."

Effect of the report on the Armenian mission.

The favorable report made by Dr. Hamlin to his mission, awakened much interest, and it was resolved, "That the Bulgarian and other Slavonic races inhabiting European Turkey, call loudly for immediate and vigorous missionary efforts; and being providentially thrown upon the American churches as the chosen instrumentality for evangelizing them, are worthy of their most devoted patronage."

Division of the field.

The mission was commenced with the understanding, that the operations of the American Board would be in the country south of the Balkan Mountains; while the missionaries of the American Methodist Episcopal Church were to occupy stations north of these mountains. The Methodist brethren desired the aid of one of the older missionaries at Constantinople in the selection of their first station, and Mr. E. E. Bliss accompanied them. They visited Varna, Shumla, Rasgrad, and Rustchuk, and decided upon occupying the first and second of these places. The acquaintance thus formed between the two missions

Tour north of the Balkan.

was ever after a source of mutual pleasure and profit. Mr. Bliss thus concludes a report of his visit: —

"This, my first acquaintance with the Bulgarians, has given me a very favorable opinion of them. Others have expressed a different opinion, but I should rank them before the Armenians in native intelligence and cultivation. Certainly a higher degree of civilization prevails among them, than among the Armenians of Asia Minor. They have better homes, better vehicles, better implements of husbandry. Wherever we went, we found much to remind us that we were in Europe, and not in Asia. Our road from Varna to Rustchuk was bordered by the posts and wires of the telegraph. Every town had its telegraphic station and corps of operators — French, English, and Polish gentlemen. More than once, through their unsolicited kindness, our approach to a stopping place was announced by the wire, and we found lodgings made ready against our coming. This, to me, was quite a strange feature of missionary travelling, very unlike my experience in Asia Minor."

Report of Mr. Bliss.

The Rev. Charles F. Morse, who joined the Armenian mission in 1857, was appointed to commence the mission. Leaving his family at Constantinople until he had completed his arrangements, he proceeded to Adrianople in March, 1858, with Hagopos, a graduate of the Bebek Sem-

Commencement of the mission.

inary, as an assistant. The population of Adrianople was then estimated at one hundred and forty thousand, of whom forty thousand were supposed to be Turks. The books in the Turkish language found in Mr. Morse's baggage, including a large number of New Testaments, were at first detained at the custom-house, under instructions from the Porte, but were released upon application of the American and English Consuls. His bookseller obtained a firman for the sale of books, and freely exposed the Turkish Testament, and Mr. Morse was himself allowed free access to the largest and finest of the mosques, — a favor not granted at the capital.

The most formidable opposition apprehended was from the Romish missionaries. They had been quick to see a double advantage in the disaffection of the Bulgarians with the Greek Church, and the fall of the Russian Protectorate, and had already erected a fine church. The French residents, their consul, and even the English consular agent, were Catholics. An intelligent Bulgarian expressed the opinion that Protestant missions furnished the only possible safeguard against Rome in that country, and one of the best informed of the American missionaries declared his belief, that the greatest contest of Protestantism with Rome, since the era of the Reformation, would be in Turkey.

Papal opposition.

The Rev. Theodore L. Byington and wife joined the mission in 1858, and were stationed at Adrianople. In the next year, the mission was strengthened by the arrival of Rev. Messrs. William W. Meriam and James F. Clark and their wives, who commenced a station at Philippopolis, in ancient Thrace. The Rev. William F. Arms and wife arrived in 1860, and were associated with Mr. Byington in a new station at Eski Zagra, seventy-five miles northwest from Adrianople, sixty north-east from Philippopolis, and twenty miles south of the Balkan Mountains. Mr. Oliver Crane was transferred from the Western Turkey Mission to Adrianople, in 1860. The population of Philippopolis was estimated at about sixty thousand, of whom twenty thousand were Bulgarians, sixteen thousand Mohammedans, fourteen thousand Greeks, and five thousand Jews. Surrounding the city, there were, within a circuit of thirty or forty miles, more than three hundred villages, including a large population, mostly Bulgarians. These villages were easy of access, and some of them would afford a healthy retreat in summer. There were numerous mosques, and five Greek and three Bulgarian churches. The Romanists were building a large church edifice. The situation of Eski Zagra was at the northern extremity of a luxuriant and beautiful plain, and contained ten thousand Bulgarians and eight thousand Turks.

The mission enlarged.

Accessible population.

Mr. Byington found a remarkable zeal for education. There were in the town six Bulgarian schools for boys, with eight hundred scholars, and four for girls with one hundred and thirty-five scholars; and in the surrounding villages there were eleven schools, with three hundred pupils. For the two principal schools they had spacious buildings, that would grace a New England town. The teachers were gentlemenly men, and enthusiastic in their work. This class of teachers had generally received their education abroad, for the most part in Russia, where they could secure it without expense. They were earnest in their efforts to introduce a higher civilization, and gave the missionaries a cordial reception. It was otherwise with the priests.

Desire for education.

The readiness of the Bulgarians to receive the New Testament in their spoken language, is deserving of special note. An English gentleman, at one of the fairs in 1857, sold four hundred copies, which was all he had. Several editions were printed under the direction of the British and Foreign Bible Society, and were exhausted in 1859. At least fifteen thousand copies had been distributed, chiefly by sale, and the demand did not seem diminished. Mr. Byington reports at Eski Zagra in September, 1860, that, at the examination of one of the schools, each of twelve members of the most advanced class was presented by the Trustees with a handsome copy of the Bible Society's edition of the New Testament. Subsequent experi-

Readiness to receive the New Testament.

ence tended somewhat to diminish the value of such facts.

A church was formed at Adrianople, on the first Church formed at Adrianople. Sabbath in 1862, with a mixed membership. Pastor Apraham, already known to the reader in connection with the church at Rodosto, came by invitation, with one of his deacons, to assist in its formation; as also did the missionaries from Eski Zagra.

Mr. Meriam at the close of 1861, stated as the results of obser[illegible]ions in his recent tours, that in villages and towns whe[illegible]lporters had penetrated with the Word of Life, the p[illegible] were no longer afraid of Protestants, but respecte[illegible] confided in them; while they venerated and clung [illegible] own form of religion; and that the obvious w[illegible] to benefit the people, spiritually and temporally, mo[illegible] thoroughly and speedily, was to have suitable native helpers quietly settled in such villages. His account of some of the incidents on these tours will prepare the reader to sympathize with this excellent missionary, and his estimable wife, in the sad events soon to be narrated.

"On reaching Tatar Bazarjik, the family of one Labors of Mr. Meriam. of our boarding scholars would not permit me to go to a public khan, but insisted that I should go to their house. I accepted the kind invitation, and while with them, at their request, conducted family worship, morning and evening. Visited a dozen families and was cordially welcomed by all. In walking the street, one morning, I heard a voice from a shop inviting me to come in, and on entering found a company of Bulgarians, with their faces all aglow with the questions they had to ask. A number of persons collected from other shops, and after an hour, all seemed still unwilling that the conversation should be broken off. Their questions showed an intelligent desire for light on the true way of salvation."

"Early Sabbath morning, a number of Bulgarians came to our room at the khan (at Otluk-Keuy), and began to ask questions about Christ, the Virgin Mary, the New Testament, Popery, Protestantism, the ceremonies of the Greek Church, etc., etc. The number of persons increased until we had an audience of forty. They gave us no time to eat until nightfall; and in the evening nine more came, and seemed convinced of the truth. We spent a week in this village. Wine is drank largely, and most of the young men are very wild, but we found some whose conversation encouraged us much. For example, there are three who hold regular meetings for the study of the New Testament on Sabbaths and fast days. Such questions as they cannot solve for themselves they reserve, until some one who can, passes through their village. They have become fully aware, by their study of the New Testament, that the Greek Church is not the one established by the Apostles. One of their earnest questions was, 'Can we find salvation in the Greek Church?' We found one enlightened priest in this village, and spent a half day conversing with him. He informed us that he was endeavoring to have the church service in the vulgar tongue, so that all might understand. He quotes Scripture readily, and is doing much good. All the other priests are miserable wine drinkers. On my refusing the invitation of one of these to drink with him, he exclaimed in astonishment, 'What! are you not a Christian'?"

CHAPTER XXXII.

THE BULGARIANS OF EUROPEAN TURKEY.

1862–1871.

BRIGANDAGE has at times prevailed in some parts of Bulgaria, especially in the Balkan Mountains. In the spring of 1862, the roads were more or less infested with highwaymen, but the one from Philippopolis to Adrianople, and thence to Rodosto, being constantly travelled, was deemed safe. By this road Mr. Byington, and Mr. Meriam with his wife and child, went to Constantinople, to attend the annual meeting of the Western Turkey Mission. Returning, Mr. Byington started a week before Mr. Meriam, and reached Eski Zagra safely, going from Adrianople to Philippopolis alone. Mr. Meriam passed over the same route with his family. Nothing noticeable occurred till they reached Hermanli, twelve hours from Adrianople, at noon, July 3d. Here they found a company of half a score or more of men, with four wagons, hesitating to proceed on account of a band of mounted brigands, said to be lying in wait to rob them. Unfortunately the courageous advice of Mr. Meriam decided them to proceed, accompanied by two armed

Brigandage in Bulgaria.

Mr. Meriam murdered by brigands.

guards. After they had started, Mr. Meriam became convinced that it would have been safer for him and his family to have gone alone; and such was the fact, for the robbers did not know of his presence, and designed only to plunder the rayahs. The brigands came upon them about three o'clock in the afternoon. The faithless guards fled at once, and some valuable horses were seized. The drivers of the two forward talaccas, of which Mr. Meriam's was one, then increased their speed, endeavoring to escape; when the robbers pursued, firing rapidly upon the wagons, piercing the covering of Mr. Meriam's, and killing or wounding two or three occupants of the next vehicle. The missionary and his family were shielded for a time by the boxes in the hinder part of the carriage, till the fall of one of the horses wheeled it round, so as to face the assailants. Mr. Meriam sprang out to protect his wife and child, and immediately fell, pierced by two balls. When the agonized wife expostulated with one of the brigands, saying, that "he loved the Osmanlees, and wished to do them good," he replied, "Why then did you flee"? Had they quietly waited, though they might have been robbed, life would probably have been spared.

Distressing circumstance of Mrs. Meriam.

Mrs. Meriam retained her presence of mind, and placing her infant upon the ground, carefully collected the papers and other articles which the robbers had scattered about, and then sat down to watch the lifeless remains of her husband. The Turkish authorities of the next village sent a conveyance to take her and her precious treasure to a khan. When the moodir saw her in her little room, with her babe and the corpse of her husband, he was much moved, and did what he could for her comfort. He sent a telegram to the governor of Philippopolis, designed for Mr. Clarke, but Mr. Clarke received no notice, and consequently no friend came to meet her. She conveyed the body in her own carriage; and spent the whole of the next night, with her babe, watching the talacca in the open air, vainly listening for the coming of the messenger whom she had so much reason to expect. On the next and last day, she prevailed on a Bulgarian boy to hasten on with a message, which brought Mr. Clarke to her relief, but only just before she entered the city. An immediate burial was necessary. The Austrian, Greek, and French Consuls were very kind, and the Bulgarian church was offered for the funeral.

Mrs. Meriam possessed an excellent constitution, but the strain had been too much for her. A premature confinement followed, and fever, which assumed a typhoid form, closed her earthly career, July 25, about three weeks after her husband's murder.[1]

Death of Mrs. Meriam.

[1] A statement, made at the time, that Mr. Meriam fired on the assassins was afterwards found to be untrue. Nor did Mrs. Meriam

It was necessary that an example should be made of the murderers. Mr. Seward, Secretary of State at Washington, took Mr. Webster's view as to the rights of missionaries, and removed the doubts of Mr. Morris, the American Minister at the Porte, which had occasioned an unfortunate delay; so that he, with Mr. Goddard the Consul General, put matters in train at Adrianople, which led the Pasha of that province to offer four hundred dollars, and soon after as much more, for information that would insure the detection of the assassins, and to distribute bands of soldiers over the country. Mr. Blunt, the English Consul at Adrianople, offered a reward of ninety dollars on his own responsibility; and with him the Austrian Consul, Mr. Camerlobe, actively coöperated.

Successful efforts to punish the assassins.

These efforts resulted in the arrest, conviction, and execution of three of the five engaged in the murder. The remaining two met with an ignominious and violent death; one having been assassinated, and the other shot down while committing highway robbery in an adjacent province.

A very effectual check was thus put to the brigandage so prevalent before, and the attention of all classes was drawn to the character, position, and aims of the missionaries.

Check to the brigandage.

receive any injury at the time of the murder. Nothing was taken from her personally, and no violence was offered her. *Missionary Herald*, 1863, p. 143.

Scarcely a year had elapsed, since Mr. Coffing had fallen by the hands of assassins in Central Turkey; and who can tell how much the punishment inflicted on the murderers of these missionaries, has contributed to the safety of their brethren, or how much it will be instrumental in preventing future massacres of native Christians, as well as missionaries, by fanatical Mohammedans.

The Rev. Henry C. Haskell and wife joined the mission in the autumn of 1862, and assisted Mr. Morse in forming a new station at Sophia, about four days' journey northwest of Philippopolis. In the following year, Miss Mary E. Reynolds took charge of a school for girls at Eski Zagra, which had been successfully commenced by a young woman from Catholic Bohemia, who spoke the Bulgarian like a native, and gave good evidence of piety. The school was designed for the education of female teachers. The health of Mrs. Crane obliged her and her husband to return home, and ask for a release from their connection with the Board. Adrianople was thus left, for a time, without a missionary. The death of Mr. and Mrs. Meriam stirred up several young men in the school at Philippopolis who became active and successful colporters in the surrounding villages. Many of the people in Sophia were found to possess the Scriptures, and a considerable number were known to read them with interest; but as soon as the fact

Further enlargement of the mission.

School for girls.

became known to their acquaintance, they were subjected to persecution.

New station at Samokov.

At Samokov, a pleasant town nine hours to the southeast of Sophia, with a Bulgarian population of ten thousand, there were encouraging indications, and that place proving to be more healthful and a better centre than Sophia, the station was removed thither in 1869.

Results of a general missionary conference.

In 1863, the missionaries of the American Board and the Methodists working in this field held a meeting at Eski Zagra, for cultivating the friendly relations already existing between them. Dr. Wood and Mr. Isaac G. Bliss were present from the Armenian Mission. They found themselves in substantial agreement as to the methods of missionary labor, and also as to the nature of the field. "While some facts of a more or less hopeful nature," writes Mr. Byington, "were reported, the general feeling seemed to be, that the Bulgarians were a very different people from what they were supposed to be, six or eight years ago, and that in our efforts for their good, patience must have her perfect work. They cannot be said to be a particularly depraved people; they are not probably addicted to the grosser sins in any unusual degree; but there seems to be among them a great want of impressibility. When the truth is presented, they at once assent to it, but without any apparent impression on the heart. The brethren generally spoke of the pleasant social intercourse which they enjoyed with the people, but upon religious matters a very painful indifference was manifested."

One great obstacle to the reception of evangelical truth among the Bulgarians, was the attachment of all classes to their national unity. The same had been found among the Armenians and Greeks. Men objected to the examination of evangelical doctrines, lest the result should be a schism in the nation; not being able to see how a change in religious belief could consist with national loyalty. Yet, though the progress of the work had not equaled the expectations awakened at the outset, it was obvious that increasing acquaintance with the missionaries was perceptibly removing prejudice. The conviction was gaining strength with many, not only that Protestants had a Christian faith, but that it was purer than their own. The girls' school at Eski Zagra had thirty pupils in regular attendance, and a score of applicants were refused for want of room. Mr. Clarke having been overworked, it was necessary to secure aid for him, and Mr. Haskell removed to Philippopolis. Mr. Ball, after a long detention at home by the decline of his wife's health, joined the Adrianople station in 1865. Some new prejudice against the missionaries was now created by accusations transferred from English newspapers, made in defense of the intolerance of

The great obstacle.

Signs of progress.

Unexpected hindrance.

the Turkish authorities, and of what certainly seemed an unfriendly policy in Sir Henry Bulwer, the English Ambassador.

Popularity of the schools.

But the school for young men at Philippopolis, and that for girls at Eski Zagra, conciliated favor. The former had fourteen pupils, who made good improvement in mental and moral character, and manifested a good degree of religious feeling, a spirit of benevolence, and a readiness to labor for the good of others. During vacation, six of them were employed as colporters. Nearly all the older students seemed ready to take their stand on the Bible, and did not fear the name of Protestant. The girls' school numbered about thirty pupils, whose progress in study had been gratifying, and there had often been deep feeling under religious instruction. Members of the common council of the town, and others who witnessed an examination of the school, sent to Mr. Byington a letter of thanks, and assured him that the missionaries would yet be recognized by the Bulgarians as benefactors of their nation.

The people not accessible to preaching.

The people could not, as yet, be drawn, in any numbers, to attend the regular religious services of the missionaries. They were banded together against receiving spiritual truth. Still something could be done by personal conversations and the circulation of books and tracts. Touring in the villages was often attended with encouragement.

Appearance of awakening interest.

The year 1867 was one of peculiar promise. The moral stupor, which for so many years had taxed the faith of the mission, seemed to be yielding to the awakening power of the Word of God, and Gospel truth was not only better apprehended by the intellect, but also was impressing the heart and conscience. Though the awakening was neither as extensive, or thorough, or spiritual as was desired, it was real, and indicated the entering upon a new stage of the work.

Girls' school at Eski Zagra.

Miss Roseltha A. Norcross became the associate of Miss Reynolds in the school at Eski Zagra. The arrival of a new teacher and many applications for admission, led to an enlargement of the school. Two sisters, however, who were among the most interesting pupils, were called to severe trials. One of them left in 1866, but the other remained, and was the best scholar in the school. Both possessed more than ordinary intelligence and amiability, and for more than two years had been heartily devoted to Christ. "The younger who had left the school," says the report of the mission, "was taken, a few days since, into a room where many of her relatives and a priest had assembled, to extort from her a renunciation of her faith, and was told that she would either have to give up, or die; that they would give her no peace so long as she persisted in her present course. But the Lord sustained her. They resorted to entreaty,

Cases of domestic persecution.

and besought her merely to make the sign of submission, telling her that she need not in her heart change her belief. But their seductions were as unavailing as their threats. It is more than a year since she left the school, and though, during this time, her closet, her Bible, and the conversation of her sister have been her only means of grace, it is evident that, in the midst of this wearing domestic persecution, a Christian character of unusual loveliness is being developed. She is as frail as a lily, but the strength of the Lord rests upon her."

Another case was that of a pupil who had left a year and a half before, to teach a Bulgarian school. "Unaided," says the mission, "except from on high, she has fought a good fight during the past year. The parents of her pupils complain because she will not conform to the rites of their Church, but the trustees of the school, not wishing to lose her services, have been wise enough not to make conformity a condition of remaining in their service. Her parents have forbidden her visiting the missionary premises, but they have not been able to separate her from her Lord, nor to prevent her laboring for the spiritual good of her pupils. Although she has been occupying, for more than a year, a position beset with temptations, and has been in a great degree deprived of the sympathy and advice of Christian friends, we still hear from her that she is kept by the power of God."

The mission suffered a most serious loss in the return of Mr. and Mrs. Byington to their native land, in consequence of the failing health of the latter.

A serious loss to the mission.

The great complaint of the missionaries had been of the indifference of the people. But after the departure of Mr. Byington, there was no ground for this at Eski Zagra. False reports were circulated with such effect, that the day-scholars were taken from the school, and the boarding-school was reassembled with difficulty. The oldest assistant teacher was forcibly abducted, but escaped and returned. A mob soon gathered, broke open an outer door, cut away some of the bars to the windows, and broke sixty panes of glass with stones. The proprietor of the house now sent for the police, which dispersed the rioters. Such outrages could not be allowed, and representations were made to Mr. Morris, the American Minister at Constantinople, and to Mr. Blunt, the friendly English Consul at Adrianople. Their prompt efforts were effectual. More than a score of the offenders were sentenced to imprisonment of different lengths, but were pardoned at the request of the missionaries. This act of clemency had a happy influence on the people, and the persecution had a good effect on the school.

Effect of false reports.

Effectual intervention.

A young man who had been for five years a student at Philippopolis, was licensed to preach the gospel on the 24th of July; and on the following Sabbath, ten Bulgarians, six of

Public celebration of the Lord's Supper.

whom were girls in the school, sat down at the Lord's table, in the presence of forty spectators. This was the more significant, as the Bulgarian council, a month before, had enjoined upon the different "trades" of the city and neighboring villages, to have no dealings with two individuals whose names and places of business were specified, nor with any others who were known as inclined to Protestantism. Such persons were therefore refused bread, or the right of baking at the public ovens, and some were reduced to great distress. The missionaries talked seriously with the leading men of the city in favor of religious *freedom*, but only a few of them conversed reasonably on the subject, and the masses were wholly opposed to it. Three men, as a means of asserting their religious liberty, went before the Turkish authorities and declared themselves Protestants, which seemed to be the beginning of a Protestant Bulgarian community. The missionaries were sometimes threatened with personal violence, but the Turkish government was ready to defend them.

Its significance.

In January, 1869, four Bulgarians were admitted to the communion at Eski Zagra, two of them pupils in the school, and two married men. The number of Bulgarian communicants in that place was now eleven.

The mission was strengthened, in 1868, by the arrival of Messrs. Lewis Bond, William Edwin Locke, and Henry Pitt Page, all

New missionaries.

ordained missionaries, and their wives. Mr. Bond was stationed at Eski Zagra, and Miss Esther P. Maltbie came thither as a teacher in 1870. Mr. Haskell welcomed the arrival, at Philippopolis, of Miss Minnie C. Beach, in 1869, and Messrs. Locke and Page commenced a new station, before noticed, at Samokov, in ancient Macedonia. Mr. and Mrs. Ball of Adrianople and Miss Reynolds of Eski Zagra found it necessary to return to the United States on account of their health; and it soon appeared that it was too late for them to recover. Mr. Ball died at Grand Rapids, Wisconsin, June 6, 1870, after a useful connection of seventeen years with the missionary work, and Miss Reynolds, at Springfield, Massachusetts, June 1, 1871, just eight years from the day of her sailing for Turkey, and after a life of singular devotedness and success.[1]

Death of Mr. Ball.

Death of Miss Reynolds.

Previous to the year 1870, the missionaries to the Bulgarians had sustained a nominal relation to the Western Armenian Mission. This connection was now dissolved, and the associated brethren took the name of the EUROPEAN TURKEY MISSION. Its stations were Eski Zagra, Philippopolis, Samokov, and Adrianople; and Dr. Riggs was reckoned as a member of it, though he continued to reside in Constantinople, his labors being chiefly for the Bulgarians. The

Connection with the Armenian Mission dissolved.

The mission as thus constituted.

[1] See *Missionary Herald*, 1871, p. 247.

Rev. Henry A. Schauffler, then in the United States, was also transferred from the Western Turkey Mission, and was expected, on his return to the field, to go to Philippopolis, where he would use the Turkish and Greek for the benefit of those who spoke these languages; and with the expectation that the work among the Bulgarians would everywhere connect itself, as soon as possible, with that of the large Mohammedan and Greek population, with whom they were intermingled.

The Bulgarians ecclesiastically free.

The Sultan, having confirmed the appointment of Bishop Anthimas, of Widdin, to be Exarch of Bulgaria, the Bulgarians thus virtually acquired their ecclesiastical independence, and so both their national spirit and their unwillingness to allow Protestantism to come in as an element of apprehended division, acquired strength. Few were yet able to see how one could be both a Bulgarian and a Protestant, and no general movement on the part of rulers and ecclesiastics towards Protestantism, was to be expected. But the Scriptures and evangelical publications were extensively circulated. Thoughtful minds were reached, and examples of what the Gospel could do to regenerate character and give peace to troubled spirits were beginning to attract attention. There was not such liberty to persecute as there had been in Asiatic Turkey. Truth was gaining a hold in cities and

First effect of this.

Promising events.

villages. The girls' school at Eski Zagra, under Miss Norcross, numbering twenty-six pupils, contained several who gave evidence of spiritual renewal, and applications for teachers had come from several towns and villages, accompanied by comparatively liberal subscriptions for their support. The hope, at Philippopolis, of getting helpers from the high school for young men, had been much disappointed, but some of its pupils were doing good. An influential merchant in Samokov was an active convert, and there was much to encourage in that region.

Early in the autumn of 1870, Miss Norcross sickened, and on the 4th of November died, greatly to the grief of her pupils and of the whole mission.[1] Miss Maltbie arrived in less than a month after she had passed away. It was soon resolved to remove the school to Samokov, as a more healthful place, and more eligible on other accounts. A regular Sabbath service was held at this station, and a weekly prayer-meeting. The audiences were very small, and but five persons were deemed worthy to be received to church fellowship. At the out-stations, though there had been no striking success, there were everywhere signs of an advance. The native helper in the beautiful town of Bansko had a school of twenty-two pupils, and a congrega-

Death of Miss Norcross.

Removal of the school to Samokov.

Promising out-station at Bansko.

[1] See *Missionary Herald*, 1871, p. 53.

tion of sixty-five, and the little company contributed to Christian objects, during the year, nearly two hundred dollars, including the purchase of a site for a house of worship. The cause was greatly advanced by the labors of an earnest and devoted Bible-woman, whom the women of Bansko helped to support.

Bansko will have the ecclesiastical distinction, hereafter, of being the place where the first evangelical Bulgarian church was formed, and fully organized. This was in August, 1871. The candidates were fifteen, nine men, and six women. In accordance with a written invitation from the people, Messrs. Locke, Bond, and Page started on Tuesday, August 22d, and went by a circuitous, though a pleasant, picturesque and easy route, passing through two cities, where they found several who were examining the truth, and reached their place of destination on the 24th. The brethren at Bansko had arranged liberally for the brethren and their horses, at their own houses, and gave them a hearty welcome. The candidates for church-membership were all examined, and answered the questions put to them more clearly than the missionaries had thought possible, considering the advantages they had enjoyed. The candidate for ordination as pastor, Mr. Evansko Touzorve, was examined on Saturday afternoon. He had been preaching there as a helper of the mission, and

A church organized.

the examination was quite satisfactory, especially on the evidences of Christianity, just then a subject of special importance in that field, owing to the influx of German and French infidelity.

Sabbath, August 27th, was devoted to the organization of the church, and the ordination of the pastor. A deacon had been previously chosen. The service was concluded with the Lord's Supper. The people were to have the services of the pastor eight months in the year, and to pay half his salary for that time, and the mission was to employ him the other four months in another part of the field. The new church could not then pay more towards the salary, having bought a lot of land, on which to build a church. The little flock was jubilant and of good courage. "What a contrast," exclaims the missionary, "between this state of things, and that two years ago, when the people seized our horses, and drove us from the village!"

One of the most important results of the mission to the Bulgarians, has doubtless been the translation of the whole Bible into their present spoken language.[1] This was published for the first time, in the year 1871. "Methodius and Cyril, who first preached the gospel to the Bulgarians a thousand years ago, gave them the Scriptures in their then spoken language, the Slavic. But this

Translations of the Bible.

[1] See Dr. Riggs' statement in the *Missionary Herald*, for 1872, pp. 76–79.

ancient tongue, the mother of the modern Russian, Bulgarian, Servian, Polish, Illyrian, etc., has long since ceased to be the vernacular of any of the nations. Hence the necessity of new translations of the Word of God in all these dialects." One of the earliest results of the waking up of the Bulgarian people, was a translation of the four Gospels by Messrs. Seraphim of Eski Zagra, and Sapoonoff of Trevna, published at Bucharest in 1828. The first edition of the whole New Testament in Bulgarian was issued at Smyrna, in 1840, at the expense of the British and Foreign Bible Society; but the literary labor was performed by a Bulgarian, the Rev. Neophytus P. Petroff, of Rila, with the aid of Hilarion, the Metropolitan Bishop of Ternovo. This edition was well received, and sold rapidly. It was faithfully, carefully, and ably prepared.

The British and Foreign Bible Society published seven editions of this Testament, or about forty thousand copies, and authorized the preparation of a translation of the Old Testament. Mr. Constantine Photinoff, of Smyrna, to whom this work was committed, just lived to complete the first draft of a translation of the Old Testament, and died in 1858, only a few days after having removed from Smyrna to Constantinople, in order to revise it for publication, with Dr. Riggs.

Meanwhile a rapid change had been going on in the Bulgarian language, and it had become manifest that the work must have a thorough revision. The translations of both the Old and New Testaments had been made in the Western, or Macedonian dialect; but the Eastern, or Slavic, was now taking the lead, and the language was evidently to be mainly moulded after that model.

It is an interesting fact, stated by Dr. Riggs, that the government censor for Bulgarian publications called on him, the day after Mr. Photinoff's death, and expressed his hearty interest in the work of translating the Scriptures, and his hope that it would not be delayed.

In the preparation of this work, Dr. Riggs was aided by two of the best Bulgarian scholars, the one trained in the use of the Western, and the other of the Eastern dialect. In the revision of the New Testament, he was also aided by the Rev. A. L. Long, D. D., of the Methodist Bulgarian mission. With such assistance, it is believed that this translation of the Bible will become a standard work. The first edition was printed in an imperial octavo volume of one thousand and sixty pages, with the references of our English Bible, which will be of special value to a people having as yet no Concordances, Bible Dictionaries, or Commentaries. Dr. Riggs brought to the annual meeting of the newly organized mission, in 1871, the first copy received from the binders.

It should be borne in mind, that only preliminary

work has been done as yet in this most inviting field.

The mission yet in its preliminary stage.

Scarcely fourteen years have elapsed since the field was first explored, and only twelve since stations began to be occupied. It is not time to expect any other results than first fruits.

Now ready to move forward.

The missionaries have become thoroughly acquainted with the field, with its wants, and its strategetic points, and are ready to move forward as fast as they shall receive the needful aid.

CHAPTER XXXIII.

THE ARMENIANS.

1861–1863.

Dr. Dwight having completed his eastern tour, visited the United States, where he arrived in November, 1861. It was arranged, that he should prepare and publish the results of his extended missionary observations. But the Head of the Church had ordered otherwise. On Saturday, January 25, 1862, while passing in the cars through Shaftsbury, Vermont, on his way to spend a Sabbath at Middlebury College, "the stormy wind, fulfilling His word," lifted the car from off the rails, and tossed it down a steep embankment; and one of the heavy trucks, following and dashing through it, at once set free the sanctified spirit of our brother, and gave him a sort of translation to the regions of the blessed. It was a sudden and unexpected close of a most useful life.

Dr. Dwight's visit to the United States.

His sudden death.

Dr. Dwight was born at Conway, Massachusetts, on the 22d of November, 1803. His family removed to Utica, New York, and there, at the age of fifteen, he was hopefully converted dur-

Life and character.

ing a revival of religion, and united with a Presbyterian church. He graduated at Hamilton College in 1825, and, while in the Theological Seminary at Andover, became deeply interested in the missionary work, and took great pains, along with some fellow-students, to illustrate the beginning of foreign missions from the United States. In his last year at the Seminary he offered himself to the American Board, and was appointed one of its missionaries. After completing his studies, he entered upon an agency for the Board, which continued until 1829. From this time, through more than thirty years, the events of his life form an important part of the history of the mission to the Armenians. That mission grew, in his time, from a single station at Constantinople to twenty-three stations, and eighty-one out-stations, extending over the greater part of Western Asia; and whereas, at the commencement of his labors, he did not know of a single convert in the whole country, at their close, there were forty-two churches, with sixteen hundred members, twelve ordained native pastors, forty-three licensed native preachers, thirty-four catechists, fifty-five teachers, and thirty-nine other helpers.

He was made to be a leader in the Lord's host. There was in him a rare combination of sound common sense, piety, resolution, firmness, candor, and courtesy, and withal an honest simplicity, a godly sincerity, and a practical tact, that seldom failed to secure for him a commanding influence; and the mission, of which he was so long a member, was sufficiently eventful to give full exercise to all his powers.

It affords much pleasure to the writer, that he is unable to recall an instance, in all the thirty years, where Dr. Dwight's opinions were seriously at variance with those of the Committee and Secretaries of the Board. It may be that, under the influence of a more extended correspondence, there was sometimes greater progress in their opinions on questions of missionary experience, than in his; but there was never any collision of thought; and it was most gratifying, on his arrival in this country, after his instructive and interesting tour of observation among the missions and mission churches, to find this eminent servant of Christ in full accord with his Committee on all the great points of missionary practice. The prominent trait, however, in his character was spirituality. This was in him an ever-growing quality. From day to day, from month to month, from the commencement of his missionary life until his death, he was wholly devoted to the kingdom and glory of his Redeemer. He walked with God, and was not, for God took him.

His views on missionary policy.

It will be appropriate, at this stage of the history, to quote some of the views of Dr. Dwight on missionary policy in Turkey, as they were embodied in a circular letter to the brethren of his own mission, and substantially communicated to the Secretaries in their personal intercourse with him just before his lamented death. Coming from such a man, after so long and varied an experience, they deserve thoughtful attention. He speaks first of the education of a native ministry.

"I am inclined to think that we have made our education at the Bebek Seminary too comprehensive, considering the actual circumstances and wants of the people. True, our course of study is nothing compared with that of American colleges; but it is much, compared with the amount of education existing in this country; and it seems to me we are in danger from two sources; namely, first, that our native preachers will be educated too far above their people; and, secondly, that they will require much more for their support, in consequence of their education, than their people can give. The plan of removing the Bebek Seminary to the interior, strikes me very favorably."

Again, as to the support of the native ministry: "I think it very evident, that the past system is fraught with too many evils to be continued. I would not favor any sudden change, but it seems to me, that the experience we have gained, by the working of the past, would lead us to begin immediately on a new plan; and the providence of God, in restricting our means, is giving us an admirable opportunity for so doing. We may urge with great weight upon the churches the support of their own pastors, and leave the responsibility there, even when the treasury of the Board shall be relieved. I begin to question, whether we ought even to give regular aid from our funds, for the support of settled pastors, or even stated supplies of churches fully organized. Would it not simplify our relations to those churches, as well as call forth much more efficient effort from themselves, if we were to leave them, as the Apostles did their native churches, to take care of their own pastors, after such have been ordained? The native churches should be expected and encouraged to take, as fast as possible, the work of evangelizing surrounding districts upon themselves; and it will be better to leave them to choose and support wholly their own laborers. The plan of having such men supported partly by the mission and partly by the native churches, does not work well. If it is necessary for the mission to assist the churches in this work, I would do it irregularly, and without any pledges as to the amount or frequency of such aid."

Exemplification of these views.

These views had been already exemplified, substantially, in the Central mission; and they have since had a more full practical development in the Eastern mission; as will appear in the progress of the history.

The actual call for missionaries.

It was not found easy to determine the number of stations or of missionaries desirable in Eastern or Western Turkey. The early theories in relation to this matter have been considerably modified by experience. It was natural to suppose, that many missionaries could labor among the million of people in Constantinople, without interfering with each other, or standing in the way of a native ministry. And so they might, could they at once have access to a considerable part of the population. But this was not true in fact, either as to missionaries, or the native ministry. It has been found, that it results in loss to place more preachers on the ground, than can find full scope for their ministry. Even should the overcrowded ministry be of the same denomination, it works badly, but far worse if made up of rival sects. For a time at least, all must operate upon nearly the same persons. In the rural districts, the missionaries reside in the centres of population, and generally where two families can dwell together, and where each missionary can have a distinct field of labor. But even there it is deemed expedient for the churches to have native pastors; nor there alone. The aim is to have constellations of churches with native office-bearers, around every missionary station. Not otherwise can the whole country be permeated by evangelical influences.

The discretion awarded to missionaries.

It is plain that in a work so unlike anything at home, missionaries ought to have large discretion as to the time and manner of organizing native churches. Nor, since these infant communities are only partially enlightened and sanctified, is there reason for discouragement should they sometimes be not perfectly harmonious with their missionary fathers. It was so for a time with one of the first churches formed at the metropolis. The missionaries had of course the sole responsibility of determining what use should be made of the funds remitted by the Board. But the pastor and a portion of the church thought they ought to have a voice in their disposal. As this could not be, dissatisfaction arose, and complaints were publicly made against their American brethren. But these misunderstandings have in good measure passed away.[1]

The Western Turkey Mission resolved, in 1862, to suspend the Bebek Seminary, with the expectation of reviving it at Marsovan. This institution was commenced by Dr. Hamlin, in November, 1840. It was a boarding-school, with a course of study believed to be adapted to the great ends of the mission, and soon became a very efficient means of gaining access to the people. Its third year, ending November, 1843, was called the "year of a thousand visits," because so many came desirous to learn the religious belief of the missionaries. The Principal was obliged to stop their coming, in order to save the school; but the

The Bebek Seminary to be removed into the interior.

Its history.

[1] See *Missionary Herald*, 1862, p. 300, 1863, p. 268; and Report of the Board for 1871, p. 23.

work among the Armenians then received an impulse which it never lost. Dr. Hamlin continued in charge of the Seminary till the year 1857; aided, at different times, by most of his brethren. Messrs. Clark, Bliss, and Pettibone, had charge of it afterward. The building at Bebek, which had been some time occupied on a lease, became the property of the Board in 1849. In 1853, the number of students was fifty, of whom fifteen were Greeks, under the instruction mainly of Dr. Riggs; and there was then a theological class of eleven Armenians. The Greek department was suspended in 1855. The students were very useful as evangelical laborers within and around Constantinople; and not a few of the graduates occupy, and have occupied, important posts of usefulness in different parts of the empire. It is recorded that, in 1857, sixty applicants were rejected for want of means to support them; and it was believed that, with adequate pecuniary means, one hundred could have received instruction as easily as fifty.

The metropolis was not found the best place to train men for the seclusion and small salaries of interior pastorates; but the school was nevertheless a most important instrument for good, and quite essential in the early progress of the mission. Of the forty-five students in the five years from 1857 to 1861, for which the Seminary was fairly held responsible, seven were preachers at the opening of 1862, and thirteen were members of the theological class.

The expediency of continuing the Seminary at the metropolis, had been discussed in the mission for several years. The other missions preferred training their native ministry within their own bounds; and the interior stations of the Western mission had strong objections to sending their pupils to be educated where expensive habits were almost necessarily acquired.

Why removed.

It was resolved, in the same year, to discontinue the boarding-school for girls at Constantinople, with the expectation of reviving it, also, at Marsovan. It was commenced in 1845. The whole number of pupils had been one hundred and twenty-eight, of whom one half became members of the church. Eighty-three were from Constantinople and vicinity, and forty-five from the interior. Thirty-seven completed the course of four years. Two of the older graduates were teachers of self-supporting schools at Nicomedia; another, whose parents lived at Trebizond, taught at Marsovan; a fourth, since married to a graduate of the Bebek seminary, devoted herself to teaching the girls in a day-school at Adabazar, in charge of the native pastor; another was mistress of a school of forty pupils at Baghchejuk; and still another had a school of forty-five girls at Diarbekir, and was otherwise a shining light. Five were wives of pastors, — at Constantinople, Broosa, Bilijik, Harpoot, and Diarbekir; three of preachers, — at Nicomedia, Bandurma, and

The boarding-school for girls.

Its usefulness.

Aidin; and several of helpers in different places. The school was located successively at Pera, Bebek, and Hass-Keuy; and its teachers were Miss Lovell, Mrs. Everett, and the two Misses West.

Exploration in the Taurus Mountains.

The summer heat at Adana was supposed to be too intense for the health of a missionary family. Mr. Coffing was therefore commissioned, by his brethren, to explore the Taurus Mountains, west and north of Marash, for a suitable summer residence. He performed this service in the autumn of 1860, accompanied by Mrs. Coffing and Deacon Sarkis. An interesting account of the tour may be found in the "Missionary Herald," for 1861.[1] Mr. Coffing requested permission, on his return, to occupy the new field, and left Aintab, with his family, for this purpose, in July, 1861; intending to reside at Hadjin, or Nigdeh in the mountains during the summer heat, and in the winter at Adana. As they went forth from Aintab, nearly the whole Protestant population, about fifteen hundred, stood on both sides of the road to bid them farewell, and as they passed, sang, —

A beautiful scene.

> "How sweet the tie that binds
> Our hearts in Christian love;"

and also an original hymn, expressive of their feelings on parting with this mission family. More than a hundred persons accompanied them during

[1] *Missionary Herald*, 1861, pp. 169, 170.

that afternoon, returning the next day; and many were the prayers offered for them, and for the dark town in the mountains whither they went. Their road through or rather upon the Taurus Mountains, was difficult, and in some places dangerous; but without serious accident they reached Hadjin on Saturday, July 14th. There they were kindly welcomed by the people, and commenced their labors with pleasant prospects of success. But, after a few weeks, the Moslem governor and the Armenian priests commenced a cruel opposition, scarcely paralleled in the missionary experiences of Turkey, and drove them from the place, with much loss and suffering. Arriving at Adana, where the native brethren gave them a kind reception, Mr. Coffing sought redress from the government, but in vain, as the Pasha was unfriendly; and the native Protestants of that city were subjected to many outrages during the winter.

Barbarous expulsion from Hadjin.

After six months, Mr. Coffing left Adana to attend the annual meeting of his mission at Aleppo, going by way of Alexandretta. The road being dangerous around the head of the gulf, he took a guard of three soldiers; but in the latter part of the route, he dismissed two of them, going on with the other, two muleteers, and a pious Armenian servant. When three miles from Alexandretta, he was fired upon by two men concealed in a thicket near the road. Two balls struck his left arm above

Murder of Mr. Coffing.

the elbow, shattering the bone and severing an artery, and one entered the body. Though severely wounded, he rode on two miles further; and then, from loss of blood, sunk down upon the beach, not far from Alexandretta, and sent to that place for help. It was promptly rendered by Mr. Levi, the American Vice Consul, Arthur Roby, Esq., the English Vice Consul, and other gentlemen, and the fainting missionary was taken to the house of Mr. Levi, where he died the next morning, March 26th, 1862. The Armenian servant died four days later from his wounds, and another, who was wounded, recovered.

Successful efforts to apprehend the murderers.

Mr. Johnson, United States Consul at Beirût, took energetic measures, in connection with Mr. Morgan at Antioch, for apprehending the murderers. They had the coöperation not only of the gentlemen above mentioned, but also of Capt. Hobart of H. B. Majesty's Ship *Foxhound*, Capt. Simon, of the French Frigate *Mogador*, and Col. A. S. Frazer, H. B. M. Commissioner to Syria. The Turkish authorities acted with commendable decision, and two young Moslem robbers of the mountains, to whom the crime was traced, were finally captured; though one of them afterwards escaped, and was protected by the Pasha of the district. The other was executed in September, 1862, and the offending Pasha was removed from office. Robbery was evidently no object with the assassins, and it was believed, that

One of them executed.

they were instigated by others. The hostile Armenians of Hadjin and Adana were, for a time, under great apprehension, and were so much impressed by the forbearance of Mr. Johnson and Mr. Morgan, that they assured the latter of their readiness to receive any preacher he might choose to send among them. The sorely afflicted widow resolved to remain in the mission, where she is still very usefully employed among her own sex. It should be added, that this is the only instance in the history of the Board, in which a missionary has suffered a violent death, inflicted because he was a missionary, from the hands of the people among whom he labored.

The result.

Mrs. Coffing remains in the mission.

Dr. Goodell attended the annual meeting of the Central mission in 1862; and so strong were his impressions that the appropriate work of the missionary was nearly accomplished at some of the stations, that he apprehended there might be more danger of the missionary's staying too long, than that he would go too soon.

Dr. Goodell's estimate of progress in the Central mission.

At Aintab, for example, he found the church supporting its own pastors and common schools, and taking upon itself the supply of nearly all its out-stations. No appropriations were asked of the Board, except for the theological class, the female boarding-school, and one out-station; for all the rest the church provided. For these objects, for their own poor, and for their taxes

Progress at Aintab.

to government, the sum total raised by the Protestants, in the then closing year, had been two thousand five hundred and fifty-six dollars, averaging one dollar and a quarter for every man, woman, and child in the community. The congregation being too large for one pastor, arrangements had been made to form a second church, and thus to have two churches instead of one. The theological school was on the point of being removed to Marash, and it was his opinion that, were it not for the female boarding-school, which would probably remain, the missionaries at Aintab should be preparing to withdraw from that place, and go to "regions beyond." While he deprecated too sudden changes, he thought the great question for the brethren at that station was: "How can we, in the most graceful manner, set up in life this first born child of ours, now come of age, and ready to act for itself?"

Progress at Oorfa.

Dr. Goodell speaks of Oorfa, along with Aintab and Marash, as advanced in Christian knowledge. About the year 1851, a native helper from Aintab spent three years in Oorfa, working at his trade as a weaver, but receiving a partial support from the mission, and reading and explaining the Scriptures to all that came. Mr. Schneider visited this place in 1854; a church was organized by Dr. Pratt in December, 1855, and Mr. Nutting commenced his residence there in 1857. Mr. White was also there a year or more, till 1859. The church was then small, and very partially sanctified. The number of church-members, in 1861, was fifteen, and nearly all the members were active, working Christians; and the real progress had been greater than the statistics indicated. Protestantism had become known, and was exerting a good influence. The congregation supported three schools, containing ninety-four pupils, of whom thirty-one were from non-protestant and non-paying parents, and thirty were girls. The Oorfa church regarded the evangelization of Germish, a neighboring Armenian village of a thousand souls, as their appropriate work.

Progress at Harpoot.

The report of the Harpoot station for 1862 states, that there was an increasing number in the city, and at nearly all the fifteen out-stations, who gave serious attention to the truth; and that there was a growing agitation among those who kept aloof from the preaching. A reform party among the old Armenians was rapidly acquiring influence; and to satisfy their demands, mid-day Sabbath services, for expounding the Scriptures in the modern tongue, were held in the churches of several villages. In the city, the party had formed a society for mutual improvement, and one of its rules was, that the Bible should be read in all their meetings. The sale of Bibles, or portions of it, in two years, exceeded two thousand, and the same was true of other volumes.

Theological school.

The Theological school contained thirty-nine pupils, — twenty-one in the first class, and eighteen in the second. It occupied the upper story of a substantial building, erected chiefly by the aid of friends in America; while the lower story furnished a neat and well lighted place of worship. Mr. Wheeler writes: "Supplied as it is, without expense to the Board, with solar reflectors and two neat pulpit lamps, it is exerting an influence for good in the villages. Already the people of three villages have covered the black mud walls of their chapels with a neat white plaster, and four villages have each purchased one of the 'wonderful lamps, by the light of which a man can read on the opposite side of the room.' At their own expense they are also furnishing their places of worship with clocks, and are beginning to learn that (to an oriental) very difficult lesson, to be prompt, and to value time." A girls' boarding-school was opened in 1862.

Girls' boarding-school.

Hadji Hagop, an old and valued helper at this station, went one Sabbath to Hulakegh, an out-station, to preach. On leaving the Protestant chapel, he met the teacher of the Armenian school with a Bible under his arm, going to the church, where they were to have a "preaching meeting," — as was the case in several villages where the mission had congregations, partly in imitation of the mission, and partly to counteract its influence, — and he asked Hagop to go with him. He went, and the leading men urged him to preach, which he

A native preacher.

consented to do. The news spread through the village, and the congregation almost immediately swelled to two hundred and fifty. He preached Christ and Him crucified for about an hour, securing most fixed attention, and it is said the women were nearly all moved to tears.

Mosul.

Mr. Walker, the resident missionary at Diarbekir, visited Mosul in 1861, and found the congregation in that city about as it was when the missionaries left. Subsequently, when visited by Mr. Williams, the Mosul church sent an earnest plea for a missionary to the Prudential Committee. Mr. Williams was with them three months, married three couples, baptized several children, and admitted one to the church.

Mr. Walker's tour was extended more than a thousand miles, and he found much that was very painful, and yet much that was encouraging, among the Arabic-speaking people in Eastern Turkey.

Ordination of a native pastor at Diarbekir.

The church in Diarbekir numbered eighty-four members in 1862, and the pupils in the Sabbath-school were two hundred and eighty-four. At Cutterbul a house had been built, to be occupied as a place of worship on the Sabbath, and for a school-house during the week, and there were hopeful indications in places near. At the annual meeting of the mission, in the following year, Baron Tomas Boyajian [1] was ordained as pastor of

[1] Known to the reader as *Tomas*. *Baron* is equivalent to *Mr.*

the first evangelical church in Diarbekir. His examination was well sustained. The ordaining services were necessarily in the open air, and were conducted in Armenian, Turkish, and Arabic. More than a thousand adults were present, besides hundreds of children, and the interest was sustained to the end. The members of the church pledged themselves to furnish nearly half the salary. Thirteen members, heretofore connected with that church, were formed into a separate organization at Cutterbul.

Contrasted with an oriental ordination.

These services were like our own; and how much more rational and appropriate must they have appeared to the people, than the ordination services prescribed in the Liturgy of the Armenian Church, as described by Mr. Goss. "In the first place, the exercises are all performed in an unknown tongue, the old Armenian. The bishop sits at one end of the church, the candidate enters at the other, walking on his knees, and thus proceeds to the altar. The skirt of the bishop is thrown over his head, and the bishop asks a few general questions, which are answered by a third person, either priest or deacon. They are such as these: 'Does this man understand the Scriptures'? 'Is he the child of a lawful marriage'? etc. An affirmative reply is given, when perhaps the man cannot read. He is then asked, if he is a disciple, not of Christ, but of certain church fathers. Also, if he will pronounce 'Anathema maranatha' upon all heretics. Then Arians, Nestorians, and other heretical sects are mentioned, and the sweeping question is put, — 'Will you pronounce all accursed who do not acknowledge Mary to be the mother of God?' The candidate repeats the names of these sects, and curses them all. Then follows the re-baptism, with the sacred oil, according to the Armenian custom with infants. The hands of the new priest are then bound together and oiled, and he is made to stand outside of the church, when the congregation come, and, kissing his hands, put their paras[1] on a plate, which is near by to receive them. The priest is then imprisoned forty days in the church, with the cuffs of his sleeves and his trousers sewed close to his limbs. In this condition, he is not allowed to brush off an insect, or to relieve his body from any unpleasant sensation whatever. He cannot change his clothes during the whole time, and his food is of the coarsest quality. His wife passes through a similar ordeal at home."

Considerable annoyance was felt, about this time, growing out of the efforts of an Armenian, named Garabed, to form a church at Diarbekir, which should admit persons to the sacrament of the Lord's Supper without requiring evidence of piety, and baptize the children of any who might desire it. He made similar efforts at Aleppo, Aintab,

Disturbing efforts of Garabed.

[1] About a mill of our money.

and Marash. He visited Jerusalem, and so far gained the confidence of English missionaries residing there, that the excellent Bishop Gobat was induced to give him ordination. But he failed to secure the confidence of the missionaries and native pastors in Central and Eastern Turkey, where he was better known; and the evidence at hand constrains me to add, that the missionaries at all the stations anticipated nothing but evil from such intrusions, at this stage of the missionary enterprise in Turkey.[1]

Progress at Bitlis.

The congregations at Bitlis were composed mostly of young men, apparently drawn together by love for the truth. About twenty were known as Protestants, and five of them had gone through a fiery trial of persecution. The Bible class, which had been broken up by that means, was now regularly attended by about thirty young men, some of whom developed rich natural endowments, and gave promise of future usefulness. Sabbath-school instruction was found a valuable auxiliary to

[1] "We desire to call your attention to the efforts of our English (Church) brethren to obtain a foothold in Aintab. It seems that large sums of money have been appropriated under the direction of Bishop Gobat, of Jerusalem, for this purpose; and a large and costly church building is being begun under the superintendence of the English Consul at Aleppo. We are surprised and grieved at this breach of courtesy on the part of these English friends, especially so soon after the earnest protests of the officers of our Board against such interference by other missionary societies." — *Letter written in* 1872.

the preaching of the missionaries, on account of the opportunity it afforded for free and familiar illustration and personal application of the truth. It also made the missionary acquainted with the superstitions and errors of the Armenian religion. The women's meeting, conducted by Mrs. Knapp and Mrs. Burbank, was well attended and influential. A school for girls, taught by the wife of the helper, was broken up by the violence of Armenian ecclesiastics. The missionaries appealed to the Pasha, and to Mr. Dalzell, the friendly British Consul at Erzroom. The result was that the priests commenced a free school for boys and girls, and also a preaching service, hoping thus to deter the people from becoming Protestants. The Porte had given orders that the Protestants in every city should have a suitable cemetery, but every effort to secure one at Bitlis had been without success.

Dr. Dwight was much interested in this city. Its population was thirty thousand, and one third were Armenians; the rest were Koords and Turks, and there were hundreds of villages within the district. The place was proverbial for salubrity, and he saw enough to convince him that the leaven of the Gospel was working powerfully among the people. Moosh, an out-station of Bitlis, was occupied by the native pastor Simon. The truth had taken some hold there, but the people were more degraded than at Bitlis.

Erzroom had several changes of missionaries in the six years previous to 1862. Being near to Russia, it suffered greatly during the Crimean war. The church was disbanded, but was reorganized by Mr. Trowbridge. Mr. Pollard removed thither from Arabkir, and was received with unexpected favor. The government now granted an eligible cemetery; and the Armenian Bishop, having had the benefit of a two years' residence in the United States, was friendly towards the American missionary.

The church at Erzroom.

The removal of Mr. Pollard left Mr. Richardson alone at Arabkir. His report for 1862, shows that there was much to encourage him. Turkish women came to the female prayer-meetings; and the opening of Protestant schools had led the Armenians to establish schools for their own children, in some of which a large proportion of the pupils were girls, though but a few years had passed since it was considered a shame for females to learn to read. Eleven young men from seven different cities and villages in this district, were connected with the Harpoot Seminary, giving the prospect of an improved class of helpers. Yet most of the former helpers had proved themselves sincere and pious; and after having done what they could to bring forward younger men of higher attainments, they were themselves humbly and gracefully returning to their former trades and callings, and laboring

Progress at Arabkir.

for the advancement of the good cause as Sabbath-school teachers and private Christians.

At the close of 1862, Dr. Wood, the Corresponding Secretary of the Board at New York, in consideration of his former experience and his familiarity with the Armenian language, was requested by the Prudential Committee to reside at Constantinople for a year or more, laboring in connection with the mission to Western Turkey. This was necessary in consequence of the sickness of several missionaries, and the special demand, at that time, for labor at that important post. He returned in the summer of 1864, after having rendered important service to the mission.

Sojourn of Dr. Wood at Constantinople.

The clerical accessions to the mission, in 1862 and 1863, were Messrs. John Francis Smith, Moses P. Parmelee, and Giles F. Montgomery, with their wives; and their respective assignments were to the Western, Central, and Eastern missions. In addition to these, Miss Arabella L. Babcock went to Harpoot, Miss Ann Eliza Fritcher to Marsovan, and Miss Mary E. Reynolds to the Bulgarian Mission.

Accessions to the mission.

In May, 1863, native pastors were ordained at Antioch, Bitlis, Adana, and Tarsus. In June, a fifth was ordained at Killis, the officiating clergy in this last case, with a single exception, being natives.

Ordination of native pastors.

CHAPTER XXXIV.

THE ARMENIANS.

1864–1866.

A reaction.

A REACTIONARY movement took place among the Mohammedans of the capital in 1864. The government had encouraged the introduction of European science. Men high in civil positions had delivered courses of lectures on history and other topics, in a surprisingly liberal spirit, and to audiences embracing hundreds of Turks. A "Literary and Scientific Gazette," published monthly under the auspices of a native "Oriental Society," discussed questions of political and social economy from an occidental stand-point; and the press was active in issuing pamphlets and books by native writers, indicating and promoting a new intellectual life. All this the devotees of the "Old School" regarded with suspicion. They were even more alarmed by the religious liberty, which had been successfully claimed for converts from Mohammedanism, who had been openly baptized, and lived unmolested as Christians. The government had some time before been led to discourage Christian education by missionaries and other foreigners, when they could do this indirectly and under plausible pretexts; and they were somewhat rigid in their censorship of the religious press. The Scriptures, however, were allowed to be printed and circulated in the Arabo-Turkish, or sacred character, and no objection was made to simple expositions of Christian truth in that language.

But when copies of Dr. Pfander's book[1] were brought to Constantinople, which defended Christianity against Mohammedanism, and assailed the latter, it was detained at the custom-house; yet copies got abroad in some way, without foreign agency, and were sought by Mohammedans who were interested in the great question it discussed. A Moslem published a bitter reply; and in July, the manifest increase of both Christian ideas and pantheistic infidelity among the people, and the growing excitement among the fanatical party, began to alarm the government. There was believed to be a somewhat large body, who wished to reform the Mohammedan faith; and it was said that a petition was presented to the government, by some Moslems calling themselves Protestants, for a mosque in which to worship in their own way.

The fears of the Sultan were aroused. For several weeks spies beset the missionaries at every step. Finally, on a set day, several Turkish converts were

[1] Dr. Pfander, was a highly respected missionary of the (English) Church Missionary Society. The work was printed in London.

arrested, and cast into prison, some of them being treated with great indignity. On the next day, the printing presses used by the missionaries were seized and put under seal, and rooms occupied by English missionaries, and the bookstore of the American mission and the two Bible Societies were also closed by the police.

Consequent movements.

These proceedings, being in direct violation of rights secured by treaty, were at once met with a decided protest from Mr. Brown, who, in the absence of the American Minister Resident, was the representative of his government; and after some delay, the British Ambassador, Sir Henry Bulwer, also sent in a remonstrance. An examination of the bookstore discovered no prohibited publications; and after two days it was allowed to be reopened. The printing offices were likewise restored. A correspondence followed between Sir Henry Bulwer and the Turkish authorities, and between him and the missionaries resident at Constantinople. The Mohammedans professed not to oppose their people's embracing the Christian religion, but only such reckless proselytism, as endangered the public peace; and they declared their willingness to release the imprisoned converts if it could be done consistently with their personal safety. But the missionaries believed that the intention of the Turks, and also the tendency of Sir Henry's movements, were seriously to curtail their own liberty and that of their converts, and greatly to embarrass the propagation of the Gospel, as well among all the nominally Christian sects, as among the Moslems.

The immediate effect of these things was to prevent attendance by the Turks on preaching, the circulation of Christian books, and personal intercourse with the missionaries. Results.

The position of the entire field, at the opening of 1864, from Constantinople to Diarbekir on the East, and to Antioch on the south, was one to interest the intelligent observer. The laborers employed in this wide and populous region, not including the Bulgarians, were — Position of the entire field.

Missionaries	36
Missionary Physicians	2
Female Assistant Missionaries	41
Native Pastors	20
Licensed Native Preachers	43
Teachers	83
Other Helpers	58
Total	283

The printing was done at Constantinople for all the missions; and that reported for the year 1863 was as follows:

In Armenian	1,821,000	pages
In Armeno-Turkish	1,128,000	"
In Arabo-Turkish	264,000	"
In Greek	6,000	"
In Bulgarian	1,896,000	"
Total	5,115,000	"

Of Turkish Scriptures twice as many copies had been distributed as in previous years. More than twenty-five thousand copies of the Word of God went into circulation, in at least twenty different languages. The following is a statement of the Scriptures prepared and printed, under the supervision of the missionaries of the Board, from 1840 to 1863:

In Modern Armenian	37,500
In Ararat	8,000
In Armeno-Turkish	6,500
In Greco-Turkish	55,000
In Koordish	13,000
In Bulgarian	4,000
In Hebrew-Spanish	23,000
Armenian Psalms	14,000
Total	161,000

Of these, there were published at the expense of the British and Foreign Bible Society, 100,000; of the American Bible Society, 54,000; and of the American Tract Society (New York), 7,000. In addition to the above printed in Turkey, 10,500 copies of the modern Armenian version were printed in New York, from electrotype plates of the American Bible Society; and 5,000 copies of the same version were printed in London, by the British and Foreign Bible Society.

The number of churches was forty-seven, with one thousand nine hundred and thirteen members. There had been received from the beginning two thousand three hundred and thirty-seven. The efforts to bring the churches to the point of self-support were not always appreciated. The people were poor, and sometimes felt their poverty more than they should, and in almost every church there were members who were ready to resent any transfer of pecuniary responsibility from the mission treasury to themselves. Moreover, it was sometimes not easy for a native pastor, with the tastes acquired during his education, to live in a manner that would put him in sympathy with his people, and encourage the hope of their soon assuming his support. Nor was it easy for the native pastor, from his different stand-point, to appreciate the responsibilities of the missionary. A union of the churches was needed, but had been delayed by their distance from each other and their poverty.

Obstacles to be surmounted.

It has been already stated that the Western mission resolved, in 1862, to remove the two seminaries from Constantinople to Marsovan. Mr. Leonard and his wife and Miss Maria A. West were already there. Mr. Dodd and family, Mr. and Mrs. Smith, and Miss Fritcher now removed thither. The delightful harmony and Christian zeal which existed at this station when the mission passed the resolution, had been followed by painful disagreements. Through the mistaken zeal of a young school-teacher, anxious to effect some changes in the school, the community were betrayed into an attempt to obtain exclusive control of the

Painful experience at Marsovan.

funds of the Board appropriated to education. This eventually led to a struggle with the mission for the possession of the meeting-house and a dwelling-house connected with it, which had been purchased by the Board a few years before. Much ill feeling existed both in the church and the community while this was in progress, and for about six weeks a large number withdrew, and set up public worship in a private house, with the teacher at their head. This separate movement was then given up, and there was soon a return of peace and mutual affection; but neither of the schools were opened before the next year.

Accessions to the mission.

The accessions to the missions in Turkey, in the time now under review, were Messrs. Walter H. Giles, Henry A. Schauffler, Lucien N. Adams, and Albert Bryant, with their wives; also Miss Clarissa C. Pond.

Working force at the metropolis.

The working force of the mission at Constantinople, consisting of Drs. Goodell and Riggs, and Messrs. Trowbridge, Herrick, and Washburn, was quite too small for the demands of that great metropolis, and for the general work of the mission which had to be performed there. The Rev. Isaac G. Bliss, agent of the American Bible Society, rendered valuable assistance in the care of the book department. Dr. Hamlin was no longer able to render the services he had performed. Robert College was allowed the use of the Seminary building at Bebek, belonging to the American Board, until another building could be erected. Its twenty students paid forty pounds each year for board and tuition. Its successful beginning in 1862, under the munificent patronage of its founder, and the care of its President, Dr. Hamlin, and Professors Perkins and Henry A. Schauffler, was a subject for general congratulation.

Robert College at Bebek.

The unhappy dissensions of the Protestant civil community had in some degree subsided; but the Pera church, maintaining its attitude of disaffection, sought patronage from the English Bishop of Gibraltar, offering to receive Episcopal ordination for the pastor, and to become a "Reformed Armenian church," which should reject the grossest errors of the Armenian Church, while it approximated closely to it in government, worship, and usages. Inquiries were instituted by the proper ecclesiastical authorities, and encouragement was withheld from the movement.

An unsuccessful disorganizing movement.

It is painful to state that Vertanes, so often favorably mentioned in the early history of this mission, and frequently actuated by a zeal which the missionaries judged too ardent, became now disaffected, and it was necessary to dismiss him as a helper.

The Pera church, at the time of writing this history, is in full fellowship with the missionaries and its sister churches.

The Protestant community at Broosa suffered severely in a conflagration, which consumed nearly the whole Armenian quarter of the city. The neat Protestant church edifice, and the dwelling of the native pastor, happily escaped.

Great fire at Broosa.

A railway connects Smyrna with Aidin, a city of about fifty thousand inhabitants, eighty miles distant. A church had been formed there previous to 1865; four persons were added to it in that year, and the brethren were grateful for their native pastor, but desired a missionary who could preach in Greek, as they could reckon up scores of Greeks who seemed ready to receive the truth.

New missionary station.

Adana remained unoccupied after Mr. Coffing's death, until March, 1863, when Mr. Goss arrived, and, afterwards, Dr. and Mrs. Goodale. The native pastor was faithful and intelligent. Though neither church nor congregation was large, there was an advance in the observance of the Sabbath, also in self-support and general benevolence. The increased price of the cotton grown on its magnificent plain, as the result of the war in America, had given an extraordinary impulse to the business of the place, and to the spirit of commerce. There was much to encourage hope in respect to this important station.

Influence of the American war at Adana.

Dr. Nutting, being transferred from the Eastern to the Central mission, was stationed at Oorfa, where his brother was laboring; Mr.

Diminished force in Central Turkey.

and Mrs. Montgomery were added to the Central mission; but the return home of Mr. and Mrs. White and of Dr. and Mrs. Goodale, by reason of a failure of health, made the number of missionaries in that field less than it had been the year before.

Yet such was the advance in Aintab, that the mission resolved, at its annual meeting in 1864, that there was no longer a call for the residence of a missionary in that city. The church had increased to three hundred and fifty members, and had two native pastors, both of decided ability, sound judgment, harmonious views, and deep-toned piety; and it was thought that the proper development of the pastoral relation, and the most economical disposal of missionary strength, would be promoted by leaving the station to native cultivation, with occasional visits of missionaries. As, however, a second church was to be formed, and a new house of worship to be built, mainly with funds from England placed under Dr. Schneider's direction, the mission approved of his remaining there till these things were done, when he was to go — as he has since gone — to another field, where he might hope, with his uncommon power as a preacher in the Turkish language, to reap a harvest like that which had resulted in the truly wonderful ingathering of souls at Aintab.

Evangelical progress at Aintab.

The division of the church took place in the following year. When the time had fully come for it, the senior pastor proposed that

Two churches formed at Aintab.

each head of a family choose between them. The result was, that the two churches, thus formed, each contained about one hundred and fifty members. The number in each congregation, small and great, was between eight and nine hundred. The preponderance was slightly in favor of the first church and congregation, of which Baron Avedis was pastor. Baron Krikore became the pastor of the new church.

On the Sabbath when the formal separation took place, the customary services were exchanged for addresses suited to the occasion by the pastors and Dr. Schneider, and there was the same intermingling of joy and sorrow which is sometimes witnessed on similar occasions in our own land. Those who went out made the sacrifice cheerfully. In the afternoon they assembled in their place of temporary worship, which was filled to its utmost capacity. "Though uncomfortably crowded, pleasure beamed in every countenance. The Confession of Faith and the Covenant were read and adopted anew by the church, all the members standing. Then they were addressed on subjects appropriate to their circumstances, with a view to rousing them to new zeal and activity. When all was over, little groups were engaged in lively conversation over the whole house, showing that all were especially interested in what had transpired."

Girls' boarding-school at Aintab.

The Female Boarding-school at Aintab, under the care of Miss Proctor, was now firmly established, having overcome much prejudice against female education, and against the regulations necessary in such an institution. It had fourteen pupils, who acquitted themselves well at a public examination in the presence of a deeply interested assembly.

In the high school for young men at the same station, under the very competent instruction of Baron Alexan, twelve candidates for the ministry were taught in secular branches, to whom lectures were delivered in the departments of theological study by Drs. Schneider and Pratt. At an examination of this school in the church, in the presence of several hundred persons, — including six Moslems of prominent social positions, most of whom listened for several hours with the deepest interest, — the scholars gave highly satisfactory proofs of mental ability and discipline; while the simplicity of their piety, and their readiness to labor where divine Providence should call them, gave good promise of their future steadfastness and usefulness. It was then resolved to remove the Theological School to Marash, and place it under the instruction of Dr. Pratt and Mr. Goss, assisted by Baron Alexan, and that none but pious young men should be admitted. The course of study was to occupy three years; and so much of their own personal expenses were to devolve upon the students, or their friends, as might test their character, and furnish a healthful stimulus to the Protestant community on the subject of education for the ministry.

High school at Aintab.

Graduating class at the Harpoot Seminary.

The Theological Seminary at Harpoot sent forth its first class of eighteen young men near the close of 1863. Eight of these had been licensed as preachers of the Gospel, and nearly all the rest were employed at out-stations, as catechists and teachers. Some were expecting to be soon ordained as pastors. The demand for additional laborers was urgent, because of the very general increase in the size, as well as number, of the congregations.

Singular method of opposition.

Social meetings for the study of the Scriptures were found to be so influential for good in the Harpoot district, that the Armenian ecclesiastics of the Old Church sought to counteract their influence by the same expedient; but the result disappointed their hopes. In Malatia, they appointed a meeting for such readings every evening in the week, in each of the twenty-four wards of their part of the city. Their intention was to have the Scriptures and the church books read in the ancient language; but the people insisted on having the Bible alone read, and read in the spoken language. So every night the Word of God, in the vernacular, was read and commented on in twenty-four assemblies of from forty to sixty persons.

Progress of self-support in the churches.

Of more significance was the fact, that many of the local communities, besides the one at Harpoot, were taking upon themselves the support of their pastors and preachers, and were beginning to relieve the Board of the expense of their schools. A missionary spirit was also springing up. The churches in the cities were beginning to care for the villages. Missionary societies were formed. In one of the outstations of Harpoot, the school boys had an evangelical society. On Saturdays they met and had prayers, singing, and the reading of a tract; and the next day they went out, two and two, to the houses of such Armenians as did not come to the Protestant place of worship, and asked the privilege of reading from the New Testament. Being children, they often found a hearing where older persons could not. A boys' missionary society in Diarbekir bore the expense of a scripture reader in a large Armenian village nine miles distant. A like association of men paid seven eighths of the salary of a helper in another village. Subsequently, a door being found open in an unhopeful village near the city, the native brethren hired a house, and each Sabbath sent one of their own number to spend the day as a scripture reader. A similar zeal was manifested at Bitlis by a number of young men, who were studying at their own charges.

And of the evangelical spirit.

But there were trials. Some of the young men in the Harpoot Seminary refused to exercise the self-denial necessary to live on the means allowed for their support, and returned to their homes; and a few of the graduating class

Trials.

preferred to enter secular business, rather than accept the salary offered. This was not without its uses, as it confirmed a wholesome principle, and was the means of bringing some men, after a time, into the service under a more just apprehension of the true value of the ministry.

Death of Mrs. Williams.

The Eastern Turkey Mission was painfully afflicted in 1865 and 1866. The three families at Harpoot each lost two children; and Mrs. Williams was called to her rest, depriving the mission of a highly valued and beloved member, and leaving her husband alone, in the sole charge of a difficult station. Mr. and Mrs. Richardson were obliged by illness to visit their native land, and the Arabkir field was placed under the permanent care of the Harpoot station.

General view of the Eastern mission.

The Eastern mission had now ten missionaries, with as many female assistant missionaries, six native pastors, seventeen licensed native preachers, twenty-five native teachers, and thirty-two other helpers. The out-stations had increased to forty-seven, eighteen of which were connected with Harpoot. The average attendance at the regular religious services was over two thousand and two hundred; and many more heard the informal preaching of colporters and other assistants. Twenty-two Sabbath-schools embraced one thousand and four hundred pupils. There were sixteen churches, with a membership of four hundred and fifty, of whom sixty-eight were admitted on profession of faith in 1864, and one hundred and twenty were women. The number of registered Protestants was three thousand five hundred and thirty. Besides four hundred adults receiving instruction, there were one thousand five hundred children in fifty common schools, of whom more than five hundred were girls. The girls' boarding-school at Harpoot had forty-two pupils. The Misses West and Fritcher, from Marsovan, had been very usefully connected for a time with this school, in consequence of the return home of Miss Babcock. Miss Clarissa C. Pond was now connected with the school, and early succeeded in gaining the language. The mission was much encouraged by a growing interest in education, especially among the women. Parents who, a few years before, thought it wholly unnecessary, if not a disgrace, for their daughters to read, and who could hardly be induced to allow them to attend school, now gladly paid considerable sums for their tuition. This advancing spirit of intelligence was seen, not only among those who were brought directly under the influence of missionary labor, but also among the Armenians generally, compelling their ecclesiastics, in some places, to open schools of their own. So, also, to keep the people away from the Protestant chapels, extra services were established in Armenian churches, in which the Bible was read and explained, and prayer was offered

Methods of opposition.

in the modern or spoken language. In the village of Ichme, they even went so far as to open an opposition prayer-meeting, a female prayer-meeting, and an evening meeting; and societies were formed in several places professedly to carry the Gospel to neighboring villages.

Liberal support of the Gospel.

There was much suffering from poverty, this year having been one of special trial in this respect, but there was great liberality on the part of the churches. In the Harpoot district, "there was a promptness in paying their pastors, preachers, and teachers," says the report of that station, "which would put to shame some richer and more enlightened communities, even in Christian America. The sums paid by the people for the support of pastors, schools, chapel building, the poor, and for other benevolent objects, amounted during the year to $1,224 (in gold), and would have been larger had not the mass of the people been unusually poor, even for them." Two things are noted that were especially cheering in regard to them: "First; so soon as they become interested in the truth, they earnestly desire a pastor of their own, and, *when necessary*, are willing to pay according to their ability for his support. Secondly; they are easily pleased, and are not fickle minded; do not desire, but rather oppose change. The preacher who has once been given to them, almost without exception they learn to love; and having learned this, they do not wish to part with him."

Mr. Williams was at Diarbekir in February, and found the church in great prosperity under the pastorate of the Rev. Tomas Boyajian. Prosperity at Diarbekir. For a year the station had had no missionary; and it was a year of high prices, almost a famine, and great stagnation in business throughout Eastern Turkey. At the same time, owing to the trouble in Constantinople, the Turkish officials were more averse to Protestants than ever before. Sickness, too, had prevailed, thirty-three having been buried at Diarbekir from the congregation over which the young pastor was settled. "Yet," says Mr. Williams, "the city work is in advance of any *one* thing at Harpoot. The congregation at the Sabbath-school, three fourths of whom are adults, numbered three hundred and thirty-nine, and I wish those whose contributions have aided in planting this vine, could have looked upon the clusters of faces which were studying the Book of Life, and heard the hum of voices asking and answering questions! They would have felt that there are some places where the missionary work is *not* a failure. The figures I have not by me, but since Mr. Walker has been absent, the church has increased, the congregation has increased; and that it is not an idle increase is shown by the fact, that this one congregation has, in the year of the missionary's absence, contributed four hundred dollars for the support and spread of the Gospel; for schools, two hundred and forty; for the poor (a year of high prices and great want), two hundred and seventy-five; and for the national head at Constantinople, forty."

The year 1865 was signalized by the death of two very useful missionaries, — Rev. Edward Mills Dodd, and Rev. Homer Bartlett Morgan. Mr. Dodd died of cholera at Marsovan, on the 19th of August. He was a native of New Jersey, and his first labors were among the Jews of Salonica, commencing in April, 1849. In 1863, he was transferred from Smyrna to Marsovan. Mr. Barnum, of Harpoot, who was there at the time of his death, speaks of him as a sincere Christian and an earnest missionary, working up to and often quite beyond the strength of his feeble constitution. "His first missionary language was Hebrew-Spanish, of which, I have been told, he had a fine command. When he was transferred to the Armenian work he learned the Turkish, which he used with much more than ordinary correctness; and some of the best sermons which I have heard in that language were from him. He devoted considerable attention to Turkish hymnology, and many of the best of the Turkish hymns now in use were contributed by him."[1]

Death of Mr. Dodd.

Mr. Morgan died at Smyrna on the 25th of August, at the age of forty-one. He was from the State of New York, and obtained his education at Hamilton College, and at the Union and

Death of Mr. Morgan.

[1] See *Missionary Herald*, 1865, pp. 380–383.

Auburn Theological Seminaries. He joined the mission to the Jews at Salonica in 1852. After that mission was relinquished, he removed, in 1856, to Antioch. Seven of the remaining nine years of his life were spent in that place, whence the great Apostle went forth on his first foreign mission; and the last two at Kessab, in a perfectly successful effort to restore unity to a divided church. The failing health of Mrs. Morgan rendered a visit to her native land imperative. Being detained ten days in the malarious atmosphere of Alexandretta by the non-arrival of their expected steamer, Mr. Morgan took the fever. Supposing it to be only an intermittent, they embarked for Marseilles, but on reaching Smyrna he was too ill to proceed farther. There, in a missionary family, he had the best of attendance, and after a week of delirious wanderings, he finished his earthly course, and was laid to rest in the cemetery of the Dutch hospital. His first wife was taken from him at Salonica, his first-born at Antioch, a second child at Bitias, and a third at Kessab; and the father sleeps in Smyrna, his old home.

"Far from thee
Thy kindred and their graves may be, —
And yet it is a blessed sleep,
From which none ever wakes to weep."

Repeated bereavements chastened the strong and decided character of Mr. Morgan. He grew in the grace of patience, and in spirituality and self-abnegation. He was an indefatiga-

His character.

ble worker, and was fitted to exert, as he did, a commanding influence on the policy of the mission. He soon made himself familiar with the Turkish language, and never wearied of studying its beautiful structure, and wrote some of the best Turkish hymns. The well known hymn, — "Not all the blood of beasts" — he clothed with not a little of the strength and power of the original.[1]

Death of Hohannes.

The year was also signalized by the death of Rev. Hohannes Der Sahagyan, pastor of the church in Nicomedia, and widely known as one of the two young men who first attached themselves to the teaching of the missionaries in Constantinople, also for his consistent piety, earnest zeal, and the severe persecutions which he suffered at different periods, as a follower of the Lord Jesus.

Interesting ordinations.

A scene at the ordination of a native pastor at Perchenj, a village two hours from Harpoot, graphically described by Mr. Williams, has its chronological place here. It was in a large garden, with the pulpit under the wide-spreading branches of a mulberry-tree, and mats and carpets spread out in front. "Around the pulpit sat the council, — lay and clerical delegates, representing most of the evangelical ministry in this part of Turkey; then the regular Protestants of Perchenj, Harpoot, and the villages about, to whom it was a 'festa,' as was evident from their dress. Outside these were the partially committed ones, who, though they did

[1] See *Missionary Herald*, 1865, pp. 383–385.

not 'dress up' for the occasion, seemed to have taken the day for it; and again, outside that company, were men drawn in by the interest of the occasion from their work, with their field dresses on, tools in hand, leaning on their long handled spades, bending forward to catch question and answer, wholly unconscious of the picturesque finish they gave to the scene.

"In the afternoon exercises, the pastor of Ichme and the pastor of Harpoot took prominent parts. The same was expected also of the pastors from Arabkir and Shapik, but unfortunately they were not present. The sermon was by Mr. Allen, and was moving and effective. It was very difficult to count the audience, at least from where I was. If I could have exchanged places with some of the boys, and hung myself among the mulberries, perhaps I could have succeeded better. Nothing in all the exercises seemed so American as the natural way in which the boys took to the trees. We jndged there were, in the forenoon, about seven or eight hundred, and in the afternoon, six or seven hundred. To the last, everything was quiet, and all went off pleasantly. As you know, the community furnish half the pastor's salary from the start."

In October, four months later, there was an ordination of much interest at Cesarea, where the churches in Constantinople, Marsovan, Sivas, and Yozgat were represented. It was in one of the most important centres of influence. Gregory the Illuminator was ordained in Cesarea, and he went forth from that place to his great work of Christianizing the Armenian nation nearly sixteen hundred years ago. There were born the great church teachers of Cappadocia, Basil of Cesarea and his brother Gregory of Nyssa. In the middle of the third century, the bishop of Cesarea protested against the usurpations of the bishop of Rome.

"Wednesday morning the council met and organized. The whole day was given to the examination of the candidate, which was held in the church, and was attended by from two to three hundred persons. The candidate occupied three fourths of an hour with a statement of personal experience and reasons for entering the ministry. This he made in a manner so clear, forcible, and satisfactory, that the council felt the need of asking scarcely a question. To the congregation it was especially impressive, showing how far removed from the religion of forms, to which they have so long been bound, is that faith which works by love. Three hours were then devoted to an examination of his theological views, and he gave unmistakable evidence of being a man accustomed to think for himself, — one who has well-defined opinions, and is prepared to defend them." [1]

Reception of Mr. and Mrs. Walker.

Mr. and Mrs. Walker, having recruited their health in their native land, were once more at their post in Diarbekir. What a change

[1] *Missionary Herald* for 1866, p. 53.

since the arrival of Mr. Dunmore among that people in the year 1851. Mr. Walker thus describes his reception: "When two or three hours distant from the city, we began to be met by companies on horseback; and farther on by those on slower mules and donkeys, and as we neared the city, a great company of men, women, and children gave us their hearty 'Hoshgelden' (word of welcome); and the children of one of the schools stood in line by the side of the road and sung theirs. Thus we were escorted by two hundred or more, through the gates of the city, and to our own home, which was swept and garnished for our coming."

The church, during a part of Mr. Walker's absence, had been without the services of its native pastor, he being at Constantinople; but one of their own number, who had been educated at the Harpoot Seminary, was engaged to supply the pulpit, and not a service had been omitted. The Sabbath-school never fell below one hundred and forty. Divine goodness spared the lives of the Protestants, with a single exception, while fifteen hundred persons were dying in the city of the cholera. The active piety of the church seemed to be quickened by their trials; and thirty, out of one hundred and one members, were wont to go out two by two, by appointment, to spend Sabbath evenings in religious conversation at different houses. The result was that their place of worship

A church in the absence of both missionary and pastor.

became over-crowded, and a new building was prepared for a second congregation that would seat four hundred and fifty persons.

Miss Maria A. West, of the Western Turkey mission, spent the winter in the family of Mr. Walker, and took a very active interest in the success of the women's weekly prayer-meetings. The attendance at these meetings sometimes arose to seventy, and the results of labor in this direction can hardly be over-estimated.

Death of a devoted native helper.

Ararkel, a very valuable helper at one of the Bitlis out-stations, died in August, 1865. He was a most active opposer of the truth when the gospel was first preached in Moosh, but one of the first to accept it, being convinced by reading the Scriptures. He was persecuted unto imprisonment, but bore all patiently. Being naturally gentle and discreet, he was peculiarly fitted to be a pioneer, and was sent as a helper to Havadorik, a village on the mountains, among Koords, known as the dwelling-place of thieves and robbers. He there labored for two years, until his death, with much success. "His mouth," says Mr. Burbank, "was always full of evangelical doctrines. His prayers were mingled with tears, and his Bible was wet with them." He died of fever, leaving two little orphan boys and an aged mother without any means of support. The Armenians cheerfully granted him a burial in their own cemetery.

CHAPTER XXXV.

THE ARMENIANS.

1865–1867.

An association of native churches and pastors, called the Harpoot Evangelical Union, was formed at Harpoot near the close of 1865. It was to serve the purpose of a Home and Foreign Missionary Society, also of an Education and Church Building Society. It could form new churches, ordain and dismiss pastors, grant licenses to preachers, and depose the unworthy. It was to hold an annual meeting, and such other meetings during the year as circumstances might require. Aggrieved church-members might appeal to it under certain limitations.

Harpoot Evangelical Union.

A similar association had been formed, September, 1864, by the churches in the Broosa and Nicomedia districts, called "The Union of the Evangelical Armenian Churches of Bithynia," embracing eight churches, and afterwards including the churches of Constantinople. Another was formed at Marsovan, at the close of 1868, and called "The Central Evangelical Union," and another in Central Turkey, called "The Cilicia Union."

Other unions formed.

The effect of these organizations has been to enlarge the views of churches and ministers, and make them feel that the work of evangelizing the people around them belonged naturally to themselves. It also greatly developed a spirit of self-denying love for their work among the pastors and preachers, and a spirit of unity and independence among the churches. "Five years ago," writes Mr. Wheeler in September, 1866, "the pastor of the Harpoot church, now President of the Union, when we put upon his people an increased amount of his salary, inquired, 'By what right do these men put this burden on my church?' But when, in this meeting, a proposition was made to get the pastor's salaries from other sources than their churches' treasury, this same man, aided by the pastor at Arabkir, so conclusively showed the folly and hurtfulness of the proposal, that the mover of it dropped it in shame. The Arabkir pastor said: 'This is to enable the pastor to be independent of the people, and to say, What have you given me that I should be your servant?' The force of this pithy argument is felt here, where ecclesiastics rule and devour the people, and where the tendency in that direction is so strong that we need to guard against it in laying the foundations of the churches. He then went on to show that it would be for the good of the churches to support their pastors. They would thus love and heed them more. 'The pastor,'

Their utility.

he continued, 'who should get his support from any source outside of his own people, would be beyond their control.' In a subsequent discussion on supporting the poor of the church, he said: 'I am fully persuaded, that every church is not only able to support its poor, but its pastor too.'"

The truth of this last remark was strikingly illustrated by the church in Shepik, the poorest and feeblest in the field, which for thirteen years had paid almost nothing for preaching, and was supposed to be a permanent pensioner on missionary bounty; but all at once it raised enough for the support of the preacher, besides nearly two hundred dollars in gold for the building of a house of worship. A blind preacher from the Harpoot Seminary had been the means of this unexpected result. He was known as John Concordance (Hohannes Hamapapar), on account of his wonderful readiness in quoting Scripture, chapter and verse. He was sent to Shepik, and hearing the complaints of the people about their poor crops and poverty, replied: "God tells you the reason in the third chapter of Malachi; where he says, 'Ye are cursed with a curse, for ye have robbed me.'" Then taking for a text, "Bring ye all the tithes into the storehouse," etc., he inculcated the duty and privilege of setting apart *at least a tenth* of their earnings for God. The people were convinced, and after paying half of

A poor church enriched.

John Concordance, the blind preacher.

His sermon on the tithes.

their crops, according to usage, to the owner of the soil for rent, and a tenth to the government for taxes, as they must needs do, they gave another tenth to the Lord's "storehouse," — a room they had set apart for receiving the tithes. And the sermon of this blind preacher, and the example of these poor people, have wrought wonders in the land.[1]

His wide influence.

During the year and a half after its formation, this union held five general meetings. The last of these was the most interesting. Eleven native pastors were present, — from the Harpoot district, and from Cesarea, Tocat, Adiaman, and Cutterbul. Nearly all the helpers of the Harpoot, Diarbekir, and Mardin fields were there, with twenty delegates from churches and from congregations that expected soon to have churches. There were also present the members of the Theological school, Mr. Livingston from Sivas, and Mr. Williams from Mardin, who had brought his students to spend the summer in the school at Harpoot.

Meeting of Harpoot Union.

On the 15th of November, 1866, Mrs. Adams died at Aintab, of consumption, much lamented.[2] Mr. Richardson, on his return from America, joined the Broosa station. Mr. Williams was then alone amid the multitudes using the Arabic that centered around

[1] Mr. Wheeler's *Ten Years on the Euphrates*, chap. x. For an abstract of John Concordance's sermon on *Tithes*, preached at Harpoot, see *Missionary Herald* for 1868, pp. 308–312.

[2] See *Missionary Herald* for 1867, p. 98.

Mardin and Mosul; and Mr. Walker was the only missionary at Diarbekir, with at least a thousand towns and villages in his district. Yet it was a year of decided progress in Turkey. The missionary force received an unwonted accession in the years 1866 and 1867. Five ordained married missionaries arrived in the last of these years, namely, Messrs. Henry T. Perry, Theodore Baldwin, Henry S. Barnum, Charles C. Tracy, and Lyman Bartlett, with as many unmarried female assistant missionaries, — Misses Roseltha A. Norcross, Mary E. Warfield, Harriet Seymour, Sarah Ann Closson, and Mary G. Hollister. Mr. Henry O. Dwight, son of the distinguished missionary, Dr. H. G. O. Dwight, arrived at Constantinople as secular agent, with his wife, a daughter of Dr. Bliss. Miss Mary D. Francis arrived in 1866, and was afterwards married to Mr. Adams.

New missionaries.

Among other signs of progress was the increase of newspapers in Constantinople, and one or two other cities of Turkey. In Constantinople, five years before, a newspaper was rarely seen in the hands of any one of the thousands of persons passing up or down the Bosphorus and Golden Horn in the steamers which take the place of the street cars of Boston or New York. Now it had become a common sight, and newsboys thronged the thoroughfares with their papers, in Turkish and other languages. The standard of journalism was

Increase of newspapers.

not high, but the thoughts of men were stirred. The influence of these papers was generally adverse to the missionary work. Partly to counteract this influence, the missionaries published, once a fortnight, a small newspaper called the "Avedaper," or "Messenger." It appeared alternately in the Armenian and Armeno-Turkish languages, and had fifteen hundred subscribers scattered over Turkey. Mr. E. E. Bliss, the editor, estimated the aggregate of readers at ten thousand. One incident may illustrate its influence. A villager living on the Taurus Mountains was so impressed with one of the sententious speeches of President Lincoln, translated in the paper, that he committed the whole to memory, that he might teach to others its lessons of "malice toward none, and charity to all."[1]

The "Avedaper," or "Messenger."

The general progress towards right religious opinions, had led to a division of the Armenians who remained in the Old Church into two parties, called the "Enlightened" and the "Unenlightened." The former was continually increasing, and had sharp contests with the Unenlightened on questions of clerical control in civil affairs. Their failure to secure even the partial reforms they sought convinced them of the necessity of more radical changes; and an Armenian paper announced a movement for the formation of a Reformed Armenian Church; on the principle of restor-

Division among the Armenians.

Reformed Armenian Church.

[1] *Missionary Herald* for 1867, p. 82.

ing the purity of doctrine and simplicity of worship, which they supposed existed in their Church at the beginning. The same paper advocated the complete separation of civil and ecclesiastical affairs; and announced that a book would soon be published, setting forth the doctrines and proposed form of worship for this new church. The new Prayer-book made its appearance early in 1867. It contained a Creed; a Ritual for Baptism, the Lord's Supper, Ordination, etc.; Forms for Daily Prayer in the churches; and Hymns and Songs. Judged by the standard of the New Testament, the book contained not a few errors of doctrine, and sanctioned many superstitious practices; yet it was a decided improvement upon the books in use in the Armenian Church. The Armenians of the Old Church regarded the changes as very radical, and the Patriarch denounced the book officially, and warned his people against it.

Reformed Prayer-book.

"The most noteworthy part of the book is its Preface, which was printed last, and may be regarded as the platform of the reformed party. After giving a sketch of the history of the Armenian Church, its original purity of doctrine and worship, and the subsequent introduction of error and superstition, through the influence of the Greek and Roman Churches, it declares that the Armenian Church has come at last to be a mere 'satellite of Rome,' and that the time has come to assert its independence, to cast off the 'ultramontane influence,' to rescue the Church of their fathers from the 'Papal claws.' Three particulars are then set forth in which a 'reformation' is needed. First, in reference to doctrine. 'The Armenian Church has,' it is said, 'doctrines introduced from abroad, which place faith in respect to salvation upon a wrong foundation, transferring man's hope from God to things created and material. Means are confounded with ends, and ends with means, and thus a thick veil is interposed between the eyes of the people and the simple doctrines of Christianity.' Secondly, 'The Church has now rites and ceremonies (unknown in purer times), which are a laughing-stock to the unbelieving, a grief to the truly pious, an offense to all enlightened men, and which have converted our churches into theatres, deprived worship of its spiritual character, and made it like the shows of a fair.' In the third place, 'The present relations of the clergy to the people are opposed to the spirit and substance of Christianity. Instead of being teachers, pastors, and fathers to the people, they claim to possess supernatural authority, rule by the terrors of that authority, teach the people only that which serves their own purposes, and are an obstacle to every good work.'"[1]

Consequent excitement.

For twenty years there had not been such a religious ferment in Constantinople, as there was at the time of issuing this Reformed Prayer-

[1] *Missionary Herald*, 1867, pp. 237–239.

book. It was not a revival of religion. The question was not, "What must I do to be saved?" but "What did our Church teach in the days of its purity?" and "What are the doctrines of the Word of God?" Meanwhile the advocates of reform were continually driven to take higher ground; and such was their progress while carrying their book through the press, that they were obliged to reprint some of the first sheets, to make them conform to their new convictions. It may be stated as an illustration, that baptismal regeneration was taught in one of the original sheets, but in the reprint it was omitted.[1] So far as is known, this book has never been used in any church; but it is an index of the reform movement, and it has been useful in awaking inquiry.

Bible-women began to be employed in Constantinople early in 1866. Five such women were supported by funds derived from the American Bible Society, and were kindly received in Armenian families. They sold many copies of the Scriptures, and met with much encouragement in their work. At this time, wherever missionaries labored in Turkey, large numbers of women were learning to read the Bible; and the majority of them were usually found at the women's prayer meeting.

Bible-women.

The progress at Harpoot, only eleven years from the commencement of the station, as described by Mr. Allen, is worthy of special

Eleven years at Harpoot.

[1] *Missionary Herald*, 1867, p. 238.

attention. The leaven of the gospel was permeating the mass of the people. Many who persistently refused to be called by the unpopular name of "Protestant," were evidently under the influence of evangelical doctrines. The rising generation was growing up with enlightened views. Many young men would have taken a stand at once on the side of truth, but for the difficulty of separating from their parents. Societies had been formed, consisting of several hundred men not reckoned among the Protestants, for the purpose of having good schools for their children, and plain practical preaching in their churches. The magnates of one church had closed its door against the native evangelical preachers, and placed two Turkish soldiers to guard it. At another church the people were more resolute, saying, "We built this church, and we will be martyred upon its threshold, if necessary to defend our right to have the Gospel preached to us." At this the chief men gave way, contenting themselves with reporting the matter to the Patriarch at Constantinople. As an additional motive, the party of progress threatened to attend the services of the missionaries, if not allowed to have a service of their own.[1]

Week of prayer at Harpoot.

Quite a number of the young men and women in the Protestant city congregation dated their conversion from the "Week of Prayer." This week was duly observed at Harpoot from the

[1] *Missionary Herald*, 1866, pp. 169–171.

first, and in 1866, with deeper religious feeling, than had ever been seen before. The morning and evening prayer-meetings were kept up till the close of May, when it was decided to discontinue the morning meetings, and to sustain the others every day, one hour before sunset. Three fourths of the congregation attended them regularly, and an earnest and tender spirit was manifest in the remarks and prayers.

During this same week of prayer, Messrs. Burbank and Knapp, at Bitlis, aided by the native preacher Simon, afterwards pastor of the church, commenced a prayer-meeting at the dawn of day, which was so crowned with spiritual blessings, that it was continued, daily, for more than six months. The attendance increased from twenty to sixty, and was at one time nearly a hundred. The church had then only five members; and at the communion season in March, each of these five men publicly confessed his sins, and formally renewed his covenant. Many were in tears. Some in the congregation, who had thought themselves Christians, when they saw the church thus making confession, were amazed, and felt that they were themselves lost, and literally cried, as did the publican, "God be merciful to me a sinner."

Week of prayer at Bitlis.

This was the commencement of the first revival of religion in Bitlis. Two meetings were held weekly for inquirers, at which between forty-

Revival at Bitlis.

five and fifty were usually present, of whom from fifteen to twenty-five were women. "Among the latter, was one over seventy years of age, who, being in the previous winter too feeble to walk through the deep snow to attend the meetings, had been carried by her stalwart son. Now she was a weeping penitent, seeking salvation at the foot of the cross, and that son was rejoicing in the hope of salvation." Forty men usually attended the sunrise prayer-meeting. Not as many of the fruits of this revival were gathered into the church as might have been anticipated, because of the very high standard — too high it would seem — which was required for admission.

Broosa after seventeen years.

There had been great progress at Broosa. When Dr. Schneider left that place in 1849, on his removal to Aintab, no church had been formed, and his audience never exceeded fifteen natives, and sometimes it was not more than eight. No Protestant community had been formed, and in those days of fierce opposition very few were ready to face the consequences of an open acknowledgment of what they were convinced was the truth. But he found all this passed away, on his visit there in 1866. There was then a church of fifty members, and a Protestant community of one hundred and fifty, chiefly young men of enterprise, and a Sabbath congregation of one hundred and fifty. They had a beautiful house of worship, a prosperous day-school, and an excellent native pastor. There were many whose beards made them venerable. Dr. Schneider believed that half the Armenians in the city were convinced of the truth.

The first evangelical church in Turkey, composed of Greeks, was organized by the Union of Bithynia at Demirdesh, in November, 1867. Mr. Kalopothakes was present from Athens. The church was composed exclusively of evangelical Greeks, and six of its thirteen members were women. Pastor Hohannes of Bilijik, on behalf of the Union, welcomed them to the fellowship of the churches; which he said had been lost through the departure of the Greeks and Armenians from the gospel, but was now recovered. The preacher was a Greek, and a native of the place.[1]

First evangelical Greek church.

The mission was sorely afflicted in September by the sudden death of Mr. Walker of Diarbekir. The cholera was prevalent in that city, and seemed to follow no laws. In the previous year, it had been almost wholly among the Mohammedans; but this year, it prevailed most in the Christian population. Mr. and Mrs. Walker removed to a khan outside the walls. "His last sermons were from the texts 'The Master has come, and calleth for thee;' and 'Except ye repent, ye shall all likewise perish.' On Monday, September

Death of Mr. Walker.

[1] The members of the church formed at Hasbeiya in 1851 (p. 376 of vol. 1st) were seceders from the Greek Church, but were regarded by the Syrian mission as of the Arab race.

10th, he went into the city, spending some time over one stricken with cholera, besides customary duties. Tuesday morning, after a somewhat restless night, he rose as usual, and proposed a mission excursion to Cutterbul, but was persuaded to remain at home and rest. The premonitory symptoms soon appeared, but nothing peculiarly alarming, and as he had been held back from over-exertion, and been very careful in diet, all were full of hope. At the first whisper of illness the Christians gathered to aid, and the faithful Shemmas, without Mrs. Walker's knowledge, telegraphed to Mr. Williams, who started from Mardin at one o'clock, P. M., on Wednesday, and riding all night reached Diarbekir after sunrise to find that six hours before, September 13, 1866, his brother had gone 'to be with Christ.'" His age was forty-five.

His funeral.

"Diarbekir was filled with mourning. Not Protestants alone, but Moslems and Armenians, all were stricken. Such a funeral, as of one who was a father to all, was never witnessed there before. The native preacher conducted it appropriately and tenderly, praying not only for the stricken there, but for those in his native land who would so feel the loss." [1]

His character.

Mr. Walker was one of the best of missionaries. "His warm and affectionate nature," says Mr. Barnum, "quickly gained the hearts

[1] *Missionary Herald*, 1867, pp. 33–37.

of the people wherever he went. His great desire was to see men coming to Jesus; and this he never forgot, whether at home or abroad. I have been with him not a little, and seldom have I seen an opportunity for a personal appeal, though only for a moment, pass unimproved."

The tribute to Mr. Walker's memory from his brother Williams, of Mardin, who knew him well, and has so lately followed him into the eternal world must not be omitted.

"His peculiar gifts were three: — 1. He remembered faces, and recalled the names which belonged to them. He knew everybody. Ordinarily he needed to meet a man but once to recognize him ever after. And this pleases men; it appeals to their self-appreciation; they feel that they have made a permanent impression. Especially is this a power among a people who look up to the missionary as occupying a higher plane of civilization. It gives him a vast influence over them.

"2. Partly as the result of this, but still distinct and beyond it, he had a marvelous faculty of making every man feel that he was especially an object of personal interest. Perhaps not that he alone was such, but that he was one of those taken into the inner sanctum of his affections. Love begets love, and believing that they were so dear to him, he was soon very dear to them. And he was never lacking in the outward expression of love. He was not afraid they would think he loved them too much.

"3. He always had something to say. I suppose there is some good done by public preaching, but it is the preacher who is ready, in the face-to-face opportunity, who comes home laden with sheaves. Mr. Walker was always ready. Meet a man when he might, where he might, just the right word was on his tongue. And that warm grip of his hand, into how many souls has it infused a new and spiritual life. So he begot his children in the gospel; and by his sermons, which were always thoughtful, he built them up into Christian characters, as a workman who needeth not to be ashamed. Our Cutterbul deacon says to me since his death, 'I *never* saw such a man.' When he left for Constantinople in 1859, perhaps one hundred men waited upon him out of the city, and he spoke to every one, and repeated nothing, but had a special word for each, exactly adapted to his case."

Mrs. Walker's return home.

Mrs. Walker returned to the United States, with her four children, in the following summer, and has since been recognized, — in connection with a benevolent lady in New York city, — as sustaining a relation of maternal guardianship to returned children of missionaries.

A contrast at Choonkoosh.

At the close of the year Mr. Wheeler and others made a visit to Choonkoosh, two days' journey from Harpoot. Many of the people came several miles to welcome them, and crowds escorted them into the city. "Nine years ago," says Mr. Wheeler, "I made my first visit here in company with brother Dunmore, and we were hooted at, stoned, and at last driven from our room, in the pouring rain and splashing mud of a dark night." Now, every house seemed open to receive them. "Their new place for Protestant worship testified to the remarkable change. The men had brought all the timber, by hand, a distance of from three to five miles, and it sometimes required thirty men to bring one piece. Women and children brought water, earth, and stones; and women were still busy in plastering the walls, so that a meeting might be held there before we left!"[1]

The foreign missionary spirit was being developed. The Harpoot Evangelical Union resolved at Diarbekir, in 1866, to send a mission into the wild region eastward of that city, where the Armenians, living among the Koords, had lost all knowledge of both the Armenian and Turkish languages, and were in the grossest darkness. A dozen small churches, with a membership of hardly more than five hundred, undertook to educate seven young men to go as their missionaries, and the movement excited much enthusiasm. At the same time, the home missionary spirit received strength. The brethren at Harpoot were endeavoring to oc-

A foreign mission resolved upon.

[1] *Missionary Herald*, 1867, p. 108.

cupy fifty or more stations, within their home field, at most of which there were a few persons somewhat enlightened and more or less desirous of instruction.

A blessing followed. The week of prayer, in the opening of 1867, was signalized by a revival at Harpoot.[1] There were indications of deep feeling in the church; and on one of the last days of the week, three of the most prominent men in the community openly identified themselves with the Protestants. One of these, named Sarkis Agha, became a very active and useful Christian. Feeling that he had been a stumbling-block to others, he lost no time in going to the market, and inviting twelve or fifteen of his most intimate friends, all men of influence, to his place of business, and telling them of his change of feeling. He expected only ridicule, but the majority were affected to tears, and requested him to read the Bible and pray with and for them.

New revival at Harpoot.

It was winter, and the travelling was very bad, so that they could not reach the more distant out-stations; but the members of the church visited the principal ones on the plain. Among these was Hooeli, about ten miles distant, where Mr. Barnum spent two days. The whole congregation appeared to be interested, prayer-meet-

The revival extended.

[1] An interesting account of this revival, by Miss Maria A. West, may be found in the *Missionary Herald* for 1867, pp. 139–142.

ings, morning and evening, were attended by from a hundred and twenty to two hundred persons; and through the entire day, till nearly midnight, the room of the missionary was thronged with inquirers. A large number of those with whom he conversed, appeared to be truly regenerated. Mr. Wheeler, on the following Sabbath, found the interest more widespread. Four hundred persons crowded into the chapel, and listened with fixed attention.

Three years before, there was not a Protestant in the place. One year before, at the dedication of the chapel, when three hundred and fifty persons were present, the audience was so rude that there was the greatest difficulty in preserving quiet.[1] Both men and women were now quiet and serious listeners. A still larger attendance was reported on the following Sabbath, when more than a hundred failed of getting into the house of worship. There was also a revival of consider-

The past and present.

[1] Mr. Barnum thus describes Miss Fritcher's meeting with seventy or eighty females in this place, two years before: "The chapel was nearly full of women, all sitting on the floor, and each one crowding up to get as near her as possible. They were very much like a hive of bees. The slightest thing would set them all in commotion, and they resembled a town meeting more than a religious gathering. When a child cried it would enlist the energies of half a dozen women, with voice and gesture to quiet it. When some striking thought of the speaker flashed upon the mind of some woman, she would begin tc explain it in no moderate tones to those about her, and this would set the whole off into a bedlam of talk, which it would require two or three minutes to quell."

able power at Perchenj, another out-station, seven miles from Harpoot.

Human nature is everywhere essentially the same. The people of Hooeli being thus strengthened, they, with a little aid from abroad, erected a larger and finer house of worship, and then began to desire a new minister. Their humble and earnest but not eloquent preacher, whose labors God had so blessed among them, would do, they said, to gather the lambs, but not to feed the sheep. Contrary to the advice of the missionaries, they called two popular men of the graduating class, one after the other, but both declined, choosing harder fields.

Effect of prosperity.

"Meanwhile their preacher was called to another place, and the people came to the city, with their donkeys, to take him and his family home. These were quietly sleeping at his house, expecting to start on the morrow, when, at midnight, nine of the principal men of Hooeli roused him from sleep, and began to beg pardon for their rejection of him, saying, 'Come, get your goods in readiness, and go with us.' It seems that they took their failure to secure the others as a rebuke from God for their pride; and having met to pray, sent these nine men to ask pardon of Garabed in person, while others wrote letters asking his forgiveness, and begging him to come back. Both parties then appealed to the missionaries, who declined to interfere, advising them to pray and decide the matter among

The Recovery.

themselves. They agreed to accept the preacher's decision as God's will, and he after prayer and reflection, decided to return to his old people. In the mean time, twenty of the women of Hooeli, impatient at the delay, met also for prayer, and with difficulty were prevented from going in a body to take their old pastor home. But the brethren kept them back, and when at length he reached the village, no other preacher ever had such an ovation in all that region, within the memory of man."[1]

[1] *Ten Years on the Euphrates*, pp. 278–280.

CHAPTER XXXVI.

THE NESTORIANS.

1864–1868.

Death and character of Deacon Isaac.

DEACON ISAAC, brother of the Patriarch, died in the early autumn of 1864, universally lamented. In character, as well as position, he was a prince among his people. I abridge the account of him by Mr. Rhea, who loved him as a friend.[1] Seen in his plain dress and simple manners, no one would have thought of him as once the mountain chieftain, ready to break a lance with Koordish robbers. Growing up amid some of the grandest scenery in the world, it had its effect on his character; and that character the grace of God moulded into symmetry and beauty. His intellect was strong, his insight into human nature remarkable. The wily Persian official, baffled by him and mortified, exclaimed: "We cannot manage *him.*" While he was accessible to little children, and poor distressed women, there was a dignity which prevented undue familiarity. The Patriarchal family were proud of him. He grew up in a land where it was no shame for noblemen to lie, yet always spoke

[1] *Missionary Herald*, 1865, p. 45.

the truth. He lived where bribery was practiced unblushingly, and his house was a court-room for the settlement of numberless cases of litigation, yet he took no reward for his services, much less to pervert justice. "He grew up where little deference was paid to woman; yet took pride in showing his respect for his wife Marta, — mentioning her name, quoting her opinions, and treating her with the utmost kindness. Their relation was a beautiful example of conjugal attachment, of untold worth in such a land and among such a people. He was naturally of a proud spirit, that could not brook an insult. Once, when insulted by a French Lazarist, he sprung to his feet, and put his hand to the hilt of his sword; but from that day he never wore the sword again."

Death and character of Miss Fiske.

Miss Fidelia Fiske died at Shelburne, Massachusetts, the place of her birth, July 26th, 1864, at the age of forty-eight. She both studied and taught at the Mount Holyoke Seminary, and partook largely of the spirit of its founder, the well-known Mary Lyon. She embarked at Boston in March, 1843, in company with Dr. and Mrs. Perkins, Mr. and Mrs. Stoddard, and some others, and reached Oroomiah in June. After laboring there with unprecedented success as the Principal of the Seminary for fourteen years, the state of her health constrained her return to the United States in 1858.

Up to her arrival at Oroomiah, the school had only day scholars, and the pupils were of course in habitual contact with the vice and degradation of their homes. She sought to make it a boarding-school; and after two years the prejudices of the people had been overcome, and the day scholars were all dropped. Her grand object was the salvation of her pupils, and of their relatives who visited the institution. After the first revival, in 1846, the school became the centre of holy influence for the women. She, and her worthy associate Miss Rice, found enough to do, day and night. When they went to a village, the women expected to be called together for prayer; and when these women returned the visit, they asked to be prayed with alone. There was a revival almost every year of her stay at Oroomiah; and probably few servants of Christ have had more occasion for gratitude, in being the means of bringing others to him, than Miss Fiske. When leaving Oroomiah on her return home, the many women and girls who gathered around to bid her farewell, asked "Can we not have one more prayer-meeting before you go, and in that Bethel?" — meaning, her own room. There they prayed, that their teacher "might come back to mingle her dust with her children's dust, hear the trumpet with them, and with them go up to meet the Lord." They were accustomed to style her "mother," and themselves her "children."

Her usefulness after her return to the United States, was probably as great as it ever had been. This was not owing to the predominance of any one quality in her character, but to a combination of qualities of mind and heart surpassing anything I have ever seen in any other person. Her emotional nature was wonderfully sanctified, and each of her powers being well developed, and all nicely adjusted one to another, the whole worked with regularity and ease. Hence that singular accuracy of judgment, and that never-failing sense of propriety, for which she was distinguished. Hence the apparent absence of fatigue in her protracted conversations and conversational addresses. Hence the habitual control of her sanctified affections over her intellectual powers, so that she seemed ever ready, at the moment, for the call of duty, and especially to meet the claims of perishing souls. She seemed to me the nearest approach I ever saw, in man or woman, in the structure and working of her whole nature, to my ideal of the blessed Saviour, as he appeared in his walks on earth.

The amount of her usefulness was as extraordinary as her character, and probably the tidings of no death have awakened so many voices of lamentation over the plain of Oroomiah, and in the glens of Koordistan.[1]

Another death occurred this year, which was also sensibly felt by the mission. It was that of Deacon Joseph, of Degala. Dr. Perkins

Death of Deacon Joseph.

[1] See *Woman and her Saviour in Persia*, by Dr. Thomas Laurie, and *The Cross and the Crown, or Faith working by Love, as exemplified in the Life of Fidelia Fiske*, by Dr. D. T. Fiske.

lamented the loss of his services in connection with the press, a kind of labor for which his qualifications were unequaled among the people. His well-balanced mind, his fine scholarship, the solidity of his Christian character, his eminent services in this department, especially the very important assistance he rendered in translating the Old Testament from the original Hebrew, would have secured him an honorable position in more enlightened lands.

Mountain tours.

In 1863 and 1864 Mr. Shedd made extended tours in his mountain field. In the first, he crossed to Mosul, and from Oroomiah to Amadia he travelled mostly on foot, in native snow-shoes and moccasins, with much fatigue and exposure. At Mosul, he enjoyed the hospitality of Mr. Rassam, and had conferences with Mr. Williams of Mardin. The second tour was in the autumn, and extended as far as Tiary.[1] The mountaineers may be viewed, he says, in two very different lights; first, as feeble, unreasonable, and lawless; poverty stricken, and lacking in self-respect, and self-reliance; connecting their interest in spiritual things too often with the hope of temporal benefits. Then there are constant feuds between villages, clans, and chiefs. The hopeful side is in the great preparatory work that has been accomplished, the general friendliness of the people, and the growing influence of the mission helpers. The following tabular view

[1] *Missionary Herald*, 1863, pp. 358-363: 1864, p. 231.

will give some idea of the mountain work in its incipient state, for, in some important respects, it was in that state as late as the year 1863: —

The mountain work.

Occupied Districts.	No. of Christian Villages.	Estimated Christian Population.	When first occupied by Helpers.	No. of Helpers the Past Year.	No. of Villages visited by Preachers the Past Year.	No. of Villages with stated Congregations.	No. of Persons in Congregation.	No. of Sabbath Schools.	No. in Sabbath Schools.	No. of Regular Day Schools.	No. of Scholars.	No. reached by Family Visitation.	No. of Communicants.	No. of Candidates.
Gawar . . .	–	–	1852	4	20	5	88	3	42	2	21	550	20	2
Tekhoma . . .	6	4000	1856	4	6	3	55	2	25	–	10	250	7	1
Amadia . . .	6	–	1857	2	5	3	55	1	25	1	8	100	4	9
Rakan . . .	3	250	1861	1	8	1	15	1	8	–	5	50	1	–
Nerwa . . .	4	300	1862	1	3	1	10	1	7	–	5	50	1	1
Jeloo	–	–	1862	4	9	2	90	2	75	1	28	560	0	2
Berwer . . .	–	–	1863	2	10	1	85	1	25	–	8	100	–	–
Total . . .	–	–	–	18	56	16	348	11	207	4	80	1660	42	15

Mr. Shedd visited the young Patriarch, in his second tour. The leaders whom he met there from different mountain districts, were surprised by the friendship shown to the missionaries by Mar Shimon, and that they heard not a word against them in the Patriarchal mansion. There were frequent interchanges of visits, and Mr. Shedd was assured that the young Patriarch was well disposed towards the mission and its labors. But there

Visit to the young Patriarch.

was no evidence that he had any real conviction of the truth.

The seminary for girls.

The seminary pupils were now working on a higher level. To a large extent, the pupils were daughters of Nestorian helpers and other pious parents, who had given them a Christian training. The contrast was striking between their general appearance and that of the earlier classes in that favored school. A considerable part of the expense was now met by the parents of the pupils.

Great usefulness of Dr. Wright.

The Rev. Austin H. Wright, M. D., was the immediate medical successor of Dr. Grant, at Oroomiah,[1] where he arrived July 25, 1840. To be thoroughly furnished for his work, he determined to master the Turkish, Syriac, and Persian languages; and it was doubtless his perfect acquaintance with these, coupled with his knowledge of medicine, and the gentle courtesy of his manners, that gave him so much influence among all classes of the people. "The influence of Dr. Wright in Oroomiah," said an intelligent Nestorian, "is that of a Prince." He is said to have spoken each of the languages above named with a precision, fluency, and grace, rarely equaled by a foreigner. In consequence of this proficiency, the intercourse with the higher classes was to a great extent in his hands. Persian gentlemen, polite and courteous in the ex-

[1] For a biographical account of Dr. Wright, see *Missionary Herald* for 1865, pp. 129–134.

treme, appreciated the dignified yet simple ease and grace with which he met them. Having gone out alone, he was united in marriage June 13, 1844, to Miss Catherine E. Myers, who joined the mission in 1843, and was then engaged in teaching. After twenty years his health and the interests of his family demanded a visit to his native land. Here he remained four years, devoting the latter half of that time to a revision of the Syriac New Testament, preparatory to its being electrotyped and printed in pocket form by the American Bible Society. To this the Psalms were afterward added. Mrs. Wright and four of the children remained in this country; but taking with him his eldest daughter Lucy, he returned to Oroomiah in September, 1864. His return was joyful to him, and to the mission, and no less so to the Nestorians; but in three short months the summons came, calling him to a higher service.

His death.

It had been arranged that he and Mr. Rhea, should translate the Scriptures into Tartar-Turkish for the benefit of the Mussulman population of Azerbijan and the regions beyond; but Dr. Wright's work was finished. His disease was typhoid fever, and during much of his sickness he was unconscious.

In the twenty-five years of his service, he performed a great variety of labors, — as a preacher, a physician, a co-laborer in the department of the press, and, not least, as a shield to the poor oppressed

Nestorians; for he was greatly respected by their Mohammedan rulers. And these duties he performed with marked ability, scrupulous fidelity, and an almost unerring judgment.

Death of Mr. Ambrose.

In this year, also, died the Rev. Thomas L. Ambrose, on the 19th of August. The three years he spent in the mountains were to him years of suffering, the result of an ardent mental and moral temperament, as well as of the labors he performed. He returned home in 1861, hoping to resume his missionary work; but feeling that his country had claims upon him, and receiving an unsolicited appointment as chaplain of a New Hampshire regiment, he entered the service, was wounded while passing from entrenchments to a hospital, and after a few weeks died in the General Hospital at Fortress Monroe. In his relations to the mission and the Nestorian people, he beautifully exemplified the spirit of his Lord, in not desiring "to be ministered unto, but to minister."

Nestorian vagrancy.

The harvests of 1865 were abundant, but there had been a famine in several of the previous years; and this had given a stimulus to the vagrancy, so frequent and annoying among the Nestorians. "Of the four thousand vagabonds," writes Dr. Perkins, "from the less than forty thousand Nestorians of Oroomiah, who made want their pretext for scattering themselves over Russia and other parts of Europe, as common beggars, hardly less greedy for lucre and for vice, than are locusts for every green thing, only a moiety return; many dying in those distant regions, from diseases induced by strange climates, or oftener by criminal indulgence; and many who survive, lying in prison for crimes, or preferring their vagabond life to the decent restraints of home. Many who do return are worse than lost to their people; coming only to spread a moral pestilence, being thoroughly demoralized; recklessly squandering their ill-gotten treasures till hunger drives them off again to beg. Happily they are now shut out of Russia by the government, and they have little hope from England. But Germany is still a golden land to them."

Mr. Rhea, another very able member of the mission, was suddenly removed from earth on the 2d of September, 1865. He was on his return from Tabriz, with his wife and children. The whole scene, as described by Mrs. Rhea in the Memoir of her husband, is one of the most touching in missionary history.[1] He was ill when they left Tabriz, and not until they had gone too far to return did his wife awake to the alarming fact, that his disease was cholera.

Death of Mr. Rhea.

She then hoped to reach Ali Shah, a village four hours from Oroomiah. It was necessary to put the

[1] See *The Tennesseean in Persia and Koordistan, being the Scenes and Incidents in the Life of Samuel Audley Rhea,* by Rev. Dwight W. Marsh, for Ten Years Missionary in Mosul, pp. 338–349.

bedding on one of the loaded horses, and then to place Mr. Rhea upon it, and for two men to hold him on; which was done by the faithful Nestorians, Daniel and Guwergis. The motion of the horse extorted frequent, though gentle, groans of pain. He was very thirsty, and both the children were crying for water. There was none. At a brackish brook he had tried to drink, but spit out the bitter draught in disgust.

"At length the moon rose, and the children became quiet. Daniel passed a rope around Mr. Rhea's back, and over his shoulders, to keep him from shaking about on the horse; and, taking off his hat, protected his head with a flannel. He grew quiet, and I said, 'He sleeps.' So we rode on and on in the still night; no sounds except from the horses' feet, or an occasional word about the precious load. 'Will the village never appear?' They said it was very near. O, how long the way seemed!

"My mind was very active, picturing that comfortable room where we should rest, the refreshing water, the quiet rest, the soft bed for the dear invalid, the quick cup of tea, his sweet words, our subsequent journey home in the takhterawan, our safe arrival there. All this time my eyes were on him, and my ears strained to catch a sound. 'How long he sleeps! How still he is!'

"At length the weary, weary road was passed. We reached the village, and stopped at a house where they said we could find a room. Daniel and I ran in to see it first, opened the windows, and spread down the shawl and pillows where he could rest; then went back to the gate, and I charged the men not to let him exert himself at all, but to take him down like a little child, and carry him carefully in. I ran forward then, opened my satchel, and got out the wine and camphor, and spreading a pillow on my lap, received him in my arms.

"Just as they deposited him in my arms he drew one long, deep sigh. I wet his lips, bathed his face, spoke to him, called his name, raised him up, kissed him, and entreated him to speak. I chafed his soft, warm hands, felt his heart, his pulse, his temples, his neck, seeking everywhere for signs of life. In vain. He was dead!"

Help came at length from the mission, and the mortal remains of Mr. Rhea found their resting place at Seir, by the side of loved ones who had gone before him.

Mr. Rhea died at the age of thirty-eight, in the very height of his usefulness. His mental abilities were very superior, and so were his acquirements, especially in Oriental languages. During his first winter's residence in Gawar, in addition to a systematic course of reading in Church History, and his study of Syriac, he went thoroughly through his Hebrew Bible. The Modern Syriac he spoke with great accuracy and fluency, and he

His character.

preached with acceptance in the Tartar Turkish. He had also made progress in the Koordish language. "As a preacher," writes Mr. Coan, "he was earnest, faithful, and pungent; the glowing words leaped from his lips, while the Word of God seemed a fire shut up within him. He poured out his whole soul in the messages he delivered. I have seldom been edified by the discourses of any one as I have been by those of this dear brother. These discourses, whether in the pulpit, the social prayer-meeting, or at family devotions, seemed drawn from his own experience of the inexhaustible treasures in Christ. They were eminently fitted to make men better." Dr. Perkins said of him, "He is one of the finest preachers I ever heard, whether in English or in the Nestorian language. The Nestorians denominate him Chrysostom, from his remarkable powers as a preacher." He was excelled by few men in the beauty and eloquence of his address on public occasions, of which there was a fine illustration on the Fourth of July, 1865, the last before his death. Though a native of Tennessee, his heart was poured out in thanksgiving that the war was really over, and that the right had gained the day.

Hostility of Mar Shimon.

The reader will not be surprised to hear that the young Patriarch, influenced by his nearest relatives, was following in the footsteps of his predecessor. In Gawar, he tried persuasion, blandishment, and compulsion; but the authorities gave him to understand that there could not be persecution. The independent tribes of the mountains were, civilly, under his power, and he was determined to keep his mountain diocese in its ancient ignorance. He diffused a vindictive spirit. No ecclesiastic ever had stronger motives to enter upon a path of reform, or fewer obstructions. But, refusing all fellowship with the gospel, he showed that the Nestorian Patriarch could no more adjust himself to the coming age of light and liberty of conscience than the Pope of Rome.

Mr. Alison, English Ambassador at the Persian Court, seasonably interposed when there were powerful combinations to effect the ruin of the mission, headed by the bigoted Minister of Foreign Affairs. The Papal party had seized upon the Nestorian church at Ardeshai, and rebuilt it; and the Shah, upon the representation of Mr. Alison, granted a site for a new church, and subscribed £100 towards its erection.

Friendly agency of the English Ambassador.

Royal donation.

This royal donation was in December, 1865. In the April following, the mission had a friendly visit from his Royal Highness, Prince Ahmed Meerza, the governor of Oroomiah, and uncle of the King. He had come to the province strongly prejudiced against the mission, but had been becoming better informed. He was on the mission premises two hours and a half, and saw

Government favor.

everything that could be shown him, in the way of schools, printing, type founding, sewing-machines, and medical dispensary. The last seemed to impress him most as to the benevolent character of the mission, and he left with strong expressions of good will.

The examination of the female seminary, at the close of its term, was highly satisfactory, especially in the Bible and in theology. In the other seminary, superintended by Mr. Shedd in the absence of Mr. Cochran, there had been much religious interest. Many of the pupils being from the mountains, Mr. Shedd's labors in the seminary had a direct bearing on his particular portion of the field. Geog Tapa had a very fine school, entirely supported by the people themselves, which almost vied with the seminaries.

Success of the girls' school.

Male seminary.

A private school.

The mission suffered another severe loss in the death of Priest Eshoo, already known to the reader, on the 19th of April, 1866. Thirty-one years before, the Koords plundered his native village on the plain of Gawar, and he removed to Degala, near Oroomiah. He was then about thirty years of age, a sedate, dignified, upright man and very righteous in his own eyes. Gentle and unassuming, he yet commanded the respect of all, and his reputation as a scholar soon secured for him the place of a teacher in the incipient male semi-

Death of Priest Eshoo.

nary. For many years he was its first teacher, and down to the close of his life sustained a relation to one or the other of these institutions. He and his lovely daughter Sarah were among the first converts in the revival of 1846. While remarkable for humility, he was firm in defense of the truth. His judgment was cool and discriminating, and he was known as a safe counselor. He was a good preacher, and several volumes of his sermons, neatly written by his own hand, showed that they were carefully studied.[1]

Dr. Van Norden and wife entered the mission in October, 1866, taking the place of Dr. Young, who had left three years before.

New medical missionary.

Mr. Labaree communicates the result of careful inquiries by Mr. Thompson, of the British Legation, who had been spending some time at Oroomiah. Mr. Thompson estimated the Nestorians in Oroomiah, Tergawer, Sooldooz, and Salmas, at twenty thousand; the Armenians in Oroomiah alone at about two thousand eight hundred; the Papal Chaldeans in Oroomiah, Tergawer, and Sooldooz at six hundred and twenty-five; but the Chaldean and Armenian population of Salmas he did not learn. He thought that the population of Persia could not be more than from five to seven millions, and his opinion was deemed of great weight, as he had made himself familiar with the civil and

Estimates of population.

[1] See vol. i. pp. 326–329.

political affairs of Persia during a long residence, and had travelled extensively through the country, with a very observant eye.

Interesting Armenian colony.

Among the new lights breaking forth in Western and Central Asia, was a community of evangelical Armenians in the Russian province of Sherwan, near the Caspian Sea. A Nestorian brother had been sent to inquire into their condition early in 1862, and there had been occasional intercourse ever since; but cautiously, lest their cause should be jeoparded. They had suffered sore persecution, and had met in glens and deep recesses of the mountains, for the worship of God and the study of his Word. Their leader, Varpet Sarkis, had been exiled, their children left unbaptized, their young people unmarried, their dead denied the right of burial, and they the privilege of commemorating the death of their Lord. In August, 1866, an Imperial Ukase was brought them by a Lutheran clergyman from Moscow, granting them full liberty to worship God publicly as their consciences should dictate, and restoring to them all their privileges. Pious Nestorians, who had gone there from Oroomiah, reported that the Lutheran clergyman remained there a week, organized a church, received a hundred and six persons to Christian fellowship, and performed the necessary baptisms and marriages; and that they were expecting the return of their beloved guide and teacher from exile. Nearly two thousand copies of the Scriptures were sold among this people within three and a half years, besides many other good books and tracts.

Mar Shimon, acting under the evil advice of his father and uncle, issued an order for the expulsion of all the helpers of the mission from Tehoma, and threatened not to leave one in all the mountains. Events providentially occasioned delay, and meanwhile Mr. Rassam, the British Vice Consul at Mosul, hearing of Mar Shimon's proceedings, addressed him a very strong letter of remonstrance, assuring him that the American missionaries were the truest and most efficient friends of the Nestorians, and urging him to invite their preachers back with the same publicity with which he had ordered their expulsion. The letter, coming from one to whom the Nestorians were greatly indebted, had the desired effect, and they were quite abashed by receiving such an emphatic rebuke from such a quarter. In addition to this rebuff, another was received, soon after, quite as mortifying. The Patriarch had written to Mr. Taylor, British Consul at Erzroom, offering to make over his people to the English Church, if the English government would extend to them its protection from Turks and Koords. The reply of the Consul was a decided rejection of the proposal, couched in language not at all flattering to the Patriarch. Thus baffled and censured, he privately signified his willingness that our preachers should remain at their places without molestation.

Patriarch thwarted in his hostility.

The mission commenced the year 1868 with the
Favoring indications. encouraging fact, that one hundred Nestorians had been received to the communion during the previous year, which was a larger number than had been admitted in any one year before. This number embraced the fruits of revivals in several villages on the plain of Oroomiah, and in the two seminaries, with individuals scattered through the Koordish mountains. Mar Yooseph, the helper in Bootan, on the Tigris, reported, that he had held his first reformed communion in that distant region, and that seven came to the table of the Lord. There had been no opposition. The native preaching force in the mission was then sixty-two, of whom eighteen were in Koordistan, under the care of Mr. Shedd; and there were seventy-eight regular preaching places. Connected with nearly all these congregations were Sabbath-schools and Bible-classes, and in not a few instances the entire congregation was connected with them. The habit of giving was very generally established, affording evidence that the people might be expected eventually to support their pastors.

CHAPTER XXXVII.

THE NESTORIANS.

1867–1870.

THE annual convention of helpers and representatives of the Nestorian churches occupied three days of October, 1867. Ninety members were in attendance. Mar Yohanan was elected moderator, and Priest Yoosep of Dizza Takka, the former moderator, preached the opening sermon. The aged preacher lamented the prevailing worldliness of the church, and earnestly enforced the duty of prayer as the great remedy. He alluded feelingly to the destruction, by a Koordish chief, of one of their oldest and best churches, which dated back more than a thousand years. A part of the materials had been used to construct a fort, and a part to build a mosque upon the site of the church. The recent increase of wine drinking, among some of the communicants, received a faithful rebuke. Carefully prepared papers were presented on practical subjects, such as education, benevolence, temperance, family worship, and the means for promoting the spiritual efficacy of their body as a communion, and

Convention of Nestorian churches.

these were followed by free and animated discussions. The duty of assuming more fully the support of the gospel and of schools among the entire people, was earnestly enjoined; and during the discussion the spirit of self-denying benevolence rose to an unusual pitch. Several pledged a tenth of their income, and the contributions on the plain rose higher than ever before.

There were pleasing episodes during these deliberations, — in the reports of Deacon Yâcob, a seminary graduate, of two and a half years' colportage in Russia, and of Deacon Eshoo concerning his successful labors for some years in Tabriz. Deacon Yâcob reported the sale of nineteen hundred Bibles and Testaments, and many other books and tracts, in Modern Russian, German, and other languages. He also spoke of revival scenes, resulting in the hopeful conversion of several adherents to the Greek Church. The Emperor of Russia, he said, encouraged the circulation of the Scriptures in the spoken language, allowed free passports to colporters, and exacted no duties for the largest sales.

"The subject of wine drinking," writes Mr. Cochran, "the greatest bane of the people in the wine-making districts, was discussed with vigor, and, with one or two exceptions, in the spirit of a determined purpose to urge forward a reform. It was manifest that, on the whole, there had been a decided growth of conviction, that total abstinence is the only safe remedy for the evil. It was gratifying to hear no complaints of the use of stronger drinks, except among those outside of our communion."

Several churches, as well as the seminaries, had enjoyed special seasons of revival. A sunrise prayer-meeting of an hour was held each day of the session, was well attended, and characterized by much fervor and importunity in prayer, and the last evening was spent in devotional exercises. The burden of prayer seemed to be for the outpouring of the Spirit on the churches and the conversion of souls, and many of the congregation were at times deeply moved.

Ordination of a Nestorian missionary.

Deacon Yâcob was ordained in the month following, that he might be able to administer the ordinances to the converts among the Malakans of Russia. Mr. Shedd wrote of him as "a man whom we delight to have among us, so full is he of the Holy Ghost and of faith." One other person was also ordained as an elder or priest, and four as deacons, in connection with meetings of district conferences composed of preachers and delegates.

A satisfactory tour.

In the first week of 1868, the "week of prayer," Mr. Labaree made a tour in five villages, and never passed that interesting season more delightfully, finding in each village cheering evidence of the special presence of the Lord. The Christians were induced to pray and labor earnestly for the unconverted around them. In each village two meetings were held each day, and were attended by considerable numbers outside of the church. Indeed that week was observed, generally, among the evangelized Nestorians, and there were indications of a blessing in the two seminaries, and in several villages.

Movement towards self-supporting churches.

It is an important step towards the support of religious institutions, when a people have once acknowledged such support to be their duty; and this admission will be the more effectual when organizations exist that can attend to the performance of the duty. In the progress of events there had grown up four ecclesiastical bodies, called *Knooshyas*, that is, assemblies, three on the plain, and one in the mountains; which had their confession of faith and rules of discipline. The local assemblies sometimes met together as one body. As in kindred bodies among the Armenians, the missionaries were admitted for counsel, but not to vote. At a meeting of one of these bodies, the duty of self-support was fully acknowledged, and the desire was strongly expressed to show their gratitude to the American churches by assuming the entire support of the gospel among themselves, and sending it to regions beyond, as did their fathers. The following resolution was adopted, namely: "That it is the duty of every member of the church, as he has received spiritual benefits from his pastor, to aid in the temporal support of the same; and also to aid in meeting the necessary expenses of the church according to his ability."

It was recommended that pastors preach on the subject of these resolutions; and that the pastor and lay-delegates, on their return home, use their influence with the brethren and congregations of their respective villages to bring the people up to their duty in these matters.

The following reflections by the venerable Dr. Perkins, written about this time, will be refreshing to the reader: "The progress of our work," he says, "is steadily onward, and is probably as rapid as would consist with its highest prosperity. This progress is not always in a uniform current. It often resembles a succession of circling eddies, caused generally by obstacles in the stream, but sometimes by the accelerated speed of the current, which, but for these self-regulating checks, might bring upon the work serious disaster. Such eddies are often our best missionary regulators, correcting mistakes or undue haste, and giving to our converts occasion and time to examine the foundations of their faith."

Progress of the reformation.

Miss Nancy Jane Dean joined the mission in October, 1868, to labor in the female seminary. Miss Rice and Mrs. Rhea had left Oroomiah in the previous May, with Dr. Perkins, and arrived at New York in August. Miss Rice had been con-

Retirement of missionaries.

nected with the female seminary twenty-two years, and her good influence was felt in hundreds of Nestorian homes on the broad plain and in the wild glens of the mountains. Mrs. Rhea's return was due to her children, but, like that of Miss Rice, it was a sad loss to the mission circle, and to the women of Persia. The return of Dr. Perkins, the father of the Nestorian mission, seemed like a removal of the foundations. "It is difficult," wrote Mr. Shedd, "to over-estimate his labors, continued now for more than a third of a century, or the value of his experience. It is a gratification to him, and to us all, that he can leave us in the atmosphere of revivals; and that, after he is gone, the many works from his pen will continue to speak to the people whom he loved. But many will sorrow at his leaving Persia, and most of all that they shall see his face no more."

What Dr. Perkins had seen accomplished.

Dr. Perkins had seen much accomplished in the thirty-six years of his connection with the mission. From eighty-five centres, and to congregations averaging nearly two thousand four hundred, the gospel had come to be proclaimed, by more than a hundred native helpers, of whom fifty-eight were fully recognized preachers; and more than nine hundred persons had professed their faith in Christ, of whom seven hundred and twenty were then connected with the evangelical communion. The seminaries had educated hundreds of youth, whose influence was seen in the general social and moral elevation of the people. In the common schools there were more than a thousand pupils; and from the press more than half a million of pages had gone forth in the year preceding his departure; making an aggregate of nearly nineteen millions (18,996,450) from the beginning.

The mission was commenced with the expectation that the revival of gospel light and influence among that people would rekindle their ancient missionary spirit. Extreme oppression and poverty have made the development of this spirit very difficult. But we have already seen among them as fine specimens of it, probably, as there ever were in the olden times. Witness the venerable Bishop Elias, Tamo of Gawar, Guwergis of Tergawer, Isaac of the Patriarchal family, Joseph the translator, Priest Eshoo of the Seminary, Oshana of Tehoma, and, more recently, Yâcob, among the Malakans of Russia, and Deacon Eshoo in the commercial capital of Persia. These were really missionary men; and there seems also to have been even a greater development of the genuine missionary zeal among the Nestorian women. There were, and doubtless there are now, men and women, who would have resolutely carried the gospel into Central Asia, had the door been open.

Rekindling of the ancient missionary spirit.

The time had now come, when it could be no longer safe for the reformed Nestorian churches to defer entering upon incipient

Foreign missions become a necessity.

the opportunity to labor for my people. I am very happy that my father and friends brought me on my way in willingness of soul. From the day that I left my own country, in every place that I have entered, until now, my heart has been excited to praise my Guide and my Deliverer, and I have also been grateful to my teachers, who brought me to labor in a desolate vineyard joyfully; I, who am so weak, and such a great sinner. In all the various circumstances through which I have passed, your counsels have been of great benefit to me.

"I think you will be glad to know, that the gospel door is wide open here. You and your friends will pray, that the Lord of the harvest would send forth laborers into his harvest.

"We left Oroomiah, May 6th, and on May 8th we reached Memikan, and remained there three days. It was our first Sabbath in the mountains, and I met that company of women, for whom our departed Mrs. Rhea used to labor. May 12th we left Memikan, and went up to the tops of the snowy mountains of Gawar. The cold was such that we were obliged to wrap our faces and our hands as we would in January. As we descended the mountain, we found it about as warm as February. That night we spent in the deep valley of Ishtazin, in the village of Boobawa, where Yohanan and Guly dwell. The people here are very wild and hard. Yohanan and Guly were not here, having gone to visit Khananis. Only a few came together for preaching. The people said, 'Yohanan preaches, and we revile.' May 13th, we left Boobawa, and soon crossed the river. Men had gone before us, and were lying in wait there. They stripped us, but afterwards of themselves became sorry, and returned our things. As we were going along this wonderful, fearful river, and beheld the mountains on either side covered with beautiful forests, we remembered Mr. Rhea, the composer of the hymn, 'Valley of Ishtazin.' And when filled with wonder at the works of the Great Creator, we all, with one voice, praised him in songs of joy fitting for the mountains. Here the brethren reminded me, that our dear Miss Fiske had trodden these fearful precipices. This greatly encouraged me in my journey. This day we went into many villages, and over many ascents and descents. At evening we reached Jeloo, and remained over night in the pleasant village of Zeer, which lies in a valley made beautiful by forests and a river passing through it. They showed great hospitality here, and were eager to receive the word of the Lord. May 14th, we left Zeer, and went to Bass. It was Saturday night, and we remained over the Sabbath in the village of Nerik. I shall always have a pleasant remembrance of the Sabbath we passed there. From the first moment that we went in till Monday morning, we were never alone, so many were assembling to hear the words of the

Lord. With tearful eyes and burning hearts, they were inquiring for the way of salvation. They would say, 'What shall we do? We have no one to sit among us, to teach us, poor, wretched ones.' Truly a man's heart burns within him as he sees this poor people scattered as sheep without a shepherd. May 16th, we mounted our mules, and went on our way. Half an hour from Nerik we came to the village of Urwintoos. An honorable, kind-hearted woman came out, and made us her guests. This was Oshana's aunt. As soon as we sat down, the house was filled with men and women. They brought a Testament themselves, and entreated us to read from that holy book. Did not my heart rejoice when I saw how eagerly they were listening to the account of the death of our Lord Jesus Christ! When the men went out, the women came very near to me, entreating for the word of the Lord, as those thirsting for water. Then I read to them from the Book.

"There are many sad deeds of wickedness among these mountain Nestorians; and when Christians hear how anxious they are to receive the words of life, will they not feel for them? We reached Tehoma May 17th. Now, from the mercy of God, we are all well and in the village of Mazrayee. I am not able to labor for the women here as I desired, because many of them have gone to the sheep-folds. It is so hot we cannot remain here, and we will go there also, soon. I trust, wherever I am, and as long as I am here, I shall labor for that Master, who wearied Himself for me, and who bought these souls with his blood."

Sarah returned to Oroomiah in the spring of 1860, and left in 1861 for Amadiah. During the winter of 1861–62, no messenger could cross the snow-covered mountains between Oroomiah and Amadiah, and she thus wrote in March, 1862, to Miss Rice.

"I did greatly long for the coming of the messenger. We were very sad in not hearing a single word from home. Now I offer thanksgivings to Him, in whose hands are all things, that He has opened a door of mercy, and has delighted us by the arrival of letters. They came to-day. Many thanks to you and your dear pupils! The Lord bless them, and prepare their hearts for such a blessed work as ours.

"Give Eneya's salutations and mine to all the school. I think they will wish to hear about the work of the Lord here. Thanks to God, our health has been good ever since we came, and our hearts have been contented and happy in seeing some of our neighbors believing, and with joy receiving the words of life. Every Sabbath we have a congregation of thirty-five, and more men than women. For many weeks only the men came; but now, by the grace of God, the women come too, and their number is increasing. I have commenced to teach the life of the Lord Jesus from the beginning. I have strong hopes that God is awakening one of them. His word is very dear to her. Her son is the priest of the village, and a sincere Christian. Four other young men and five women are, we trust, not far from the door of the kingdom. We entreat you, dear sisters, to pray in a special manner for these thoughtful ones, that they may enter the narrow door of life.

"From the villages about us we have a good report. They receive the gospel from Oshana and Shlemon, who visit them every Sabbath. In my journeys through these mountains, I have seen various assemblies of men and women listening to the gospel; poor ones, exclaiming, 'What shall we do? Our priests have deceived us; we are lost, like sheep on the mountains. There is no one to teach us.' They sit in misery and ignorance. They need our prayers and our help. I verily believe that if we labor faithfully — God help us to labor thus — we shall soon see our Church revived, built up on the foundation of Christ Jesus, and adorned for Him as a bride for her husband. With tears of joy we shall gaze on these ancient ruins becoming new temples of the Lord. Soon shall these mountains witness scenes that will rejoice angels and saints. Those will be blessed times. Let us pray for them, and labor with Christ for their coming."[1]

[1] *Woman and her Saviour in Persia*, pp. 216–221. Similar illustra-

Death of Priest Abraham.

Priest Abraham, the father of this excellent woman, died in 1871. He was one of the first to coöperate with Dr. Perkins, and was faithful unto the end.

Failure of the original plan of church organization.

There was the more call for some new missionary movement from the fact, that, whatever may be affirmed as to the wisdom of the plan adopted for reforming the Nestorian Church, in the earlier stages of the mission, experience had shown that the Old Church, as such, could not be reformed. It was proper that, from time to time, the favorable facts on this subject should be stated in this history, as they appeared to the men then on the ground, — to Dr. Lobdell;[1] to Dr. Dwight;[2] to Mr. Coan;[3] to Dr. Perkins;[4] indeed to the whole body of the mission. But the experience of six and thirty years had shown, that the dead Church could not be galvanized into spiritual life. There was no way for the truly enlightened but to leave it, and form reunions on the Apostolic basis.

Mar Yohanan.

The necessity had become obvious, but it was a trying process. It was too much for Mar Yohanan. He must be spoken of kindly, for he had long stood in friendly relations with the

tions could be multiplied from this remarkable volume, some of them scarcely less interesting than the above.

[1] Chapter xxvii. [2] Chapter xxix.
[3] Chapter xxix. [4] Chapter xxviii.

mission, though the evidence of his piety was never entirely satisfactory.

Priest John, of Geog Tapa, gave unquestioned evidences of piety in early life. But in 1868, if not earlier, his gold had become dim, and his proceedings and their consequences must have a place in this history. Erratic proceedings of Priest John.

Becoming extravagant in his habits, and thus involved in debt, he was disaffected because the mission could not accede to exorbitant demands, and relieve him from pecuniary embarrassments. So he went abroad to collect money for this purpose, and made his way to England, where he succeeded in interesting several of the dignitaries of the Established Church. Returning home in the autumn of 1869, he made such a report of his visit, and excited such expectation of the coming of Episcopal clergymen, and large patronage for ecclesiastics and civil protection for all classes, that many of the simple-hearted people were carried away. The mission had been hoping to get some of the evangelical churches, ere long, upon a self-supporting basis; but the hopes thus excited of their burdens being assumed by the Church of England, put back for a time this work of self-support.

The narrative is continued in the language of Mr. Cochran: "Priest John returned from England flushed with the apparent success of his mission. At Geog Tapa, the next Sabbath after our communion, at early dawn he baptized fifteen children with much display. More than two hours were spent in reading the English Liturgy, chanting Psalms, and explaining and vindicating the usages of the English Church. He announced his intention to give the communion to all who desired it. This innovation upon the evangelical usage of more than a dozen years (though he had once previously practiced indiscriminate baptism), was not inappropriately followed by the suspension of the Sabbath-school and preaching service, and the turn-out of the whole village, headed by Malek Yonan and Priest John, to meet the son of the master of their village, who happened to return on that day from a long absence in the army. In the delay of the young Khan's arrival, a young deacon, more zealous than discreet, proposed a service by the roadside, but many voices cried, 'We have become Episcopalians, and don't want any more preaching.' This public and flagrant violation of the Sabbath, headed by the two leading Christians of the village, painfully illustrates the material found there, and sadly contrasts with the better days of the excellent and lamented Malek Agha Beg and Mar Elias.

"We have heard nothing from friends in England, but from other sources infer the probability of at least a visit of Episcopalians to Mar Shimon, and possibly to Oroomiah, the coming spring. Priest John states, that Dr. Perkins did him harm in England by his published statement, that he (Priest John) had come, not as an accredited agent to secure Episcopal interference, but rather on a private and personal begging expedition (the truth of which is well known in Oroomiah, and confirmed by a written stipulation lodged with friends here, that his companion should receive one third of the avails of the excursion). To destroy the force of Dr. Perkins' statement, Priest John has secured the signature of a large number of names, including Patriarchs, Bishops, Maleks, and principal men among the people. The paper was circulated privately, but we learn that only one of our employees, and very few, if any, of our communicants, could be persuaded to sign it.

"If asked, what is the true state of feeling among our communicants, an extensive and familiar acquaintance with them enables me to testify with great confidence, that, with the exception of a very small high-church party, headed mainly by Mar Yohanan, I discover no special tendency to Old Churchism of any kind, and if let alone, they are more than satisfied with the gospel simplicity and spontaneity of worship."

The best people stand firm.

Under date of January 10th, 1870, Mr. Cochran adds, "Geog Tapa continues to witness novel scenes under the eccentric and reckless Priest John. At the close of the fast of the nativity, the communion was administered to the whole village, and numbers from surrounding villages were also invited in. Many who had not communed for from ten to thirty years, as well as the more superstitious and the lowest rabble, participated. Four priests, all of whom are of doubtful piety (though two were in our communion), officiated, clothed in white. The whole Old Church service was read in ancient Syriac, and long Psalms were chanted in the same. The baser sort were exultant, but the thoughtful, even of those not with us, were sad. Every artifice was used to draw in our communion, but we were rejoiced to find that all except ten, — consisting of the family of Priest John, and the priests and deacons who officiated, — refused to partake with them.

"I have preached there three times since. Yesterday was our communion. The house was crowded at both services. It was judged that seven hundred were inside, and not less than one hundred and fifty outside. I preached in the morning on the spiritual character of a true church, and newness of life as the condition of admission, and that the ordinances belong exclusively to the church, and not to those outside. All listened attentively, though a disturbance was feared. In the afternoon I 'fenced' our communion fully, but Priest John had the effrontery to partake. I have since learned that had it been withheld, he, with the rabble, would have taken it by force. A perfect separation seems called for, and with it a casting out of unworthy members from the church. But the heart of the body is right, and will, I trust, stand by the truth."

"Enlightened villagers," adds Mr. Shedd, under date of January 20, 1870, "besides members of the evangelical communion, did not partake. It shows the movement for high-church aid in its true colors. Such aid on the part of the English bishops is nothing more nor less than salarying Mar Shimon and his ecclesiastics, for reading their old prayers and using their dead forms and rites, as they have done for ages past. We rejoice in so simple an issue, and are sure it can do no injury to vital Christianity."[1]

The time having come for separate and independent church organizations, these painful occurrences seem to have been providentially designed to promote that result.

The new organizations thus facilitated.

Mr. Cochran thus writes: "The progress of the gospel and providential occurrences, are bringing us into many new relations to the old Nestorian Church, and grave questions, affecting the purity and future growth of our churches, are now forcing themselves upon us. So long as the Old Church did not oppose evangelical labors, so long as she freely opened her doors to our services, consenting to a separate administration of the ordinances for the hopefully pious, and silently tolerating many ecclesiastical and social reforms, and an abandonment of the liturgical service; in short, so long

The past not to be condemned.

[1] *Missionary Herald*, 1870, p. 190.

as we could see, under the preached gospel, the hold on the old superstitions steadily lessening, and the masses being leavened with evangelical truth, we were more than content to labor on without a separate church organization.

Separate churches a necessity.

"But experience in other fields, as well as our own, has proved that such labors can only be prosecuted for a time. From year to year we have found the old ecclesiastics more restive under their loss of support, and more jealous of the progress of spiritual life. Mar Shimon, as you are informed, has for years openly opposed the gospel, and now so intimidates the interior mountain districts under his immediate control, that it seems preposterous to attempt to prosecute labors there, unless on a separate foundation. And we now find the opposition on the plains, and all over the field, not less positive, and daily becoming more concerted and potent.

"Mar Yohanan has also, for years, secretly, and often openly and most offensively, opposed spiritual and reformatory labors. Priest John, a most untiring and reckless man, is arousing a furor of zeal for Old Churchism,—a fanaticism that will not be likely to subside with the spasmodic efforts he may make. He and others are now administering the communion every few weeks to the whole people, without distinction of character. They also enjoin the fasts and saints' days, resume the use of the liturgy in ancient Syriac, burn incense daily, bow before the altar, and make the sign of the cross; though some, as yet, refuse to come into all these measures.

"With the return of these old superstitions, there is also a painful throwing off of moral restraint, and intemperance and kindred vices have greatly increased.

"In these circumstances the question has arisen, first in Geog Tapa, and subsequently in other places; Can 'the evangelicals' further unite in the morning and evening service conducted by priests — and there happen to be five or six in that village — who are reviving these superstitions? Almost the whole church are surprisingly united in the decision to withdraw. This has been done for the last two months, and we find upwards of one hundred members there, who are firm, and daily waxing stronger in faith and opposition to the old superstitions."

Signs of revival.

These and other distractions seriously hindered the spiritual growth of the churches in the winter of 1869 and 1870. But in the spring, a very thorough work of grace was enjoyed at Degala, and it was believed that there were more than twenty genuine conversions, mostly among the aged and middle-aged. The church in that place paid half the salary of its pastor, and was expected soon to pay the whole. Mar Yooseph, the young bishop at Bootan, wrote that his congregation had increased to one hundred and fifty, and that, for much of the time, Christ and his salvation formed the only theme of conversation. He had hopes concerning considerably more than a score of new converts. Deacon Toma, who had spent a year in the Seminary, was with him as a helper, and promised to become another Deacon Guwergis.

The foreign mission field for the Nestorians.

The immediate foreign mission field of the Nestorians, is among the Armenians in Russia, and the same people at Tabriz, Hamadan (the ancient Ecbatana), Teheran, and Ispahan in Persia, with the numerous villages in the intervening regions; descendants, to a great extent, of Armenians carried captive, in the year 1605, from the regions of Ararat by Shah Abbas the Great. They furnish the field providentially offered to the Nestorians, as the Koords do for the Armenians in Turkey. Hamadan is about three hundred miles southeast of Oroomiah, on the great caravan road between Tabriz and Bagdad. On the 28th of May, 1870, the mission resolved, that they considered it a duty urged upon them to embrace at once within their efforts the Armenians and the Mussulman sects of Central Persia, by planting a station at Hamadan; and they expressed the hope that the Board would heartily endorse this action, and help them to carry it out without delay, and also to occupy Tabriz.

The members of the mission, in the spring of 1870, were the Rev. Messrs. Coan, Labaree, Cochran, and

Shedd, and Dr. Van Norden, with their wives, and Miss Dean, principal of the female seminary. The mission was now known as the "Mission to Persia," in view of plans to reach the entire population of the country. To Mr. Cochran was assigned the superintendence of twenty out-stations in Oroomiah, Sooldooz, and Tergawer, and the field outlying these, together with the male Seminary. To Mr. Coan was committed the press, the editing of the "Rays of Light," care of the treasury, and the oversight of the city church, and of two out-stations. To Messrs. Shedd and Labaree, jointly, was given the care of twenty out-stations in Oroomiah and Salmas, besides Tabriz and Hamadan, with the Armenian work in general; and, separately, to Mr. Shedd the mountain field, and to Mr. Labaree the Mussulman work. Dr. Van Norden was to carry on his medical department, and to translate the Gospel of John into Turkish.

The Missionaries.

Assignments of fields of labor.

In the autumn of this year the Mission to Persia was formally transferred to the care of the Presbyterian Board of Foreign Missions; reserving, however, the Armenian work in the northern portion of the field, from its intimate connection with the mission to the Armenians of Turkey.

Transfer of the mission.

It remains only to speak of the honored founder of the mission.

Dr. Perkins lived through the entire connection of the mission with the American Board, and died at Chicopee, Massachusetts, on the 31st of December, 1869, when he had nearly attained the age of sixty-five; having been born on the 12th of March, 1805. He graduated at Amherst College in 1829, taught the next year in Amherst Academy; spent the two following years in Andover Seminary; and was tutor in his Alma Mater for the greater part of another year. The engagement last named was shortened by his call to commence the mission among the Nestorians. His life, from the time of his sailing from Boston, with Mrs. Perkins, in September, 1833, for six-and-thirty years, is largely the history of the Nestorian mission.

Death and character of Dr. Perkins.

The careful reader of this history will not need a portraiture of his character. He was evidently made for the position he so long occupied. He was an acknowledged leader in the Lord's host; a Moses and a Joshua, with traits of character resembling those both of Elijah, and of the Apostle Paul. To idleness, vagrancy, and drunkenness, besetting sins of the Nestorians, he was the old prophet; and in his longing desire to make them savingly acquainted with the gospel, he was the apostle. Their spoken language he reduced to a written form, and gave them, in their vernacular, the Scriptures of the Old and New Testaments; with a commentary on Genesis and on Daniel. Is it too much to pronounce him the Apostle to the Nestorians? He came to his end as a shock of corn fully ripe; and glorious results of his self denying, and in some respects suffering mission, he will assuredly behold in the heavenly world. Where in his native land could he have labored, with the prospect of so large a spiritual harvest, taking no account of the widely reacting influence of his labors on the churches at home? And we might propose the same inquiry with respect to the departed Stoddard, and Rhea, and Grant, and Fidelia Fiske, and others, both among the dead, and the living.

CHAPTER XXXVIII.

SYRIA.

1857–1860.

Death of Dr. Smith.

DR. ELI SMITH, whose name has an honorable place among the translators of the Scriptures, died at Beirût, Sabbath morning, January 11th, 1857.[1] Thirty years had elapsed since his first arrival in Syria, and he had before been connected for several months with the press at Malta.

The work performed by him.

In 1829, he made an exploring visit, with the author, to the Ionian Islands, the Morea, and the Grecian Archipelago; and the next year, he and Dr. Dwight explored Armenia, and a part of the Nestorian country. The other more important events of his life are so far known to the reader, that they need not be repeated.

The mind of Dr. Smith was rich in general prin-

[1] Dr. Smith expressed a decided opinion, in his last sickness, that no memoir of his life and labors should be published, since he had never kept a journal, and there were not sufficient materials. In this he was probably correct, considering what the public would have expected. A well written obituary, somewhat extended for that publication, may be found in the *Missionary Herald* for 1857, pp. 224–229. See, also, pp. 123–125.

ciples, and in well-considered applications of them to the missionary work; though, in this latter respect, he was restricted more than his brethren among the Armenians, by the less pliable nature of the materials on which he was called to operate. After having explored countries which others were to oc ; after contributing largely to the accuracy,
value of Dr. Robinson's "Biblical Re-
nd after securing the formation of type
acceptable to the most fastidious Arab;
lf to prepare a new translation of the
the Arabic language. With this in view,
ied the study of Arabic and kindred lan-
es to a greater extent than was necessary to
come either a good speaker, or a good preacher. His learning was both extensive and accurate, and he was continually adding to his stores by a wide range of judicious reading. To a good knowledge of the ancient classics, he added an acquaintance, more or less perfect, with the French, Italian, German, and Turkish languages. With the Hebrew he was familiar; and the Arabic, by far the most difficult of all, was to him a second vernacular.

Dr. Smith was eminently a man of business, and was accustomed to give attention to the minutest details. He spent much time in superintending the cutting, casting, and perfecting of the various fonts of type, made from models that he had accurately drawn from the best specimens of Arabic caligraphy.[1]

[1] See vol. i. p. 233.

For many years he read the proof-sheets of nearly every work that was printed at the mission press; and he bestowed much thought and labor upon the mechanical apparatus and fixtures of that establishment.

To him every pursuit was subsidiary to a faithful translation of the Word of God into the Arabic language. Yet he did not neglect the regular preaching of the gospel, which he regarded as the first duty of every missionary; and having early become a fluent speaker in the Arabic, this was ever his delight. "Almost as a matter of course, his preaching was expository and didactic. In clear, lucid, logical exposition of divine truth, he had few equals. His language, though select and grammatical, was always simple, and within the comprehension of the humblest of his hearers. In regard to matter, his discourses were eminently Biblical, sound, and evangelical. In form and costume, his theology was that of Edwards, and Dwight, and Woods, — the theology of the Puritan fathers of New England. Upon this system of divine truth his own hopes of eternal life rested, and it was this which he earnestly labored, for thirty years, to infuse into the Arabic literature, and transplant into the hard and stony soil of Syria's moral desert."

The author, having had the best opportunities for knowing Dr. Smith, bears testimony to his excellent judgment, and to the great value of his correspondence with the executive officers of the Board, in the forming period of the missionary work.

It did not please the Lord to grant the earnest desire of Dr. Smith to live and complete his translation of the Scriptures; and it must be admitted, that his ideal of perfection in the work was such, that it is doubtful whether he ever could have been satisfied that his entire translation was ready for publication. Only Genesis, Exodus, and the first sixteen chapters of Matthew, had received his final revision, and were acknowledged by him as complete. But, with the help of Mr. Bistâny, his assistant translator, he had put into Arabic the entire New Testament, the Pentateuch, the Historical Books of the Old Testament, and the books of Isaiah, Jeremiah, Lamentations, Hosea, Joel, Amos, Obadiah, Jonah, Micah, and Nahum. He had revised, and nearly prepared for the press, the whole of the New Testament, and all except Jeremiah, Lamentations, and the last fourteen chapters of Isaiah, of the books named in the Old Testament. With these finished specimens, and with so large a portion of the remainder translated and carefully revised, together with the helps to translation which he had accumulated, his brethren believed that he had laid the foundation for one of the best versions of the sacred Scriptures to be found in any language.

Dr. Van Dyck had been connected with the mission since 1840, and very soon made himself master of the spoken Arabic, in which he greatly excelled as a preacher. It soon appeared, that he was the man to succeed Dr. Smith as translator of the Scriptures, and the mission arranged his removal, for that purpose, from Sidon to Beirût; so that in due time he was enabled to bring the great work to successful completion.[1]

Dr. Van Dyck succeeds him as translator.

Mr. Aiken had joined Mr. Wilson at Hums, a new station north of Damascus, where he was bereaved of his wife before she had been six months in the field. The arrangement for 1857 was that Beirût should be occupied by Messrs. Van Dyck and Ford, and Mr. Hurter, the printer; Abeih by Messrs. Calhoun and Bliss; Sidon by Mr. Eddy; Deir el Komr by Mr. Bird; Bhamdûn by Mr. Benton; Tripoli by Messrs. Jessup and Lyons; and Hums by Mr. Wilson. Dr. Thomson and Mr. Aiken were in the United States; the latter with health so impaired as to forbid his resuming his mission. He had previously married Miss Cheney. In the following year, Miss Jane E. Johnson and Miss Amelia C. Temple arrived to take the care of a girls' boarding-school at Sûk el Ghurb, on Mount Lebanon; but the former was soon found unable to endure the climate. Dr. Thomson, while in this country, published a valuable work on Biblical literature, in two volumes, entitled "The Land and the Book." Dr. and Mrs. De Forest had come to this country in the hope of a

The Missionaries.

[1] See chapter xl.

restoration of his health; but on the 24th of November, 1858, this excellent missionary was released from long and severe physical sufferings by a peaceful death. Death of Dr. De Forest.

The health of Mrs. Wilson made it necessary, for a time, to leave Hums without a resident missionary. The principal operations, both here and at Deir el-Komr, were through schools for both sexes, which had been embarrassed by Syrian and Greek opposers, but in no case suppressed. The female department of the school at Deir el-Komr commenced with a dozen pupils, but in six months the attendance exceeded fifty. When Mr. Bird came to that place, he thought there were not six females in the nominally Christian population, who could read; but a year had not passed before half the pupils in his girls' school could read their Bibles. There were other mountain schools under the care of the station, and in one there were more than sixty pupils. The Schools.

The following contrast of the state of things in 1857 with what it had been fifteen years before, indicates a preparatory work in no small degree encouraging. "Then, the missionary could hardly purchase here the necessaries of life; and when he left, he was followed by stones and execrations. Now, he is welcomed and honored. Then, fear kept even his friends from venturing to visit him; now, priests and even a bishop are ashamed not to return his calls. Then, the Prot- Progress in fifteen years.

estant sect could not be vilified enough; now, it is spoken of with favor in public and in high places. The old Emir Beshir, once the persecutor and terror of Protestants, has passed away, and his dilapidated palace is used as barracks for Turkish soldiers. His prime minister, or secretary, who did much injury to the cause of evangelical religion, and whose mansion was, as it were, the stronghold of the enemy, is no more. What remains of this Ahithophel's house is the abode of the missionary, and furnishes apartments for Scripture schools, and a Protestant chapel. His sons-in-law were leaders in the movement which brought us to Deir el-Komr, and are among our firmest friends. His grandchildren learn the folly of popery by the knowledge of the Bible they acquire in our schools.

"Time was, when every one trembled at the anathema of the clergy. Now, the latter dare not show their impotence by pronouncing it. Some of the people would be glad to be thus dissevered from a church which they abhor, for they would thus not only gain their end, but retain the sympathies of many who would else oppose them. Those who send their children to our schools, have been refused admission to the confessional and the eucharist; the Maronite bishop, however, has at length yielded the point, and tries to win, rather than compel. Their high school he has made free of charge, and has promised to open a girls' school beside. In the

Greek Catholic communion, on the other hand, the men and some of the women remain "suspended;" yet they are of good courage, some glad of so excellent an excuse to get rid of the confessional, and others incensed at the glaring injustice that would admit the drunkard and the notoriously vicious, but exclude the respectable and the moral. We have here the anomaly of those being thrust out of the church, who are still its very pillars, its substantial supporters, whose names are known, and whose influence is felt, throughout the region.

"We have reason to thank God and take courage. Still we long to see a work more purely spiritual. Light is being diffused, but there is not the corresponding religious interest. The truth is viewed by many as a beautiful theory, the heart remaining a flint. We have to regret the fact, that some of the best minds in the place are tinged with skepticism. Happily the most influential are, notwithstanding, our firm friends, and are in favor of good education and good morals."

Ain Zehalty, a village situated in the heart of Lebanon, has been already mentioned.[1] Mr. Bird says, "We now have there five church-members. There have been regular Sabbath services under the charge of the native helper, Khalil. The audience has been on the increase, and is now not only larger than that in Deir el-Komr,

Ain Zehalty.

[1] Vol. i. p. 383.

but is composed of better materials. Those who come desire instruction, and are regular attendants and declared Protestants." An Ain Zehaltian, when out of his village, if not a Druze, was set down at once as a Protestant. The day school in that place had forty scholars, and half as many attended the evening school for adults. This school was for the special purpose of studying the Bible, and the pupils had gone through the historical books of the Old and New Testaments. Their custom on Saturday and Sabbath evenings was to read the devotional parts, and hold a prayer meeting.

Church at Hasbeiya.

Mr. Ford made a visit to Hasbeiya in February, 1857, with Mr. Jones, Secretary of the Turkish Missions Aid Society. He had never before been in that region, and speaks highly of the native laborers. Of the church-members he says: "When compared with the rock from which they were hewn, and the hole of the pit from which they were digged, they show the genuineness of the work of grace in their hearts." "The signs of the times," he adds, "in the community around, are most encouraging. I will only refer now to a remarkable stirring up of the Maronites to defend themselves against the inroads made by the gospel upon their hitherto solid ranks. Their ecclesiastics

Attitude of the Maronite clergy.

have always maintained an attitude of proud contempt, as though conscious of the strength of their hold upon their people, and they have rarely deigned to come into personal contact with the despised preachers of the gospel. But the serious diminution of their numbers in various parts south of us, and the diffusion of spiritual light among the rest of their flocks, have forced them down from their assumed elevation, and now they select the ablest of their priests, ordain him bishop, and send him on a crusade through Deir el-Komr, Hasbeiya, Merj Aiun, and so on to Alma, where the spirit of Asaad es-Shidiak, the modern martyr of Syria, seems to be revived in the hearts of a simple people, preparing them to brave death itself for the Gospel's sake. This bishop has sought public discussions with Mr. Bird, at Deir el-Komr, and also with Mr. Wortabet, at Hasbeiya. In the latter place there had been two such discussions held just before we arrived. In the first, the bishop was effectually caught in his own craftiness, and so completely worsted, that he and his friends came to the second session prepared to regain by violence the advantage they had lost in argument; and the result was a stormy debate, terminated abruptly by an assault upon some of the Protestants present."

Kefr Shema.

Kefr Shema, a promising out-station, became a station by the removal thither from Aleppo of Mr. and Mrs. Eddy. No objection to their residence was made by the people, though it was not four years since they had combined in a desperate attempt to drive all Protestants from the village. The missionaries were visited and welcomed by many.

A high-minded Christian.

Honorable mention is made of Antonius Yanni, the only native Protestant in Tripoli, who had been two years connected with the mission church, and had suffered much for the cause of Christ. He had refused the honorable and highly lucrative post of vice-consul for Russia, because its acceptance would necessarily have made him subservient to the corrupt Greek Church, and an attendant upon its services.

Religious toleration.

There had been preaching for several years at Aramon, three miles from Abeih. But the congregation was broken up in midsummer by a mob. Mr. Calhoun, who was regarded with great respect by the people, visited the place, and in a very kind, gentle manner, told the people that religious freedom was guaranteed to all, and that they of the mission should be allowed to worship in their own hired house. The people listened with attention. On Monday Mr. Calhoun referred the case to the English Consul-general, and to the acting Consul for the United States. Late in the week, two officials from the government in Beirût, and two from the governor of the mountain district, met Mr. Calhoun at Aramon. "When the time for service arrived, the officials publicly stated, that there is to be perfect religious freedom for all;—to-day, to-morrow, this year, next year, and for all time. This they repeated over and over again, as the will of the Sultan, and then ordered some one to go upon the house-top and proclaim aloud, after the manner of the Mohammedans, *that it was time for prayers, and that all who wished to come might come.* Services were then conducted as usual, with an attentive audience; and at the close, in a place appointed, the officials demanded that the persecutors should ask pardon of the persecuted, which was accordingly done, many kissing the hand of the man whose house they had entered, and which we had hired. The governor also called some of the men to his own village, and threatened them with severe punishment if they should again molest any one on account of his religion. He then, Mohammedan as he was, repeated, in substance, the sentiment advanced, in the presence of his officers, by Mr. Calhoun, that religion pertains to the individual conscience and to God alone." Henceforward Mr. Aramon, the first teacher in the seminary, met with no opposition in a regular preaching service.

Prospect of a native ministry.

The number of pupils in the Seminary, at the close of the year, was twenty-five, and some of them were of unusual promise. A theological class, of four middle-aged, married men, was kept up during the summer, and then they went forth preaching the gospel, or laboring as teachers and colporters. Thoroughly-educated young men, otherwise qualified to preach the gospel, could only be obtained to a limited extent. But men of riper age, of good common sense and simple-hearted piety, could be fitted, by a few months of direct Biblical training annually, to preach to the uninstructed peasantry, — a labor for which there was the loudest call.

On the 12th of January, 1858, a deputation of four young men was received by Mr. Eddy, at Sidon, from a large village east of Tyre, called Cana. These brought a letter, signed by twenty-six persons, professing their dissatisfaction with their own corrupt Church, in connection with which they obtained no knowledge of God or of heaven, and asking that a preacher might be sent to them at once, and a teacher for their children. They denied being actuated by any worldly motive, and were sent back with two New Testaments, and the assurance that some one would be sent to instruct them as soon as possible. They were, accordingly, visited by Daher Abud, a faithful native helper, who was much gratified with the zeal and interest he found among them. In February, Mr. Eddy went himself, and was warmly welcomed. About forty men attended his preaching, whose eagerness to hear and converse detained him over the next day.

A new call for the gospel.

From thence he went to Alma, a village of five hundred inhabitants, a long day from Cana, beautifully situated upon the summit of a high range of hills, two miles from the sea. The

Church at Alma.

evangelical movement had commenced there two years before, and there was a Protestant community of about forty, including nine members of the church. "This was considered, in some respects," writes Mr. Eddy, "one of the brightest spots in the Syrian field. The great adversary of souls tried in vain, by the terrors of persecution and the seductions of flattery, to recover the people to himself. Failing in this, he sought to sow discord among brethren, and thus to conquer them; and for several months past he has rejoiced in seeing this 'house divided against itself.' I felt much anxiety as to the issue of my visit, and had made it the subject of special prayer. I spent three days among the people, one of which was the Sabbath. The conversation and the preaching were mainly directed to the end of securing peace, and a day of fasting and prayer was observed. On the morning of the fourth day the clouds parted, and the Saviour revealed himself in love. Then, amid tears, and confessions, and promises, and prayers, the covenant of peace was signed, and thanksgiving offered to God, and we separated."

Mr. Eddy visited Cana twice in the summer, and found the people, young and old, eager to be instructed in the Word of God. So many children attended the school from Catholic families, that the priest sent word to the bishop in Tyre, that if he did not interpose his authority, all

Successful ministry at Cana.

the village would turn Protestant. Accordingly the bishop came, bringing with him several wealthy and influential men of the city. The Protestants were all invited to assemble at the house of the head man of the village, and then these friends of the bishop, in company with the head man and the priest, labored most of the night to induce them to return to their church. It would have been beneath the dignity of the bishop to have interceded directly with them, especially if he had not succeeded. The effort was a failure. Next the Prior of all the convents in that part of the country, hearing of the bishop's ill success, came, and sought to obtain, by love and promises, what the bishop had failed to accomplish by threats. But he too returned disappointed; and coincident with his departure, two persons came out from the Catholic Church and joined the Protestants.

First completed Protestant church in Syria.

The month of November found Mr. Eddy again at Alma, to dedicate the first completed Protestant church in Syria. The enrolled Protestants numbered then about fifty. Dr. Van Dyck, before leaving Sidon, had selected a site for the building and seen the foundation laid, and had since collected from native Christians and foreign residents nearly the amount required for the church, which was of stone, thirty-two feet long and twenty-two feet broad, and capable of holding from one hundred and fifty to two hundred persons. It cost about three hundred dollars; thirty of which were contributed by the people of Alma out of their deep poverty, besides a large amount freely bestowed in labor. No opposition was made by the government to its erection.

After the dedicatory sermon, the Lord's Supper was administered to the nine church-members, who renewed their vows to the Lord; and these, with other appropriate services, made it a Sabbath long to be remembered.

In the summer of 1859, Mr. Eddy again visited Cana, taking Mrs. Eddy with him to secure access to the women. He pitched his tent, the first night, on the banks of the ancient Leontes, six or seven miles north of Tyre, and the next day at noon they were at Cana. The poor women, ignorant, yet eager to be taught, had never before enjoyed such an opportunity, and prized it exceedingly.

The missionary's wife at Cana.

The people had passed through severe sufferings. Several of the women had been beaten, and the men had a bitter tale to tell of oppression by their governor. He demanded a duplicate payment of taxes, and when the head man of the Protestants respectfully showed him a receipt, with his own seal affixed, he ordered him to be severely beaten and placed in confinement. He then sent officers to bring others of the Protestants before him, but, suspecting his intention, all except two

Persecution.

fled into the open country. These two, when brought, were thrown down upon the ground before the governor, and beaten with staves without mercy upon their backs and feet, he encouraging his servants to deal harder blows with commands and threats. Thus beaten till their backs were livid and swollen, they were wounded also by being kicked and stepped on by those who beat them, to make them lie still. When hardly left alive, chains were placed upon their necks and feet, their hands were placed in wooden stocks, and they were cast into prison, where they spent the night with companions who had been previously beaten. Next morning they were brought before the governor, and two of them were again beaten, when they were dismissed with a threat, that if they left the village he would pull down their houses. They however, despite his threats, made their way to Tyre, whence they embarked in a vessel to Beirût, to seek redress from the Pasha, and sympathy from the missionaries. When they appeared before the Pasha's court, their backs were ordered to be uncovered, and their wounds exhibited; and the greatest indignation was expressed by the members of the council against him who had so barbarously treated them, in violation of the laws of the realm."

The governor was sent for, and the indications were, that he would be expelled from office. But he was not. The Pasha suddenly changed his tone towards the Protestants, ordered one of them to be cast into prison on a false charge by the governor, and forbade the council to proceed further against him. The Cana people were detained two months from their homes. The proffered interposition of the English Consul was rudely rejected, and their release, when it was effected, was with no regard to the claims of justice. The visit of Mr. and Mrs. Eddy at that time must have been very seasonable and acceptable.

From Cana they proceeded to Alma, where they remained about a week. The women here, being more numerous and more enlightened, and some of them members of the church, were prepared to receive greater benefit from the instruction of a Christian sister. Three additions were made to the church. The people, though poor, had here also been compelled by their governor to pay their taxes twice.

Among the women at Alma.

The Seminary at Abeih was now made more directly a training school for native preachers and helpers; and a female boarding-school was opened at Sûk el-Ghûrb, a village six miles north of Abeih, under the direction of Miss Temple. The training of female helpers was its leading object, and the removal of Mr. Bliss thither made a home for the pupils.

Training of helpers.

Ain Zehalty continued to be a marked village, and the papists made great efforts to reclaim it. A Maronite bishop at one time,

Ain Zehalty again.

and a wily Jesuit at another, repaired thither, at the urgent request of the papal party, to uproot the dangerous exotic. The coming of the bishop was with great boasting on the part of his adherents, but, much to their chagrin, he declined commencing a controversy with Khalil, the native helper there; and was afterwards so hotly plied with texts of Scripture by some of the church-members whom he ventured to attack, that he fled for refuge to the more accommodating "traditions of the elders." It was supposed that the disciple of Loyola would carry all before him; but the undaunted Bible-men were more than ready to meet him, which they did effectively; and his visit was productive of more good than harm.

Struggles in the department of education.

The report of the mission for 1858, furnishes many striking evidences of the influence exerted, especially in the department of education. Soon after the opening of the first Protestant school at Tripoli, the Greeks opened a school for boys, which soon became large and prosperous. And when the Protestant girls' school became a success, a board of directors was organized, under the direction of the Greek bishop, to break up the other, if possible. Not finding an educated woman in Syria who was not a Protestant, the Greeks applied to two Protestant young ladies to take their school, but without success. To secure the needful pecuniary means, they constrained the

Patriarch to surrender a part of the convent revenues for this purpose. The Russian government, moreover, took up the subject of education in Syria, and remitted twelve thousand piasters (four hundred and eighty dollars) to the Greek school directors in Tripoli for the city schools; but with the injunction, that the tenets of the Greek Church should be the chief subject of instruction.

Accessions to the churches.

Nineteen persons were added to the churches of the mission during the first half of the year 1859. This of course involved various local indications of progress, for which the limits of this history afford no space. A new place, however, is brought to our notice by Mr. Eddy, named Deir Mimas, a large village on the river Litany. A few had here professed Protestantism about two years before, and had encountered a storm of persecution from members of the Greek Church, and from the Mohammedan governor of their district. Yet they had constantly increased in numbers and strength. The missionary spending several days there, was delighted to find an audience each evening of more than one hundred, after their severe labors, all eager to hear. The number of men professing Protestantism was above sixty, and counting the women and the children, the number was one hundred and fifty, the largest in Syria. Their enemies were on the alert, and it was a sad fact, that no competent native

New Protestant community at Deir Mimas.

teacher could be found to reside among them. They were then dependent on a native teacher, who came to them each Sabbath from a distance, having first preached in his own villlage.

A cheering annual meeting.

The annual meeting of the mission in this year was one of unusual interest. "From the beginning to the end of the meeting, it was apparent that there was much of a spirit of prayer among the native brethren. The native female prayer meeting in Beirût was more fully attended than usual, and the union meetings in Arabic and English, held in the chapel, in which the missionaries and native brethren united and large audiences assembled, were occasions of deep interest. The statements made in the meeting when the annual reports were read, at which W. A. Booth, Esq., of New York City, and Hon. Alpheus Hardy, of Boston, a member of the Prudential Committee, were providentially present, filled the minds of all with the conviction, that never before in the history of the Syria mission have we had so much encouragement, or such strong proofs that God is with us, and that the work is going forward in this land."

Friendly aid from United States Ambassador.

Before this meeting, the mission had been favored with a visit from the Hon. James Williams, United States Ambassador at Constantinople, whose friendly and most useful agency was duly acknowledged by the mission. His reply to them may be found in the "Missionary Herald."[1]

[1] See *Missionary Herald*, 1860, p. 163.

The translation of the New Testament was now completed and published under the care of Dr. Van Dyck. The pocket edition was admitted to be one of the most beautiful books, in its typographical execution, in the Arabic language. It had this advantage, that it could be carried and read without attracting notice; which was something in a land where Bible readers met with so much determined opposition.

Arabic New Testament published.

CHAPTER XXXIX.

SYRIA.

1860–1863.

THE year 1860 was noted for a civil war in Syria, and for savage massacres on Lebanon, at Hasbeiya, Damascus, and elsewhere, which awakened the indignation of the Christian world. The Druzes were prominent in these massacres, and so suffered greatly in character; yet the Turks were believed to have been the instigators. The war commenced in June; but the government for months had foreborne to check private assassinations and angry collisions, until the condition became unbearable.

Another civil war in Syria.

All the Greek and Papal Christians united against the Druzes, with the declared purpose of not leaving one of them on Lebanon, but they had miscalculated their power. The Protestants decided to take the side of neither party. It was believed at Beirût, that the main object of the foreign Jesuits and native Catholic clergy was to exterminate the Protestants, who had their homes chiefly among the Druzes. The Druzes were aroused to desperation, and thirty or forty Maronite and Greek villages were burned early in June. The inhabitants who escaped massacre fled to Beirût. Not one of these fugitives was a Protestant.

The missionaries safe.

The missionaries at Abeih, Deir el-Komr, and Sûk el-Ghûrb were not molested, and Messrs. Calhoun and Bird and their families remained at their several stations. It was thought best for those at the Sûk to descend to Beirût. Disturbance having arisen at Sidon, an English war steamer was sent thither to look after the foreigners. The steamer brought Mrs. Eddy and her children to Beirût, but Mr. Eddy and Mr. and Mrs. Ford decided to remain at Sidon.

Massacre near Sidon.

In the country and gardens near that city, hundreds of unarmed men and defenseless women and children, many of whom had fled thither for their lives, were afterwards savagely butchered by Moslems and Druzes. The missionaries then asked for a guard from the city governor, which he refused until the American Cousul in Beirût demanded it.

Mr. Bird at Deir el-Komr.

Mr. Bird, at Deir el-Komr, supposing that all was quiet around the city, left home to look after the little company of Protestants in Ain Zehalty. In his absence, the Druzes attacked Deir el-Komr on every side, and when Mr. Bird returned towards evening, he saw the town in flames, but could not enter. One of the more than one hundred houses burned, was a school-house belonging to the mission. The Druze Begs declared it was a mistake, and promised to rebuild it. The Christians had fought until their ammunition was exhausted, and then surrendered. Mr. Bird found his family unharmed, though the fighting and burning had been very near them. The Pasha coming up from Beirût made such arrangements that Mr. Bird and family decided to remain.

Destruction of Zahleh.

The Druzes were now masters of Mount Lebanon south of the Damascus road, and there was no power left in that district to oppose them, save in the town of Zahleh. It was from this town that a company of horsemen went to Hasbeiya, sixteen years before, to compel the Protestants there to recant; and from this same town, not many months before, Mr. Benton and his family had been expelled with great violence by a mob. Its time had now come. Mr. Lyons passing that way in October, with relief for the survivors of the massacre, thus speaks of Zahleh: "It presents one of the saddest spectacles in all the wide field of desolation. Only a few months before, I had seen this then flourishing town in all its beauty and pride. Now, nothing remained but a vast collection of roofless houses, with blackened, shattered walls, and shapeless heaps of stones and rubbish. Shops, magazines, costly dwellings, and elegant churches, all had shared in the common ruin."

The Protestants in Hasbeiya began to be troubled, early in the year, by premonitions of a coming storm. Mr. Eddy was there in May, accompanied by Mrs. Eddy and Miss Temple, who devoted themselves to labor for the spiritual good of the women in that community. Hardly had they returned to Sidon, when Hasbeiya was surrounded by hostile Druzes. They were driven off at first, but on the 3d of June the commander of the Turkish soldiers told the Christians to retire within the palace, and he would protect them. On the 11th the Druzes surrounded the palace, and the Turkish commander opened the gates, and allowed the Druzes to cut them in pieces. Some saved their lives by crawling under the dead bodies, and others by escaping over the walls. The Protestant church was partially destroyed, but not burned; its walls and roof remaining uninjured. At Rasheiya the Druzes told the Christians to give up their guns, and they would be safe. In the night, they set fire to the houses, and killed nearly all of one hundred and thirty men. More than one thousand persons were murdered in Hasbeiya and the surrounding region. Of these only nine were Protestants.

Massacre at Hasbeiya.

At Damascus, on the 9th of July, the wild Moslems, from one of the suburbs of the city, with Koords, Druzes, and Arabs, burst upon the Christian quarter, plundering, butchering, and burning; not opposed, but aided, by the Turkish

Massacre at Damascus.

soldiers, who could have suppressed the insurrection at any time. The slaughter continued several days, and the killed were estimated at five thousand. The whole Christian quarter of the city was plundered of its great wealth, and the houses and churches were laid in ruins.

Relief for suffering thousands.

Those who escaped these massacres fled towards Beirût and Sidon, destitute of everything. Appeals were at once made to the Christians of England and America, and the missionaries, acting for the "Anglo-American Relief Committee," were the chief almoners. The expenditure in August for food, clothing, bedding, shelter, hospital, and soup, was at the rate of about sixty thousand piasters a week, or two thousand four hundred dollars, and yet it seemed to make little impression on the mighty mass of misery. Dr. Thomson had the especial care of the clothing, bedding, shelter, and soup-kitchen, Dr. Van Dyck of the hospital and the sick in general, Mr. Jessup of the distribution of bread to about six thousand persons daily, and Butrus Bistany and Michael Aramon, two of the native brethren, had the daily distribution among about two thousand five hundred poor. The funds up to this time had come chiefly from the people of England, and English merchants at Beirût gave much time to managing the large financial business connected with so vast a charity. Dr. Thomson declares that the male children were generally murdered, and that the killed were largely mere boys; and who, he asks, were to support the thousands of widows, with their fatherless daughters? The country had no factories, and scarcely any kind of business by which such widows could gain a support. The silk, grape, and wheat harvests had been destroyed, the olive was likely to perish from neglect, there were no animals for the plough, no implements for husbandry, nor was life safe in the fields. He adds: "There was never, perhaps, a darker hour for missions in Syria; yet we are becoming acquainted with the people more rapidly than ever, and should we be permitted to visit them months hence, we shall have a most friendly welcome."

Rasheiya and Deir Mimas were burned. Cana and Alma, being far from the Druze district, were not invaded. Tripoli was undisturbed. The destroyers in the neighborhood of Baalbec were not Druzes, but Moslems and Metawales. It is a remarkable fact that, excepting perhaps in Damascus, no injury was offered to a missionary; and Protestants, when recognized as such, were generally safe. The arrival of ships of war and a detachment of the French army at Beirût, with apprehensions of an alliance of Christian powers for the protection of the Christian population, had, at first, a restraining, and finally, a controlling influence, on the Turkish government. The Prime Minister was sent to

Remarkable escape of missionaries and native Protestants.

Foreign interposition.

Damascus, and inflicted terrible justice on one or two hundred of the guilty there.

Effects of the war.

The direct effects of the war upon the missionary work were doubtless injurious. Immorality increased, the baser passions were aroused, and the hearts of many were hardened through suffering. But priestly and feudal power, the two greatest obstacles to the Gospel, were weakened, and new civil rights were secured to the Protestants. The respect for Protestant Christianity was increased, and prejudices were dissipated by witnessing its beneficent fruits; while multitudes were brought within the reach of the Gospel, who, but for these troubles, would never have heard its messages.

The connection of Mr. and Mrs. Benton with the Board and the mission terminated in June, 1861, though they remained in Syria some time longer.

Scripture translations.

The Arabic New Testament having been completed and published, the mission resolved to proceed, as soon as possible, with the translation and publication of the Old Testament, under the direction of Dr. Van Dyck. The British and Foreign Bible Society requested permission to adopt this version, instead of the one formerly issued by them. The result of a friendly negotiation was, that the American and the British and Foreign Bible Societies agreed to publish the version conjointly, from electrotype plates furnished by the former. The price of the

Coöperation of American and English Bible Societies.

reference edition was fixed at ten piasters, and of the pocket edition at five, or about forty and twenty cents, which placed them within reach of nearly all who could read.

The importance of this work cannot easily be overestimated. Imperfect translations, and type which seemed to caricature their alphabet, had done much to prejudice Arabic scholars against the Christian Scriptures. By the labors of the mission, these objections were now removed. The educated Arab finds a book printed in characters modeled after the most approved specimens of Arab caligraphy. He soon perceives the style to be that of a man who is master of this wonderful language in all its grammatical and idiomatic niceties and rich resources. As a literary work it secures his respect, and thus invites a candid perusal. If he reads it, he finds the truths of Christianity clearly and correctly stated. Its beneficial influence will yet be felt, it is hoped, not only by the Christian sects of Mount Lebanon and Syria, but by the many millions who speak that language in other parts of the world. This work alone, worth many times what the mission had cost, could not have been accomplished, except by Christian scholars residing permanently among Arabs, and for substantially missionary purposes.

Importance of the version.

The sale of the Scriptures, notwithstanding the poverty of the people, was unprecedented. In 1859, it amounted to four hundred and forty-eight copies; in 1860, to four thousand two hundred and ninety-three, — a nearly ten fold increase.

Sale of the Scriptures.

Dr. Van Dyck was preparing a voweled edition of the New Testament, suitable for Mohammedans, written in the style of the Koran, which required much care and labor. This was completed in 1863.

A voweled New Testament.

The field manifestly brightened in the two or three years after the war. There was an interesting development of the missionary spirit. Not less than six different missionary societies were formed, embracing nearly all the Protestants of the various towns and villages, and a commendable degree of liberality was shown by the natives in collecting and contributing. A hundred dollars thus raised will not appear a small amount to any one, who knows the extreme poverty of most of the congregations. There had been a great influx of population at Beirût, and preaching services, during some months, were held daily. The Sabbath-school numbered two hundred, and the children sang the same songs in Arabic, which American children love to sing in their own language. The mountain stations reported unusually large and attentive audiences. Ain Zehalty was wholly under Protestant influences. Its civil ruler was a member of the Protestant church, and its church edifice, purged of its altar and pictures, was no longer used for the idolatrous

The field brightening.

Greek service. The Gospel was preached in nine places in connection with the Sidon station, the congregations had doubled their number, and schools of both sexes were demanded. There were cases of unusual interest among the young men. Hasbeiya and Rasheiya were not yet safe for the return of their people, but their Protestants retained an ardor in the cause which was very encouraging. Ibl and Deir Mimas were still centres of evangelical light, and the people of Boaida, numbering one hundred, were all professed Protestants, and placed themselves under Biblical instruction. Mr. Ford and his family spent the summer in the district of which Deir Mimas is the centre, and more than thirty women were taught to read by Mrs. Ford. The field was open for schools, for preaching, and for influencing individuals, families, and communities. The only drawback was the want of laborers.

Brief extracts from a letter of Mr. H. H. Jessup, written in March, 1863, portray the work at that time.

"Delegation after delegation, of men from various villages and different sects, call upon and write to us, entreating us not to neglect them. They ask for preachers, and we have none to send. They ask for schools, and we have not the means to support them. We are in *great straits*, and lay the case before our Christian brethren at home, throwing the responsibility upon those to whom God has given the means, and especially upon the young men in a course of preparation for the ministry."

"The people of the village of Ain Kunyeh, near the Lake of Merom, on the upper waters of the Jordan, have with one consent turned away their priest, shut up their place of worship, and are entreating one of our Protestant helpers to come and teach them the way of life."

"A few Sabbaths since, while we were assembled for divine service in the Beirût chapel, a crowd of thirty men came in, and with difficulty found seats, so full was the chapel already. Upon inquiry, after service, we learned that they are from the village of Rasheiya-el-Wady, north of Mount Hermon, and are a part of the residue of the people who escaped the massacre in that place in 1860. They ask for a teacher, or native preacher, but we can give them only the most indefinite promises."

"Twenty men from the village of Koryet-el-Hosson, near the famous castle Kolat-el-Hosson, half-way between Tripoli and Hums, write that they too have seen the light, and wish some one to come and instruct them; but what can we do for them, when the twenty-five men of Sheikh Mohammed, who petitioned us some time since, have been sent away empty?"

"This morning a white-bearded priest called, with his aged brother, and several younger men. They declared their wish to become Protestants, and beg most earnestly for a school. They belong to a large and powerful family, and the Lord may use them as the entering wedge, to open that strong Greek district to the gospel. What shall we answer them?"

Daoud Pasha, the new papal Governor, secured in 1862 by foreign intervention for Mount Lebanon, was at first supposed to be a bigot, and a tool of the Jesuits, but he soon proved himself an impartial and excellent ruler. He had several Protestants in office about him, in very important situations. Instead of objecting to missionaries establishing schools, he encouraged all efforts to educate the people.

A good governor.

Among other evidences of an advance it may be stated, that in Hums two hundred and fifty persons avowed themselves Protestants, and sought earnestly for a Christian instructor. It was immediately decided to send them Suleeba Jerwan, who had lived two years in that place with Mr. Wilson, and was well acquainted with the people; and the native missionary society at Beirût decided to support him as their first missionary. This was done with a cordiality and earnestness that was most promising. Hasbeiya women and girls pledged weekly contributions for the spread of the Gospel, some promised two cents a week, and some half a cent; but even these small sums were large for them, and they gave with a hearty gladness that was most cheering. Two hundred and thirty Marou-

Further evidence of progress.

ites in Bteddin had for months adhered steadfastly to the Protestant faith, and a flourishing school existed among them. In Cana the Protestant community had been augmented threefold, and the same was true of Deir Mimas. There had never been a time when so many were inquiring on the subject of religion; and a greater number avowed themselves Protestants within twelve months, than in the whole previous forty years. A new church edifice was built in Merj-Aiyun, costing about five hundred dollars, without drawing from the resources of the Board, and a new church had been formed in that district of seventeen members, most of them from the Hasbeiya church. In the Sidon field six persons had been admitted to the church, and there were twenty-two hopeful candidates. In Beirût and Abeih, there were seventeen such candidates, besides nine admitted to the communion. Bible classes were largely increased, and an unusual number of adults were learning to read, that they might study the Scriptures. Thirty of the best Sabbath-school songs published in America, had been translated into Arabic, and published at the expense of a sewing society at Beirût, and thus gospel truths, in an attractive form, were reaching the children all over the land.

The president of the missionary society at Beirût stated in May, 1862, that in the two previous months, they had not only sent a missionary to Hums, but had sent also a colporter to Jezzin, maintained religious meetings every Sabbath at Kefr Shima, and employed a city missionary in Beirût.

But with these signs of prosperity, there seems to have been a need of chastening. The clergy of the Greek church at Hums, excited, as was supposed, by foreign influence, set their people so against the Protestants, that it was feared few would be able to stand. The native brethren were stoned and beaten in the streets, and abused by all classes. Quite a large number returned, nominally, to the Greek church; but many of these commenced a Bible class in the Greek church itself, thus bringing the truth to many, who would not otherwise have heard it. About fifteen men stood firm, and met nightly with Suleeba, for reading the Scriptures, prayer, and conference. The priests had expected the utter overthrow of Protestantism, and were enraged at the firmness of these brethren, and forbade all dealings with them. Letters to Suleeba from the missionaries were taken from the mail, read, and destroyed, and the Protestant places of meeting were assailed with stones. In the midst of these trials, Suleeba wrote expressing his gratitude to God for sustaining grace. Some alleviation was experienced through the efforts of Colonel Fraser, Her Britannic Majesty's Commissioner, so that the Protestant community became regularly organized, with a representative in the Mejlis, and a tax roll distinct from other sects.

Persecution.

The Protestants in Ain Zehalty were also called to suffer. An order having come from Constantinople, requiring the restoration of all church edifices to their original sects, Daoud Pasha issued an order for giving up the edifice at Ain Zehalty. He must have acted under a misapprehension, since the building had never been the property of the bishop, but was built and still owned by the family of Khalil, the Protestant preacher. The Catholics were a very small minority in the village, yet the edifice appears not to have been recovered. Another convenient house of worship was soon after provided by Protestant friends.

Mr. H. H. Jessup wrote respecting Hums:—

A significant event.

"Quite recently, one of the more enlightened among the Greeks was taken ill, and sent for Suleeba, the native helper. He went, and found quite a company of relatives and friends. The sick man asked him to read a portion of Scripture. The passage selected contained the ten commandments, and while he was reading the *second*, the wife of the sick man exclaimed,—'Is that the Word of God? If it is, read it again.' He did so, when she arose and tore down a wooden picture of a saint at the head of the bed, declaring that henceforth there should be no idol worship in that house; and then, taking a knife, she scraped the paint from the picture, and took it for use in the kitchen. This was done with the approbation of all present.

The case is the more remarkable, as it was the first instance in Syria, in which a woman had taken so decided a stand in advance of the rest of the family."

The manifest agency of the Holy Spirit is the highest encouragement in the missionary work. "One of the members of the Beirût church," Mr. Jessup writes, "has passed through an interesting religious experience this summer. He was for a time troubled with blasphemous thoughts, till he gave himself up as lost. His language was not unlike that of Bunyan in his "Grace Abounding;" and only after protracted struggles in prayer, the study of God's word, and finally resolving to go forward and do his duty in both light and darkness, did he find relief. The case was interesting as indicating the presence of God's Spirit, in leading him through a most severe struggle into ultimate peace in believing. Several young Protestants of Hasbeiya, resident in Beirût, are now passing through very deep conviction of sin. I have rarely seen persons so completely broken down by a sense of their lost condition. On Monday I spent several hours with two young people, who were passing through deep waters. They burst into tears, exclaiming, "We are lost, we are lost!" The Spirit of God was striving with them. Never have I felt more deeply the need of Divine aid, than when trying to lead these heavy-laden ones to Christ. Yet the missionary can have no more delightful labor than this."

Evidence of Divine agency.

The mission was strengthened, in 1863, by the arrival of Rev. Messrs. Samuel Jessup, Philip Berry, and George Edward Post, M. D., and their wives. Miss Temple retired from the mission in consequence of the obstructions to the higher education of girls growing out of the massacres, but with the esteem of all her associates. Mr. Lyons, broken down by overwork, was also under the necessity of withdrawing from the field. The girls' boarding-school had been transferred from Sûk el Ghûrb to Sidon, where it was under the care of Miss Mason.

Changes in the mission.

The population of Beirût was now not less than seventy thousand. A bank, a carriage road to Damascus, steamers plying to almost every maritime country in Europe, telegraphs in several directions, numerous schools and hospitals, and three printing presses, made it the commercial and intellectual capital of Syria.

Growth of Beirût.

The tendency was to intellectual rather than spiritual progress, and there was a growing demand for education. The Jesuits were striving to reap the benefit of this, by opening colleges and seminaries in various parts of the country; nor could the fact be overlooked, that zealous Protestant educators, from different parts of Europe, were becoming so numerous at Beirût as to embarrass the mission in its natural development. The exigency at length constrained the mission to consider whether

Demand for education.

advantage should not be taken of the offer of Christian friends at home to found a Protestant College at Beirût.

Proposal for a Protestant College.

This was well, as will appear in the sequel. But it is impossible not to see, that the progress of the mission, in the years immediately following 1863, — in the increase of converts, and the multiplication of churches, with native preachers and pastors, — was not such as the facts already stated gave reason to expect. This the brethren on the ground foresaw, and their anxious appeals for help abound on the pages of the "Missionary Herald," and were enforced by appeals from the Prudential Committee. The "Annual Report" for 1863 thus states the deficiency of laborers at that time: —

What hindered a more rapid progress in the mission.

"The field north of Beirût, a hundred miles long and fifty wide, has no missionary, although hundreds in Hums, and the large district of Akkar, are looking to the mission for instruction. A score of villages, in each one of which a faithful preacher would find an audience, do not receive a visit once a year from a gospel minister. Mount Lebanon, with its four hundred thousand inhabitants, scattered through its thousand villages, into nearly every one of which more or less light has penetrated, and from which cries for help constantly come, has but two missionaries; and one of them is confined, for the most part, to the Abeih Seminary. The southern district, comprising one half of the Syria mission field, with its ten regular preaching places, crippled by the disability of its oldest native helper and by the death of another, has but two missionaries, one of whom is just commencing to learn Arabic. Within the last eight years, thirteen missionary laborers, male and female, have entered the Syria field, while twenty-five have left it. During this period, the work has increased tenfold. Many who have fallen asleep took part in sowing, where now the harvest is so great that the few who remain cannot gather it; and unless the Lord of the harvest send more laborers, much precious fruit will be lost."

It is painfully evident, that the degree of missionary spirit in the churches at home then fell short of the providential calls for evangelical labor in this field. Yet it is by no means certain what would have been the effect of a very large, sudden increase in the working forces. Without the restraining grace of God, it might have been the occasion of a fierce and malignant outbreak of opposition.

The deficiency of laborers sufficiently accounts for the slow progress, and even the decline there was in not a few of the places named; as in Tripoli, and Hums, not to speak of promising villages in the western and southern sections. Churches, towns, cities in the most favored portions of New England would suffer a decline in religion and morals, if left, as these places necessarily were, with no more of the means of grace.

CHAPTER XL.

SYRIA.

1863–1869.

MRS. HENRY H. JESSUP died at Alexandria, after a prolonged sickness, on the 2d of July, 1864, whither her husband had taken her on his way to the United States. Mr. George C. Hurter, after laboring twenty-three years as printer and secular agent with great usefulness, found himself constrained by domestic circumstances to withdraw from the mission. Mr. Bird was prostrated with a dangerous sickness for several months at Abeih, but a merciful Providence spared his valuable life.

Personal.

A boarding high-school was established at Beirût by Mr. Butrus Bistany, with nearly a hundred and fifty pupils. The charge for tuition and board was large for that country, yet the school was self-supporting. The pupils were made up of Greeks, Maronites, Greek-Catholics, Druzes, Moslems, and Protestants. A girls' boarding-school in the same city, under native instruction and government, promised also to be soon self-sustaining

Boarding schools.

The common schools of the mission were twenty-five, with five hundred and forty-eight pupils. The Seminary at Abeih had thirty-three pupils, a larger number than ever before. Five were in the theological department, and several others gave good evidence of piety. The graduates of this institution were now scattered over a wide region. The boarding-school for girls at Sidon, under Miss Mason, had ten pupils, and was making a favorable impression. It became evident, however, that pupils could not be obtained there sufficient to warrant so large an outlay, taking also into view the unhealthiness of that climate, and Miss Mason returned home, though with great reluctance. The girls' boarding-school at Beirût, under the care of Mr. Aramon and Miss Rufka Gregory, was prosperous.

Printing.

The printing, in 1862, amounted to eight thousand volumes and nine thousand tracts, making an aggregate of 6,869,000 pages, more than two thirds of which were Scripture. The number of pages from the beginning, was about 50,000,000. Somewhat more than six thousand volumes of Scripture were distributed during the year.

Completion of the Arabic translation of the Scriptures.

The translation of the Scriptures into Arabic was completed on the 22d of August, 1864, and the printing of the whole Arabic Bible in March of the next year. This event, of the highest importance to a large portion of the human race, was appropriately celebrated by the missionaries and their native brethren. In the upper room where Dr. Smith had labored on the translation eight years, and Dr. Van Dyck eight years more, the assembled missionaries gave thanks to God for the completion of this arduous work. "Just then," writes one of them, "the sound of many voices arose from below, and on throwing open the door, we heard a large company of native young men, laborers at the press and members of the Protestant community, singing to the tune of 'Hebron' a new song, 'even praise to our God,' composed for the occasion by one of their number in the Arabic language. Surely not for many centuries have the angels in heaven heard a sweeter sound arising from Syria, than the voices of this band of pious young men, singing a hymn composed by one of themselves, ascribing glory and praise to God, that now, for the first time, the Word of God is given to their nation and tongue in its purity." The hymn was composed by Mr. Ibrahim Sarkis and translated by Dr. H. H. Jessup, as follows: —

"Hail day, thrice blessed of our God!
Rejoice, let all men bear a part,
Complete at length thy printed word,
Lord, print its truth on every heart.

"To Him who gave his precious word,
Arise and with glad praises sing;
Exalt and magnify our Lord,
Our Maker and our Glorious King.

"Doubting and darkness flee away
Before thy truth's light-giving sun,
Thy powerful word, if heeded, may
Give guidance to each erring one.

"Lord, spare thy servant, through whose toil
Thou giv'st us this, of books the best;
Bless all who shared the arduous task,
From Eastern land, or distant West.

"Amen! Amen! lift up the voice;
Praise God whose mercy 's e'er the same;
His goodness all our song employs,
Thanksgivings then to His Great Name."

Multiplication of copies.

Ten different editions of parts of the Scriptures were printed as the version was gradually prepared for publication, and over thirty thousand copies had been put into circulation, nearly all by sale. The demand for the volume, in one form or another, after the version was completed, was greater than the mission presses could meet, though worked by steam. The American Bible Society wisely undertook to electrotype several editions of different sizes, and Dr. Van Dyck came to New York to superintend the work. But after the royal octavo edition had been stereotyped, it was thought best for him to return to Syria, with the understanding that the Bible Society would enable him to electrotype the version in other forms, at Beirût.

The press was now unable to meet the demand

which had arisen for the books, as well as for the Bible. The issues were called for on the southern and eastern coasts of Arabia, and in India, and a box of them was sent to the interior of Africa.

The administration of Daoud Pasha, the Christian Governor of Mount Lebanon, continued to be marked by commendable justice, vigor, and liberality, and there was a sense of security to which the land had long been a stranger. Industry and thrift began to appear, and all the interests of society received an impulse. Much, however, depended on the foreign Protestant Powers exerting a proper influence on the councils of the Turkish government in favor of religious liberty.

Improved government of Lebanon.

The only ordination of a native preacher by the mission, up to this time, was that of the Rev. John Wortabet, in 1853, afterwards pastor of the Hasbeiya church. On the 10th of May, 1864, Mr. Suleeba Jerwan received ordination at Abeih. He had gone successfully through a four years' course of study in the Seminary, and had for some time proved himself faithful and efficient as a teacher and preacher.

The native ministry.

The Druzes had a prosperous high school at Abeih, under the special patronage of His Excellency Daoud Pasha, supported by the income from their religious establishments. Both of the instructors were Protestants and graduates of the Abeih Seminary. Though not a religious

Druse High School.

institution, such a school must have had an important bearing on the future of that singular people. In 1866, the Principal left, and was succeeded by another Protestant, also a graduate of the mission Seminary. Referring to the Druzes, the brethren of the Abeih station close their report for the year 1864 with the following remarkable declaration: —

Value of Druze protection.

"While it is true that the government of the mountain was never better, and we are free to open schools wherever parents dare send their children, it is no less true that the Protestants are a small and hated minority. Providence has made the Druzes a wall of defense, for the present. To them, under God, it is due that we pursue our labors on this mountain."

Death of Tannûs El Haddad.

Tannûs El Haddad, the oldest and most esteemed native helper in the mission, died in 1864, after more than thirty years of efficient labor. "A guileless, spiritual man, whose lovely spirit disarmed the enmity even of those who hated his religion. The church of Christ in Syria owes much to the holy life and faithful teaching of this man of God. The missionaries owe much. He long upheld their hands by the strength of his affection and sympathy."

Native pastor at Hums.

The installation of Suleeba Jerwan as pastor of the church in Hums, occurred in 1865. The Protestants there had long resisted the settlement of a native pastor, hoping to obtain the residence of an American missionary, but their welcome to the native pastor was now cordial. His wife was an excellent young woman, formerly a pupil in Mr. Bird's family, and his assistant in the instruction of her sex. Both pastor and people had a varied experience in after years, not unlike what is often seen in Christian lands.

Remarkable awakening at Safeeta.

In the spring of 1865, the oppression of the Turkish government became so unbearable at Safeeta, in the district of Tripoli, that a large number of the people resolved to seek relief in Protestantism. A deputation of sixty heads of families, representing nearly five hundred souls, was accordingly sent to the missionaries at Tripoli. Their motives were wholly secular, and they were not at all aware of the spiritual object of the missionaries. This had to be explained, and they were told, that it was beyond the power of the mission to afford civil protection. The government allowed them to register their names as Protestants, and they listened with marked attention to the spiritual instructions of Dr. Post; Mr. Samuel Jessup, the other missionary, being then at Hums. On leaving, they asked for books, and to be more thoroughly inducted into the new way.

The region of Safeeta was new to Protestant missions, but was populous and fertile, and bordering on the Nusaireyeh. Among the names handed to

Dr. Post, as interested in this movement, were one hundred and fifty of this strange people, and there were a number of them in the deputation; but all of this class soon fell away. Dr. Post visited Safeeta in May, and arrangements were effected with the government, which opened the door for Christian teaching. He had audiences of one hundred and fifty every night, listening with reverent attention to words they had never heard before. "I taught them hymns," he writes, "and heard them repeat passages of Scripture and answer religious questions. On Sunday they commenced coming at five, A. M., and kept pouring in upon me all day long, till ten P. M.,—just allowing me time to eat, and not even leaving the room while I did that. Our large meetings in the evenings were by the light of the moon, as an open light would have been extinguished, and we had no lantern. A most interesting feature was the number of women in the audiences, an exceptional thing in all new religious movements in Syria." Two horsemen came from distant villages, to inquire about the new faith and sect. The motive was doubtless secular, but there is always hope where the Gospel gains a hearing.

The fires of persecution soon began to burn with fury. The Greek bishop bribed the Turkish government, and the people were driven from their homes; everything was broken that could be broken, everything eaten that could be eaten,

Remarkable persecution.

and women were left to the brutal lusts of the Turkish soldiers. It was surprising with what tenacity the people held out against all this. A few had become earnest inquirers; but without a more general acquaintance with the truth they could not be expected long to stand such an onset. Some relief came after a few weeks, through the death by cholera of the Greek bishop.

Failing to find relief from English intervention, the newly made Protestants went *en masse* to the governor of Tripoli; and failing to meet him, they then crossed the mountains to the Governor-general at Damascus, taking with them their wives, that the sight of their distress might move the heart of the Moslem ruler. At last they secured a hearing from him, and he promptly removed the oppressive tax-gatherer at Safeeta, and gave the poor people some money in token of his sympathy. But returning to their homes, they were still oppressed by their local governor. Mr. Samuel Jessup writes in October, that poverty and want had come upon them beyond anything seen elsewhere in Syria, excepting at Hasbeiya. Some had no means of buying their daily bread. They were promised a restoration of all that had been taken from them, if they would return to their old faith, but they stood firm. They desired a school for their girls, and a married teacher was sent them for a boys' school, so as to accommodate a female teacher in his family.

Some months later, the cattle of a Protestant strayed, and while driving them home he was met by one of their persecutors, of the house of Beshoor, who, with some savage Nusairiyeh, threw him on the ground, stamped upon him, and drew a sword, threatening to kill him if he did not desist from his unclean religion. They dared not do more through fear of witnesses. Again, the plowmen of this same house plowed up the wheat belonging to the Protestants, ruining their hopes of a coming harvest, and leaving them without means to pay their taxes; which they must pay or go to prison. They also gathered all the olives of the Protestants, reducing them to the greatest straits for the means of living. The Moslem governor received large bribes to exterminate the sect, and would give them no hearing, but quartered his soldiers on them, who ate up all their scanty food, and distrained even their miserable cooking utensils, that they might sell them for barley for their horses. Many lived from day to day on what they could beg, or borrow. Still, after a year of such trials, they remained firm; which is the more wonderful, as only a few of them gave evidence of piety, and the time had not come for organizing them into a church. The school was doubtless helpful, being a decided success. Even the shepherds took tracts and primers, and studied them while tending their flocks.

In January, 1867, the whole Protestant community

of Safeeta were arrested, men, women, and children, and imprisoned in a small room, and a fire of cut straw was made on the floor to torture them with smoke. This wanton cruelty was based on a false demand made on them for money. Their sufferings were so great that they were finally released. In the evening, while assembled for worship, with their native preacher, government horsemen broke open and plundered their houses, and in the night drove them all, old and young, mothers and children, boys and girls, into the wilderness.

The terrible experience of this people in the summer of 1869, somewhat more than two years later, is too suggestive and interesting to be passed in silence. I give the facts as related by Mr. Samuel Jessup.

"For four years, a large number have been Protestants, and the oppressors have added persecution to oppression. Many fell away at first, but since then we have seen no special signs of apostasy until lately. Their enemies recently made a desperate effort to crush out Protestantism from that region. They took the leading men, one by one, and led them through fire and perils of all kinds; promising, at every step, to give immediate relief, if they would only return to the Greek Church. They fulfilled their promises to some who yielded, and then increased the pressure on the others. At length, seizing the opportunity when our teacher was absent, they made another grand onset. On Sunday morning, the Greek bishop and the abbots of the neighboring convents, with priests and people from all the region around, together with a great number of horsemen and footmen, made a grand parade, and came down like locusts upon the Protestants. Their former oppressor is dead, but his son, Tamir Beshoor, is making his little finger thicker than his father's loins. He headed a grand parade, and brought with him a supply of new garments, which he had purchased as bribes for the occasion. With the bishop and others, he entered the house of every Protestant, and by bribes and promises, followed by fiendish threats, carried off many captives. Some few had previously sold themselves, and agreed to take their stand on this occasion, and then they headed the crowd, and declared that every Protestant had decided to return, and that Protestantism was dead. Where they found a house locked, they forced it open, and sprinkled holy water in it.

"But though their success was far too great, it was not complete. They succeeded in taking with them, that morning, twenty-one males. Eleven of them have not been to the Greek church since that time, but continue to meet with our brethren for prayer; and though it is now an important Greek fast, they do not observe it. The other ten either dare not or care not to come back to us, though all came to see me.

"Before finishing their work that Sunday morning, they sent men to our school-room, broke it open, sprinkled it with holy water, and stole our bell."

The firmness of some of the church-members is thus described: "After exhausting their catalogue of promises and threats on one, he said to them, — 'Take my property, my house, my clothes, my family, even my body, and do with them what you will, but my soul you cannot have, and nothing will induce me to leave Christ.' Another said, when they came to his house, — 'Come in, and let us read in the New Testament together, and perhaps you will see that we are right.' One girl, who had been two years in the Sidon school, saw her parents and relatives all fall into the procession; but when special effort was made to induce her to yield, she said, — 'Though you should cut my body in pieces, I will never go with you.'

Firmness of the persecuted people.

"I reached Safeeta a few days after, and found that those who had stood firm had been obliged to flee for safety, and did not dare return until I went there. The wrath of their persecutors seems to have reached its height, and the poor people know not what to do. Appeal to the government seems useless, for it is from the government that their chief oppressor gets his power to persecute. All who went back came to call on me, and most of them attended the services. They said, in palliation of their course, 'We are flesh and blood, and have families to support. We have waited for deliverance for years, and now Tamir (the chief oppressor) says, Come back and I will restore to you all; remain as you are, and I will strip you of the little you have left, and drive you out of the country. And so we went back, but our hearts are with you, and we will come here too, though they compelled our bodies to go with them.' One woman showed a striped gown, threw it on the ground, and trampling on it said, with tears in her eyes, 'With that they bought my husband.' Some of the women, with tears and entreaties, tried to keep their husbands and friends from going, telling them that death was better."[1]

The persecution closed.

Twenty men were standing firm at Safeeta in February of the following year, though there had been little abatement of persecution. In April Dr. Jessup wrote, that it had just terminated, and the brethren at the Tripoli station had good hopes that there would be peace in that long persecuted community. This was owing, in great measure, to the interference of the American and English Consuls-general, and their influence with the Governor-general of Syria.

Decline and recovery of the church at Hums.

The people of Hums becoming dissatisfied with their pastor, Suleeba, his connection was dissolved, three years after his settlement. The church remained in a divided condition for a year or more, without any celebration

[1] *Missionary Herald*, 1869, pp. 407–409.

of the Lord's Supper. In the summer of 1869, Mr. Samuel Jessup visited the city, and finding the Protestants in a better state of feeling, invited the communicants to assemble at the Lord's table. All came and seemed to enjoy it as a season of rest and refreshment, after a long and weary wandering. They were ready to take a native pastor who suited them, and pay the larger part of his salary. They needed one well acquainted with the historical defenses of the Gospel, because of the inroads of European Jesuits and French infidel literature. Suleeba found demands for his faithful labors in other places. "The news," says Dr. Jessup, "from 'scattered and peeled' Safeeta and from distracted Hums, is alike cheering, and indicative of progress in the right direction."

Native missions.

The Tripoli station sent forth two of the Safeeta church-members as missionaries to visit the villages to the north and east, sending two together, as it would not be safe for one to go alone. The native missionary society at Beirût employed a zealous colporter, whose tours took a wide range, from Acre on the south to Hamath and even to Aleppo on the north, and his monthly reports showed that, throughout the country, there was not only urgent need of such labor, but also an increasing number prepared to profit by the visits of the gospel messenger. During the latter part of the year, another person was employed in similar work near Beirût. He also testified to a great increase of desire among the people for religious instruction.

Administration of Daoud Pasha.

Daoud Pasha, after inaugurating important reforms and improvements on Lebanon, was promoted to a seat in the cabinet at Constantinople. He had started a newspaper, "The Lebanon," established telegraphic lines, commenced a carriage road, encouraged education, and made his pashalic the safest in the empire for travelling. His successor was Franco Pasha, a Latin Catholic. The Beirût Arabic official journal, in speaking of his arrival, says, that "although attached to his own religion, he is free from bigotry, and will guarantee liberty of conscience to all."

Accessions to the mission.

The mission was strengthened in 1867 by the arrival of Samuel S. Mitchell and Isaac N. Lowry, and their wives; and in 1869, of James S. Dennis, and Misses Eliza D. Everett, and Nellie A. Carruth. Messrs. Berry and Mitchell were constrained, by the failure of health after a short service, to leave the mission. Miss Carruth, also, though deeply interested in the work, and after valuable service in the girls' school, felt constrained soon to return to the United States.

Books published.

Among the books printed in this time, were Edwards' "History of Redemption;" Bickersteth's "Scripture Hand-book," with additions by Mr. Calhoun; a large Psalm and Hymn Book; Curwen's "New System of Musical Notation;"[1] a Children's Hymn Book; Bistany's Arabic Dictionary, and his Elements of Grammar; and an Arabic Almanac, probably the first ever printed in Arabic, although "Al-Manakh" (the climate) is an Arabic word. The press was now under the direction of Mr. Henry Thomson, a son of Dr. Thomson, who relieved the Beirût station of a heavy burden of care. The necessary preparations were completed in 1868 for electrotyping the Arabic Scriptures in Beirût.

Accession to the publishing department.

[1] By this, musical notes written in a syllabic form can be given, like the Arabic, from right to left. The staff, notes, and signatures are dispensed with, and single letters are arranged in succession, with separations by dots and marks. As a result, the ordinary Arabic types can be used to print the most intricate music.

CHAPTER XLI.

SYRIA.

1869–1870.

THOUGH the Seminary at Abeih had a few students preparing for the ministry, under Mr. Calhoun, it could not properly be called a Theological Seminary. Only at Hasbeiya, Hums, and Ain Zehalty had native pastors been found for the churches. There were five churches without pastors. The eight churches had two hundred and forty-five members. The thirty-one common schools numbered a thousand male and one hundred and seventy female pupils. Eight of the teachers were church-members, and four of these were females. The demand for education was beyond the ability of the mission to supply.

But few students in theology.

At the recommendation of the Prudential Committee, a Theological Seminary was commenced at Abeih in May, 1869; and Dr. Jessup from Beirût, and Mr. Eddy from Sidon, were associated with Mr. Calhoun in its instruction. Seven students composed the first class, and, with but one exception, evinced a good Christian spirit,

Institution of a theological seminary.

studied hard, and seemed anxious to live an active and useful Christian life. The five winter months of their vacation were spent in evangelical labors.

As far back as 1865, there was a prosperous female boarding-school at Beirût, under the care of Mr. Aramon and Miss Rufka Gregory, natives of Syria. In the following year, this school had thirty boarders and twenty day scholars. It was the first Protestant school in Syria that demanded pay for the education of girls, but its receipts for tuition and board equaled about half the expenses. "Among the causes," say the brethren of the Beirût station, "which operated to prevent the raising of the rates of board and tuition to a self-supporting basis, was the existence of competing schools furnished with European teachers, rendering it difficult for the seminary to induce parents to pay the full expense. This was a grave difficulty, and one which, in one form or another, has met every attempt to establish the principle of self-support in Syria, in all departments of our work; but it only makes it the more important that this native institute, with native teachers and adapted to native tastes and habits, should be steadily sustained, lest the impulse already given in the direction of self-support, be lost." A building was completed for the school in 1867, at the cost of about $9,000, chiefly the result of contributions in the United States, but without any organic connection with the mission. Of its

Female boarding-school.

seventy-six pupils fifty-seven were boarders, and the income was $3,220 in gold, which was $1,000 short of its expenses. There was still the impediment of unwise competition. The pupils were from Moslem, Greek, and Greek-Catholic, as well as Protestant families; though it was well known that the institution was an evangelizing agency, and that all were expected to attend Protestant worship on the Sabbath, and were daily taught in the Bible.

In the absence of Miss Gregory on account of failing health, Mr. and Mrs. Aramon carried on the school, with the assistance of ladies from the mission. The school increased in numbers and the examination in 1868 was attended by a great throng of the people, from all classes and all sects. It was a noticeable fact that Mohammedan parents in Beirût were beginning to insist earnestly upon the education of their girls. The Beirût Arabic official journal, the "Kadethat el-Akhbax," published a list of schools in the city,—possibly somewhat exaggerated,—in which it was said, that there were two thousand girls and three thousand boys and young men in the various Protestant, Greek, Maronite, Catholic, and Mohammedan schools.

The school passed under the care of Misses Everett and Carruth on their arrival in Syria, and substantial progress was made towards self-support, but less than would have been but for the French, English, and German schools, which tended to draw away the girls, and the families they represented, from the influence of the missionaries.

There was, also, a female boarding-school at Sidon, which had been growing in numbers and influence. The scholars were all Protestants, selected with care from the various schools of the country. "They have come," wrote Mr. Eddy, "from all parts of the land, — from Hums and Safeeta on the north, from Mount Lebanon on the east, and the district of Merj Aiyun on the south; and besides the good they gain for themselves while here, they will carry light and civilization, and we trust religious influence with them to their widely scattered homes." The school was in the immediate charge of Mrs. Watson and her daughter, English ladies, and more recently Miss Jacombs, for five years a teacher on Mount Lebanon, and supported by a society of ladies in England. It was fully in sympathy, however, with the mission, and had the sympathy, prayers, and aid of English Christians. The number of pupils was twenty.

THE SYRIAN PROTESTANT COLLEGE.

The desire for education had visibly increased, and was due, in part, to commercial intercourse with western nations, and the interference of foreign powers in the political affairs of the country; but far more to the schools, books, preaching, and personal influence of missionaries. Schools had been multiplying for elementary and high school

Demand for a college.

instruction, but there was no provision for a liberal education. The Jesuits, indeed, had institutions, but their teaching was partial, fitted to repress inquiry, and exclusively to foster their own ecclesiastical and sectarian ends.

The demand for a Protestant college was discussed

THE SYRIAN PROTESTANT COLLEGE.

at a meeting of the mission, in the spring of 1861, and again in the following August, when an outline of the proposed scheme was presented.[1]

[1] In this statement concerning the College, I make such use as my limits will allow, of an able document, drawn up by Prof. D. Stuart Dodge, and kindly sent me, at my request, by the President, Dr. Daniel Bliss. It bears date May, 1872.

"The objects deemed essential, were to enable natives to obtain, in their own country, in their own language, and at a moderate cost, a thorough literary, scientific, and professional education; to found an institution, which should be conducted on principles strictly evangelical, but not sectarian; with doors open to youth of every Oriental sect and nationality, who would conform to its regulations, but so ordered that students, while elevated intellectually and spiritually, should not materially change their native customs. The hope was entertained, that much of the instruction might at once be intrusted to pious and competent natives, and that ultimately the teaching could be left in the hands of those, who had been raised up by the College itself."

Its objects.

The curriculum embraced a period of four years; and the studies were the Arabic Language and Literature, Mathematics, the Natural Sciences, the Modern Languages, Turkish Law and Jurisprudence, and Medicine, — the last to have special prominence, since the East was filled with ignorant native quacks and medical jugglers. A leading place would also be given to Moral Science, and Biblical Literature, with the Scriptures as a constant text-book. Theology, as a system, would be left to the care of the several missions.

Range of its studies.

It was thought that the American Board could not undertake so large a literary work in any one mission, and that the College should be separate from and independent of the Board and its missions, as such; but that, being on so broad a basis, other evangelical bodies among the Arabic-speaking race might be invited to share in its advantages and control. Denominational distinctions set aside, those engaged in similar missionary operations could unite in an enterprise designed to advance their common interests.

Why an independent institution.

The College was to be at Beirût, the chief seaport of Syria, and a place of enterprise and growing importance, occupying a central position in respect to all the Arabic races. The local Board of Directors was to be composed of American and British missionaries and residents of Syria and Egypt, with several consular officials and leading merchants; of which a quorum should always reside in Beirût and its immediate vicinity.

Its location and government.

The Rev. Daniel Bliss, six years a missionary of the American Board on Mount Lebanon, was cheerfully released by the Prudential Committee from his connection with the mission, that he might take the Presidency of the College, and visit the United States and England to obtain the needful endowment.

To secure public confidence, it was found indispensable to have the institution incorporated in America, with a responsible Board of Trustees. A charter was accordingly obtained, in April, 1863, in accordance with the laws of the State of New York, and in May, 1864, additional power to hold real and personal estate was granted by act of the Legislature. A constitution was framed, binding the institution to evangelical and unsectarian principles; formally constituting the body, appointed by the mission, a local Board of Managers, with large liberty in administration; and defining the relations between the Boards in America and Syria and those of the various officers to be connected with the College. It further provided, that the Board of Trustees should have the right to exercise final authority in all matters, and that funds for endowments should be retained in the United States, the income only to be transmitted to the East.

Its endowment.

An endowment fund of $100,000 was secured from a small number of contributors, the Trustees and their immediate friends being the largest donors.[1] In addition to this, Dr. Bliss obtained £3,000 in England; Lords Shaftesbury, Stratford de Redcliffe, Dufferin, Strangford, and Calthorpe, among the nobility, indorsing the enterprise; and the Turkish Missions Aid Society rendered valuable assistance. The "Syrian Improvement Committee" gave £1,000, from funds remaining after the relief of sufferers from the Lebanon massacres.

Dr. Bliss returned to Syria early in 1866. The

[1] Among the more active and influential of these, as I learn from other sources, was the Rev. D. Stuart Dodge. In 1872, the endowment fund was reported to be $130,000.

first college class consisted of fourteen members. A preparatory department was afterwards added, and eighty names have been enrolled in the two departments. The students have evinced, in most instances, an aptitude and zeal for study, that would be creditable in more favored lands. The charge for tuition is twenty-five dollars for the collegiate year of nine months; and fifty-five dollars additional for those who board in the institution. The sects represented are the Protestant, Orthodox-Greek, Papal-Greek, Latin, Maronite, Druze, Armenian, and Coptic.

Its students.

All boarders are required to be present at morning and evening prayers, and to attend Protestant worship and Bible classes on the Sabbath; and Bible lectures or Scripture recitations are of daily occurrence. A voluntary prayer-meeting is maintained by the students.

The religious influences.

Most of the thirteen who have graduated from the Academic Department, are acceptably employed as teachers of a higher grade in Syria and Egypt. Two have entered the Medical Department, and two are studying Law. The first Commencement was in July, 1870, and the addresses were in three languages. The College has a Medical Department, and the first medical class was graduated in July, 1871.

First graduating class.

A building fund of about $70,000 having been contributed chiefly by the donors to the endowment fund, a plot of nearly twenty acres of ground was purchased at Râs-Beirût, in the immediate vicinity of the city; facing Lebanon, overlooking the Mediterranean, healthy, accessible, yet sufficiently retired; and the edifice is in the process of erection. The corner stone was laid, December 7, 1871, by the Hon. William E. Dodge, and appropriate exercises, in English and Arabic, accompanied the ceremony. The College edifices.

The Medical Hall is located at some distance from the College edifice. These buildings may be seen from almost every quarter of the city, and from the villages on the western slopes of Lebanon; and they will be the first objects to greet the eyes of all who enter the harbor, and will stand as the exponents and dispensers of sound Christian learning.

The connection of this mission with the American Board continued until the latter part of the year 1870, wanting only two years of half a century, when the reunion of the Presbyterian Church gave rise to the question of a transfer of the mission to the Presbyterian Board. The events above described, connected with the Syrian Protestant College, favored such a result, and the question was kindly, though reluctantly entertained. On the 20th of September, 1870, the following paper was received at the Missionary House: — Transfer of the mission to the Presbyterian Board.

"The Syria mission, at a special meeting held in

Abeih, August 16, 1870, had laid before them two documents, one from the Prudential Committee of the American Board of Commissioners for Foreign Missions, and the other from the Committee of Conference of the General Assembly of the Presbyterian Church with the American Board, — touching the transfer of the mission from the American Board to the Presbyterian Board of Foreign Missions; and having given the subject their serious and prayerful consideration, they have adopted the following action: —

"1. That the mission regard the subject thus presented as one which has not originated with themselves, but as having been brought before them by the Providence of God; and as not to be decided at all by them on personal grounds or ecclesiastical preferences, but to be decided solely in view of its bearings upon the cause of Christ in this land, and among the churches at home.

"2. That the mission appreciate the delicacy and kindness with which the Prudential Committee of the American Board of Commissioners for Foreign Missions conveyed the consent of the Board to the withdrawal of its members from their service, with the view of forming a new connection, if they deem it expedient, and the hearty assurance of their readiness to continue the support of the mission should they decide to remain as heretofore.

"3. That they also equally appreciate the cordial

invitation extended to them by the Committee of the Presbyterian Church, and the pledge conveyed to the mission, that they shall enjoy, in the new proposed connection, all the freedom of action, 'in respect to their policy and ecclesiastical relations,' which they have hitherto possessed.

"4. That the mission find great difficulty in considering calmly and impartially a question involving their separation from the American Board, the severing of ties which have existed until within two years of half a century, which have been interwoven with the earliest recollections of childhood, which have grown strong by personal connection and active coöperation during years of service, and which we had anticipated would only be dissolved by death. No language can express how much of pain to their hearts the thought of this separation involves. Their relations to the Secretaries, to the Prudential Committee, and through them to the churches, have been most tender and happy.

"In these relations they have found the largest liberty and the fullest sympathy, and personally, the mission have no cause to desire a change.

"The feelings of the mission on this point will be more fully expressed by individual communications from its several members, to the Prudential Committee.

"5. In view, however, of the weighty considerations which have been set before the mission for this change of their connection, considerations whose reasonableness and justice are apparent to their minds, and in view of the expressed opinion of what is their duty, on the part of the reunited Presbyterian Church, they cannot but feel that the call is from God, and the step to be taken is one demanded by the highest interests of Christ's Church.

"6. That the mission express their conviction, that no change is demanded in the ecclesiastical connections of any of its members.

"In accordance, therefore, with these views of this whole subject, —

"*Resolved*, 1st; that the mission present to the Prudential Committee a request for a release from their connection with the American Board, with a view to placing themselves under the direction of the Presbyterian Board.

"And 2d, That the mission accept the invitation conveyed in the letter of the Rev. J. F. Stearns, D. D., Chairman of the Committee of Conference of the Presbyterian Board of Missions, dated June 19, 1870, to place themselves under the care of the Presbyterian Board.

"Although the official ties which have bound us to those with whom we have been so long and so happily associated may thus be severed, we feel that the bonds of sympathy and of prayer remain unchanged, and will continue so to remain until, in the higher work of praise, our hearts and voices shall be again and forever *united.*"

In accordance with this action the individual members of the mission sent a request to be released from their connection with the American Board, and they were released by vote of the Prudential Committee.

The members of the mission, at that time, were Drs. Thomson, Van Dyck, and H. H. Jessup, and Messrs. Calhoun, Eddy, Bird, Samuel Jessup, I. N. Lowry, and James S. Dennis. The author would naturally have great pleasure in quoting from their letters of farewell, but can only refer the reader for them to the "Missionary Herald."[1]

Feeling awakened by the transfer.

RESULTS OF THE PAST.

The history of the mission of the American Board to Palestine and Syria cannot be closed better than by the retrospective summary made by the mission at the close of their relations with the Board. They are speaking of the results of past labors.

"To Protestant influence, in great part, may we ascribe the changed feeling, which has come over the minds of the Mohammedans towards Christians. The Christian religion has become understood by them to be not wholly the system of idolatry, which they once regarded it, nor professing Christians as devoid of morality as they once seemed. As a consequence, there has been a sensible quenching of the flame of Moslem bigotry, and a greater respect

[1] *Missionary Herald*, 1870, pp. 391–398.

for Christians, their rights, their Bible, and their religion. The relative positions of the crescent and the cross are not what they were when the missionaries came to Syria. The Bible has gained ground, and the Koran has lost it, as a controlling influence in the land. Some Mohammedans are among the attendants upon our preaching, and these would doubtless be more numerous, but for the risk to property and to life, which inquirers from among them incur.

"Not without results have the children of the Druzes been taught in our schools during all these years, and so many conversations been held with adults of that sect. The leaven of the Gospel has penetrated even to the secret inner sanctuaries of their religion; and the white turbans of the initiated Druzes seen in our Sabbath congregations, the inquirers who come to our houses, and the baptized converts from among them, show that not in vain to the Druzes has the light of the Gospel again dawned upon Syria.

"But principally among the nominally Christian sects have the indirect results of missionary labor extended. These are visible in the changed power of the clergy. Once excommunication was a terror above all terrors. Now it is so powerless a weapon, that those who once wielded it so effectively are ashamed to challenge ridicule by exposing its weakness.

"Protestantism, once regarded by the mass of the people as the blackest of heresies, finds everywhere its defenders and vindicators, even where it lacks followers, and no longer can the lies gain currency, with which the clergy were accustomed to frighten away their flocks from gospel influence.

"The religious instruction given in their churches has been modified. More Bible is taught, and less tradition. The preaching is more of Christ, and less of the saints. The adoration of pictures has greatly lessened. All sects have been compelled to introduce schools, and to educate both boys and girls, to educate their priests, and to remove the restrictions from reading the Bible.

"The circulation of the Scriptures, and of religious books, has been wide-spread, and we have heard of some who have been enlightened by these silent teachers, and have through them found Christ as their Saviour, and died in joyful trust in Him; though they never had an opportunity to publicly profess their faith in Him.

"Among all sects, Mohammedan, Druze, Greek, Maronite, and Catholic, the glaciers of prejudice, which for centuries have been forming, are now melting under the warmth of the Gospel.

"The gift of the Bible to this people in their own tongue, is the rich golden tribute which the West has returned to the East, in acknowledgment of its obligation to the land whence the Bible came.

"Brighter than the light, which kindles early and lingers late upon the crests of Lebanon and Hermon, crowning them with glory, is the light of the Gospel, which has shone into dark hearts, in hamlet and city, recalling the memories of a past not inglorious, and presaging a fairer splendor in the future.

"Not in vain have Hebard, and Smith, and Whiting, and De Forest, and Ford, sowed the seed of the Word in tears, even though they went home with few gathered sheaves. From the heights of heaven they now behold the springing harvest. Not in vain have others toiled here, whose summons has not yet come. They bless God for what their eyes see and their ears hear of the Lord's working around them. Reluctantly have those yielded to the sad necessity of returning home, who, having just thrust in the sickle, found their strength unequal to the toil.

"The churches in America, which have aided in sustaining the mission by their offerings and their prayers, have seen fewer results, than have crowned their labors in other fields; their faith has been sorely tried; but they have been permitted to hear, from time to time, of souls ransomed from darkness and sin; echoes of the songs of triumph sung by departing saints have been borne to their ears, and they have felt that their labors have not been unrewarded.

"By God's grace we have laid anew the foundations of God's living temple, Christ being the chief corner-stone, and we have seen some courses already built upon it. We have set up and maintained the banner of the cross in the face of its pretended friends and its avowed foes. We have collected a little army on the Lord's side, and armed them with the sword of the Spirit. We have prepared an arsenal of spiritual weapons for future conflicts, in the Scriptures and other religious books translated and committed to the people. We have established outposts of schools and seminaries, have raised strongholds of the truth in churches planted here and there throughout the land. We have taken possession of the land in the name of King Immanuel, and we aim to subdue and hold it wholly for him."[1]

[1] From the *Foreign Missionary of the Presbyterian Church*, April, 1871, p. 305–307.

CHAPTER XLII.

THE ARMENIANS.

1867–1869.

THE year 1868 added five to the ordained missionary force of the missions; namely, Messrs. Alpheus N. Andrus, Carmi C. Thayer, John Edwin Pierce, Royal M. Cole, and Theodore S. Pond. Messrs. Milan H. Hitchcock, Edward Riggs, Henry Marden, and John Otis Barrows, were added in 1869. These were all accompanied by their wives. Besides these, there were George C. Reynolds, M. D., and wife, and ten unmarried women; namely, Misses Rebecca A. Tracy, Charlotte Elizabeth Ely, Mary A. C. Ely, Harriet G. Powers, Cyrene O. Van Duzee, Olive L. Parmelee, Isabella C. Baker, Flavia S. Bliss, Ursula C. Clarke, and Ardelle M. Griswold. Mardin was now manned, for the first time, with three missionaries, Messrs. Williams, Andrus, and Pond, with Misses Parmelee and Baker, two unmarried young women. Dr. Van Lennep and Mr. Ladd closed their labors in connection with the mission in 1869.

New missionaries.

It was not alone at Harpoot, that the year 1869 opened with a revival of religion. Aintab, Bitlis, Marash, and Mardin were favored

Revival at Marash.

with the like blessing. The "Week of Prayer" at Marash was described as a jubilee. Both houses of worship were opened, each day, an hour before sunset, and in each was a gathering of at least two hundred and fifty; where the many spontaneous prayers, and the pastor's vain endeavors to close the services within the hour, showed that the attendance was not a mere form. Twenty-nine out of fifty-two candidates were admitted to the first church, and twenty-one out of forty to the second. Nearly all these were able to read; and the examination was deemed more remarkable than the number received.

In respect to Mardin, I cannot refrain from quoting the expressive words of Mr. Williams, whose pen had much of graphic power. "The community here received the proposal to observe the week of prayer most joyfully, and preferred two meetings a day to one, — the first at sunrise, the second an hour and a half before sunset, each an hour long. Our first meeting was in a pouring rain, thirty present. This is the first pleasant day, and seventy-six were present in the morning. One of the preachers opens the meeting by singing, reading, remarks, and prayer. This occupies from twenty-five to thirty minutes, and then the meeting is thrown open to others, and six or eight prayers, short and pertinent, fill the time till the hour is up. We never before have been able to start a prayer-meeting here, and now they move off in a line, as if they had done

Revival at Mardin.

nothing else all their lives. I think as many as twenty-five persons have led in prayer."

Native candidate for a foreign mission.

A church had not yet been formed, but the Protestant community undertook the entire support of their preacher, and also of one of their own number as a missionary to the Koords. The latter is thus described by Mr. Williams: "A great, six feet, brawny fellow, with unwashed clothes (he is a tanner), long, disheveled hair, large, open features, and eyes black as coal, that shine like stars; but so simple in his trust, so tender in his love to Jesus, and earnest in his efforts to do good! He learned to read with steady, earnest application, and his questions are so spiritual, so humble, so childlike, that it is as the sun whenever he enters my door.

"One evening Oosee (Hosea) came in with clothes torn, fez[1] gone, face bloody, hair wildly disheveled, but the same genial lustre beaming from his eyes, accompanied by another Protestant, Daoud (David), who was earnest, almost imperative, that I should at once go to the governor and enter complaint. Asking for particulars, I learned that, returning from his garden soon after sunset, Oosee was set upon by a crowd of Papists, and escaped in the plight I saw him. Daoud insisted that unless those men were at once imprisoned, no one would be safe. I asked Oosee how he felt about it. 'Just as you say,

[1] Red Turkish cap.

Khowaja,'[1] was his reply. I read to him parts of Rom. xii. and xiii., and showed him that he was justified in entering complaint, that he had a right to protection, and that those who had set upon him doubtless deserved punishment; but said I, 'Would those men have touched you when you were a Papist?' 'Not one.' 'Why?' 'They dare not. Why, they knew I could thrash the whole of them, and would have feared I'd kill them. They knew me.' 'And now?' 'Now they think I'm a Prote, and wont strike back.' 'Did you?' 'Not a bit; I only tried to get away from them.' 'And if now, instead of throwing them into prison, you forgive them, and treat them as if nothing had happened, do you think they will see any difference between Oosee the Papist, and Oosee the Prote?' 'Of course they will.' 'To what will they charge the difference?' 'To my new religion.' 'Will not that lead them to admit the power of the Gospel? Will it not honor Christ?' 'Yes, I believe it will.' 'Well, Oosee, just as *you* say. If you on the whole wish it, I will go to the governor and enter complaint, — you have a clear right to this, — or I will let it drop just here, as you please.' 'No, Khowaja, I'll not complain, I forgive them. I'll go home and treat them as if nothing had happened. That is what Jesus says, and I'll do it. Perhaps they will come to Christ.' He has never since been molested.

[1] Gentleman — a title given to the missionaries in Eastern Turkey.

"When it was decided to take a new class of training pupils in Arabic, Oosee was the first to whom I spoke about joining it. The proposition was wholly unexpected, and I wish you could have seen the joy that shone in his eyes and beamed from every feature! I asked him if he thought his wife would consent to his going. 'We will ask Jesus,' he said. 'If he wants me to go he will make her willing. I don't think she'll oppose.' To some, who attempted to dissuade him on the ground that the allowance was insufficient for his family, he said, 'If only they will let me study, we will consent to live in the yard; no matter about a house, we'll get on any way; anything for Jesus.' Some days after, I said; "How about the wife?' 'O, she says go, and if need be we'll sell our vineyard to meet expenses. She is more anxious to go than I.' The vineyard would possibly bring, if sold, forty dollars in currency."

A church was organized at Mardin in February, which engaged to choose and support a pastor. On Sabbath afternoon, when it was organized, and the sacraments were administered, there were present three hundred and fifty persons, in a room which Mr. Williams says, "I had always insisted would hold one hundred and fifty, if properly packed." While candidates were being examined, the wife of Oosee presented herself. "No one had thought of her as a church-member, but before her examination was through, each

Church organized at Mardin.

Wife of Oosee.

had written against her name 'accepted.' We were as much delighted as surprised at her answers, and the meek, loving spirit she showed." Oosee did not go on the proposed mission, not deeming himself sufficiently educated; but is understood to have adorned his Christian profession down to the present time.

Struggle with the people of Zeitoon.

The reader has already some acquaintance with the people of Zeitoon, inhabiting the mountains north of Marash. Until subdued by the Turks in 1862, they were famed for their defiance of all law. The town contained about twelve thousand inhabitants, all of them Armenians. The men were described as of athletic make, quick step, and piercing eyes, showing in all their bearing that they breathed the free air of the mountains. The town is about thirty-five miles from Marash, built against the side of a high rock, the houses hanging one above another, so that the roof of the house below is the front yard of the house above.

Two years after their subjugation, Dr. Pratt made a professional visit, to attend one of their leaders then dangerously sick, and suffered no molestation. Two years later, at the earnest solicitation of several Protestants, Mr. Montgomery attempted a visit, with Pastor Avedis of the second church of Marash, and a deacon of the first church. The town being then under Turkish authority, they anticipated no special danger. "At evening, as we were entering the city," writes Mr. Montgomery, "to visit the governor of the place, according to custom, a furious mob of men and boys dragged us from our horses, and at once began beating and stoning us with frantic rage, rending the air with savage yells. Our Protestant guide was driven out of sight amid volleys of stones, the mob crying, 'Kill him! kill the wretch!' The deacon was allowed to secrete himself; but for Avedis and myself there was no escape till the mob had spent their fury, stoning us, and afterwards kicking and beating our prostrate bodies, while we were looking for escape only through death."

Deadly assault.

At this crisis, a great strong man, yelling so as to appear in sympathy with the mob, rushed up to where Mr. Montgomery was lying, and threw him on his horse, saying to him in an under tone, "Don't be afraid, trust me;" and then with curses hurried him out of the way, and took him and the pastor in the dark to his own house, where, as he dared not to keep them, he got them ready, as well as he could, to return at once to Marash.

The rescue.

"Thus we were saved," continues Mr. Montgomery, "after having been in the hands of the mob over two hours. We had a hard ride that night, hatless, our clothes bloody and torn, and our bodies so bruised that we could scarce sit on our horses; but we were enabled to pick our way homeward by the rough mountain paths."

It was subsequently known that this outrage was instigated by the priests at Marash, with the connivance of the governor. Meanwhile the Zeitoon people were fearful lest they had gone too far, and the Protestants began to breathe more freely; and many, who had failed to declare themselves before, now stood up openly for the truth.

The Gospel gains a footing.

In the summer of 1868, a native preacher was sent to Zeitoon by the home missionary society of Marash, and was allowed to remain unmolested, with ample opportunities for preaching the Word. At the close of the year, Mr. Trowbridge, having removed from Constantinople to Marash, made a visit to Zeitoon, and remained there laboring freely from Thursday till Monday. His guide homeward was a Zeitoon Protestant,—"a tall, gaunt man, past middle life, who has suffered much there for Christ's sake. At one time the people blackened his face with a coal, put him astride of a donkey with his face towards the tail, and thus paraded him through the streets; a crier shouting before him, 'Thus shall it be done to all who reject the worship of saints, and do not honor the Virgin Mary.' There is now no persecution."

Coast of the Black Sea.

Hopeful indications once more appeared among the Greeks at Erzroom and Trebizond, and also at Kerasun and Ordo, on the coast of the Black Sea west of Trebizond. Mr. Parmelee visited the two places last named, and put a helper named Harootune at Ordo, around whom the people gathered, earnestly desiring to learn the way of life. Even the women, who were precluded by their notions of propriety from assembling with the men, anxiously inquired when the helper would bring his wife, that she might teach them also. Persecution arose, but as usual it was overruled for good.

Death of Dr. Goodell.

Dr. William Goodell, after more than forty years of successful missionary service, returned in 1865, in feeble health, to spend the evening of life in his native land. With his wife, who had been his faithful companion from the first, he made his home with his eldest son, a physician in Philadelphia. There, beloved and revered, he lived until February 18, 1867, when he was removed to his heavenly home, at the age of seventy-five.

His life and character.

To the early friends of Dr. Goodell it seemed that his providential call was to be a preacher of the Gospel; and such he really was all through life, and the printed volume of his sermons in Armeno-Turkish, translated also into Armenian and Bulgarian, has had a very extensive circulation.[1]

[1] The report of the Nicomedia station for 1871, contains the following: "In Diermendere, a basket-maker has learned Turkish, and is supplied with books and tracts in that language for use among the Turks. The book he thinks most of, and which he begs may be put into the Arabic character, is Dr. Goodell's sermons. A Baghchejuk brother, whose business takes him often among the Turks in the vicinity of Armash, always takes these sermons with him. He says that the Turks always listen with interest, and sometimes with tears.

But Divine Providence so ordered the events of his early missionary career, that translating the Scriptures became his principal work. He began at Malta to translate the New Testament from the original into the Armeno-Turkish. That done, he entered upon the Old Testament; and he completed the last revision of the Bible in 1863. It was a great and good work, and will transmit his name for grateful remembrance to future ages.

Dr. Goodell had few equals as an agreeable letter-writer. The author was in official correspondence with him through his whole missionary life, and never ceased admiring his vivacity, humor, and felicity of expression, the aptness of his thoughts, and his very appropriate quotations of Scripture. He had the power, beyond most men, of passing at once and by an easy transition, from the merriest laughter to the most serious topics. His addresses to children had a resistless charm, and his power of turning a conversation into channels of his own choice was invaluable, in dealing with conceited disputatious orientals. "Indomitable in his purpose to do good, affable and courteous in manner, of ready tact, and abounding in resistless pleasantry, he

He is often requested to read the same sermon over and over again." The Marsovan report for the same year contains the following: "At Vizier Keopreu a change in public sentiment has taken place to such a degree, that the Armenian teacher is preaching Dr. Goodell's sermons to attentive audiences of his own people."

gained access wherever he chose to go, and wielded an influence powerful for good upon all with whom he chose to associate. He commanded the respect of foreign ambassadors and travellers, of dignitaries in the Oriental Churches, bankers, and the highest in society, as well as the common people. Even enemies were constrained to honor him. Few possess in so high a degree the admirable faculty of doing good without offense, and of recommending personal religion to the world."[1]

Prolonged tour in Eastern Turkey.

Mr. Herman N. Barnum's account of a tour to Diarbekir, Mardin, Sert, Bitlis, and Moosh, in 1867, brings the Eastern field vividly before us. His new associate, Mr. Henry S. Barnum, together with the pastors connected with the Evangelical Union, and nine recent graduates of the Seminary, accompanied him as far as Diarbekir, where they arrived on Saturday. There was a union service of the two congregations, on the next day, in the yard of one of the chapels, at which as many as eight hundred were present. The church in Diarbekir, though its pastor had been absent for two and a half years, and there was only one native preacher for the two congregations, yet had maintained the ordinances, and secured frequent accessions to the community. They supported their preacher, and also several schools, sent money to their absent pastor, and supported two students at

At Diarbekir.

[1] See *Missionary Herald* for 1867, pp. 129–133; also 1865, p. 350.

the Theological Seminary, whom they had sent thither to be educated for the mission in Koordistan. They chose several of their more intelligent members to assist the preacher in keeping up the services of the two congregations; thus proving their ability to care for themselves under very unfavorable circumstances.

The Union was in session four days, and its meetings were well attended. The evangelizing of Koordistan received a good deal of attention. The five young men who were preparing for it, had locations assigned them, their salaries fixed, and thus the native pastors were acquiring experience in missionary superintendence. Seven young men, just graduated from the Seminary, were carefully examined for licensure, especially in their religious experience and their motives for entering the ministry.

Meeting of the Evangelical Union.

The last day of the session was the most interesting, when one of the pastors read an essay upon the "means of promoting an awakening among the unconverted;" which was followed by remarks from nearly all the pastors present. The interest was greatest when some gave expression to their deep feeling of responsibility, and to the conviction that their own want of earnestness and spirituality was the reason of so much indifference among the unconverted.

From Diarbekir the missionaries and six of the pastors went to Mardin, whence, after ordaining one pastor, they went a journey of five days to Sert. There they took part in another ordination, and the formation of a church. Elias, the new pastor, had labored long and faithfully in this place, and refused a most pressing call from Mardin, though in worldly things it was much more desirable. He believed he could be more useful where the poor and oppressed looked to him as their spiritual father. Out of seven persons who offered themselves as candidates for church-membership, six were organized into a church. The congregation was small and poor, but a long series of persecutions had wonderfully purged them of selfishness. They had paid largely for their house of worship, had provided the pastor elect with a new suit of clothes for the ordination, and, considering their deep poverty, had made extraordinary subscriptions towards the required half of his salary. They now adopted the system of tithes cheerfully, which had been so successfully advocated by John Concordance.

At Mardin.

At Sert.

A remarkable church and pastor.

From Sert Mr. Williams proceeded to Mosul, and the rest to Bitlis. There the congregation had long desired for their pastor Baron Simon, who received ordination as an evangelist years before at Constantinople. He has been repeatedly mentioned as Pastor Simon, and was a man

At Bitlis.

of experience and sterling worth. There were no missionaries then at Bitlis. From hence they passed on to Moosh. The plain on which the town is situated, is sixty miles long and ten or twelve wide, and contains about seventy nominally Christian villages. The travellers were exposed to a snow-storm while crossing the plain. "It was genuine winter weather," writes Mr. Barnum, "yet I think I never saw anywhere else, not even in the warm sunshine of Egypt, so much nakedness, total or partial. Adults of course had the semblance of clothing, though it was often a mass of rags, sewed or tied together; but the poor children! It makes my heart ache to think of them. Some had a tolerably whole shirt and drawers, some had no drawers, and what was once a shirt was now a few shreds, hanging from the shoulders. Many had merely a rag, as a sort of jacket, with holes to put the arms through, and others had not a thread upon their bodies. The people seem to be almost bedless. Wherever we went, we found that the beds were a piece of carpet, or felt, or only a little straw, with a piece of carpet as a covering. In the six or seven villages visited by us, we did not notice a woman, or a child, who had either stockings or shoes. They walked about in the snow, and over the frozen ground, with bare feet. The soil is fertile, and the people own the land themselves, — not the Turkish Aghas, as is the case in many other parts of the

Extreme poverty on the plain of Moosh.

country, — so that it must be mere thriftlessness, rather than any stern necessity, which makes them so destitute. They have not learned to raise cotton, and consequently do not have on hand the material for making clothes, except some kinds of woolen garments; and as they do not like to pay money for cotton cloth, they live in this truly barbarous state. Our pastors had never seen any destitution like this among their Christian brethren, and it made a deep impression upon them."

Mr. Barnum adds: "The spiritual condition of the people is as bad as the physical. In the three or four monasteries surrounding the plain, there are said to be fifty vartabeds — men of more or less education. What a work they might do in these seventy villages, in improving the condition of the people, if they only had the heart for it. They are in a great measure responsible for this state of things. They come down periodically from their haunts of dissipation, and gather up and carry off whatever the people can spare; and this has helped to discourage enterprise. The great want now is the pure Gospel. This will not only save their souls, it will give them true civilization and refinement. To us it seemed that the people were ripe for the reception of the truth, for they are growing tired of their present condition. The pastors turned away from Moosh plain with the determination to induce the Evangelical Union, if consistent with the work undertaken in Koordistan, to do something for these people."

Spiritual oppression and poverty.

This journey of five hundred and fifty miles occupied thirty-eight days, and was too much for the new missionary, who reached home "jaded and worn," and had a serious illness. Before his recovery, and probably in consequence of her care of her husband, Mrs. Barnum was prostrated by typhus fever, which proved fatal on the 31st of December, 1867, a little more than three months after her arrival at Harpoot. But even in so short a time she had greatly endeared herself to her associates.[1]

Death of Mrs. H. S. Barnum.

North of the territory traversed by Mr. Barnum, is the Erzroom district. Of the sixty thousand inhabitants of the city of Erzroom in 1868, fifteen thousand were Armenians. The hundred villages scattered over its plain are smaller and more scattered than those on the plain of Harpoot. But then the territory connected with Erzroom is nearly as large as New England west of Maine, and has a population of half a million, two thirds of whom are Armenians. Touring in this territory is easy, as compared with the Harpoot district; since the roads, almost everywhere, admit of the use of wheels, and on the public thoroughfares the khans are comparatively good. A wagon road was then in a sluggish process of construction from Trebizond across the mountains.

District of Erzroom.

The church in Diarbekir continued to grow, even

[1] *Missionary Herald* for 1868, p. 136.

during the three or four years' absence of the pastor. They were active in communicating the truth to their neighbors, and were especially interested in securing the introduction of the Gospel into the surrounding villages, and into Koordistan. But since then, the energy bestowed upon these outside enterprises has been turned toward the building of a large church, by means of funds collected by the pastor chiefly in England, and to strictly home affairs.

The mission to Koordistan.

The young men sent on the mission to Koordistan addressed themselves chiefly to the Armenians and Jacobites, without neglecting the Moslems, Koords, and Yezidees. These sects, in their social intercourse, used only the Koordish language; but in their prayers, the Armenians used the ancient Armenian, the Jacobites the ancient Syriac, and the Koords the Arabic, all wholly unintelligible to them. And it was a new thought to them, that God could be addressed in the Koordish language.

Mission to the Moosh village.

A company of native missionaries was sent from Harpoot, in the summer of 1868, to the benighted region of Moosh. This was a result of the tour just described, and was a self-denying enterprise, but the sacrifice was cheerfully made.

The Seminaries at Harpoot.

The two Seminaries at Harpoot were now full. Including the students brought thither for a time from Mardin, and the Koordish students, there were fifty in each Seminary; and these, with their children, made a colony of one hundred and fifty.

It became manifest, soon after the Crimean war, that the Papal ecclesiastics in Turkey, emboldened by the increased prospect of French protection, grew relentlessly cruel where they had power, in their persecutions of the Protestants. A painful illustration of this occurred at Mardin in the summer of 1868, upon the arrival of a new Papal Patriarch. He and the Papal Armenian bishop resolved to make a determined effort to crush out Protestantism. The charges upon which the proceedings were based, were pretended arrearages in the payment of taxes, whereas none of the taxes were due.

Cruel persecution at Mardin.

On July 25th, six Protestants were arrested, and taken, not to prison, but to the cavalry camp, to bring water for the horses, sprinkle the ground, build mangers, clear privies, etc. Suleeba, the Protestant preacher from Diarbekir who was laboring there at the time, went to the Muteserif or governor of the city, and represented the injustice of the proceeding. As a result, he was ordered to prison himself, but was soon released. After various other efforts with the Muteserif and the Pasha to secure justice (in which he was opposed by the Papal Syrian Patriarch, and by priests and leaders of the other sects at Mardin), and after presenting receipts which had been given the Protestants for their taxes, Suleeba was delivered to the soldiers, with the rest. He writes: —

"A gendarme took me to the camp. On seeing me the soldier said, 'This is their priest; bring some *large* jars (water jars) for him.' They fastened two jars to my neck, one before and one behind, and gave two into my hands.[1] A soldier was assigned to each one of us, and each one carried a long stick of wood, an inch in thickness, and with these they freely beat us. In filling the jars which were fastened to us, the soldiers would pour nearly as much into our necks as into the jars, so that we were thoroughly drenched all the time. Once I was so much fatigued that I begged permission to set down the jars and rest, but the soldiers would not allow me. I dropped one of them, as I could not hold it any longer, for the road was long and my hands grew weak. In trying to recover it I fell to the ground, and the soldier beat me severely with his stick."

It was on Monday that Suleeba was sent to the camp, and things remained thus till Friday. "A little after sunrise on that day, a gendarme came and said, 'The Protestants are wanted at the palace.' We were taken to the Muteserif, and he began to curse us in the vilest manner for not giving the

[1] The four jars, when full of water, weighed more than one hundred and fifty pounds.

money. I said, 'Examine our accounts, and if you find that we owe anything we will pay it.' He then ordered a stick to be brought, — it was a strong one, thicker than my thumb, — and telling a soldier to take me by the head and bend me forward, he gave the stick to a centurion, who gave me ten or twelve blows. I still feel the soreness, though he was not violent in his beating."

"About nine o'clock they called us to the Mejlis, or city council. After a careful examination of the documents, in which the Pasha's scribe, Fettah Effendi, took a prominent part, the Mejlis said with one voice, to those on the other side, 'You have no claim whatever on the Protestants.'" This decision was not accepted by the enemies of the Protestants. In the afternoon of the same day, Suleeba writes: "The Patriarch and the Papal Armenian Bishop called on the Pasha. They stayed about half an hour. Before they left, a lieutenant came from the Pasha, accompanied by two priests, and said to the Muteserif, 'The Pasha orders that you instantly deliver each one of the Protestants to two gensdarmes, and collect the money from each one *at once*, according to this paper.' The Muteserif replied, 'There is no claim upon these men. What shall we collect?' He replied, 'This is the Pasha's order.' The Muteserif said, 'We have just examined these men's accounts, and have found that the Protestants do not owe a para. Tell the Pasha so.' The Lieutenant replied,

'The Patriarch and Bishop were with the Pasha just now, and he told them that this money should be collected.' The Muteserif then turned to Fettah Effendi, of Diarbekir, and urged him to go and explain to the Pasha, but he did not wish to go. He then called out, much excited, 'Come, gensdarmes, take these men and kill them.' I then said, 'How much money do you want? Tell us, and we will give it.' The Muteserif said, 'I don't know.' I said, 'You are delivering us over to these soldiers. Tell us how much you want and we will give it, and save ourselves from them.' The Muteserif then asked Fettah Effendi, who had looked over our documents, and who had said that the Protestants owed nothing, 'How much are these men to pay?' He said, 'I don't know.' He then turned to the members of the other sects and said, 'How much do you want of these men?' They said, 'Let them come to the market [where the chief of police was receiving taxes], and we will see.' So we were hurried off there. This was less than an hour before sunset. We were taken to the shop occupied by Daoud Agha, the chief of the police. A great crowd gathered as we went along, and afterwards, which completely filled all the streets in that vicinity. As we entered, Daoud Agha, who is an old enemy of the Protestants, said to his men, 'Bring me two bottles of raki and three or four candles, and I will collect this money before morning."

The reader will remember the interesting account Mr. Williams gave of the conversion of an influential merchant at Mardin named Meekha.[1] This is the old man, Muksi Meekha, whom the chief of the police delivered over to the gensdarmes, with the charge to collect six thousand piasters from him. Mr. Barnum thus describes the treatment he received: "They took him out into the street and began to beat him with their gun-stocks. This is done by taking the gun in both hands and striking with it endwise. He promised to give security for the payment of the money in the morning, and begged to be allowed till morning to raise the money, as the shops were all shut; but they said, 'We must have the money now.' He wandered through the market in the vain hope of finding somebody who would advance the money, the guard all the time beating him, and so severely that he several times fell down, and his outer garment was torn into shreds; and he has since that time, now more than a week, kept his bed most of the time. At last he met a member of the Mejlis (a Turkish member), who told the guard that if it was money they wished they must take *kefil* from him, and wait till morning, as it was now evening, and nobody could raise money at that time; 'but,' he said, 'if your object is to kill him, take him back to the chief of police and butcher him there.' They then took him back to the crowd, and

[1] See Chapter xxvii.

he found a man who gave a part of the money and a note for the payment of the rest in the morning, and he was released. He thinks that he would have been killed but for the intervention of the Turk.

"Each one of the prisoners was then passed over to two gensdarmes. Some of these were at once delivered, by their friends advancing the money; but four of them, besides Muksi Meekha, were treated just as he was, and all of them have kept their beds most of the time since.

"The police were at the same time sent to the houses of all the other Protestants, and they were brought, and the money which the sects demanded collected from them, by their paying the money or getting security for its payment in the morning. In this way, in the space of a few hours, and that evening, nineteen thousand piasters were collected."

Only a very small portion of this money was ever refunded.

Revival at Oorfa.

Mention was made, in connection with Dr. Goodell's visit to the central mission in 1862, of the progress of the evangelical reformation at Oorfa. Two years later, Mr. Nutting, the resident missionary, announced an interesting revival of religion among his people. Both church and congregation were aroused, and the missionary had never seen more thorough conviction of sin, than was apparent in many. They had been studying the Westminster Assembly's Catechism for two years, and recently had attended lectures on the Epistle to the Romans; "and the fundamental truths thus lodged in their minds," writes Mr. Nutting, "had been greatly blessed." They met entirely the expense of their own religious and educational institutions. In February, 1865, the church numbered forty-two, and as many more were known to be inquirers.

About this time there arose considerable uneasiness in the mission from an apprehension of doctrinal errors in a candidate for the pastorate of this church. To what extent such errors actually existed, was never determined with certainty, but there was a spirit of alienation and division, which was regarded with concern. The churches in Oorfa and its four out-stations contained a total, in 1870, of one hundred and sixty-one members, of whom twenty-five had been received in the previous year. The Report of the Board for 1871 declares the difficulties of former years to have happily passed away; except that unsound doctrinal views continued to disturb the harmony of the church at Severek, and that this place was noted, in early times, for the prevalence of similar errors.

Apprehended doctrinal errors.

Mr. Wheeler returned from his visit to the United States in October, 1868, accompanied by Mrs. Wheeler, and the Misses Parmelee and Baker; and they were met, six hours or nearly twenty miles out, by the Harpoot and village pastors, and quite a delegation from the city. The last day

Reception of Mr. Wheeler at Harpoot.

was a constant succession of welcomes. As they drew near the city, they saw a large crowd on the hill, with a white flag. It was the theological students drawn up in a line; and next, the women and girls of the school; and then men, women, and children crowded to greet them. It was the spontaneous expression of love to those who had told them of Christ and his salvation.

Progress of civilization at Aleppo.

The return of Dr. David H. Nutting from the United States to the Central mission, in the autumn of 1868, led him to speak of the progress of civilization at Aleppo. "All the stations of this mission are now connected with this city by telegraph, while it is connected with Constantinople. A line from here to Killis, Aintab, and Marash, has just been constructed. We have French and Russian, as well as Turkish, posts. A semiweekly paper called the "Frat" (Euphrates), is printed here, in three languages — Arabic, Armeno-Turkish, and Arabo-Turkish. The streets are being repaved and widened in some places, and street-lamps are put up. A carriage-road from here to Alexandretta, the sea-port, is to be built immediately."

Death of John Concordance.

John Concordance, the blind preacher at Havadoric, died at that place in March, 1869, greatly beloved and lamented, and not by his own people alone. The Armenians vied with the Protestants in attending to the burial services, and especially in seeing that Hohannes' particular requests were carried out to the letter, and both classes were genuine mourners at his grave. His influence in the matter of consecrating one tenth of one's income has been extensively felt; and he practiced what he preached. His salary was only eight dollars a month, and although he had a wife and child to support from this, he never failed of giving one tenth into the "store-house;" thus leaving but little more than seven dollars for the monthly support of himself and family.

In the year 1868, Dr. Schneider, after a residence at Aintab of a score of years, returned again to Broosa. It was natural for him to review the progress of the good work at Aintab during his connection with it, and his statement will interest the reader.

Aintab after twenty years.

"I preached my first sermon in Aintab to a company of twenty-five or thirty in the year 1848. Now, the average audience is near one thousand, and often rises to twelve or fifteen hundred. Then, there was a church of only eight members; now, there are two churches, containing three hundred and seventy-three members. Then, the entire community of Protestants numbered only forty souls, while at present there are nineteen hundred, small and great. The number has become so large, that a division into two separate congregations became a necessity; and while there was then hardly any native laborer, now two able native pastors are settled over these two churches. In the beginning, next to nothing was done in the way of self-support and general benevolence; while now, these communities pay the salaries of their pastors and school-teachers, and all their other expenses. Besides this, nearly five hundred dollars in gold were given for general benevolence, and more than nine hundred towards a second church edifice. All this in a community where a day-laborer receives thirteen and a half cents per day, and a mason or carpenter thirty-two cents. In view of their poverty, and the exactions of the government, this is extraordinary liberality. More than one half of the male members of these churches give a tithe of their income to benevolent objects.

"In the beginning, we worshipped in a private house; but for many years a large church edifice has been filled, and a second one, for the benefit of the second church, will be completed in a few months. At first, there was no school through the week, or on the Sabbath; now, there are seven common schools, with nearly four hundred pupils, and a Sabbath-school averaging a thousand, which has been as high as sixteen hundred. More than a score of pastors and preachers have been trained at Aintab, most of whom are still in the service, and a large number have been sent forth as teachers and colporters into the surrounding regions. Finally, when the Gospel was first preached in Aintab, the

Protestants were despised and persecuted; while now, they are not only recognized as a regular community, with rights and privileges, but they have acquired for themselves a name, respect, and influence."

CHAPTER XLIII.

THE ARMENIANS.

1869–1872.

THE year 1870 commenced at Marash with another revival. A thousand persons were present at the prayer-meeting on the 3d of January, which was admirably conducted by Pastor Murad. The missionaries, though present, did not deem it necessary to assist him. Fifty-three new members were received into the two churches, and a much larger number offered themselves for admission. Successful efforts were made to reach the women, who were visited in their own homes by the wives of students in the theological school, and by the older scholars in the girls' school. The number of houses thus visited during six weeks, was three hundred and eight, and there were fifty-five prayer-meetings.

Another revival at Marash.

A revival was also in progress at Bitlis. For many weeks there had been a sunrise prayer-meeting every day, and it was fully attended for eight months; its location being changed occasionally to accommodate different parts of the

Another at Bitlis.

city. The meeting on the 18th of February was the most interesting and profitable. Nearly ninety persons were seated on the floor of a room thirteen feet by twenty. Pastor Simon had charge of the meeting, and so ready were the people, that it continued two hours and three quarters before he could bring it to a close. As many as seventeen spoke, and about as many prayed. During the meeting, a prominent church-member called the attention of the weeping congregation to the importance of making a covenant with God *now;* and after reading a beautiful and appropriate hymn, he requested all who were ready to make such a covenant to rise. Nearly all rose, and while they were standing, he offered an earnest prayer for the aid of the Holy Spirit in keeping that covenant. It was an impressive scene. Forty were added to the church as the result of this revival. The people paid the debt on their chapel and parsonage, and enlarged the former. They also gave a site for the building to be erected by the two Misses Ely for the girls' boarding-school, in which were twenty pupils, for the most part wives of native helpers.

New church and pastor at Havadoric.

Some time in the month of April, the good people of Bitlis observed a day of fasting and prayer for the village of Havadoric, where the blind preacher, John Concordance, had labored, and where he died. After a few weeks, Mr. Knapp visited the place, with Pastor Simon, and they found delightful evidence of the presence of the Holy Spirit. It was in contemplation to organize a church in that place, and the church in Bitlis had sent three delegates, who walked forty-five miles over the muddy roads. Ten hours were spent, the day after their arrival, in examining more than a score of persons for the new church, and eleven were approved, including two women. After the church had been organized, Avedis, a graduate of the Harpoot Seminary, was ordained as pastor. Fifty were present at the Lord's supper from Bitlis, Moosh, and Khanûs.

Great change in Hadjin.

The barbarous expulsion of Mr. and Mrs. Coffing from Hadjin, in 1862, will be remembered.[1] This was attributed, at the time, to the priests and the Turkish governor, and not to the people. Mr. Adams from Adana, and Mr. Trowbridge from Marash, went there in 1870, in company with Hagop Effendi, the Civil Head of the Protestants in Turkey, who was then on an official tour through the empire. They found the door for Christian effort wide open, as Messrs. Montgomery and Perry had done the year before. Though situated on the northern side of the Taurus mountains, Hadjin is more conveniently cared for by the Central mission than by the Western, and that section of country had been transferred accordingly. Native laborers had gone there, and a great change had taken place. Thirty-two had been enrolled as Protestants, and no

[1] See p. 221.

mention is made of opposition. At the evening services on the house-top, where the missionary's tent was pitched, not only the Protestants, but large numbers of the Armenians, listened with eager attention. From early morn until dark on the Sabbath, there was hardly an intermission in the preaching, exposition, or reading of the Word of God.

In the autumn of 1869, Dr. Schneider, by direction of the mission, attended the examination of the Theological School at Marsovan. He writes, "The examination continued through most of three days, and as a whole was quite satisfactory. The appearance of the students in theology was peculiarly gratifying. The readiness and propriety of their answers proved that they had bestowed thought on the various points brought up, and saw their relations to one another. Their public addresses, when they received their diplomas, were all excellent, while some were of quite a superior order, and exhibited no common degree of oratorical power." He was also much gratified by the appearance of the girls' boarding-school.

Theological school at Marsovan.

Seven days' travel, on his return to Broosa, brought him to Angora, a city of from forty to fifty thousand inhabitants. The probable estimate gave ten thousand to the Catholics, three hundred to the Greeks, a thousand to the Armenians, and five hundred to the Jews; the remainder were Mussulmans. Many books had been

Angora.

sold there, much light disseminated, and a small body of Protestants earnestly entreated for a missionary to reside among them, or at least for an educated native preacher. No uneducated man could sustain himself there against the powerful array which the Roman Catholics could bring to bear upon him by means of their educational establishments. Among the obstacles to be encountered, were the extreme worldliness of the people, and their devotion to sensual pleasures. Angora is within the limits of the ancient Galatia, and very probably was the site of one of "the churches of Galatia." It appears not yet to be occupied as a station.

Erzingan.

Another interesting place was Erzingan, within the Erzroom district, visited by Mr. and Mrs. Cole in the autumn of 1870. They travelled the whole distance of a hundred miles in a gig; with many risks, it is true, but with no disaster. The city was supposed to contain as many as ten thousand Armenians, forming a third part of the population. Mr. Dunmore, the brave pioneer, had spent three months there, and various helpers had been stationed there from time to time. The missionary and his wife were received with the utmost kindness, and had crowded meetings during the nine days they were there. Mrs. Cole had several interesting meetings, also, with the women. "Thus time passed," writes Mr. Cole, "and you may be sure it was a continual feast to the soul, and we felt quite reluctant to turn homeward."

The mission sent by native churches to the Koords, like most new missions, had a tardy success; and, after four years, the zeal of the native churches began to flag, and some of the native pastors proposed to stop the work in Koordistan, and devote themselves more fully to the "home field." Knowing that the influence of such a course would be disastrous, Mr. Wheeler threw himself into the breach, and was off for a three weeks' tour in Koordistan. Redwan, the seat of the mission, was eighty miles east of Diarbekir. He was accompanied by Hagop Effendi, Civil Head of the Protestants, and two native preachers; and was rejoiced to find at Redwan a congregation of eighteen men, thirteen women, and twenty-two children. They had learned, or begun to learn, to read in the Armeno-Koordish, into which the four Gospels had been translated; and some were learning the Armenian language, so as to be able to read the whole Bible. Their chapel, of sun-dried brick, ten feet by twenty, was crowded on the evening of their arrival. "They sang 'Sweet hour of prayer,'" writes Mr. Wheeler, "and 'There is no other name so sweet,' translated from Armenian by their preacher, who had also translated, with the help of Pastor Mardiros of Harpoot, 'Forever with the Lord,' 'How lost was my condition,' 'My faith looks up to Thee,' 'Safely through another week,' 'My days are passing swiftly by,' and others. Per-

Crisis in the mission to Koordistan.

Visit of Mr. Wheeler.

The mission.

haps it was all romance, but somehow that little, close, low, dark, foul-aired chapel seemed to me almost a heavenly place, as we joined,—they in Koordish and I in Armenian,—in singing those sweet hymns." At an expense of forty dollars in gold, the people bought a fine lot for a larger building, including chapel, school-room, and parsonage, which they hoped to put up in the following year. They desired also the formation of a church, and the ordination of a pastor. "Do you wonder," adds Mr. Wheeler, "that I returned with a light heart to tell the churches these good news from their mission field?" The Harpoot church immediately decided to send a school-teacher to Redwan, so that the preacher might give himself entirely to his work.

Visit to Sert.

Mr. Pond, of Mardin, went to Sert four days distant in Koordistan, and experienced the usual trials by the way,—sleeping in "stifling stables, with a perfect menagerie of animals and fowls, and creeping creatures too numerous to catalogue."

The church at Sert he found full of brotherly love, simple faith, and a desire for knowledge. It had given freely to the brethren in Redwan, and paid the entire salary of its own pastor. "Indeed," says the missionary, "but for this church in Sert, we should almost despond for the Arabic-speaking portion of our field. In Mardin, it is true, we have a flourishing church and community, but not so refreshing in its simplicity and strength of faith and love. The pastor of the Sert church is one of the best men for the pastoral work I have ever seen in Turkey, and is the chief cause, under God, of the cheering state of his flock."

Mr. Pond next visited Mosul, and found it no longer an unpleasant part of their field. "Once, and that not long ago, it was the least hopeful spot in all our bishopric. For over thirty years has the Gospel been preached there, and by such men as Grant, and Lobdell, and Williams, Marsh, and Hinsdale. The church contained at one time twenty members, but had dwindled to ten."

Mosul again visited.

A pastor was to be ordained at Mosul, and Mr. Andrus, missionary from Mardin, Pastor Jurgis of Mardin, Pastor Elias of Sert, and delegates from these two churches were there to aid in that service. The pastor elect was ordained, the dead branches in the church were cut off, and eight new members were added, while as many more were ready to join at the next communion.

Dr. Williams died at Mardin on the 14th of February, 1871, at the age of fifty-three, broken down by an accumulation of labors and cares, which, until near the close of his life, he had been compelled to bear alone. It was a great loss to the mission, but especially to Mardin; and he

Death of Dr Williams.

was called from earth just when the clouds, which had made his field seem dark to him, began to break. He saw it, and rejoiced. He said he was like Moses, who was permitted to look into the promised land from Pisgah, but was not allowed to enter it.

His character.

Mr. H. N. Barnum, who knew Dr. Williams intimately, while admitting that he was unduly disposed to distrust his own powers and judgment, says that, aside from this, he was a rare man. "He had great self-control, and was so undemonstrative, that those who did not know him intimately can scarcely be said to have known him at all. He possessed genuine refinement; and with his marvelous fund of information in almost all departments of knowledge, his fine command of language, and his good nature and enthusiasm, he was, in his more cheerful moods, a fascinating member of our social circle. His clear mind had been carefully cultivated, and his acquisitions were very exact. However much he distrusted his own judgment, his associates confided in it. He was forward to acknowledge any mistake, and correct it, and he was enthusiastic in his zeal for the policy of self-support in the missionary work. His students held him in the highest admiration, and very few missionaries have secured the affection of the people for whom they labor so fully as he did. Had he remained at home, I am sure he would have stood conspicuous among the clergy. He was very careful in the use of missionary funds, and in everything maintained a conscience void of offense. He was, withal, eminently spiritual. His many trials had wrought in him a deep and thorough work of grace."

"The *one* attraction of heaven for Mr. Williams," writes his bereaved wife, "was *Jesus*. 'Like Jesus,' and 'without sin,' and 'to be with Jesus and see Him as He is,' were phrases ever on his lips. He used often to speak of the great host gone before, and of the loved ones constantly gathering there; but it was rare to hear him speak of joy at the prospect of meeting them. It was always '*Jesus*, the joy of loving hearts.' Neither did he long for heaven as a place of *rest*, until very near the end. He loved toil, and felt a great desire to live and labor for the Master." "At last," she says, "he did grow very weary, and often exclaimed, 'So tired, O, so tired.' In one of those weariest hours, he asked me if I remembered Bickersteth's description of Paradise. 'Well,' he said, 'I can't bear to think of it. To think of climbing over those mountains, it is so wearisome. I think, 'In my Father's house are many mansions,' and I want to be taken right into one of them, and laid down to rest — to rest — O, how sweet.' His intellect was clouded in the last hours."

I find some facts, received in 1871, concerning the women in the region of Cesarea, indicating a decided progress. "Three years ago,

The women in the region of Cesarea.

with the exception of Cesarea, Yozgat, and Moonjasoon, the truth seemed to have gained but very slight hold upon the women at our several out-stations. But few were ever found in the Sabbath congregation, scarcely any could read, and some bitterly persecuted their husbands. But now a marked change is visible, and the women form no inconsiderable part of all our congregations; large numbers are learning to read; female prayer-meetings are held at nearly or quite every out-station; and an earnest desire for improvement is everywhere apparent. As a consequence, a corresponding change is observed in the conduct of these women. They become better wives and mothers, and their influence is felt for good upon those around them."

Messrs. Wheeler and Reynolds made a visit to Van in the summer of 1871, preparatory to the occupation of that important post. Most of the ninety miles from Bitlis to Van, was within sight of the lake; its waters reposing in quiet beauty amid the mountains, on whose loftiest peaks there still lingered patches of snow. They reached the city in September, and were there a week. They found more readiness to receive the Word of God, and its teachers, and to have intercourse with them, than they had expected. They were also agreeably disappointed in the number, who were desirous that missionaries should reside among them. The region southeast of Van, which they had supposed was ex-

Missionary visit to Van.

clusively a Koordish-speaking section, they found to contain a number of Armenian villages, speaking their own language, with Bibles in the modern tongue, and men accustomed to read them. At the time of writing these pages, missionaries are understood to be on their way for the permanent occupation of Van, should such be the will of Providence.

Occupation of Van.

The church at Cutterbul, and indeed the whole region around Diarbekir, experienced a severe bereavement early in 1872, in the death of its first pastor Abd en Noor. "He was a thoughtful man," writes Mr. Andrus of Mardin, "and a more independent thinker than many. He had made him a place in the village, so that even the young men of the Jacobite community looked to him as their father. He was very anxious to improve the condition of his race, was faithful both as a preacher and as a pastor, and in the latter capacity was more especially active during the past winter. He was one of the eight pupils received into the first class formed by Dr. Williams in Mardin, in September, 1862 (was then about thirty years old), and remained three years in the class, supplying the pulpit in Cutterbul during the winter months, where he had been preaching before he entered the school."

Death of a native pastor.

The impressions made on Dr. Clarke, Foreign Secretary of the Board, by occurrences in 1871, on his way from Adana to Aintab, are significant of the work of grace, now in progress in the region distinguished by the early labors of the Apostle Paul. His route was across the Cilician and Antioch plains, over the Amarus mountains and another range, and for the most part through a region of wonderful fertility, needing only proper cultivation.

"The journey," Dr. Clarke writes, "was not without some items of missionary interest, as showing how widely the truth is diffused. The first night out we encamped a little distance from a village that bears the name of Missis, built on the ruins of the ancient Mopsuestia — a place of some note in the early history of the Church. As we were setting up our tent, two Armenians from the village accosted us with the question, — 'Are you the men that are bringing light into this dark land?' On being assured that we were just those very men, they gave us a hearty welcome, and did their best to assist us in every way, remaining till dark, and coming again in the early morning. This they did as a labor of love, and to receive some words of counsel and cheer. They were Protestants, but not church-members, who had come here for business — one from near Antioch, and the other from the neighborhood of Harpoot. Here, where no preacher of the truth had ever been stationed by us, these men were faithful to the light they had, spending the Sabbath together in studying the Scriptures and in prayer, and speaking to all who would listen of the Gospel of Christ.

One of the men had formerly been a keeper of a drinking shop. One day, while plying his trade, he called out to a passer-by to come in and drink. The reply, 'I cannot, I am a Protestant,' arrested his attention, and eventually led him to give up his wicked traffic for an honest calling.

"On another day we met a party of laborers coming down into Cilicia from Eastern Turkey, whom we at first mistook for Koords. But coming nearer, Mr. Trowbridge recognized them as Armenians, and at once asked if there were any Protestants among them. 'O yes,' cried several; and in proof they drew Testaments from their bosoms. One of them, a leading Protestant from Haboosi, on learning who I was, at once beset me to hurry on to the dedication of their new church, that was to come off in a few days. He, poor man, had been obliged to come away, but was very anxious to have me go. I was really sorry I could not do so, and thus be a witness to some of the ripe fruits of the great work in the villages about Harpoot. What may not be accomplished by such a party of Christian laborers, going into villages and neighborhoods unreached by other means? It is thus that the good seed is now scattered broadcast over the land.

"We had hoped to reach Hassan-Beyli for the Sabbath, but the distance proved too great, and as it was three hours off from the main road, we had to give up a visit to this mountain eyrie, — now a centre of Christian influence, a few years ago a nest of robbers. But they would not let us off so. Tuesday morning, by six o'clock, we were surprised to see a half dozen of those stalwart men, who had left their mountain crags, three hours before, to come down and exchange Christian salutations. As I looked at them, I could not but wonder at the work of grace manifest in them. After words of exhortation through an interpreter, on mounting my horse I took them each by the hand, while the grasp tightened and eyes flashed and filled at the words—'Christ, Hallelujah, Amen.'"

CHAPTER XLIV.

THE ARMENIANS. — EDUCATION.

1872.

THE common school is as much a necessity in mission fields, as it is that the people should be able to read the Word of God; and it has everywhere been a primary object of attention; but always, and more especially of late years, with the aim and expectation, that it will speedily derive its support from the parents of the children. Common schools a necessity.

Properly conducted, the tendency of the common school is to development. Teachers are learning all the while; new branches of study are introduced; there is greater thoroughness in the teaching and discipline; till at length the Academy is evolved, and perhaps the College.

This would be the natural order of development, were general education the leading object of missionary societies. But the unevangelized nations must be evangelized, and chiefly by their own people. Consequently one of the first efforts is to raise up teachers and preachers.

Enough has probably been said, in this history,

respecting the common schools. So, also, of the Seminary at Bebek, instituted in 1840,[1] and the Girls' Boarding-school in the metropolis, instituted in 1845.[2] The Bebek Seminary was in some respects the forerunner of "Robert College." But however suitable its proximity to the capital may have been, regarding it as an incipient college, the location was not well adapted, on the whole, for a school to raise up young men for pastoral work in the towns and villages of the interior. Hence its discontinuance in 1862, and the opening of a training Seminary in Marsovan, in 1865. The delay of three years was owing to peculiar and unexpected causes. The Girls' Boarding-school at Constantinople was also discontinued for similar reasons, and was reopened at Marsovan in 1865.

The Bebek Seminary.

A highly intelligent Armenian gentleman thus addressed Dr. Hamlin: "The Bebek Seminary has given birth to influences, which have waked up our young men all over the land; and you are regarded as a public benefactor, although you can never be regarded as our religious guide. Still, in sentiment, you have — not eight thousand, but eight hundred thousand followers. We shall never be called Protestants; it is not an Armenian term; but we hope to see the day when the Armenian Church will be as evangelical as yours."

The present Theological Seminaries are at Har-

[1] See Chapter xxxiii. [2] See Chapter xxxiii.

poot, Marsovan, Marash, and Mardin. There are, besides these, theological classes at Cesarea, Broosa, Sivas, Harpoot, Bitlis, Erzroom, and Eski Zagra. The first of the four seminaries above named originated in 1859, the second, in 1865, the third in 1868; and the fourth, in 1870. Like similar institutions in the United States, they are intended to receive only such as not only give evidence of piety, but are promising candidates for the gospel ministry. The course of study at Harpoot illustrates, substantially, the education given, or contemplated, in each of those institutions.

The existing Theological Seminaries.

For the *first* year, Exegesis, the Synoptic Gospels and Pentateuch, the Turkish and Ancient Armenian languages, Algebra, Physiology, Reading, Writing, and Spelling Armenian.

For the *second* year, Exegesis, Isaiah, Daniel, and Revelation, Geometry, Natural Philosophy, and Astronomy, Rhetoric in Ancient Armenian, Evidences of Christianity (Turkish).

For the *third* year, Exegesis, Acts, Pauline Epistles, except Romans and Hebrews, Mental Philosophy, Moral Philosophy, and Theology.

For the *fourth* year, Exegesis, Pastoral Epistles, Romans, Hebrews, and Gospel of John, Sermonizing, Pastoral Theology, Church History, and Logic.

Weekly exercises in composition and declamation through the first three years; and lectures on Physical Geography, Geology, History, and Chronology, and lessons in singing, distributed through the course at convenience.

The female boarding-schools.

The female boarding-schools are mainly designed to educate teachers, Bible-readers, and wives for native teachers and pastors. They are in Marsovan, Aintab, Marash, Harpoot, Mardin, Bitlis, Erzroom, and Samokov. The pupils in the theological seminaries and classes, and in the female boarding-schools, as reported in the year 1871, were as follows: —

Tabular view of the higher schools.

		Theological Seminaries.	Theological Classes.	Female Boarding-schools.
WESTERN TURKEY.	Marsovan.	26		38
	Cesarea.		5	
	Broosa.		13	
	Sivas.		2	
CENTRAL TURKEY.	Aintab.			20
	Marash.	35		
EASTERN TURKEY.	Harpoot.	17	25[1]	34
	Mardin.	5		5
	Bitlis.		9	20
	Erzroom.		6	8
	Total.	83	60	125

Thus the number in training for the gospel ministry, in 1871, was one hundred and forty-three, and the number in the female boarding-schools was one hundred and twenty-five.

[1] More properly called a "Normal school."

The Marsovan Seminary commenced with eight pupils, and the number was increased in two years to twenty-four. Classes were organized at the stations, to prepare candidates for admission to the seminary, and to train such helpers as were not to take the full course of study. The plan of instruction in the seminary has recently been enlarged so as to include the training of native agents for the Greek-speaking races of southwestern Asia Minor. Eight young men, who graduated in 1869, received licenses to preach from the "Central Evangelical Union," and were in great demand. Thirteen were thus commissioned in 1870, in which year a convenient seminary building was finished.[1]

Marsovan Theological Seminary.

Mr. Wheeler has given a full and interesting description of the theological and female Seminaries at Harpoot, in his valuable work, entitled "Ten Years on the Euphrates," and to that the reader is referred.[2] Eighteen pupils graduated in 1863, seven in 1865, and eleven in 1867; of whom thirty-two became pastors, preachers, or helpers.

The Harpoot Seminaries.

Theological classes were taught at Aintab and Marash, as early as 1860. It was resolved, eight years afterwards, in view of the

Marash Theological Seminary.

[1] See Chap. xxiv. p. 17; Report of the Board for 1870, p. 21; and *Missionary Herald* for 1869, pp. 87, 122, 257; and for 1871, p. 109.

[2] *Ten Years on the Euphrates*, pp. 162–221.

greater number of students at Marash, that the Theological Seminary, then about being established, should be at that station. The examination of the students of this seminary in 1869, drew together an audience of a thousand persons. Thirty-three students were here in the following year, and it was necessary for the resident missionaries to give themselves almost wholly to their instruction; while the work in the city and at the out-stations was committed to the churches in Marash. That was a year of growth and prosperity to these churches; sixty-six new members being added to them on profession of faith. A new class of eighteen members was received in October.

Mardin Seminaries.

The Seminaries at Mardin are conducted on the same principles as those at Harpoot. They are comparatively new, and are designed to reach the race speaking the Arabic language.

Training-school at Tocat.

The training-school at Tocat was broken up by the fire, which consumed the mission premises in 1859.

High school at Aintab.

A very valuable high school was taught for some years at Aintab, by Mr. Alexan; who was transferred to Marash, in 1864, as assistant teacher in the new Theological Seminary.

Marsovan female seminary.

Thirty-five pupils attended the female Seminary at Marsovan in 1869, and many of them were hopefully converted. In 1870 there were forty pupils.

A majority of the young men in the Seminary at Harpoot were married, and one main design of the female seminary at that station was the education of their wives. These kept house for their husbands, and attended school about seven hours a day, five days of the week. Their younger children were committed to the care of a woman employed for the purpose, while the older ones went to one of the city schools. Of the ninety-four connected with the seminary previous to 1867, forty-one were hopefully converted while in it. Their chief text-book was the Bible; and some of them, besides learning to read intelligently, and to write, keep accounts, and know something of geography and astronomy, became intelligent students and expounders of the Bible, and, with hearts warm with love to Christ, proved themselves wise and efficient in winning souls to Him.[1] This institution has had several valuable teachers from the United States, prominent among whom was Miss Maria A. West.

Harpoot female seminary.

The Female Boarding-school at Aintab was commenced under the care of Miss Proctor in 1861, with eight pupils. The number was increased to fourteen in 1864, and to twenty-five in 1867, of whom ten gave evidence of piety. It is one of the best schools in Turkey.

Female Boarding-school at Aintab.

Mrs. Coffing's labors among the women of Marash, in 1867, and in the four schools of which she had

[1] *Ten Years on the Euphrates*, p. 189.

the oversight, were of great value. In 1868, she had charge of a girls' high school, which was an institution of much promise. The pupils were thirty-eight, six of whom were wives of students in the Theological Seminary. Of the hundred girls who had been in this school from the beginning, twenty-one were hopefully converted while in the school. In 1872, a boarding department was added for the benefit of girls from the out-stations.

Marash female high school.

THE ROBERT COLLEGE.

This college has no direct connection with the American Board, nor with the mission as such; yet our history would be incomplete without some account of it.

The college may be said to have grown out of the efforts of Dr. Hamlin to furnish employment to Protestant Armenians, whose evangelical principles had thrown them out of business. For this end a flour mill and bakery were established with unlooked for success; and when the Crimean war broke out, very large quantities of bread were furnished by this Protestant bakery to the English troops and hospitals at Constantinople.

Its origin.

Christopher R. Robert, Esq., of New York, was then travelling in the East, and his attention was attracted to a large boat load of excellent bread *en route* from the bakery to the English camp. This led to further inquiries, and to an acquaintance and permanent friendship between himself and Dr. Hamlin.

The project of a college was first suggested by the sons of Dr. Dwight, one of the most honored founders of the Armenian mission; and a meeting for consultation, called by them, was held at the house of Mr. Robert in New York, in October, 1857. Several such meetings were held, but no agreement was reached as to the principles which should govern the College.

Mr. Robert, finding that nothing was to be done, then proposed to Dr. Hamlin to take up the work in coöperation with himself; which, after consulting his brethren and the officers of the American Board, he decided to do. I now quote from a statement kindly furnished me by Dr. Hamlin.

"While all agreed in the necessity of a higher education, there were various views in regard to the proposed College. Some regarded these three obstacles as insuperable. (1) The variety of races, — Turkish, Armenian, Greek, and Slavic, — which have no common sympathies, and would not unite in one institution. (2) Variety of religious faith, — Islamism, Romanism, the Oriental Orthodox, and Armenian Churches, — which could never agree in one institution. (3) Variety of language, — Greek, Armenian, Turkish, and Slavonic, — each of which would seek preëminence.

Obstacles to be overcome.

"It was decided, however, to make the experiment.

The College was to be a Christian institution. The Bible was to be read, and prayer offered, morning and evening, at which all should be present. There would be Christian worship and Bible teaching on the Sabbath, but freedom of conscience would be sacredly regarded.

To be a Christian institution.

"The American civil war, breaking out in 1861 prevented any attempt to obtain an endowment in the United States, and Mr. Robert, who had already advanced $10,000 for the purchase of a site, then deposited $30,000 in the hands of trustees, in order to commence the work.

The founder.

"The Turkish Government, at the instigation of Jesuit and French diplomacy, prevented the College from using the beautiful site it had purchased, although official leave to build there had been obtained from the department of Public Instruction. After much delay, expense, and fruitless effort, the College was opened in the building belonging to the American Board, and formerly known as the Bebek Seminary. It was called 'Robert College;' though without Mr. Robert's knowledge, because the name, having no special significance to the people there, would excite no local prejudice.

"The College, thus founded in 1863, slowly but steadily gained the confidence of the communities around it. During the fourth year of its existence, the building was filled with students, and was considerably enlarged. On the

Fully established.

fourth of July, 1869, the corner-stone of a new and large building was laid on the purchased site, leave having been obtained after seven years' effort. The new building, capable of receiving two hundred and fifty students, was entered, and the college opened publicly, September 15th, 1871. It has so rapidly filled with students, that the Trustees have resolved

ROBERT COLLEGE.

to raise an endowment, and erect another still larger building, confident that it also will soon be filled.

"All the supposed obstacles have disappeared. There are seventeen nationalities and six religions represented in the College, and there are no peculiar difficulties of government. Two forces contribute mainly to unify the whole. How obstacles were surmounted.

(1) All are subject to the daily influence of Christian instruction. (2) All study the English language in the preparatory department, and the College course is wholly in that language.

"Another feature of the college should be noticed.

The College self-supporting.

It is self-supporting. It was designed to offer a sound Christian education to those who would pay for it. Two hundred dollars in gold are paid by every student for board and tuition forty weeks in the year. This is more for Turkey, than twice that sum would be in the United States.

"Mr. Robert has given nearly $175,000 for this

Gifts by the founder.

institution, or more than fivefold what he originally contemplated.

"Nothing but the very highest education that can

The demand for Liberal education.

be attained, will now satisfy the Turkish community. Jesuit colleges have fallen into disrepute. They cannot meet this demand fairly, and satisfy it. New ideas of religious freedom pervade these communities; the old bonds are broken, and the college that gives the best culture, moral and mental, will be the most patronized by all. Missionary Societies cannot properly prosecute the work in this highest department of education. And yet foreign missions would be a failure if their work should stop in those classes where it usually begins. It must pervade and control the intelligence and enterprise of the land, and it cannot culminate in this result without the Christian College, and ultimately the Christian University."

PROPOSED COLLEGE IN THE INTERIOR.

As one result of the establishment of "Robert College" at Constantinople, a desire was awakened among the Protestants of Central Turkey for a similar institution, though on a less extended scale, and somewhat differently constituted; to be established either at Aintab, or Marash. Both places were anxious for the location, and set forth their claims with much ability, but the decision inclined in favor of Aintab. The subscriptions pledged by the people of that city, on condition of securing the college, were regarded by Dr. Schneider as equivalent to $60,000 of American money, or more than twenty dollars for each church-member, Nor were the offerings at Marash less liberal, in proportion to their means.

How the idea originated.

The idea appears to have had its origin with the people of Marash; who state that their own condition, the number and power of their enemies, and the baneful influences of infidelity among them, made them feel that the standard of education in the Theological Seminary ought to be so raised as to meet the exigency. The failure of this proposal suggested the college; and the plan of one, elaborated by a committee, was brought before the "Union." By that time, however, the Protestants of Aintab had become fully awake to the importance of the measure, and the claims of the two cities were so earnestly pressed, that the Union declined deciding between them, and referred the decision to the Prudential Committee of the American Board.

The very able pleas by the Protestants of the two cities drawn up in the spring of 1872, are before me, in the English language. The Aintab document opens with an interesting statement of their past progress in the matter of education. "We well remember," they say, "what our condition was, twenty-five or thirty years ago. We had then not even a thought about the necessity or advantages of education. A population of ten thousand Armenians was content with a single common school, where only reading and writing were taught. When, however, through the agency of the American Board, the Bible was translated into our modern language, it soon changed our opinions as to the importance of education, we can hardly explain how. Soon, the evangelical Armenians, not to speak of members of the Old Church, were not content with even three or four schools, nor were they satisfied with educating their sons, but began to plan for the education of their daughters. We discovered that mere reading and writing were not enough, and saw plainly the necessity of a higher grade of studies. Whereas once, we were hardly willing to send our children to schools where all the expense was borne by the missionaries, we were now anxious to open

Interesting statement from Aintab.

schools of a still higher character, and support them ourselves. We now realized, under the light of God's Word, that if men are to be good Christians, good fathers and mothers, and useful members of society, they must be educated. In this respect, our desires have been greatly strengthened by watching in our churches the constantly increasing demand for a stronger class of preachers and teachers. All the churches within the bounds of the Union are convinced of the necessity of a more thoroughly educated ministry. Hence the desire for a college in this section of the country."

To be located at Aintab.

The decision was in favor of Aintab in view of its greater financial ability, its centrality, its comparative healthfulness, the abundance of good building materials, the lower price of skilled labor, the prospective railway communication between the coast and the interior, the proper distribution of educational advantages (the Theological Seminary being already at Marash), and the interest felt by all classes at Aintab, including the Old Armenians and the Moslems.

CHAPTER XLV.

THE ARMENIANS. THE PRESENT CONDITION.

1872.

IT seems often to be required of missions, though not properly, that they shall exert a vastly greater reforming influence on unevangelized countries, than the Gospel has yet done in Christian lands. When we speak of "the conversion of the world," we are generally understood as meaning the introduction of the "Millennium." But what we refer to is not the millennial state, but such a diffusion of gospel agencies and influences through the unevangelized world, as we see in the most favored Christian communities.

Unreasonable demands on foreign missions.

This is all that can reasonably be expected from missionary efforts. The Millenium, whether it be near or remote, doubtless implies such a previous extension of gospel agencies as we are now attempting, but will be the actual result of a universal outpouring of the Spirit, such as we are taught to expect when the time comes for the ultimate triumphs of the Christian dispensation.

How the Millennium is made possible.

The question naturally arises, in closing this

History, how far progress has been made in evangelizing Turkey, or in preparing the way for its future evangelization. From the nature of the case, there can be only an approximation towards an exact reply; and perhaps none can be given more satisfactory, than is furnished by the narrative already recorded in these pages. Yet a brief notice of some of the more important facts, may reasonably be expected here.

Evangelizing progress.

It must not be supposed, that some of the first facts that will be mentioned are regarded as direct results of missionary effort, or as indications of evangelizing progress; but even these mark a progress in the condition of society, which is very cheering, and full of promise with reference to future efforts for the introduction and establishment of a true and pure religion; while others noticed have a more direct and full connection with the missionary work.

Where there has been intellectual and social progress on a large scale, we naturally look for material improvements. Turning, first of all, to the great metropolis, Dr. Wood testifies to such improvements as these: "The streets are named, and doors designated by numbers. Scavenger carts are supplanting the dogs. The terrible conflagrations have secured broad avenues, and handsome stone and brick structures, in place of mean wooden buildings, on streets so narrow that the sun could hardly enter them. Spacious flag-

Changes in the metropolis of Turkey.

stone sidewalks are taking the place of the rough pavements of horrible memory, and macadamized roadbeds help one to climb the steep hill-sides of Constantinople. 'Tramways' are built or building, a boon of inexpressible value to the aged and feeble, and a thousand dwellings have been demolished for the track of the Belgrade and Vienna Railroad, entering at the Seven Towers, and carried along the Marmora, and around the Seraglio Point, to its terminus on the Golden Horn. The demolition of much of the sea-wall to make way for it and furnish materials for embankments, is a suggestive symbol of the social and religious reconstruction, which is tearing up old foundations, and using the labors of ages past for that which is to be."

Dr. Wood next instances the significant telegraph lines, running to all points of the compass, of which he counted twelve on one side of a street, and four on the other. "The spectacle of small craft on the waters, sea-going steamers of the largest class, smaller passenger-boats for the Bosphorus and ports on the Marmora, and the magnificent iron-clads anchored in front of the Sultan's palaces, impresses both residents and strangers with a vivid sense of the greatness, wealth, and power, which, in spite of mismanagement, corruption, misrule, and all the elements of weakness and decline in the country, are here concentrated."

"Costumes," he says, "are changing, and customs

and ideas change with them. Even Turkish women are adopting Frank articles of dress, worn beneath the external covering, and go about tottering on high-heeled shoes of latest Parisian style; and Armenian women appear in public with unveiled faces, attired like ladies of Europe. Thirteen newspapers — three of them dailies, three tri-weeklies, and seven weeklies (one of which issues a daily bulletin), for Armenians alone, at the capital — attest a new intellectual life, by the fact of their existence, and by the freedom of their discussions.

"Schools for girls are multiplying; even a normal school for Turkish girls has been established under government patronage; but a still greater zeal is displayed for the education of boys. The notions of the people concerning education are, indeed, very faulty, and much of the instruction given is poor enough in quality; but the waking up on the subject heralds a brighter day in the future. That this is far greater among the Christian populations, than in the Mohammedan and Jewish, and that the former are gaining more and more upon the latter in the possession of wealth, is suggestive of coming events, of the highest interest and importance."

Dr. Clarke, Foreign Secretary of the Board, writing in the same year (1871), after his visit to the East, mentions the following indications of progress: "Hundreds of miles of railway, begun and under contract; telegraphic communi-

National progress.

cation between the principal towns; postal arrangements for the conveyance of money, as well as letters, established within a few years between many places; police regulations, securing protection to life and property as never before; the suppression of robber-hordes, which had infested different sections; and the beginning of a newspaper press. The public mind in the great centres is waking up to what is going on in the outside world. The war in our own country, by its derangement of commerce, led to much inquiry; and the later conflicts in Europe have excited a lively interest in many minds. And not the least significant matter is the change of sentiment in reference to France and French influence. Already is it said by native merchants, that their children must learn English, or German, instead of French; and the power of Romanism, upheld so long by French consuls, is sensibly weakened. And Protestantism is quietly doing its work of enlightenment, — directly, in thousands of minds, and indirectly, in thousands more."

Influence of the Protestant faith.

Mr. Adams, of Adana, writing a year earlier, affirms that the Christian populations are far more ready to hear and read the Gospel than is commonly supposed, and that the Protestant faith has found its way into the remotest corners of the land. He says, we should not measure the success of missions by "tabular views" alone, for it often happens that a missionary's strongest grounds of hope are quite outside of the largest array of figures. "As I write this," he adds, "a statement of Hagop Effendi occurs to me. He said: "I have travelled a great deal among the Protestants of Syria and Turkey, and the strongest impression I have does not arise from the schools, books, or churches, as pledges that Protestantism is to be a success in Turkey, but from the prodigious extent to which the country at large is leavened by Protestant truth. The grandest results of your labors are not apparent."

Another testimony is by Mr. Leonard, of Marsovan, under date of January, 1871. "Evidence," he says, "of a gradual reform in the Oriental churches, especially the Armenian Church, chiefly as the result of evangelical labors, crops out in almost every city. Consecrated pictures leave church walls for the garret; silver crosses go into the refining pot; auricular confession is neglected; many superstitious ceremonies and foolish restrictions, imposed by the priesthood, are regarded only as a curious relic of the past. We note, also, a growing friendliness towards Protestants, and occasionally very sensible efforts, in emulation of them, to educate the people."

Reform in worship.

Mr. Leonard doubtless had a special reference to the Armenian Bishop of Amasia, who, having secured a majority of the people in his favor, swept two churches of their gold and silver images, crosses, and vestments, and appropriated the avails to the erection of school-houses and the support of teachers. The minority appealed to the Patriarch at Constantinople; but he is known to have been in sympathy with the reforming party in the church before his election, while at Van and Moosh, and is said to have sanctioned the whole proceeding, and to have followed his sanction with an exhortation to preach the Gospel.[1]

The missionaries hopeful.

Another testimony is from Mr. Wheeler, of Harpoot, written in April of the same year: "Henceforth we shall need less money, and more prayer; for this finishing of the work is, in some respects, even more perilous than was its beginning. The people expect and demand a thousand things, which they cannot *now* have; and sometimes the more earnest ones are inclined to take the missionaries by the throat, with a 'Pay us that ye owe!' We are encouraged by the reflection that such experiences necessarily enter into such a work of awakening and reform, as is here going on."

The degree of progress.

The testimony of Hagop Effendi, the Civil Head of the Protestants of Turkey, should also be adduced. He says: "The fact that eighty-five per cent. of the adults in the Protestant community can read, speaks greatly in favor of its members. Any one acquainted with the social con-

[1] *Report of the Board* for 1871, p. 27.

dition and religious ideas of the Orient, who will take pains to compare them with the liberal institutions now introduced, can readily imagine the state of society that must necessarily follow such a change. As yet, the people do not possess the intellectual and moral elements necessary for the maintenance of the liberal institutions of Protestantism independent of foreign aid." "Those," he adds, "who have become Protestant in principle, far exceed in number the registered Protestants. The indirect influence of Protestantism has been greater and healthier than is apparent." He then instances the strictly sober habits of the Protestants, among whom the use of strong drink is very rare, and habitual drunkenness is hardly known. And he was everywhere gratified to find, throughout the empire, a great improvement in domestic relations, as compared with the condition of families before they became Protestants.

The districts of Harpoot, Aintab, and Marash are probably more advanced in the matter of self-governing, self-supporting, evangelical churches, than any other considerable portions of the field in Western Asia. The Rev. Herman N. Barnum, of the Harpoot station, while in the United States, drew up, at my request, a statement of some of the more important results of missionary labor in his own district, which may be regarded as illustra-

Illustrations of progress.

tive of the results of missionary labor in other districts.

He states these as rules, — that no church is to be organized without a native pastor; that no church is to receive aid from the mission for more than one half the salary of the pastor, and none for more than five years. Eighteen churches have been formed in the district, with six hundred and fifty members, and most of them on this plan. The church at Harpoot was self-supporting from the outset. Wherever a fully organized and self-supporting church existed, the peculiar work of the missionaries was regarded as completed in that place; the church and pastor, rather than the missionaries, being henceforth held responsible for the evangelization of the surrounding community. The missionaries aid, if necessary, by their counsel and in other ways, but what they do is through the church. His response as to the character of the churches, which I necessarily abridge, is deemed applicable, substantially, to the seventy-four churches among the Armenians. He says: —

The Harpoot churches.

"1. They are becoming intelligent. Making the Bible a study, they become established in Christian doctrine.

"2. Church discipline is better maintained than it is in American churches. Their 'watch and care' are delightful to witness. Many of these Christians came out of the grossest corruption, but the fellowship of the church is a shield and a support.

"3. They are self-denying. The support of their own institutions, including the building of their school-houses and houses of worship, with very little missionary aid, necessitates the sacrifice of comforts which they cheerfully forego. Experience in Turkey has abundantly proved, that dependent churches are nearly worthless for evangelizing agencies. When the institutions of the Gospel are supported for them, they regard the work of extending it as belonging especially to the missionaries; and hence, however lavish the expenditure, they often complain that money is not more freely spent, and the work prosecuted on a grander scale. Complaints against missionaries come chiefly from churches doing little for themselves. On the other hand, self-supporting churches regard the work of propagating the Gospel as their own, and whatever is given them, they gratefully receive as aid in doing their own work.

"4. These churches resemble the primitive churches in their disposition to work for others. They are imbued with a spirit of labor. They go from house to house, reading and preaching the word. This is the theme in the shop, the field, and by the way-side.

"The chief source of discomfort is in the Armenian character itself, in which there is a lack of stability, and a want of perseverance. But there is ground for hope, that even this national trait may be overcome by the power of the Gospel.

"In Harpoot and its seventy out-stations is a Protestant community of about five thousand souls, characterized by a remarkable reformation in the outward life. Many of them are doubtless Christians, who, in the great care which the churches use in receiving members to their fellowship, are in a certain sense on probation. The Protestant name has become a synonym for integrity and uprightness.

The Harpoot community.

"The extent, to which the Gospel has affected the communities not Protestant, cannot be appreciated by one not in actual contact with them. It manifests itself partly in the weakened power of superstition, the multiplication of schools, the number of adults who have learned to read, the increase in general intelligence and knowledge of the truth, the decrease of intemperance and vice, the promotion of enterprise and good order; and, in short, the beginnings of a civilization, that has a Christian aspect. There have been sold at Harpoot about four thousand copies of the Bible, and twenty thousand portions of the same, with nearly fifty-five thousand volumes of other books, religious and educational, from the mission press. Large numbers of these have gone into the hands of the unevangelized, and are silently exerting an influence. This class of persons is always represented in our congregations.

They hear the truth discussed everywhere, and thousands of them have accepted it intellectually, who have not yet separated themselves from their own religious communities. All this suggests the possibility of a rapid development, when the Spirit shall be poured out from on high.

"Were the Harpoot field limited to the district seventy miles square, of which the city is the centre, it might now be safely left, with its seminaries and hundreds of villages, to the eleven churches and the native laborers found there, with an annual grant, for a few years, from the American Board. As it is, there is good hope that, by the blessing of God on the means in use, the whole district, embracing more than twenty thousand square miles and half a million of souls, may, in a few years, be relinquished as a missionary field."

General statements.

Some estimate may be formed of the influence exerted by the press, when it is considered that more than ten and a half millions of pages were issued, in the single year 1870, in the Armenian, Armeno-Turkish, Græco-Turkish, and Bulgarian languages; and that nearly three hundred millions of pages have been issued by these missions since they began their operations. The number of missionaries among the Armenians, in 1870, was forty, and of female assistant missionaries sixty.

When the missionaries entered Turkey, religion was administered wholly by the hierarchy, and had everywhere a stereotype form. Death was the penalty for heresy among the Moslems; and it was scarcely less in the prevailing sentiment of the nominal Christian sects. The history relates how far this obstacle existed, and how far it has been overcome. Whatever be true as regards the ecclesiastics, the people have now accepted, in some good degree, the principle of religious freedom, and so has the government of the Sultan.

Before the institution of Protestant missions, the school-books among the Turks, Armenians, and Greeks were in the ancient languages, and the schools were consequently of little practical value. One of the first things done by the missionaries was the publication of school-books in the languages spoken by the people; and this simple movement took wonderfully with both Christians and Moslems, and has wrought a mighty revolution in the empire.

The principle of self-support in native churches appears now to be the well-defined policy of all the missions in Turkey, to be realized in practice at the earliest possible day. In some of the missionary districts, the forming of the church and the ordination of the pastor are expected to occur at the same time; and when aid is given it is only for a limited series of years; and the schools, and all other necessary agencies, are to be transferred at the earliest moment from the mission to the people themselves. As a general rule, the missionaries do not now take the lead in the building of school-houses and places of worship. They aid as may seem necessary; but the responsibility and chief pecuniary burden are left with the people; except where the power of precedent, from a different course, is too strong to be overcome at once.

The result.

The various testimonies embodied in this chapter will not affect all minds alike. Yet all must admit, that the Gospel has gained a deeper, firmer hold on the Armenians, than it ever had before, from the days of Gregory "the Illuminator" until now. A mental, moral, and social revolution is in progress, and mainly as a consequence of the republication of the Gospel by missionaries in the past half century; and there is no probability of any event occurring that shall be sufficient to arrest it. Doubtless great evil would result from extensive inroads of sectarian zeal. But there is hope of triumph even then, — from the Bible in their own language, brought by the press within reach of thousands of families, with fathers, mothers, and children able and free to read it; from self-governed, self-supported, self-propagating churches, scattered over the empire, each with its indoctrinated native pastor; from woman holding such a place in the family and social circle, as she never held before; and from common schools, and normal schools, and high schools, and theological seminaries, and even colleges, all independent of the hierarchy, and beyond the power of the Jesuits; with the logic of free thought, and a free conscience.

It would seem that it may not be needful greatly to enlarge the present number of missionaries among the Armenian people. The native ministers and native churches are the main thing. And it must be admitted, that the Gospel, through the grace of God, has been republished, and its institutions replanted, extensively and most hopefully in the Armenian Church of the Orient. "In the midst of fermentation," writes the Constantinople station in 1872, "the leaven of truth is making its way; and so is, also, that of infidelity; but the latter is temporary in its influence, the former permanent. There is far more Protestantism outside of the Protestant church than within it. Protestant ideas of truth, of liberty of conscience, of progress, are spread far and wide, and are convulsing these nations."

CHAPTER XLVI.

THE MOHAMMEDANS.

The Mohammedans approached through the Oriental Churches.

THE necessity for republishing the Gospel among the Oriental Churches, in order to approach the Mohammedans successfully, was stated in the Introduction to this History.[1] It seems proper now to give some illustrations of the effect this republication is likely to have upon that people.

A large portion of them of Christian origin.

A large portion of the Mohammedan population of Turkey is undoubtedly of Christian origin, and therefore less firmly wedded to the Moslem faith and ritual, than are the Osmanly Turks. Three fourths of the four millions in European Turkey, are believed to be of this class. The Kuzzelbashes in Eastern Turkey have a tradition that their Christian ancestors were compelled to become Mohammedans, and they are now regarded by the Turks as little better than infidels; nor are the Koords in much higher repute. Of the Druzes enough was said in the first volume.[2]

Though the penalty of death for embracing the Christian religion has been abrogated in Turkey,[3]

[1] See Volume i. pp. 1–6. [2] See Chapter xv.

[3] See Chapters ix. and xxv.

yet the convert from Mohammedanism does not feel himself free from danger of secret assassination. Far greater security of life and property is enjoyed by Protestant Armenians and Bulgarians, than by Protestant Turks. Indeed, it is not long since Protestant Turks had no security whatever; and in Persia, they have none now. When Koord, Kuzzelbash, and Turk shall feel as free to inquire, and to act on conviction, as the members of the nominally Christian sects, there are facts encouraging the belief, that large numbers of Moslems may be expected to embrace the Christian faith.

Degree of security for Moslem converts.

There is no more satisfactory way of illustrating this than by a simple statement of some of the more important facts. Indeed, it is requisite to the completeness of this history, that these be now stated, since they were designedly omitted in the preceding pages, in their various connections, in order to be recorded here.

Mohammedan susceptibility to Christian influence illustrated.

I begin with the year 1854, when the Imperial Firman of 1850 became known in the provinces.[1] Mr. Dunmore, on his way from Arabkir to Diarbekir, with Priest Kevork, spent the first night at a Moslem village. They had travelled in the rain, and were scarcely dry, says Mr. Dunmore, "when a company of Turks asked us to read to them from the New Testament, and tell them something of our be-

[1] See Chapters xxiv. and xxv.

lief. Kevork read to them from the Gospels, explaining, as he passed along, the precious teachings of our Lord, and closed with prayer. All listened attentively, and pronounced it, 'Good,' 'True,' 'Just.'"

At another place, Mr. Dunmore found Turks desirous to hear the Gospel. "More than once," he says, "in passing through the streets, rich Moslem merchants called us into their shops, expressed their sympathy with us, and an earnest desire that we would remain. They called the Armenians to discuss questions with us, but the latter did so only when constrained by fear, or shame. We were frequently followed by a number of respectable Moslems, as we went from shop to shop to converse with the Armenians; and one day so many gathered about us that we could scarcely proceed on our way; all exclaiming, 'Right,' 'True,' 'Good,' to all that we said."

The Hutti Humaïoun was promulgated in 1855. In that year the Turkish Scriptures were sold openly on the bridge between Galata and Constantinople, no man forbidding.

In September, 1857, Dr. Hamlin described the official examination, at his house, of a family converted from Mohammedanism. It was made at the instigation of the mother of the wife, who was almost frantic at the baptism of her daughter and grandchild. "Our dear friends," wrote Dr. Hamlin, "stood firm as a rock, and at length the officers arose and said to me, as nearly as I can state; 'We are fully convinced that no compulsion has been used in this case, and, so far as we can see, the accusations of the mother are false. It is the will of his Majesty, our Sovereign, and it has become the law of the empire, that every subject, without exception, should enjoy entire religious freedom. The Mussulman is now as free to become a Christian, as a Christian is free to become a Mussulman. The government will know no difference in the two cases. It will only undertake, whenever an accusation of restraint or compulsion is brought, to ascertain the true state of the case; and then only in order to secure the most unexceptionable freedom of choice.'"

In May of the following year, Dr. Hamlin wrote, that Selim Effendi, a converted Mussulman employed as an evangelist among his countrymen, had many inquirers. "I think he conversed with eleven last week; among whom a woman expressed a very decided desire to embrace Christianity, but she was afraid of her son. Her son had sometimes expressed the same wish, but he was afraid of his mother! Selim introduced them to each other."

"Let the following statements be appreciated," said Dr. Schauffler, in September, 1858, "and the difference between the present and the former state of things will be better understood. (1.) The Imans and Ulemas are obliged to resort to moral suasion and entreaty. No threats of persecution are employed; the government takes no responsibility in these matters; the police has nothing to do with them. (2.) Although there are fewer purchasers of the New Testament, yet men buy it publicly, fearing no civil penalty. 'Why do you buy this infidel book?' says a bigot to a Mohammedan purchaser of the Gospel. He replies: 'I chose to buy it, and with my own money; you are welcome to mind your own business;' and so the matter ends. (3.) We hear of no search being made for the books in circulation among Mussulmans. No New Testaments have been burned yet, that we know of, by the Turks, as many copies have been by the Greek or Catholic priests and bishops."

Mr. Dunmore wrote, in the same year, after visiting thirty villages, mostly Kuzzelbash and Turkish: "I really felt ashamed, that in touring I had ever passed by a Turkish village, without stopping to point them to the Lamb of God, which taketh away the sins of the world? And I testify what I have seen, when I say, that the Turks are approachable; and many of them ready to listen to the Gospel; while others are anxious to search the Scriptures, and are restrained only by the pressure of fears, which, as yet, the Hatti-humaioun has scarcely begun to remove in this region."

I quote again from the same missionary: "At a Koordish village of twenty houses we spent two hours in preaching the Word to a company of thirty. One of them, who seemed to have received a few rays of light from enlightened men, boldly declared, that he believed the time was near, when the sword would no more be used to keep men in Moslem bonds, but that they all would soon be free to embrace the Gospel, if they wished. We spent a night at a Kuzzelbash village of forty houses. Immediately on our arrival, we had an audience of thirty or forty; and during the long evening, fifty or more listened to the great truths of the Gospel. We preached 'Christ crucified; the way, the truth, and the life;' and they received the word with eagerness. When the evening was far spent, we bowed together before the mercy-seat, after which our audience reluctantly retired. These are but samples of our visits among Kuzzelbashes and Turks on this tour."

Dr. Hamlin, speaking of Turks near the close of 1858, says: "There have been, here and there, some burnings of the New Testament; not publicly, but in private, or in small social circles. Among Mussulmans themselves a spirited debate has repeatedly arisen as to the moral character of the act. Some have approved, others have most decidedly condemned it, affirming that the New Testament is the Word of God. What impressed us most strongly is the bold manner in which orthodox Turks have declared it to be the Word of God, and that to burn it is a sin."[1]

[1] See *Missionary Herald* for 1858, p. 380.

Dr. Dwight wrote in May, 1859: "The work among the Turks is looming up; and if not hindered by some untoward event, or by our neglect, it will by and by assume very large proportions. That Turkish officials through the country have been instructed not to persecute Mohammedans who embrace Christianity, is very evident. The governors of Sivas, Cesarea, and Diarbekir have, to our knowledge, within a short time, and with actual cases before them, publicly declared, that a Mohammedan who became a Christian could not be molested."

Mr. White visited a place on the north of the Taurus Mountains in May, 1860, and had many calls from Mussulmans. "Every day they came," he says, "with an apparently sincere desire to learn the truth; and held long conversations on man's sinfulness, and how it was possible for God to forgive sin. 'We have lost God;' 'We have lost the road;' 'We cannot find God;' were expressions they used very often. At almost every meeting, from three to five Mussulmans were present. One is known all over the city as a Protestant; and a second is a member of the Governor's Council."

Mr. Herrick, speaking of the Turkish department in the Bebek Seminary, wrote thus, in the same year: "Quite a number of Mohammedans have renounced Islam, and become true Christians; many more are soberly inquiring after the truth; and many others are turning, unsatisfied, from a religion which cannot save, or wavering in a merely nominal devotion to Islamism. That which is most striking is the clear evidence, often, of the work of God's Spirit in individual cases, and in general movements."

Dr. Schneider gives this testimony concerning the Mussulmans at an out-station of Aintab: "There is a willingness among the Moslems here to listen to arguments in favor of Christianity, that is uncommon. By intercourse with Protestants, and the reading of the Scriptures, many of them have obtained glimpses of the truth, and a few are more or less convinced that Christianity is true. While I was there, fifteen Mussulmans and several women attended a service. Apparently there is no place in this region where there is so much prospect of a speedy work to be done among the Mussulmans."

The inducement to labor among the Moslems, was much increased in the year 1860. At one large town in the heart of Asia Minor, a Moslem said to a Protestant, "Since you came here, you have caused us to fall into doubt and fear." At another, a Turk and his wife appeared to be true Christians. Though the man was zealous in making known the Gospel, the Moslems agreed to ignore his being a Protestant. At Diarbekir, a Turk declared himself a Christian, and a captain of the army at Harpoot did the same. Many Turks in the latter region purchased the New Testament, and some the whole Bible. The military

Pasha of this district bought a Bible publicly, and so did the civil Pasha; thus showing the effect of the thorough evangelization of that community. At Constantinople, Dr. Dwight reported his having read the Scriptures and bowed in prayer with a high officer of the army in the palace of a Pasha, in the Mussulman quarter of the city, and in the presence of servants; the officer appearing to be strongly under the influence of evangelical ideas and feelings. Six Moslem converts were baptized that year at the capital. One of these was an Iman, seventy years of age. There had then been fifteen baptisms of adult converts from Mohammedanism in Constantinople.[1] The Grand Vizier subsequently required the Serasker to call Abdi Effendi, the baptized Iman above mentioned, and examine him. This was done, and the old man made the following confession and statement: "We are no ghiaours (*i. e.* we worship neither pictures, nor crosses, nor saints); we assemble and read out of this book (drawing out of his bosom the New Testament); we sing out of this one (producing a Turkish Hymn Book); and we listen to preaching from the Gospel, and engage in prayer for all men. If there is anything wrong in this book, please point it out to me." He supposed (on inquiry) that there might be some forty men who were like him, and mentioned some of their names.

[1] In part, by English missionaries.

General character of the illustrations.

It would be easy to multiply illustrations like the foregoing of the susceptibility of Mohammedans to Christian influence; and the reader will notice that they are of the same general nature with the early manifestations of interest among the Armenians. There have been, also, Turkish converts, who braved death in their Christian profession, and remained steadfast unto the end.

The Gospel yet in its incipient stage of influence.

No churches have been formed by our missionaries exclusively of Turkish Christians; and it can hardly be said, that the Board has yet had an organized mission to this people. Of the four missionaries sent especially to the Turks, Dr. Schauffler has devoted himself chiefly to translating the Scriptures into the Osmanli-Turkish; Mr. Herrick, besides doing service by his commentaries and other literary labors in that language, has been mainly employed in the Turkish department of the Theological Seminary, first at Bebek, and then at Marsovan; the younger Mr. Schauffler was born on the ground, as we may say, and began his labors amid the strifes of the Armenians in Constantinople with the missionaries, which was a great hindrance to his work, and the health of his family not allowing him to remain in Turkey, he is now a pioneer in the new mission to Austria; and Mr. Hutchison had scarcely entered the Turkish department of the Bebek Seminary, when the failure of his wife's health required a return to the United States. The mission of the Rev. James L. Merrick to the Persian Mohammedans, in 1834, was little more than a tentative exploration of the field, and was not continued.[1]

With a field so inviting as the Armenian alongside of the Mohammedan, it was not easy to obtain missionaries to the Moslems. Then again, missionaries to the Armenians soon became engrossed by their labors. "The Mohammedans," wrote Dr. Schauffler in 1859, "never will be cared for by missionaries to the Armenians or the Bulgarians. We can all render each other important services, but no missionary can take charge of two nationalities. Each one, soon after coming, finds his hands so full of business for which he feels responsible, that he cannot do much besides. Moreover, every man gets his sympathies enlisted for the people of his charge. This is probably necessary to enable us to labor with energy, and suffer with patience; but this needful concentration of feeling precludes the idea of universality in missionary labor."

Why so little effort hitherto.

Experience has also developed the great law here,

[1] It should be stated that the English Church Missionary Society has had a missionary to the Mohammedans in Constantinople since 1862, and reports five converts who are communicants. For the reactionary movement among the Turks at Constantinople, in consequence of the distribution of Dr. Pfander's *Defense of Christianity against Mohammedanism*, see page 234 of this volume.

as well as elsewhere, that the main work of winning races to Christianity must be performed by men of the same race. A Moslem will listen more patiently to a Christian Turk ("renegade" though he be), than he will to an Armenian; nor has it been found easy to enlist the Protestant Armenians effectively in labors for the Turks. It may be otherwise when the work is more advanced, and the Armenians are elevated to a higher social level. But a ministry raised from among themselves, is indispensable to the most efficient evangelization of the Turks.

Demand for laborers of the same race.

It would seem, therefore, that, up to the present time, the original plan of the mission to Turkey has been more promising of good, than any other; namely, that of operating upon the Mohammedans through regenerated churches planted in the communities where they dwell; and the greatest usefulness of these churches, for obvious reasons, must be expected in the interior, rather than in the capital. Thus far, there has been no material or very obvious change in the missionary policy; and the risk of such a change, and its probable advantages on the whole, should be carefully estimated. The Protestant nations of Europe are substantially with us in our evangelical labors among the Oriental Churches; and the churches we gather are "our epistle," "known and read" by the Mohammedans. Gradually, it may be, some of the

Experience favors the plan hitherto pursued.

missionaries now in the field, who are familiar with the Turkish language, and have their Armenian churches supplied with pastors, will turn their attention mainly to the Moslems, in the exercise of a sound discretion, both as regards the Turks and the Christians. It may be found that both classes may be happily inclosed in the same fold. The missionary now occupies a higher and more influential position with both, than he did years ago. The Turk, too, is better appreciated as he becomes known. He has more of manliness, self-respect, and religious feeling, than some races for whose salvation our labors have been blest. The masses are by no means hopeless, and the middle class is full of promise.

The probable future.

The relation of the missionary.

The Turks not an unhopeful race.

The future is in the hands of the great Head of the Church; who has so crowned with success the past labors of his servants in Turkey, as to warrant the expectation, that whatever is needful to the effectual republication of the Gospel in those Bible lands, may be attempted with the glad assurance of success.

MISSIONARIES.

MISSIONARIES.

When no date occurs in the right hand column, it is because the missionary is still in the field.

In several instances, the date of the wife's arrival in the field precedes the arrival of the husband. The explanation is that the wife, previous to marriage, had been connected with the mission as a teacher.

Dr. Eli Smith's Exploring Tour is included in his thirty years' missionary service. So in the case of Dr. H. G. O. Dwight, and some others.

Cyprus is included in the Mission to Greece and the Greeks; the population consisting largely of that element.

The asterisk (*) placed before a name, denotes that the person is deceased. When it is placed before a *date*, in the right hand column, it denotes that the person died *at the time there indicated*, and in the field.

The Assyria Mission terminated in November, 1860, when it was merged in the Mission to the Armenians. The persons composing that mission remained at their stations.

It should be specially noted, that this table is not designed to state the time of a missionary's connection either with the Mission, or with the Board, but only of his residence in the field.

MISSION TO PALESTINE.

Ordained Missionaries.	Wives of Missionaries.	Time of Entering.	Time of Leaving.
*Pliny Fisk	. . . .	Jan. 15, 1820.	*Oct. 23, 1825.
*Levi Parsons . . .	. . . .	Jan. 15, 1820.	*Feb. 10, 1822.
*Jonas King, D. D. .	[See Mission to Greece.] .	Nov. 2, 1822.	Aug. 26, 1825.
*George B. Whiting .	[See Mission to Syria] .	Oct., 1834.	Autumn, 1843.
	Mrs. Matilda S. Whiting	Oct., 1834.	Autumn, 1843.
Wm. M. Thomson, D. D.	[See Mission to Syria] .	April, 1834.	
	*Mrs. Eliza N. Thomson	April, 1834.	*July 22, 1834.
*John F. Lanneau .	[See Mission to Syria] .	May 1, 1836.	June 11, 1846.
Charles S. Sherman .	. . . .	Sept., 1838.	July 1, 1842.
	Mrs. Martha E. Sherman	Sept., 1839.	July 1, 1842.
Missionary Physician.			
*Asa Dodge, M. D. .	. . . .	Sept., 1834.	*Jan. 28, 1835.
	Mrs. Martha Dodge . .	Sept., 1834.	1838.
Assistant Missionary.			
	Miss Betsey Tilden . .	June 16, 1836.	March 1, 1843.

Messrs. Beadle and Keyes were at Jerusalem from July 17, 1840, to January, 1841.

THE PRINTING ESTABLISHMENT AT MALTA.

Ordained Missionaries.	Wives of Missionaries.	Time of Entering.	Time of Leaving.
*Daniel Temple . .	[See Mission to Armenians]	Feb. 22, 1822.	Dec., 1833.
	*Mrs. Rachel B. Temple	Feb. 22, 1822.	*Jan. 15, 1827.
	*Mrs. Martha E. Temple	Feb. 25, 1830.	Dec., 1833.
Assistant Missionary.			
Homan Hallock . .	[See Mission to Armenians]	Dec. 10, 1826.	
	Mrs. Elizabeth Hallock .	Mar. 26, 1828.	

MISSION TO SYRIA.

Ordained Missionaries.	Wives of Missionaries.	Time of Entering.	Time of Leaving.
*William Goodell, D. D.	[See Mission to Armenians]	Oct. 16, 1823.	May 2, 1828.
	*Mrs. Abigail P. Goodell	Oct. 16, 1823.	May 2, 1828.
Isaac Bird	. . . .	Oct. 16, 1823.	Aug., 1835.
	Mrs. Ann P. Bird . . .	Oct. 16, 1823.	Aug., 1835.
*Eli Smith, D. D. . .	. . . .	Feb. 18, 1827.	*Jan. 11, 1857.
	*Mrs. Sarah L. H. Smith	Jan. 28, 1834.	*Sept. 30, 1836.
	*Mrs. Maria W. C. Smith	June 17, 1841.	*May 27, 1842.
	Mrs. Henrietta S. Smith	Jan. 12, 1847.	May, 1857.
Wm. M. Thomson, D. D.	[See Mission to Palestine]	Sept., 1834.	
	Mrs. Maria Thomson . .	Aug. 3, 1835.	
*Story Hebard . .	. . . .	Mar. 14, 1836.	*June 30, 1841.
	*Mrs. Rebecca W. Hebard [formerly Miss Williams]	Nov. 18, 1835.	*Feb. 18, 1840.
Elias R. Beadle . .	. . . .	Oct. 15, 1838.	Sept. 27, 1842.
	*Mrs. Hannah Beadle .	Oct. 15, 1838.	Sept. 27, 1842.
Samuel Wolcott, D. D.	. . . .	April 1, 1840.	Jan. 2, 1843.
	*Mrs. Catharine E. Wolcott	April 1, 1840.	*Oct. 26, 1841.
*Nathaniel A. Keyes	. . . .	April 2, 1840.	April 5, 1844.
	*Mrs. Mary Keyes . . .	April 2, 1840.	April 5, 1844.
Leander Thompson .	. . . .	April 1, 1840.	March 1, 1843.
	Mrs. Anne E. Thompson	April 1, 1840.	March 1, 1843.
C. V. A. Van Dyck, D. D.	. . . .	April 1, 1840.	
	Mrs. Julia A. Van Dyck .	Dec. 22, 1842.	
*George B. Whiting	[See Mission to Palestine]	Autumn, 1843.	*Nov. 8, 1855.
	*Mrs. Matilda S. Whiting	Autumn, 1843.	Mar. 14, 1856.
*John F. Lanneau .	[See Mission to Palestine]	Feb., 1844.	Feb. 17, 1846.
	Mrs. Julia H. Lanneau .	Feb., 1844.	Feb. 17, 1846.
Simeon H. Calhoun .	. . . .	July 8, 1844.	
	Mrs. Emily P. Calhoun .	March 6, 1849.	
Thomas Laurie, D. D.	[See Mission to Nestorians]	Dec. 11, 1844.	May 9, 1846.
William A. Benton .	. . . .	Oct. 20, 1847, }	Con. terminat-
	Mrs. Loanza G. Benton .	Oct. 20, 1847, }	ed June, 1861.
*J. Edwards Ford .	. . . .	March 8, 1848.	June, 1865.
	Mrs. Mary Ford . . .	March 8, 1848.	1865.
David M. Wilson . .	. . . .	March 8, 1848	May 4, 1861.
	Mrs. Emeline Wilson . .	March 8, 1848.	May 4, 1861.
Horace Foote . . .	. . . .	Aug. 24, 1848.	Autumn, 1854.
	*Mrs. Roxana Foote . .	Aug. 24, 1848.	Autumn, 1854.
*Wm. F. Williams, D.D.	[See Assyria Mission] . .	March 6, 1849.	
	*Mrs. Sarah P. Williams	March 6, 1849.	*July 1, 1854.

MISSION TO SYRIA. — Continued.

Ordained Missionaries.	Wives of Missionaries.	Time of Entering.	Time of Leaving.
William W. Eddy .	. . . .	Jan. 31, 1852.	
	Mrs. Hannah M. Eddy . .	Jan. 31, 1852.	
William Bird . . .	. . . .	April, 1853.	
	Mrs. Sarah F. Bird . .	April, 1853.	
J. Lorenzo Lyons	. . . .	Feb. 25, 1855.	June, 1863.
	Mrs. Catharine N. Lyons	Feb. 25, 1855.	June, 1863.
Edward Aiken . . .	. . . .	April, 1856.	May 1, 1858.
	*Mrs. Susan D. Aiken .	April, 1856.	*June 20, 1856.
	Mrs. Sarah C. Aiken . . [formerly Miss Cheney]		May 1, 1858.
Daniel Bliss, D. D. .	. . . .	April, 1856.	
	Mrs. Abby M. Bliss . .	April, 1856.	
Henry H. Jessup, D. D.	. . . .	Feb. 7, 1856.	
	*Mrs. Caroline Jessup .	April, 1858.	*July 2, 1864.
	Mrs. Harriet E. Jessup .	Nov. 22, 1868.	
Samuel Jessup . .	. . . .	Jan. 24, 1863.	
	Mrs. Ann E. Jessup . .	Jan. 24, 1863.	
Philip Berry . . .	. . . .	Oct. 7, 1863.	Oct., 1865.
	Mrs. Magdalene Berry .	Oct. 7, 1863.	Oct., 1865.
Geo. Edw'd Post, M. D.	. . . .	Dec., 1863.	
	Mrs. Sarah P. Post . .	Dec., 1863.	
Samuel S. Mitchell .	. . . .	June 12, 1867.	1868.
	Mrs. Lucy M. Mitchell .	June 12, 1867.	1868.
Isaac N. Lowry . .	. . . .	Nov. 23, 1867.	1869.
	Mrs. Mary E. Lowry . .	Nov. 22, 1867.	1869.
James S. Dennis . .	. . . .	Feb. 10, 1869.	
Missionary Physicians.			
*H. A. DeForest, M. D.	. . . .	Mar. 23, 1842.	May 8, 1854.
	Mrs. Catharine S. De Forest	Mar. 23, 1842.	May 8, 1854.
Assistant Missionaries.			
George C. Hurter . .	. . . .	April 15, 1841.	Spring, 1864.
	Mrs. Elizabeth Hurter .	April 15, 1841.	June 7, 1861.
	*Miss Rebecca W. Williams [afterwards Mrs. Hebard]	Nov. 13, 1835.	*Feb. 8, 1840.
	*Miss Anna L. Whittlesey	May 2, 1851.	*May 1, 1852.
	Miss Sarah Cheney . . [now Mrs. Edw'd Aiken]	April, 1853.	May 1, 1858.
	Miss Jane E. Johnson .	Aug. 31, 1858.	May 15, 1859.
	Miss Amelia C. Temple . [now Mrs. Geo. Gould]	Aug. 31, 1858.	Spring, 1862.
	Miss Adelaide L. Mason .	April 11, 1860.	June, 1865.
	Miss Eliza D. Everett .	Nov. 22, 1868.	
	Miss Nellie A. Carruth .	Nov. 22, 1868.	1869.

MISSION TO GREECE AND THE GREEKS.

Ordained Missionaries.	Wives of Missionaries.	Time of Entering.	Time of Leaving.
Josiah Brewer . . .	. . . .	Dec. 27, 1826.	Spring, 1828.
*Elnathan Gridley .	. . . .	Dec. 27, 1826.	*Sept. 27, 1827.
*Jonas King, D. D. .	[See Mission to Palestine]	April, 1831.	*May 22, 1869.
	Mrs. Anna A. King . .	April, 1831.	1869.
Elias Riggs, D.D. . .	[See Mission to Armenians]	Jan., 1833.	
	Mrs. Martha Jane Riggs	Jan., 1833.	
Samuel R. Houston .	. . . .	Nov., 1834.	1840.
	*Mrs. Mary R. Houston .	Nov., 1834.	*Nov. 24, 1839.
*Lorenzo W. Pease .	. . . .	Nov., 1834.	*Aug. 28, 1839.
	Mrs. Lucinda Pease . .	Nov., 1834.	Spring, 1841.
James L. Thompson	. . . .	May, 1836.	Autumn, 1841.
Daniel Ladd . . .	[See Mission to Armenians]	Oct., 1836.	
	Mrs. Charlotte H. Ladd .	Oct., 1836.	
*Nathan Benjamin .	[See Mission to Armenians]	Nov., 1836.	
	*Mrs. Mary G. Benjamin	Nov., 1836.	
George W. Leyburn .	. . . .	June, 1837.	1842.
	Mrs. Elizabeth W. Leyburn	June, 1837.	1842.

MISSION TO THE ARMENIANS.

Ordained Missionaries.	Wives of Missionaries.	Time of Entering.	Time of Leaving.
*William Goodell, D. D.	[See Mission to Syria] .	June 9, 1831.	Summer, 1865.
	*Mrs. Abigail P. Goodell	June 9, 1831.	Summer, 1865.
*H. G. O. Dwight, D. D.	. . . .	Feb. 27, 1830.[1]	Jan. 25, 1862.
	*Mrs. Elizabeth Dwight .	June 5, 1832.	*July 8, 1837.
	*Mrs. Mary Dwight . .	Sept. 4, 1839.	*Nov. 16, 1860.
*Daniel Temple . .	[See Print. Estab. at Malta]	Dec. 28, 1833.	Summer, 1844.
	*Mrs. Martha E. Temple	Dec. 28, 1833.	Summer, 1844.
Thomas P. Johnston	. . . .	Jan. 19, 1834.	1853.
	Mrs. Marianne C. Johnston	Jan. 19, 1834.	1853.
Benj. Schneider, D. D.	. . . .	Jan. 19, 1834.	
	*Mrs. Eliza C. Schneider	Jan. 19, 1834.	*Sept. 29, 1856.
	Mrs. Susan M. Schneider	Oct. 1, 1858.	
John B. Adger, D. D.	. . . .	Oct. 25, 1834.	1846.
	Mrs. Elizabeth K. Adger	Oct. 25, 1834.	1846.
Philander O. Powers	. . . .	Jan. 12, 1835.	Summer, 1861.
	*Mrs. Harriet G. Powers	Jan. 12, 1835.	April, 1841.
	*Mrs. Sarah L. Powers .	Jan. 11, 1848.	June, 1861.
Philander O. Powers	[Reappointed	June 25, 1866.	
Henry A. Homes . .	. . . .	Dec. 26, 1835.	Dec. 10, 1850.
	Mrs. Anna W. Homes .	June 17, 1841.	1849.
William C. Jackson .	. . . .	Feb. 1, 1836.	1845.
	Mrs. Mary A. Jackson .	Feb. 1, 1836.	1845.
Cyrus Hamlin, D. D.	. . . .	Feb. 4, 1839.	
	*Mrs. H. A. L. Hamlin .	Feb. 4, 1839.	*Nov. 14, 1850
	*Mrs. Harriet M. Hamlin [formerly Miss H. M. Lovell]	April 18, 1845.	*Nov. 6, 1857.
	Mrs. Mary E. Hamlin [formerly Miss M. E. Tenney]	Jan. 22, 1856.	

[1] Dr. Dwight arrived at Malta at the date here indicated, but did not settle at Constantinople till June 5, 1832. The intervening time was employed partly in an exploring tour, and partly at Malta, in labors tributary to the mission.

MISSION TO THE ARMENIANS. — Continued.

Ordained Missionaries.	Wives of Missionaries.	Time of Entering.	Time of Leaving.
H. J. Van Lennep, D.D.	. . . .	April 13, 1840.	Summer, 1869.
	*Mrs. Emma L. Van Lennep	April 13, 1840.	*Sept. 12, 1840.
	*Mrs. Mary E. Van Lennep	Nov. 24, 1843.	*Sept. 27, 1844.
	Mrs. Emily A. Van Lennep	June 16, 1850.	Summer, 1869.
Josiah Peabody . .	. . . .	July, 1841.	July, 1860.
	Mrs. Mary L. Peabody .	July, 1841.	July, 1860.
George W. Wood, D. D.	. . . .	April 28, 1842.	Sept. 4, 1850.
	*Mrs. Martha B. Wood .	April 28, 1842.	Sept. 4, 1850.
George W. Wood, D. D.	[Reappointed]	1871.	
	Mrs. Sarah A. H. Wood .	1871.	
Daniel Ladd . . .	[See Mission to Greece] .	Sept. 8, 1842.	Aug., 1867.
	Mrs. Charlotte H. Ladd .	Sept. 8, 1842.	Aug., 1867.
*Azariah Smith, M. D.	. . . .	Jan. 11, 1843.	*June 3, 1851.
	Mrs. Corinth I. Smith .	Sept. 20, 1848.	1853.
Edwin E. Bliss, D. D.	. . . .	April 16, 1843.	
	Mrs. Isabella H. Bliss .	April 16, 1843.	
E. Riggs, D. D., LL. D.	[See Mission to Greece and the Bulgarians] . . .	1844.	
	Mrs. Martha J. Riggs .	1844.	
*Nathan Benjamin .	[See Mission to Greece] .	August, 1844.	*Jan. 27, 1855.
	*Mrs. Mary G. Benjamin	August, 1844.	1855.
*Joel S. Everett . .	. . . .	April 18, 1845.	*March 5, 1856.
	*Mrs. Seraphina Everett	April 18, 1845.	*Dec. 27, 1854.
Isaac G. Bliss, D. D. .	. . . .	Aug. 24, 1847.	
	Mrs. Eunice B. Bliss . .	Aug. 24, 1847.	
Oliver Crane . . .	. . . .	March, 1849.	1854.
	Mrs. Marion D. Crane .	March, 1849.	1854.
Oliver Crane . . .	[Reappointed]	1860.	1863.
	Mrs. Marion D. Crane .	1860.	1863.
*Joseph W. Sutphen	. . . .	Jan. 16, 1852.	*Oct. 9, 1852.
	Mrs. Susan H. Sutphen . [afterwards Mrs. Morgan]	Jan. 16, 1852.	1865.
Wilson A. Farnsworth	. . . .	Jan. 22, 1853.	
	Mrs. Caroline E. Farnsworth	Jan. 22, 1853.	
William Clark . . .	. . . .	Jan. 22, 1853.	Aug., 1859.
	Mrs. Elizabeth W. Clark	Jan. 22, 1853.	Aug., 1859.
Andrew T. Pratt, M. D.	. . . .	Jan. 22, 1853.	
	Mrs. Sarah F. Pratt . .	Jan. 22, 1853.	
George B. Nutting .	. . . .	Feb. 9, 1853.	Summer, 1868.
	*Mrs. Sarah E. Nutting .	Feb. 9, 1853.	*July 9, 1854.
	Mrs. Susan A. Nutting .	Autumn, 1856.	Summer, 1868.
*Fayette Jewett, M. D.	. . . .	April 20, 1853.	*June 18, 1862.
	*Mrs. Mary A. A. Jewett	April 20, 1853.	Summer, 1862.
*Jasper N. Ball.	. . . .	Sept. 21, 1853.	Aug., 1861.
	*Mrs. Caroline W. Ball .	Sept. 21, 1853.	Aug., 1861.
*Jasper N. Ball. . .	[Reappointed]	Jan., 1865.	1869.
	Mrs. Martha Ann Ball .	Jan., 1865.	1869.
*George W. Dunmore	. . . .	May, 1851.	1861.
	Mrs. Susan Dunmore .	May, 1851.	1856.
Albert G. Beebee . .	. . . .	Sept., 1854.	March, 1860.
	*Mrs. Sarah J. Beebee .	Sept., 1854.	*Oct. 28, 1858.
George A. Perkins .	. . . .	Sept., 1854.	Spring, 1861.
	Mrs. Sarah E. Perkins .	Sept., 1854.	Spring, 1861.
Sanford Richardson .	. . . .	Sept. 25, 1854.	
	Mrs. Rhoda A. Richardson	Sept. 25, 1854.	
*Edwin Goodell . .	. . . .	Sept. 25, 1854.	1855.
	Mrs. Catharine J. Goodell	Sept. 25, 1854	1855.
Benjamin Parsons .	. . . .	Sept. 25, 1854.	1860.
	Mrs. Sarah W. Parsons .	Sept. 25, 1854.	1860.

MISSION TO THE ARMENIANS. — CONTINUED.

ORDAINED MISSIONARIES.	WIVES OF MISSIONARIES.	TIME OF ENTERING.	TIME OF LEAVING.
Alexander R. Plumer	. . . .	Feb. 8, 1855.	1859
	Mrs. Elizabeth P. Plumer	Feb. 8, 1855.	1859
Ira Fayette Pettibone	. . . .	Aug. 4, 1855.	1863
Ira Fayette Pettibone	[Reappointed]	May, 1866.	
Justin W. Parsons .	[See Mission to the Jews]	Sept., 1855.	
	Mrs. Catharine Parsons .	Sept., 1855.	
*Edward M. Dodd .	[See Mission to the Jews]	Sept. 28, 1855.	*Aug. 19, 1865.
	Mrs. Lydia H. Dodd . .	Sept. 28, 1855.	June, 1866.
Orson P. Allen . .	. . . .	Dec. 9, 1855.	
	Mrs. Caroline R. Allen .	Dec. 9, 1855.	
*Homer B. Morgan .	[See Mission to the Jews]	Jan., 1856.	*Aug. 25, 1865.
	Mrs. Susan H. Morgan .	Jan. 16, 1852.	1865.
Tillman C. Trowbridge	[See Mission to the Jews]	Jan. 22, 1856.	
	Mrs. Margaret Trowbridge	1861.	
George A. Pollard .	. . . .	Jan. 22, 1856.	1868.
	Mrs. Mary H. Pollard .	Jan. 22, 1856.	1868.
Crosby H. Wheeler .	. . . .	March 2, 1857.	
	Mrs. Susan A. Wheeler .	March 2, 1857.	
Charles F. Morse . .	[See Mission to Bulgarians]	March 2, 1857.	
	Mrs. Eliza D. Morse . .	March 2, 1857.	
Oliver W. Winchester	. . . .	March 2, 1857.	June, 1865.
	Mrs. Jeannette S. Winchester	March 2, 1857.	June, 1865.
*Jackson G. Coffing .	. . . .	March 2, 1857.	*Mar. 26, 1862.
	Mrs. Josephine L. Coffing	March 2, 1857.	
George H. White . .	. . . .	March 2, 1857.	Autumn, 1868.
	Mrs. Joanna White . .	March 2, 1857.	Autumn, 1868.
Julius Y. Leonard .	. . . .	Sept. 4, 1857.	
	Mrs. Amelia A. Leonard	Sept. 4, 1857.	
George Washburn .	. . . .	August, 1858.	
	Mrs. Henrietta L. Washburn	April 15, 1859.	
Joseph K. Greene .	. . . .	Feb. 22, 1859.	
	Mrs. Elizabeth A. Greene	Feb. 22, 1859.	
Herman N. Barnum	. . . .	Autumn, 1858.	
	Mrs. Mary B. Barnum .	July, 1860.	
William F. Arms . .	. . . .	1860.	1864.
	*Mrs. Emily F. Arms . .	1860.	*March, 1861.
Alvin B. Goodale, M. D.	. . . .	Mar. 25, 1860.	1864.
	Mrs. Mary E. Goodale .	Mar. 25, 1860.	1864.
*Zenas Goss . . .	. . . .	Mar. 25, 1860.	*Aug. 28, 1864.
William W. Livingston	. . . .	Sept. 8, 1860.	1871.
	Mrs. Martha E. Livingston	Sept. 8, 1860.	1871.
*Wm. F. Williams, D.D.	[See Mission to Assyria] .	Nov., 1860.	*Feb. 14, 1871.
	*Mrs. Caroline P. Williams [for. Miss C. P. Barbour]	Oct. 4, 1861.	*Jan. 15, 1865.
			Dec. 25, 1857.
	Mrs. Clarissa C. Williams [formerly Miss C. C. Pond]	Oct. 15, 1864.	1871.
*Augustus Walker .	[See Assyria Mission] . .	Nov., 1860.	*Sept. 18, 1866.
	Mrs. Eliza M. Walker .	Nov., 1860.	July, 1867.
George C. Knapp . .	[See Assyria Mission] . .	Nov., 1860.	
	Mrs. Alzina M. Knapp .	Nov., 1860.	
Lysander T. Burbank	. . . .	Oct. 18, 1860.	1871.
	Mrs. Sarah S. Burbank .	Oct. 18, 1860.	1871.
John Francis Smith	. . . .	July 8, 1868.	
	Mrs. Laura E. Smith . .	July 8, 1868.	
Moses P. Parmelee, M.D.	. . . .	Aug. 14. 1868.	
	*Mrs. Nellie A. Parmelee	Aug. 14, 1868.	*Feb. 17, 1870.
	Mrs. Julia Parmelee . .	Sept., 1871.	
Giles F. Montgomery	. . . .	Dec., 1868.	
	Mrs. Emily R. Montgomery	Dec., 1868.	

MISSION TO THE ARMENIANS. — CONTINUED.

Ordained Missionaries.	Wives of Missionaries.	Time of Entering.	Time of Leaving.
*Walter H. Giles . .	. . . .	Nov. 17, 1864.	*May 21, 1867.
	Mrs. Elizabeth F. Giles .	Nov. 17, 1864.	
Lucien H. Adams .	. . . .	June 9, 1865.	
	*Mrs. Augusta S. Adams	June 9, 1865.	*Nov. 18, 1866.
	Mrs. Nancy D. Adams [formerly Miss N. D. Francis]	June 26, 1868.	
Albert Bryant . . .	. . . .	Oct. 28, 1865.	June, 1868.
	Mrs. Mary E. I. Bryant .	Oct. 28, 1865.	June, 1868.
Henry T. Perry . .	. . . .	Jan. 11, 1867.	
	Mrs. Jennie H. Perry .	Jan. 11, 1867.	
Theodore A. Baldwin	. . . .	Aug. 9, 1867.	
	Mrs. Matilda J. Baldwin	Aug. 9, 1867.	
Henry S. Barnum .	. . . .	Aug. 10, 1867.	
	*Mrs. Lucretia L. Barnum	Aug. 10, 1867.	*Dec. 31, 1867
	Mrs. Helen P. Barnum .	1869.	
Charles C. Tracy . .	. . . .	October, 1867.	
	Mrs. Lemyra A. Tracy .	October, 1867.	
Lyman Bartlett . .	. . . .	Nov. 8, 1867.	
	Mrs. Cornelia C. Bartlett	Nov. 8, 1867.	
Alpheus N. Andrus .	. . . .	May 30, 1868.	
	Mrs. Louisa M. Andrus .	May 30, 1868.	
Carmi C. Thayer . .	. . . .	July, 1868.	
	Mrs. Mary F. Thayer .	July, 1868.	
John Edwin Pierce .	. . . .	Sept., 1868.	
	Mrs. Lizzie A. Pierce .	Sept., 1868.	
Royal M. Cole . . .	. . . .	Sept., 1868.	
	Mrs. Lizzie C. Cole . .	Sept., 1868.	
Theodore S. Pond .	. . . .	Dec. 18, 1868.	
	Mrs. Julia J. Pond . .	Dec. 18, 1868.	
Milan H. Hitchcock .	. . . .	June 5, 1869.	
	Mrs. Lucy A. Hitchcock	June 5, 1869.	
Edward Riggs . . .	. . . .	July, 1869.	
	Mrs. Sarah H. Riggs . .	July, 1869.	
Henry Marden . .	. . . .	Oct. 15, 1869.	
	Mrs. Mary L. Marden .	Oct. 15, 1869.	
John Otis Barrows .	. . . .	Dec. 28, 1869.	
	Mrs. Clara S. Barrows .	Dec. 28, 1869.	
Missionary Physicians.			
Henry S. West, M. D.	. . . .	Feb., 1859.	
	Mrs. Lottie M. West . .	Feb., 1859.	
D. H. Nutting, M. D.	[See Assyria Mission] .	Nov., 1860.	
	Mrs. Mary E. Nutting .	Nov., 1860.	
*H. B. Haskell, M. D.	[See Assyria Mission] .	Nov., 1860.	Summer, 1861.
	Mrs. Sarah J. Haskell .	Nov., 1860.	Summer, 1861.
James A. Milne, M. D.	. . . .	Aug., 1867.	1868.
	Mrs. Arabella Milne . .	Aug., 1867.	1868.
Geo. C. Reynolds, M. D.	. . . .	Nov. 26, 1869.	
	Mrs. Martha W. Reynolds	Nov. 26, 1869.	
Mary L. Wadsworth, M. D.		June, 1871.	
Assistant Missionaries.			
Homan Hallock . .	[See Print. Estab. at Malta]	Dec., 1833.	1841.
	Mrs. Elizabeth Hallock .	Dec., 1833.	1841.

MISSION TO THE ARMENIANS.—CONTINUED.

Assistant Missionaries.		Time of Entering.	Time of Leaving.
	*Miss Harriet M. Lovell [afterwards Mrs. Hamlin]	April 18, 1845.	*Nov. 6, 1857.
	*Mrs. Sarah C. Hinsdale [widow of Rev. A. K. Hinsdale]	1845.	1855.
	Miss Melvina Haynes	Jan. 22, 1853.	July, 1856.
	Miss Maria A. West	Jan. 22, 1853.	
	Miss Isabella H. Goodell	1855.	
	Miss Mary E. Goodell [afterwards Mrs. H. N. Barnum]	1855.	
	Miss Mary E. Tenney [afterwards Mrs. Hamlin]	Jan. 22, 1856.	
	Miss Sarah Elizabeth West	Jan. 22, 1856.	Sept., 1862.
	Miss Myra A. Proctor	July 28, 1859.	
	Miss Arabella L. Babcock	Sept., 1862.	May, 1864.
	Miss Ann Eliza Fritcher	July 8, 1863.	
	Miss Clarissa C. Pond [afterwards Mrs. W. F. Williams]	Oct. 15, 1864.	1871.
	Miss Nancy D. Francis [afterwards Mrs. L. H. Adams]	June 25, 1866.	
	*Miss Mary E. Warfield	April 27, 1867.	*Feb. 12, 1870.
	Miss Harriet Seymour	April 27, 1867.	
	Miss Sarah Ann Closson	Nov. 8, 1867.	
	Miss Mary G. Hollister	Dec., 1867.	
Henry O. Dwight	. . . .	Dec., 1867.	
	Mrs. Mary A. Dwight	Dec., 1867.	
	Miss Rebecca D. Tracy	Sept., 1868.	1870.
	Miss Charlotte Elizab. Ely	Sept., 1868.	
	Miss Mary A. C. Ely	Sept., 1868.	
	Miss Harriet G. Powers	Sept., 1868.	
	Miss Cyrene O. Van Duzee	Sept., 1868.	
	Miss Olive L. Parmelee	Oct., 1868.	
	Miss Isabella C. Baker	Oct., 1868.	
	Miss Flavia S. Bliss	Nov., 1868.	
	Miss Ursula C. Clarke	Nov. 18, 1868.	
	Miss Ardelle M. Griswold	Oct. 15, 1869.	
	Miss Caroline E. Bush	Aug. 27, 1870.	
	Miss Julia A. Rappleye	Nov. 11, 1870.	
	Miss Sarah L. Wood	Nov. 11, 1870.	
	Miss Julia A. Shearman	Jan., 1871.	1872.
	Miss Cornelia P. Dwight		
	Miss Mary S. Williams	May, 1871.	
	Miss Mary M. Patrick	Sept. 21, 1871.	

ASSYRIA MISSION.

Ordained Missionaries.	Wives of Missionaries.	Time of Entering.	Time of Leaving.
Dwight W. Marsh	. . . .	Mar. 29, 1850.	Summer, 1860.
	*Mrs. Julia W. Marsh	May 9, 1858.	*Aug. 12, 1859.
*Wm. F. Williams, D.D.	[See Mission to Armenians]	May, 1851.	
	*Mrs. Sarah P. Williams	May, 1851.	*July 1, 1854.
	*Mrs. Harriet B. Williams	Nov., 1857.	*Dec. 25, 1857

ASSYRIA MISSION. — CONTINUED.

ORDAINED MISSIONARIES.	WIVES OF MISSIONARIES.	TIME OF ENTERING.	TIME OF LEAVING.
*Henry Lobdell, M. D.	. . . .	May 8, 1852.	*Mar. 25, 1855.
	Mrs. Lucy O. Lobdell . .	May 8, 1852.	Summer, 1860.
*Augustus Walker .	[See Mission to Armenians]	April 27, 1853.	
	Mrs. Eliza M. Walker .	April, 1853.	
George C. Knapp . .	[See Mission to Armenians]	April 5, 1856.	
	Mrs. Alzina M. Knapp .	April 5, 1856.	
MISSIONARY PHYSICIANS.			
D. H. Nutting, M. D.	[See Mission to Armenians]	Sept., 1854.	
	Mrs. Mary E. Nutting .	Sept., 1854.	
*Henri B. Haskell, M. D.	[See Mission to Armenians]	April 19, 1856.	
	Mrs. Sarah J. Haskell .	April 19, 1856.	

MISSION TO THE JEWS.

ORDAINED MISSIONARIES.	WIVES OF MISSIONARIES.	TIME OF ENTERING.	TIME OF LEAVING.
Wm. G. Schauffler, D.D.	[See Mission to Mohammedans]	July 31, 1832.	
	Mrs. Mary R. Schauffler	Feb. 26, 1834.	
*Eliphal Maynard .	. . . .	April 2, 1849.	*Sept. 14, 1849.
	Mrs. Celestia A. Maynard	April 2, 1849.	1850.
*Edward M. Dodd .	[See Mission to Armenians]	April 2, 1849.	
	Mrs. Lydia H. Dodd . .	April 2, 1849.	
Justin W. Parsons .	[See Mission to Armenians]	June 24, 1850.	
	Mrs. Catharine Parsons .	June 24, 1850.	
*Homer B. Morgan .	[See Mission to Armenians]	Feb. 16, 1852.	
	*Mrs. Harriet G. Morgan	Feb. 16, 1852.	*Sept. 10, 1852.
	Mrs. Susan H. Morgan . [formerly Mrs. Sutphen]	Nov. 7, 1853.	

MISSION TO THE MOHAMMEDANS.

ORDAINED MISSIONARIES.	WIVES OF MISSIONARIES.	TIME OF ENTERING.	TIME OF LEAVING.
James Lyman Merrick	[See Mission to Nestorians]	Oct. 25, 1835.	Dec., 1842.
	Mrs. Emma Merrick . . .	Mar. 11, 1839.	Dec., 1841.
Wm. G. Schauffler, D.D.	[See Mission to the Jews]	May, 1858.	
	Mrs. Mary R. Schauffler	May, 1858.	
William Hutchison .	. . . .	Nov. 14, 1858.	April, 1859.
	Mrs. Foresta G. Hutchison	Nov. 14, 1858.	April, 1859
George F. Herrick .	. . . .	Dec. 2, 1859.	
	Mrs. Helen M. Herrick .	Aug., 1861.	
Henry A. Schauffler .	[See Mission to Bulgarians]	June 3, 1865.	
	Mrs. Clara E. Schauffler	June 3, 1865.	

MISSION TO THE NESTORIANS.

Ordained Missionaries.	Wives of Missionaries.	Time of Entering.	Time of Leaving.
*Justin Perkins, D. D.	. . . .	Nov., 1835.	May 28, 1869.
	Mrs. Charlotte Perkins .	Nov., 1835.	1857
*Albert L. Holladay .	. . . .	June 7, 1837.	Spring, 1846.
	Mrs. Anne Y. Holladay .	June 7, 1837.	Spring, 1846.
*William R. Stocking	. . . .	June 7, 1837.	June, 1853.
	Mrs. Jerusha R. Stocking	June 7, 1837.	June, 1853.
*Willard Jones . .	. . . .	Nov. 17, 1839.	1844.
	Mrs. Miriam Jones . .	Nov. 17, 1839.	Winter, 1844.
*A. H. Wright, M. D.	. . . .	July 25, 1840.	*Jan. 4, 1865.
	Mrs. Catharine A. Wright	June 14, 1843.	August, 1859.
*Abel K. Hinsdale .	. . . .	June, 1841.	*Dec. 26, 1842.
	*Mrs. Sarah C. Hinsdale [See Mission to Armenians]	June, 1841.	Oct. 21, 1844.
*Colby C. Mitchell .	. . . .	June, 1841.	*June 27, 1841.
	*Mrs. Eliza A. Mitchell .	June, 1841.	*July 12, 1841.
*James Lyman Merrick	[See Mission to Mohammedans.]	Dec., 1842.	Summer, 1845.
	*Mrs. Emma Merrick . .	Dec., 1842.	Summer, 1845.
Thomas Laurie, D. D.	[See Mission to Syria] .	Nov. 11, 1842.	Nov. 10, 1844.
	*Mrs. Martha F. Laurie .	Nov. 11, 1842.	*Dec. 16, 1843.
*David T. Stoddard .	. . . .	June 14, 1843.	*Jan. 26, 1857.
	*Mrs. Harriet Stoddard .	June 14, 1843.	*Aug. 2, 1848.
	Mrs. Sophia D. Stoddard	June 26, 1851.	July, 1858.
*Joseph G. Cochran	. . . .	Sept. 27, 1847.	*Nov. 2, 1871.
	Mrs. Deborah W. Cochran	Sept. 27, 1848.	
George W. Coan . .	. . . .	Oct. 13, 1849.	
	Mrs. Sarah P. Coan . .	Oct. 13, 1849.	
*Samuel A. Rhea . .	. . . .	June 26, 1851.	*Sept. 2, 1865.
	*Mrs. Martha Ann Rhea	July 1, 1852.	*Sept. 16, 1857.
	Mrs. Sarah Jane Rhea .	Oct. 25, 1860.	May, 1869.
*Edwin H. Crane . .	. . . .	Oct. 20, 1852.	*Aug. 27, 1854.
	*Mrs. Ann E. Crane [afterwards Mrs. P. O. Powers]	Oct. 20, 1852.	Nov., 1857.
*Thomas L. Ambrose	. . . .	Nov. 27, 1858.	August, 1861.
John H. Shedd . .	. . . .	Nov. 11, 1859.	
	Mrs. Sarah Jane Shedd .	Nov. 11, 1859.	
*Amherst L. Thompson	. . . .	July 2, 1860.	*Aug. 25, 1860.
	Mrs. Esther E. Thompson	July 2, 1860.	Summer, 1861.
Benjamin Labaree .	. . . .	Oct. 25, 1860.	
	Mrs. Elizabeth E. Labaree	Oct. 25, 1860.	
Henry N. Cobb . .	. . . .	Oct. 25, 1860.	Autumn, 1862.
	Mrs. Matilda E. Cobb .	Oct. 25, 1860.	Autumn, 1862.
Missionary Physicians.			
*Asahel Grant, M. D.	. . . .	Oct. 15, 1835.	*April 24, 1844.
	*Mrs. Judith S. Grant .	Oct. 15, 1835.	*Jan. 14, 1839.
*F. N. H. Young, M. D.	. . . .	Oct. 25, 1860.	Summer, 1863.
T. L. Van Norden, M. D.	. . . .	Oct. 6, 1866.	
	Mrs. Mary M. Van Norden	Oct. 6, 1866.	
Assistant Missionaries.			
*Edwin Breath . .	. . . .	Nov. 7, 1840.	*Nov. 18, 1861.
	Mrs. Sarah Ann Breath .	Oct. 13, 1849.	Summer, 1862.
	*Miss Fidelia Fiske . .	June 14, 1843.	July 15, 1858.

MISSION TO THE NESTORIANS. — Continued.

Assistant Missionaries.		Time of Entering.	Time of Leaving.
	Miss Catharine A. Myers [afterwards Mrs. Wright]	June 14, 1843.	August, 1859.
	Miss Mary Susan Rice .	Nov. 20, 1847.	
	*Miss Martha Ann Harris [afterwards Mrs. Rhea.]	July 1, 1852.	*Sept. 16, 1857.
	Miss Aura Jeannette Beach	July 2, 1860.	Sept., 1862.
	*Miss Harriet N. Crawford	July 2, 1860.	May, 1865.
	Miss Nancy Jane Dean .	Oct. 19, 1868.	

MISSION TO THE BULGARIANS.

Ordained Missionaries.	Wives of Missionaries.	Time of Entering.	Time of Leaving.
Charles F. Morse . .	[See Mission to Armenians]	Mar. 26, 1858.	1870.
	Mrs. Eliza D. Morse . .	Mar. 26, 1858.	1870.
Theodore L. Byington	. . . .	Sept. 4, 1858.	1867.
	Mrs. Margaret E. Byington	Sept. 4, 1858.	1867.
*William W. Meriam	. . . .	April 22, 1859.	*July 8, 1862.
	*Mrs. Susan Meriam . .	April 22, 1859.	*July 25, 1862.
James F. Clarke . .	. . . .	Oct., 1859.	
	Mrs. Isabella G. Clarke .	Oct., 1859.	
William F. Arms . .	. . . .	July, 1860.	June, 1862.
	*Mrs. Emily Arms . . .	July, 1860.	*Mar. 31, 1861.
Oliver Crane . . .	[See Mission to Armenians]	Sept. 19, 1860.	Aug., 1868.
	Mrs. Marion D. Crane .	Sept. 19, 1860	Aug., 1868.
Henry C. Haskell .	. . . .	Dec. 13, 1862.	
	Mrs. Margaret H. Haskell	Dec. 13, 1862.	
*Jasper N. Ball . .	[See Mission to Armenians]	Jan., 1865.	1869.
	Mrs. Martha A. Ball . .	Jan., 1865.	1869.
Lewis Bond . . .	. . . .	May 29, 1868.	
	Mrs. Fannie G. Bond . .	May 29, 1868.	
Wm. Edwin Locke .	. . . .	June, 1868.	
	Mrs. Zoe A. M. Locke .	June, 1868.	
Henry Pitt Page . .	. . . .	Nov. 26, 1868.	
	Mrs. Mary A. Page . .	Nov. 26, 1868.	
Elias Riggs, D.D., LL.D.	[See Mission to Armenians]	1871.	
	Mrs. Martha J. Riggs .	1871.	
Henry A. Schauffler	[See Mission to Mohammedans.]	1871.	
	Mrs. Clara E. Schauffler	1871.	
Assistant Missionaries.			
	*Miss Mary E. Reynolds	July 8, 1863.	1869.
	*Miss Roseltha N. Norcross	April 27, 1867.	*Nov. 4, 1870.
	Miss Minnie C. Beach .	Oct. 15, 1869.	
	Miss Esther T. Maltbie .	Nov. 11, 1870.	
	Mrs. Anna V. Mumford .	1871.	

ADDENDA.

The foregoing Tabular View of the Missionaries was made partly for the author's convenience on commencing the second volume, by the very accurate gentleman who prepared the List of Publications that follows. Such a statement is very difficult to make; and it may be, after all the subsequent corrections, that there are omissions and errors. Should they be seasonably pointed out, the corrections will be made in a subsequent edition.

The following should have had a place, under the head of the *Mission to the Armenians*, namely:—

Rev. William A. Spaulding, who sailed in November, 1871.
Mrs. Georgia D. Spaulding.
Rev. Joseph E. Scott, who sailed in February, 1872.
Mrs. Annie E. Scott.

Assistant Missionaries.

Miss Laura Farnham, who sailed November, 1871.
Miss Phebe L. Cull, who sailed November, 1871.

PUBLICATIONS.

CATALOGUE OF PUBLICATIONS

ISSUED FROM THE MISSION PRESSES CONNECTED WITH THE MISSIONS OF THE BOARD TO THE SEVERAL ORIENTAL CHURCHES.

Compiled by Rev. John A. Vinton, Winchester, Mass.

THE sources of information were the "Missionary Herald" from 1821, and the Annual Reports of the Board from the beginning of these missions to the year 1871.

IN ITALIAN.

The Sabbath.
Dr. Payson's Address to Mariners.
Prayers for the Seven Days of the Week.
Dr. Ashbel Green's Questions and Counsel.
The Dairyman's Daughter, 78 pages, 1,000 copies.
William Kelley, 32 pages, 500 copies.
The Progress of Sin, 16 pages, 500 copies.
Dialogue between a Traveller and Yourself, 12 pages, 500 copies.
The Novelty of Popery.
An Address to the Children of Israel, 25 pages, 1,000 copies.
Christ's Sermon on the Mount, 16 pages, 1,000 copies.
The Negro Servant, 28 pages, 1,000 copies.
The Young Cottager, 72 pages, 1,000 copies.
The Shepherd of Salisbury Plain, 12 pages, 1,000 copies.
Serious Thoughts on Eternity, 12 pages, 1,000 copies.
Dialogue between Two Sailors, 18 pages, 1,000 copies.

Previous to November, 1827, the number of books and tracts printed at the Mission Press in Italian, was 43; number of consecutive pages, 1,430; of copies, 55,500; whole number of pages, 1,700,000.

IN MODERN GREEK.

The Dairyman's Daughter, 119 pp.
The Negro Servant, 32 pp.
Payson's Address to Mariners, 22 pp.
Short Prayers for Every Day in the Week, 70 pp.
Tract on Redemption, by Dr. Naudi, 72 pp.
Sixteen Short Sermons, 48 pp.
Progress of Sin, 20 pp.
Dialogue between a Traveller and Yourself, 14 pp.
Life and Martyrdom of John the Baptist, 28 pp.
Serious Thoughts on Eternity, 16 pp.
The Young Cottager, 87 pp.
The Shepherd of Salisbury Plain, 73 pp.
William Kelley, 45 pp.
Watts's Catechism for Children, 16 pp.
Address to the Children of Israel, 34 pp.
Chrysostom on Reading the Scriptures, 26 pp.
Content and Discontent, by Mrs. Sherwood, 24 pp.
Serious Address to Young and Old, 27 pp.
Life of James Covey, a converted Sailor, 16 pp.
Life of the Virgin Mary, from the Bible only, 20 pp.
An Appeal to the Heart, 34 pp.
Exhortation to Seamen, 20 pp.
Christ's Sermon on the Mount, 16 pp.

The following were printed from 1830 to 1833 : —

Historical Selections from the Old Testament, 84 pp.
Life of Abraham, 36 pp.
Life of Joseph, 60 pp.
Life of Moses, 36 pp.
Life of Samuel, 24 pp.
Life of David, 64 pp.
Life of Elijah.
Life of Elisha.
Life of Daniel, 36 pp.
Life of Esther, 20 pp.
Abridgment of the Old Testament, 140 pp.
Abridgment of the Gospels, 48 pp.

Abridgment of the Acts, 60 pp.
Lessons for Children.
Bickersteth's Scripture Help, abridged.
Lyttelton on the Conversion of St. Paul.
The Ten Commandments.
Ecclesiastical History.
Dialogues on Grammar.
The Alphabetarion, 120 pp.
The Greek Reader, 156 pp.
The Little Philosopher, 72 pp.
The Child's Assistant, 60 pp.
The Child's Arithmetic, 48 pp.
Adams's Arithmetic.
History of Greece.
History of Rome.
History of England.
History of France.
History of the Middle Ages.
History of the Sandwich Islands.
The Priest and Catechumen, a Dialogue, 12 pp.
Peter Parley's Geography, with lithographed maps, 108 pp.
Pinnock's Catechism of Greek History, with remarks, 150 pp.

The amount printed in Modern Greek, while the press remained at Malta, was about 350,000 copies, mostly 12mo, comprising 21,000,000 pages. Many of the editions were of 4,000 copies each. In the year ending October 1831, 4,760,000 pages were printed.

After the removal of the press to Smyrna, in December, 1833, there were printed in Modern Greek, —

Woodbridge's Geography, 296 pp.
Scriptural Teacher, 116 pp.
Questions on the Pentateuch, 88 pp.
Several Hymns for the Mission Schools.
Child's Book on the Soul.
Tract on Self-Examination.
Difficulties of Infidelity.

The Magazine of Useful Knowledge — a monthly publication commenced in 1836 or 1837, and continued till 1843, when it was transferred to Mr. Nicholas Petrokokino. It had, in 1839, 1,200 subscribers.

About thirty million pages in Modern Greek had been printed by the mission between July 1822 and 1837.

At Smyrna, in 1847 and 1848, were printed, Barth's Church History, 354 pages, 3,000 copies; 1,062,000 pages.

At Constantinople, after the removal of the press, in 1853; Hymn Book, 112 pages, 2,000 copies; 224,000 pages.

In 1854, a tract of 20 pages, 2,000 copies; 40,000 pages.

In 1860, tracts, 5,000 copies, 40,000 pages.

In 1863, tracts, ... 6,000 pages.

Printing in Modern Greek, at Athens, under the supervision of Dr. King: —

Up to 1844, 32 books and tracts, 3,717 consecutive pages, 128,-215 pages in the whole.

In 1845, 2,000 copies, 664,000 pages.

In 1846, 3,000 copies, 190,500 pages.

In 1853 to 1856, a collection of the publications of the American Tract Society, vol. I.—V., making 2,500 consecutive pages of the five volumes.

In 1855, Chrysostom on Reading the Scriptures, 180 pages.

Two volumes of Sermons, 48 in number, by Dr. King.

A volume of Miscellanies, including his Farewell Letter to his Friends in Palestine and Syria.

IN GRÆCO-TURKISH (THE TURKISH LANGUAGE IN GREEK LETTERS).

Christ's Sermon on the Mount, 16 pages, 450 copies.

History of Moses, of Samuel, of Elijah, of Elisha, of Daniel, of Esther; each a volume by itself; total, 524,000 pages.

From 1840 to 1853, were printed 55,000 copies of the Scriptures.

In 1854 and 1855, the Bible in 8vo, 7,000 copies, 2,456,000 pages.

In 1864, 72 pages, 3,000 copies; in all, 216,000 pages.

In 1867, the Tract Primer, 5,000 copies, 340,000 pages.

In 1869, a Hymn Book, 264 pages, 2,000 copies; 528,000 pages.

IN ANCIENT ARMENIAN.

The New Testament, 836 pages, 2,000 copies. At Smyrna, 1838.
The Four Gospels, printed separately, 1,000 copies.
The Acts and Epistles, of the same edition, 1,500 copies, in 1843.
The Psalter, 274 pages, total 548,000 pages; 3,000 copies printed in 1841; 2,000 copies in 1846.
The New Testament, 2,000 copies, 1,464,000 pages; in 1853.
The Christian Teacher, 136 pages, 500 copies; in 1838.
Daily Food for Christians, 62 pages, 1,000 copies; in 1838.
In 1869, printed 268 consecutive pages and 4,250 copies.

IN MODERN ARMENIAN.

Abercrombie on Mental Culture, 84 pages, 1,500 copies; 126,000 pages. Printed in 1844, at the expense of the author.
Against Infidelity, 16 pages, 3,000 copies.
Almanac for 1837, 3,000 copies.
Almanac for 1839, 1,000 copies.
An Arithmetic, 1866.
An occasional paper, 4to, 20 pages, 500 copies.
Answer of Evangelical Armenians to the Patriarch's Manifesto, 104 pages, 1,000 copies.
Anxious Inquirer.
Assembly's Shorter Catechism, with references, 104 pages, 2,000 copies.
Astronomy, 104 pages, 3,000 copies.
Avedaper (The), or Messenger, a religious periodical in Modern Armenian, and in Armeno-Turkish. Published since January, 1855; once in two weeks, with a circulation, in each language, of 1,000 copies.
Balbaith's Confession, in the form of a letter from a converted Jew, giving reasons for his profession of Christianity, 62 pages, 4,000 copies.
Baptism and the New Birth, 112 pages, 1,000 copies.
Baxter's Saints' Rest. 1854.
Bible Dictionary. 1854.
Bible Hand-book, 240 pages, 300 copies.
British Martyrology. 1850.
Child's Entertainer, 296 pages, 1,000 copies, containing Watts's

Divine and Moral Songs in Armenian verse, evangelical anecdotes, some natural history, etc. 1838.

Child's Instructor, 74 pages.

Concordance to the Bible, 8vo, 504 pages, 2,000 copies.

Dairyman's Daughter, 48 pages, 3,000 copies.

Evidences of Christianity.

False Claims of the Pope, 77 pages. It has been published in English by the American Tract Society.

Five Wounds (The) of Conscience, by Flavel, 1,500 copies.

Forever! 4 pages, 4,000 copies.

Friendly Letters to Sufferers by the late Fire, 16 pages, 500 copies.

Good Works; a Tract on Justification, 48 pages, 4,000 copies.

Grammar, English and Armenian; 112 pages, 500 copies. Another edition of 272 pages, 1,000 copies.

Guide to Parents, 61 pages, 1,000 copies.

Guide to Repentance, 288 pages, 1,000 copies.

Handbills, (four) each one page, containing, The Decalogue: A Contrast between the Deaths of Haliburton and Voltaire; The Christian Sabbath; The Death-bed of a Modern Freethinker; 4,000 copies.

History of the Church of God.

History of Joseph, 326 pages, 3,000 copies.

History of the Reformation, by Merle d'Aubigne. In 2 vols. 8vo, with an Appendix of 50 pages, 1,000 copies. 1846. An enlarged edition was printed in 1866.

Holy Spirit, a Work on the, 1850.

Hymns, 25 pages, 500 copies.

Jones's (Rev. C. C.) Catechism, 203 pages, 4,000 copies.

Joy in Heaven, 24 pages, 3,000 copies.

Key to Reading, 8 pages, 1,500 copies.

Lancasterian Cards, 80 to the set. 100 sets.

Light of the Soul, 46 pages, 3,000 copies.

Lives of the Patriarchs and Prophets, 300 pages, 1,000 copies.

Lord's Supper, Treatise on the, 84 pages, 1,000 copies.

Mary Lothrop, 96 pages, 3,000 copies.

Messenger, The. See *Avedaper*.

Mother at Home, 288 pages, 300 copies.

Monthly Evangelical Preacher, commenced January, 1845, and suspended at the close of the year, 284 pages, 1,000 copies.

Monthly Magazine, four vols., for 1839–1842. The first year, 1,100 copies, each following year, 1,500. Relinquished for want of funds. Resumed 1844, continued till 1846.

New Testament, 646 pages, 5,000 copies in 1842 and 1843. A new translation, carefully executed by four of the best scholars in the Armenian nation, and compared by Dr. Adger, word by word, with the original Greek.

New Testament, with marginal references, and parallel passages. Prepared by Dr. Adger and Dr. Riggs. 948 pages. 1848 and 1849.

New Testament, in the Ararat or Eastern Dialect of the Modern Armenian, with Scripture references, 8,000 copies.

New Testament, in the Ararat or Eastern Dialect of the Modern Armenian, with the Ancient Armenian, in parallel columns.

Old Testament, in four volumes, 500 copies.

Old Testament, imperial edition, 5,000 copies.

Payson's Thoughts, 180 pages, 2,000 copies.

Pentateuch, 684 pages, 1,500 copies.

Progress of Sin, 24 pages, 2,000 copies.

Pilgrim's Progress, with notes, 814 pages, 1,000 copies.

Protestant Confessions, 265 pages, 1,000 copies.

Psalter, in the Western Dialect of the Modern Armenian, 275 pages, 3,000 copies.

Psalter, in the Ararat or Eastern Dialect of the Modern Armenian, 275 pages, 5,000 copies.

Reply to Archbishop Matteos.

Scripture Rule of Faith, 364 pages, 1,000 copies.

Scripture Texts, 56 pages, 500 copies.

Scripture Text Book, 622 pages, 1,000 copies.

Sermon for the Whole World, 16 pages, 2,000 copies. It is the Sermon on the Mount.

Sin no Trifle, 16 pages, 2,000 copies.

Spelling Book, 60 pages. At least four editions.

Sunday-school Hymn Book, 8vo, 134 pages, 8,000 copies.

Sunday-school Hymn and Tune Book, 8vo, 128 pages, 5,000 copies.

The Two Lambs, 48 pages, 2,000 copies.

Tract on Self-Examination, 52 pages, 1,000 copies.

Upham's Intellectual Philosophy.

Vivian's Three Dialogues, between a Minister and his Parishioner, 2,000 copies.
What must I do? 20 pages, 2,000 copies.
What is it to believe? 12 pages, 5,000 copies.
Whateley's Evidences of Christianity, 192 pages, 2,000 copies.

There were also many common school books.

The sum total of printing in the Modern Armenian, in the year 1869, was 1,865 consecutive pages, and 25,920 copies.

IN ARMENO-TURKISH.

Printing in this language was commenced at Malta in 1828. In August, 1829, the number of publications was nineteen. The printing of the Armeno-Turkish New Testament was begun January 8, 1830, and the last sheet was corrected before the close of January, 1831. A second edition of the same was printed at Smyrna in 1843, consisting of 4,000 copies. The Old Testament was printed at Smyrna in 1841, 3,000 copies. The Pentateuch was printed in a separate form, 2,000 copies. The Book of Psalms, in a separate form, was printed in 1844, 2,000 copies.

The following publications have also been issued: —

Abbot's Young Christian, 350 pages, 2,000 copies.
Arithmetic, 66 pages, 3,000 copies.
Avedaper (Messenger), a monthly magazine. See *Avedaper* in the preceding list.
Barth's Church History, 408 pages, 1,000 copies.
Bogue's Essay, 444 pages, 1,000 copies.
Capadose, Dr., Memoir of, 52 pages, 1,000 copies.
Catechism on Christ, 82 pages, 1,000 copies.
Chrysostom on Reading the Scriptures, 106 pages, 2,000 copies.
Commentary on Matthew, 1,000 copies.
Essay on Fasts, etc., 220 pages, 1,000 copies.
False Claims of the Pope, 112 pages, 2,000 copies.
Forever! 11 pages, 1,000 copies.
Gallaudet's Child's Book on the Soul, 156 pages, 1,000 copies.
Gallaudet's Natural Theology, 233 pages, 2,000 copies.
Good Works, A tract on, 44 pages, 2,000 copies.
Grammar, 213 pages, 3,000 copies.
Guide to the Use of the Fathers, 318 pages, 2,000 copies.

History of a Bible, 34 pages, 2,000 copies.
Hymn Book.
Intemperance, Tract on, 46 pages, 2,000 copies.
Jones's (Rev. C. C.) Catechism, 305 pages, 1,000 copies.
Light of the Soul, 48 pages, 2,000 copies.
Mary Lothrop, 172 pages, 2,000 copies.
Narrative Tracts, in one vol., 152 pages, 1,000 copies.
Neff's (Felix) Dialogues on Sin and Salvation, 140 pages, 1,000 copies.
New Testament, with marginal references.
Old Testament, with marginal references, royal 8vo.

From 1840 to 1863, 6,500 copies of the Scriptures were printed, —

Physiology, Treatise on, 272 pages, 3,000 copies.
Pike's Persuasives to Early Piety, 70 pages, 2,000 copies.
Reader, No. 1, 63 pages, sixth edit., 5,000 copies. 1867.
Reader, No. 2, 72 pages, 5,000 copies. 1869.
Reader, No. 3, 84 pages, 5,000 copies. 1869.
Sabbath, A work on the, 116 pages, 2,000 copies.
Scripture Titles of Christ, 104 pages, 1,000 copies.
Serious Inquiry, 20 pages, 2,000 copies.
Sermon for the Whole World, 28 pages, 2,000 copies. It is the Sermon on the Mount.
Sermons, fourteen in one vol., 316 pages, 1,000 copies.
Spelling Book, 64 pages, 1,000 copies.
Theological Class Book.
The Ten Commandments, a handbill, 2,000 copies.
Without Holiness no Man shall see the Lord, 11 pages, 1,000 copies.

In Armeno-Turkish there were printed in 1869, 398 consecutive pages and 16,000 copies.

IN ARABO-TURKISH (SOMETIMES CALLED THE OSMANLI-TURKISH. TURKISH IN THE ARABIC CHARACTER).

Under the direction of Dr. Schauffler, an edition of the New Testament, of very beautiful typography, was issued in 1862. Also, Matt. v. in separate form.
A Commentary on Matthew and Mark, 400 pages, 1,000 copies. 1864.

The Decalogue, one page, 1,000 copies. 1867.

The Beatitudes, one page, 1,000 copies. 1867.

Selected Texts, one page, 1,000 copies. 1867.

Selected Texts, one page, 1,000 copies. 1867.

On Belief and Worship: an Explanation of the Christian Religion as understood and professed by Protestants, 128 pages, 3,000 copies.

The Primer, 64 pages, 5,000 copies. 1869.

Notes on the Decalogue, 80 pages, 3,000 copies.

Teachings of the New Testament, concerning the Judgment, 16 pages, 5,000 copies.

Firman of the Porte in relation to the Protestant community, 300 copies.

In this dialect, in 1869, were printed 161 consecutive pages, 13,300 copies — total, 531,300 pages.

In the Koordish Dialect, previous to 1863, 13,000 copies of the Scriptures had issued from the mission press.

IN BULGARIAN.

In the year 1844, a small volume in this language was issued at Smyrna. It was Part I. of Gallaudet's Child's Book on the Soul, 61 pages, 2,000 copies.

In 1851 and 1852, several Tracts were printed, in all 8,000 copies.

In 1853, the Book of Psalms.

In 1860, 59,000 copies, in part of the New Testament, and in part of other books and tracts, making 3,332,000 pages.

In 1861, the New Testament, Biblical Catechism, Child's Book on the Soul, etc., 1,195 consecutive pages, and 60,000 copies.

In 1863, 1,896,000 pages. Up to this time, 4,000 copies of the New Testament.

In 1864, 303 copies of tracts, etc., 39,000 consecutive pages.

The issue of the Old Testament, following the New, commenced 1866.

The Zornitza, or Day Star, a small monthly sheet, was commenced about 1866, having 750 subscribers.

After this time, the printing was as follows: —

	PAGES.	COPIES.	TOTAL COPIES.
The Bible, commenced, imperial, 8vo. .	624	5,000	3,120,000
The Pentateuch	352	1,000	352,000
Book of Genesis	167	1,000	167,000
Book of Proverbs	91	2,000	182,000
Hymn and Tune Book, finished . .	44	3,000	132,000
Dr. Goodell's Sermons	522	3,000	1,566,000
Sermon on the Sabbath	12	2,000	24,000
Commentary on Matthew	240	3,000	720,000
Spiritual Worship	156	2,000	312,000
The Bible and Tradition	35	3,000	105,000
Protestants the Ancient Orthodox . .	43	3,000	129,000
Baptism	28	3,000	84,000
The Lord's Supper	34	3,000	102,000
The Pope and the Roman Catholic Church	74	3,000	220,000
Answer to Infidel Objections . . .	36	3,000	108,000
Bruch on Prayer	48	3,000	144,000
The Way of Salvation	8	3,000	24,000
Poor Joseph	8	3,000	24,000
The Two Lambs	18	3,000	54,000
On Fasting, third edition	16	3,000	48,000
The One Thing Needful, second edition	7	3,000	21,000
The Enlightened Priest, second edition	22	3,000	66,000
Index to Sermons	4	3,000	12,000
The Heavenly Voice, and What it is to believe in Christ	16	3,000	48,000
Confession of Faith	8	1,000	8,000
Zornitza, "The Day Star," 12 Nos. 4to.	96	2,000	192,000
	2,709	70,000	7,964,000

In the Bulgarian, in 1869, were printed 519 consecutive pages, and 19,000 copies.

IN HEBREW AND HEBREW-SPANISH.

The Psalms, 3,000 copies, 1836. An edition in 1858, 5,000 copies.

The Pentateuch, 500 copies. Second edition of 2,000 copies.

The Old Testament, printed at Vienna, 3,000 copies.

The same, second edition, 5,000 copies, printed at Smyrna.

Oppenheim's Hebrew Grammar, at Smyrna, 2,000 copies. It was designed to lead the Jews from a fanciful to a grammatical construction of the Hebrew Oracles.

A Hebrew Vocabulary.

A Hebrew-Spanish Primer, of 20 pages.

A Hebrew-Spanish Lexicon, in part; extending to 187 consecutive pages; number of copies 8,000. So far in 1851. It appears to have been since completed.

In 1855, just before the close of the Jewish mission, 319 pages of Hebrew-Spanish literature were printed in Constantinople, 5,000 copies.

Between 1840 and 1860, 23,000 copies of the Hebrew-Spanish Scriptures, under the supervision of missionaries of the American Board.

IN ARABIC.

Previous to the arrival of the Mission Press at Beirût, the following tracts had been issued from it at Malta: —

Farewell Letter of Rev. Jonas King to his friends in Syria, in 1825.

Asaad Shidiak's Statement of his Conversion, and of his Persecutions.

Mr. Bird's Reply to the Maronite Bishop of Beirût, 535 pages.

In 1836, amounting to 380,800 pages, as follows: —

Spelling Cards, 8 pages, 500 copies.

Watts's Catechism for small children, 16 pages, 1,000 copies.

A Lithographic Copy-book, 200 copies.

Elements of Arabic Grammar, 168 pages, 1,000 copies.

Hymn Book, 24 pages, 200 copies.

Alphabet, lithographed, 200 copies.

The Dairyman's Daughter, 96 pages, 2,000 copies.

Since 1836, the issues of the press were as follows: —

Extracts from Chrysostom, 166 pages, 2,000 copies.

Extracts from Thomas à Kempis, 60 pages, 2,000 copies.

Smith's Arithmetic, 84 pages, 1,200 copies.

Proverbs of Solomon, 4,000 copies.

On Self-Examination, 40 pages, 4,000 copies.

Sermon on the Mount, 12 pages, 6,000 copies.

Tract on the Cholera, 12 pages, 4,000 copies.

Child's Book on the Soul. Part I., 104 pages, 2,000 copies.

Epistle to the Ephesians, 24 pages, 3,000 copies.

The Psalms of David, 276 pages, 5,000 copies.

Confession of Faith, 60 pages, 400 copies,
On Temperance, by Mrs. Whiting, 96 pages, 2,000 copies.
Child's Book on the Soul. Part II., 116 pages, 2,000 copies.
Little Henry and his Bearer, 84 pages, 2,000 copies.
The Acts of the Apostles, 150 pages, 2,000 copies.
Arabic Syntax, 74 pages, 2,000 copies.
The Passion of Christ, as in Matt. xxvii., 16 pages, 6,000 copies.
Thomas à Kempis, revised, 343 pages, 2,000 copies.
The First Sixteen Psalms, for Schools, 23 pages, 1,000 copies.
The Office and Work of the Holy Spirit, 256 pages, 2,000 copies.
Spelling Book, 63 pages, 2,000 copies.
The Westminster's Assembly's Catechism, 43 pages, 2,000 copies.
Good Works, their place, 87 pages, 2,000 copies.
Nevins's Thoughts on Popery, 156 pages, 2,000 copies.
Watts's Catechism for Children, 2,000 copies.
The Assembly's Shorter Catechism, with proofs, 1,500 copies.

In 1842, the Arabic printing at Beirût amounted to 1,708,000 pages. In 1843, to 13,000 copies, and 1,282,000 pages. Number of pages from the beginning, 6,077,000.

After the year 1845, the printing proceeded from year to year, and the number of copies and pages was reported as formerly; but the titles do not occur in the printed Reports, except as follows: —

The Spelling Book, from Bible; 59 pages, 1,500 copies.
Letter to the Syrian Clergy, 20 pages, 1,200 copies.
The Book of Genesis, 136 pages, 1,200 copies.
Union Question Book, Vol. I., 1,500 copies.
An Arithmetic, by Butrus el Bistâny.
Mrs. Whiting on Temperance, second edition.
Mr. Johnston's tract on Good Works, their Place, second edition.
Mr. Bird's Reply to the Maronite Bishop, second edition.
Mr. Calhoun's Companion to the Bible.
Dr. Van Dyck's Geography.
Dr. Alexander's Evidences of Christianity.
Dr. Van Dyck's Algebra.
Dr. Van Dyck's Sermon on the Second Commandment.
A small Arabic Grammar.
Dr. Meshakah on Skepticism.

Dr. Schneider on Rites and Ceremonies.
A new edition of the Psalms of David.

The New Testament, in the version made by Dr. Eli Smith, assisted by Butrus el Bistâny, and revised by Dr. Van Dyck, with references, and also a Pocket Edition of the same, without references, of 5,000 copies, was issued from the press in March 1860.

The printing of the WHOLE BIBLE IN ARABIC was finished in March 1865. Upon this great work Drs. Smith and Van Dyck had labored with zeal and energy sixteen years, from 1838. Of this translation, ten different editions, of the whole, or of parts, had been printed in 1865, comprising over 40,000 copies.

Two hundred copies of the first three chapters of the Gospel by John were printed in raised letters, for the use of the blind.

Printed in 1866: volumes of all kinds, 28,484. Copies of Tracts, 23,000. Copies of Scripture, 14,554. Pages of Tracts, 888,000. Pages of Scripture, 2,872,000.

Printed in 1867:—

Edwards's History of Redemption.
Bickersteth's Scripture Hand-book.
A large Psalm and Hymn Book.
A Psalter, versified.
A Children's Hymn Book.
A Monthly Missionary Arabic Journal.
Mr. Bistâny's Elements of Grammar.
Two editions of his Arabic Lexicon.

In 1867, were printed 16,800 volumes of all kinds, and 20,700 Tracts.

In 1868, 726,000 pages of Scripture, and 1,300,000 of other works.

In 1869, 5,147,000 pages of all kinds.

The reports for subsequent years are defective.

MODERN SYRIAC. (THE LANGUAGE OF THE NESTORIAN PEOPLE.)

The printing, in the year 1843, was 860 volumes, 6,940 tracts, and 611,580 pages.

In 1844, the Four Gospels, and the Dairyman's Daughter, were printed. Whole amount, 437,800 pages.

The New Testament, with the ancient and modern Syriac in parallel columns, was printed in 1846. In that year, 2,500 books and tracts, and 1,114,000 pages, were printed; of which about 1,000,000 pages were quarto. Among the books was a new and enlarged edition of the Nestorian Hymn Book, a Spelling Book, and a Question Book.

The Pilgrim's Progress was commenced in 1847.

A monthly paper, entitled "The Rays of Light," was begun in 1848, and has continued till the present time.

In 1853 and 1854, an edition of the New Testament entire, was printed; also a Hymn Book, and a volume entitled Scripture Facts.

In 1855, Green Pastures for the Lord's Flocks, 392 pages.

In 1856, Barth's Church History, and a Scripture Geography. Whole number of volumes printed this year, 3,000; 880,000 pages.

In 1857, 934,000 pages, of which 768,000 were of Scripture, in large quarto.

During the eighteen years following the arrival of the press, from 1840 to 1858, 68,000 volumes were printed, comprising 13,493,020 pages.

In 1860, the New Testament, with references, had been printed.

The Old Testament is spoken of as having been previously printed in that form.

A Christian Almanac was issued in 1862.

The Word of God was largely printed from year to year

In 1866, Rays of Light, a monthly paper, 8vo, 384 pages, 400 copies. Wayland's Moral Science.

Volumes printed in 1866, 1,250. Tracts, including the monthly paper, 5,500. Pages of Scripture, and other works, 381,300.

Whole number of volumes from the beginning, 91,350. Number of pages, 18,052,050.

In 1867, Dr. Perkins's Commentary on Genesis; also a Christian Almanac.

In 1869, Rays of Light, monthly, 104 pages, 400 copies.
Night of Toil, 221 pages, 500 copies.
Signet Ring, 65 pages, 200 copies.
Revival Hymns, 32 pages, 200 copies.

Dialogue on the Papacy, 12 pages, 200 copies.

Almanac, 44 pages, 200 copies.

Dr. Perkins's Commentary on Daniel, 154 pages, 500 copies.

Printed in 1869, 632 consecutive pages, 2,200 copies.

Total pages from the beginning, November 1840, to the close of 1869, 19,529,150.

INDEX.

END OF VOLUME II.

CPSIA information can be obtained
at www.ICGtesting.com
Printed in the USA
LVHW040103230323
742312LV00002B/74

9 783382 128357